# BURNING ISSUE

## by the same author:

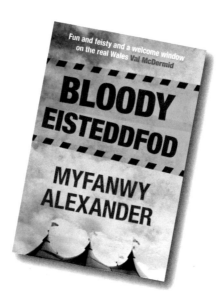

The National Eisteddfod is held at Meifod and there is more than enough work for Dyfed Powys Police.

A darkly comic tale of lust, violence, revenge and strict metre poetry set in the heart of rural Wales.

*'Fun and feisty and a welcome window on the real Wales.'*
*– Val McDermid*

Gwasg Carreg Gwalch, £9

# Burning Issue

*Myfanwy Alexander*

## Author's Note
Though places and institutions in this novel are based in reality, all characters are entirely fictional. The candidates in this story are not intended to refer to any candidates standing for election in Montgomeryshire at any time.

First published in Welsh, *Pwnc Llosg*: 2016
First English edition: 2021

© Myfanwy Alexander / Gwasg Carreg Gwalch

ISBN: 978-1-84527-750-5

Published with the financial support of the
Books Council of Wales

Cover design: Siôn Ilar

Published by Gwasg Carreg Gwalch,
12 Iard yr Orsaf, Llanrwst, Wales LL26 0EH
tel: 01492 642031
email: books@carreg-gwalch.cymru
website: www.carreg-gwalch.cymru

*To Sarah Morris,*
*who is rather fond of the metaphorical use of birds*
*and has the eye of a red kite herself,*
*with many thanks.*

# Characters

Because so many people share so few surnames, farm names or nicknames are commonly used.

| | |
|---|---|
| Daf Dafis (Deifi Siop) | Inspector at Dyfed Powys Police |
| Gaenor Jones | His partner, former wife of |
| John Jones, Neuadd | Wealthy farmer, brother of |
| Falmai Dafis | Daf's ex-wife, deputy head of the primary school |
| Sion Jones, Neuadd | Son of Gaenor and John |
| Carys Dafis | Daughter of Daf and Falmai |
| Rhodri Dafis | Son of Daf and Falmai |
| Mali Haf Dafis | Baby daughter of Gaenor and Daf |
| Heulwen Breeze-Evans | Plaid Cymru Parliamentary Candidate |
| Phil Evans, Dolfadog | Heulwen's husband |
| Jac Evans, Dolfadog | Son of Heulwen and Phil, husband of Lowri |
| Gruff Evans, Dolfadog | Son of Heulwen and Phil |
| Nansi Bockarie | Daughter of Heulwen and Phil, wife of |
| Rev Seth Bockarie | Evangelical Christian pastor |
| Margaret Hamer, Tanyrallt | Farmer and breeder of ponies |
| Rhys Bowen, Weirglodd | Tory Assembly Member, butcher and businessman |
| Mostyn Gwydyr-Gwynne | Tory MP and landowner, fiancé of |
| Haf Wynne | Radical lawyer |
| Lisa Powell | Civil servant |
| Janet Cilgwyn | Plaid Cymru Assembly Member |
| Carwyn Watkin, Brynybiswal | Farmer |
| Sheila Francis | Detective Constable, Dyfed Powys Police |
| Steve James | Detective Sergeant, Dyfed Powys Police |
| Darren Morgan | Sergeant, Dyfed Powys Police |
| Neville Wyn Roberts | Constable, Dyfed Powys Police |
| Nia Owen | Constable, Dyfed Powys Police |
| Belle Pashley | Owner of specialist hydrocarbon-detecting dogs |
| Father Joseph Hogan | Catholic parish priest, Welshpool |
| Milek Bartoshyn | Factory worker, brother of |

| | |
|---|---|
| Basia Bartoshyn | Cleaner |
| Felicity Jones | Vet |
| Gwilym Bebb | Solicitor and county councillor |
| Chrissie Humphries, Berllan | Agricultural contractor, mechanic, farmer |
| Bryn Humphries, Gwaun | Chrissie's second husband, twin of her first |
| Rob Humphries, Berllan | Chrissie's son, best friend to Rhodri Dafis |

# Glossary

In this story, all conversations take place in Welsh unless specifically stated. Here is a list of unfamiliar words found in the text, some of which are Welsh words often used in English, others unfamiliar concepts

| | |
|---|---|
| AS | Assembly Member (The Assembly is now called the Senedd) |
| Assembly/ the Bay | The Welsh devolved legislature |
| *Boncyn* | A small hill or slope (not as fun as it sounds) |
| Cade | A bottle-fed lamb. Also known as *oen swci* hence the use of *swci* as an insult for a person lacking in resilience |
| *Catffwl* | A fool. See also *lembo* |
| *Cariad* | A term of endearment, 'love' |
| CEOP | Child Exploitation and Online Protection |
| *Cerdd dant* | A traditional Welsh type of singing, usually to harp accompaniment |
| Clemmed | Hungry |
| *Cog* | A male version of *lodes*. *Cog bêch clên* = tidy little lad, *cogie* = boys |
| *Cont* | An obscene word used as a greeting in north Wales |
| CSM | Crime Scene Manager |
| *Cwtch* | Hug or cuddle, both a verb and a noun |
| *Del* | pretty one |
| *Duwcs* | Gosh, a mild expletive |
| Eisteddfod | A cultural competition. Local ones may be called after chapels, such as Eisteddfod Seilo |
| Estyn | The education and training inspectorate for Wales |
| *Fech, fach* | Female form of *bach* = small; with a Montgomeryshire accent, the 'a' becomes an 'e' |
| *Ffermio* | What Match of the Day is to football, *Ffermio* is to agriculture |
| *Helm* | An open shed |
| *Hwntw* | A mildly insulting term for someone from south Wales; pl. *hwntws* |

| | |
|---|---|
| Jac Sais | English Jack, a mild insult |
| Kit | A small farm building |
| *Lembo* | Dullard, blockhead |
| The List | 40 of the 60 Welsh Senedd Members are elected by the 'first past the post' system. The other 20 are elected from party regional lists, so can be said not to have 'won' their seats. |
| Living tally | Cohabiting, from the Welsh *talu*, to pay |
| *Lodes* | A fond term for a girl, specific to Montgomeryshire dialect. Literally, a wench. *Da lodes* means good girl. |
| *Llanc* | Male equivalent of *lodes* |
| Lleifior | The Montgomeryshire farm at the heart of the classic novels of rural life written by Islwyn Ffowc Elis |
| Meibion Glyndŵr | Participants in the arson campaign of the 1980s called themselves the 'Sons of Glyndŵr', the 15th-century rebel against English rule |
| Menter Maldwyn | A local group promoting Welsh culture |
| Merched y Wawr | 'The Daughters of the Dawn' are even more formidable than the WI, their equivalents |
| Nain | Grandmother |
| *Nefi blw!* | A mild expletive – Navy Blue. |
| *Noson Lawen* | A long-running light entertainment show, no longer filmed in sheds |
| *OMB* | 'Oh, Mam bach' the equivalent of OMG |
| On tack | Rented on a short-term lease |
| OSPRE | Objective Structured Performance Related Examination |
| *Papur bro* | Community newspaper eg *Plu'r Gweunydd* or *Plu* |
| PCSO / CSO | Police Community Support Officer |
| *Pedair Wal* | Popular former TV show, property porn with a sense of history |
| Penyberth Three | D. J. Williams, Saunders Lewis and Lewis Valentine – three pre-war language activists who burnt down a military establishment which had displaced a Welsh community in Llŷn, the north-western peninsula. |

| | |
|---|---|
| Plaid | 'Plaid' means a political party but 'Plaid' with a capital 'P' means Plaid Cymru, the Welsh Nationalist Party |
| *Plantos* | Children |
| Plygain | Ancient carol service, traditionally held at dawn |
| *Potsh* | To fuss with something or interfere |
| *Prynhawn Da* | A weekday afternoon lifestyle programme |
| Sali Mali | Heroine of the most popular books for small children |
| *Sang-di-fang* | Messy, untidy |
| SIO | Senior Investigation Officer |
| *Smic* | smidge |
| The Smithfield | Welshpool livestock market, largest sheep market in Europe |
| SOCO | Scene of Crime Officer |
| Sprot | To take a sprot, or sprut, is to take a look |
| Surree | A survival of the Shakepearean 'sirrah', an affectionate greeting to a man or boy |
| Taid | Grandfather |
| Teg Wawriodd | A traditional carol, sung at Plygain services |
| The Thin Language | A mildly insulting term for the English language |
| Ti a Fi | See *ysgol feithrin* |
| *Twmffat* | Idiot |
| *Twt lol* | Nonsense |
| *Tyrd i mewn* | Come in |
| *Washi* | My lad (north Wales) |
| Wil Cwac Cwac | From children's books and TV, think Puddleduck with attitude |
| WilJil | An insulting term for an effeminate man, now thankfully rarely heard |
| *Wtra, sietin, bing* | *Wtra* lane, *sietin* hedge, *bing* small farm building, all words found only in Montgomeryshire, are unfamiliar even to Welsh speakers |
| Urdd | The Welsh youth group which organises cultural and sporting competitions. Fiercely competitive, spawns pushy parents |
| YFC | Young Farmers' Clubs |
| *Ysgol feithrin* | Nursery school. Mothers and younger children attend Ti a Fi |

# Chapter 1

## *Monday, April 11, 2016*

His second pint of Monty's in his hand, Daf Dafis was enjoying one of the simple pleasures of life. Since moving to a house opposite the pub, it was easy enough for him to pop across, just for an hour, to collect the day's news for Gaenor and to relax after a challenging day in his role as an inspector with Dyfed Powys Police. But if he was honest, there was another reason for his appearance at the bar of the Goat. Daf wanted to show the whole world, or the inhabitants of Llanfair Caereinion anyway, that he was not in hiding after his decision, eight months back, to leave his wife Falmai to live with Gaenor, who just happened to be married to John, who just happened to be Falmai's brother.

The family at Neuadd, one of the most respectable in the area, had never faced such a scandal. It had begun as an affair between two middle-aged people who were just bored with their lives, but it grew into passionate love and Daf was reluctant to carry on living a lie. Besides, Mali Haf had made her appearance and even if Gaenor had tried to fool John, her baby daughter's face proclaimed her paternity to the world.

'So,' Chrissie Berllan had said as they picked up their respective sons from the under-16 training session at the rugby club. 'It was John Neuadd who was the Jaffa after all.'

Licking his lips because his mouth had gone unaccountably dry and trying not to look at the way Chrissie's boiler suit was deliberately missing the top poppers to reveal a good deal of cleavage, Daf asked, 'Jaffa?'

'Seedless, Mr Dafis, seedless. I've heard he'd called her barren on times. Not so barren now she's changed the bull, hey?'

Of course, the scandal was meat and drink to the local gossips but a new pattern of life had somehow been created.

Daf had worried about his son Rhodri because no boy of fourteen wants his family to be the centre of all the talk of a small community but when asked, the lad responded, 'Oh, some lad from Newtown did start on about Gaenor but Rob Berllan shoved his head down the bog and we haven't heard anything since.'

'Rob shouldn't have done such a thing,' responded Daf, hiding his delight at this. 'He could get excluded for something like that.'

'Not when you're chairman of the exclusion committee, Dad,' was Rhodri's reply.

When Daf was young, he'd spent a lot of time with his Uncle Mal, his father's brother. A tall, broad-shouldered man, he had a mental age of seven. He loved playing simple games like Snakes and Ladders or Ludo but his favourite was Spillikins. Very often on a Sunday morning, Mal would take down the wooden box from the mantelpiece and ask Daf, 'How about a go on the Spills, surree?'

In the box were forty little sticks which would be thrown onto the table, the aim of the game being to pick them up, one by one, without disturbing the others. Since leaving Falmai, Daf had often remarked on the similarity between life and a game of Spillikins: in both it was almost impossible to alter one thing without disturbing others. But somehow or other a pattern had formed from the chaos.

Rhodri and his sister Carys had chosen to live with Daf and Gaenor but Daf's biggest shock was the attitude of Sion, Gaenor's nineteen-year-old son. He was a carbon copy of his father, a farm boy to his bones and, though Gaenor had envisaged that she would have difficulty explaining her decision to him, she'd been pleasantly surprised.

'Don't worry,' Sion had responded cheerfully. 'It's the perfect excuse for me not to go to college. And Mum, you do have a right to be happy and, if you have to leave Dad, I'd rather you went to live with Uncle Daf because this way, I don't have to get used to a stranger.'

Yet, people did still avert their eyes sometimes and conversations seemed to die away when Daf came within earshot. Given that Gaenor, like most mothers of babies only weeks old, wasn't doing much socialising, Daf was determined to show his face in the pub every now and again, to demonstrate that he had nothing to be ashamed of. And the pub was so handy. As a man who'd grown up in the town, he wasn't missing the open countryside now that he could just step over the street and enjoy a pint or two. There was always good company to be had in the Goat but, that night, Daf had the pleasure of meeting one of his greatest friends, Huw Mansell.

Huw was a quiet, intelligent man with a pitch-black sense of humour. Daf had very little bitterness in his nature but every time he had encountered Huw Mansell since moving in with Gaenor, he was glad not to be married to Falmai any longer.

In Falmai's opinion, Mansell, with his standing in the community, his lovely Welsh and his well-connected family, had the potential to be the perfect man, but he was let down by his fatal lack of snobbery. For years, Falmai had been searching for the perfect wife for him, and for years, Daf had endured endless barbecues at Neuadd where the latest young teacher at the primary school was paraded as a prospective future partner for the highly eligible doctor. Eventually, however, Huw Mansell had settled the matter himself and Falmai was deeply disappointed in the choice he made: a girl he'd met at the bar in the Gwladys Street stand at Goodison Park.

Dana, named after the Irish Eurovision winner, was the polar opposite of Falmai's idea of a suitable wife: she was not only English but common, with no idea how to behave. Once, Dana had been invited to share a table with Falmai at a charity Sunday lunch. After downing a full bottle of Apple Sourz, Dana had explained to her astonished audience that she had only agreed to go on a date with Huw in the first case as a tribute to the great Wales and Everton player Neville Southall. It was her last invitation to a charity lunch.

'Daf, what's the score with micro-pigs?' the doctor asked. 'Is there a lot of paperwork involved?'

'What the hell do you want with a micro-pig?' Daf replied. 'You haven't got a farm.'

'The clue's in the name, plod; they're little pigs, to keep as pets. Plenty of room in our garden.'

'You'll still need a Holding Number from the Rural Payments Agency.'

'I've got no interest in subsidies. I just want to get a present for Dana.'

'A small pig can be every bit as much of a risk as a large one, in terms of infection. You'd better register, to be safe.'

'OK, I will.'

'What on earth does Dana want with a micro-pig anyway?'

Mansell shrugged his shoulders.

'God knows. But her birthday's coming up and I haven't got the time to take her anywhere warm so it looks like it's going to be the micro-pig.'

Daf smiled at the thought of Dana taking her micro-pig for a walk through Llanfair on a lead. Sunday morning, maybe, as Moriah Chapel was emptying out. He couldn't wait.

'You haven't tried the Mischief, Daf,' Huw observed.

One of the attractions of the Goat was the range of local beers. Daf was no expert but he liked to drink beers which were something other than a cocktail of chemicals. He had ventured to the Beer Festival in Bishop's Castle with Mansell a couple of times without learning much in the process but he did know that the pint in front of him was a good pint.

'Next time,' he promised, draining his glass.

'Just another cheeky one won't hurt.'

'No, I'd better be going.'

Daf was not prepared to admit the reason he was unwilling to have the other pint: the Neuadd Land Rover was parked opposite, outside his house. Daf did not consider himself the jealous type but he was anxious about John Neuadd. To give

Falmai her due, she accepted that her relationship with Daf was over, but John was desperate to lure Gaenor back to the vast, empty black-and-white farmhouse on the hill. Daf had expected a little more self-respect from his former brother-in-law, but John was heartbroken and prepared to change, offering everything to his wife if only she would return. Daf trusted Gaenor implicitly but still...

The front door opened straight into the sitting room and so it took only moments for Daf to discover who the visitor from Neuadd was. Sion was sitting by the stove, his baby sister in his strong arms.

'Hey, Daf, how was the Goat?' he asked, offering one of his large red knuckles for the baby to gnaw at.

'Grand, thanks. How's the lambing coming on?'

'All arrived by now.'

Gaenor came in from the kitchen with two mugs and a packet of biscuits. Realising for the hundredth time how lovely her face was and how gentle the look in her eyes, Daf felt a cold shudder down his spine. The truth was, he lived with a fear of losing her, which was the basis of his baseless anxiety.

'Hello *cariad*,' she said, seeing him in the doorway. 'You take this coffee and I'll make myself another one.'

'I'd rather have a drop of Bushmills after a couple of pints. You sit down.'

Before she did so, Gaenor had to check that Mali Haf was settled in the lap of her totally inexperienced brother. She was as happy as a lark, gazing up into his big brown face. To Daf, there was some kind of enchantment around his daughter. He attempted to remember if it had been like this with his older children but he could not.

On returning from the kitchen, glass in hand, Daf noticed a peculiar look on Gaenor's face, as if embarrassment was mixed with her usual kindliness.

'Fair play to him,' she was saying to Sion.

Sion turned to Daf. 'I was just telling Mum that Dad's gone on a date tonight.'

Daf searched Gaenor's face but found no trace of any longing there. He put his arm round her shoulders.

'Fair play to him indeed,' he declared. 'Anyone we know?'

'Some woman from over Llansantffraid. He met her last week at some Country Landowners do.'

'CLA? Is she posh then?'

'Shouldn't think so. Can't imagine Dad going with anyone who wasn't well used to the smell of silage.'

Daf had lost a fair bit of sleep before resolving to wreck the foundations of his family. Were he and Gaenor putting their own happiness before their duty to their children? He need not have worried; in the months since he'd left that bungalow built on Neuadd's land, the children had flourished, somehow. Carys was in love, Rhodri growing in self-confidence as children do in a home full of warmth, and Sion had matured. For the first time in his life, Sion had to look after himself, cook his own meals, make his own doctor's appointments. He was still immature compared to his cousin Carys but Daf was glad to see him develop: he would not have relished the role of stepfather to someone who got on his nerves.

'Did you see the Six o'Clock News?' asked Gaenor, breaking the atmosphere of leisurely quiet. 'My old friend Rhys Bowen was on, looking very sharp in a good suit, going on about the local economy.'

'Don't tell me that you're a friend of that bloody Tory!' exclaimed Daf. 'If it wasn't for the fuss over the windfarms, he would never have been elected last time. The people of Montgomeryshire will never send him back to the Assembly.'

'Rhys is a lovely bloke,' retorted Gaenor, with a nostalgic look on her face. 'He was two years older than me in school and I had a dreadful crush on him then.'

'Dear God, Llanfyllin must have been Ugly City if Rhys Bowen was the school idol.'

'He wasn't quite so chunky in those days,' chuckled Gaenor, delighted to have a chance to tease Daf.

'Never mind how much of a pin-up he was, Rhys Bowen knows his stock,' was Sion's contribution to the discussion. 'When he comes to the Smithfield, he only buys the best. I reckon I'll vote for him.'

'And I will,' agreed Gaenor. 'For old times' sake.'

Daf rose to his feet, feigning annoyance. 'A nest of Tories under my own roof!' he exclaimed. 'Shocking!'

'OK then, Daf, who's your choice?'

'I've always been loyal to Plaid.'

Gaenor made a scornful noise in the back of her throat. 'I'd rather Rhys Bowen than that bloody Heulwen Breeze-Evans. The perfect farmer's wife!'

'Just because she wins the cookery cup in Llanfair Show every year and you can never get better than Highly Commended, Mum.'

'No. Well, OK, yes, but there are plenty of other things as well. She's a snob.'

'High time Plaid had a local candidate,' pronounced Daf. 'And Mrs Breeze-Evans has worked very hard in the community over the years, what with the schools, and the County Council and the Enterprise Project...'

'Fair enough,' answered Sion, 'but have you ever met anyone who called her a friend?'

'I admit she doesn't shake hands and take everyone to the bar for a pint like Rhys Bowen, but she has achieved quite a bit locally.'

'What about the Liberals?'

'Some bloke from off. No, it'll be a straight fight here between Rhys Bowen and Heulwen Breeze-Evans in this election. I'm sorry I can't turn out to help campaign but as a policeman, I'm not allowed.'

'As the father of a six-week-old baby, you're not allowed.'

'I had no idea you were that much of a Plaidy, Daf,' observed

Sion. 'We've always been big Liberals at Neuadd but to me, as a farmer, it makes sense to back a butcher, and if the butcher just happens to be some bit of a fair chap as well, I'm not fussed what party he supports.'

Daf opened his mouth to begin a lecture on the advantages of independence for small nations but Sion was spared by the ringing of Daf's phone. The station.

'Sorry, I'm not on duty, Steve.' But it only took two sentences of Steve's report for Daf to change his mind. 'I'll be down there with you right away.'

As he was putting his phone in his pocket, Daf was aware of six eyes looking at him.

'I've got to go. Big fire down in Welshpool.'

'You can't drive, Daf – that was a fair-sized whisky and you've had two pints.' Gaenor said exactly what Daf himself had been thinking.

Sion stood up gingerly, trying not to disturb Mali Haf.

'I'll run you down, Daf,' he offered. 'Then one of your team can drop you back later.'

'Thanks a lot, lad. You ready to go now?'

'No worries.'

On the way down to Welshpool, Daf received three more phone calls, another from Steve to check he was on his way, one from WPC Nia and the third from Joe Hogan.

'Daf, how're you doing?'

'Good thanks, Joe. Isn't it a bit late for a social call?'

'You do know that there's a building on fire in Canal Street?'

'On my way there now.'

'Glad to hear it because a couple of members of my flock live in the flat upstairs. I want to make sure they get fair play, OK?'

Joe Hogan, priest of the Catholic parish of Welshpool. An intelligent and observant man, he was principled without being naïve. In Daf's opinion, his life was a total waste: no family, no money and nothing to look forward to but a future of more hard work, but Joe was the most contented man Daf had ever met. He wasn't a man living in a philosophical bubble, either; as chaplain to the prison in Shrewsbury before it closed and as the leader of a parish full of sinners, he and Daf had worked together on many occasions. When he spoke of fair play, Daf knew what to expect: trouble with travellers or Polish lads.

Before they'd even reached Welshpool, the smell of smoke had reached Daf's nostrils. Above the town in the distance, a smoky orange glow tainted the sky.

'Quite some fire, then,' said Sion, under his breath.

Totally typical of the Neuadd family, thought Daf, to state the most obvious thing possible. Then he recalled Sion's generous offer of a lift and how happy Mali Haf was in her brother's arms and he started to feel guilty.

'Let me out by the station, could you, Sion?' he requested. 'And thanks again for the lift. I'll buy you a pint when you're on your next big night out in Llanfair.'

Sion laughed, showing the straight white teeth which were evidence of Gaenor's care, and years of costly braces.

'We don't do big nights out in Llanfair, Daf,' he replied, 'but it would be grand to crash on your sofa every now and then. The new house is right handy.'

'Any time, but don't bank on getting much rest; Mals isn't that good at sleeping.'

By now, they had reached the roundabout by the train station. Sion started to make a left turn.

'No, not here!'

'But Daf, you asked for a lift to the station.'

'The police station, Sion lad! I don't need to get on a train!'

Not for the first time, Daf wondered if there was something slightly odd about Sion because he never seemed to understand any wider meaning behind the words spoken to him. Daf recalled raising this with Carys who had responded, 'The whole Neuadd family are on some spectrum, Dad, don't worry about it.'

The car park outside the police station was full, so Daf jumped down onto the pavement.

'Thanks a lot, *lanc*.'

'Any time, Daf. I'm always looking for a bit of excitement in my life, as well you know.'

There was a fair bit of coming and going in the station reception area. Daf saw WPC Nia Owen making a beeline for him.

'Hell's bells, Nia, what are you doing here?'

'I was in bed, if you must know. And I'm pretty pissed off with Steve. He's completely lost his head and called everyone in. We don't need a family liaison officer just because a bloody shop is on fire.'

'Oh, it's a shop, is it?'

'I reckon so but I've only just arrived: I don't know any more than you do.'

Given that Nia was normally so keen on a bit of overtime, her attitude came as a surprise to Daf, then he glanced at the clock above the desk. Quarter past ten. An early night for Nia, perhaps?

'Were you asleep when Steve phoned?' he asked, all innocence. 'Or were you perhaps participating in a little … matrimonial activity?'

'Shut your head, boss. You stink of whisky … better chew a bit of gum before meeting any members of the public.'

Nev, who had overheard this conversation, raised his eyebrows.

'Poor you, Nia. Were you having a lovely little cuddle?'

'The harassment levels in this station are unbelievable,' responded Nia, before adding, with a smile, 'And Nev, don't make a big deal out of it. Everyone has a sex life, you know. Apart from you, of course.'

The external door opened and Steve came in, bringing in a cloud of smoke.

'Can you get up there straight away, boss? A couple of big Polish lads have come out of the Wellington: it seems their flat is above the fire and they're kicking off big time. There's a lot going on.'

In Daf's opinion, Steve was a good officer, one of the best, but there was a new note in his voice that night, a hint of fear. Daf stepped outside with him for a moment.

'What is it, *lanc*?' Daf asked.

'My Taid's place went on fire when I was a kid; I was staying there. Fires freak me out, to tell you the truth.'

His hand was shaking. Daf had never seen him in such a state before. He decided to divert him from his anxiety.

'You know what we need? An anchorman down here. Been onto the Trunk Road Agency? And Housing's 24-hour line? Get the Flash opened up for emergency accommodation. You man the fort here, OK? And don't mind if Nia's a bit sharp; you interrupted her and the other half on the job when you phoned.'

Steve hid his weakness behind a storm of laughter and Daf started his walk up towards the fire. He called back, 'Send Nia and Nev up after me, OK?'

Steve nodded and vanished into the station. Just before he was out of earshot, Daf heard an unusual sound from Steve's direction; a deep sigh, as if he were taking his first breath after being in deep water. Daf felt somewhat uneasy. One of his strengths was supposed to be his understanding of his team and yet, after working closely with Steve for almost ten years, he had had no idea about this fear of fire.

The heat hit Daf like a wall. He turned his head for a moment to fill his lungs with clean air before walking down the smoky street. There was ash everywhere and the stench of melting plastic. He noted the three fire engines: it looked like the situation was under control. A brick-built Victorian building was on fire, and a shudder ran through Daf's body as he realised that the Plaid Cymru office was at street level; it was as if their discussion of politics had sparked this. Like sheepdogs, the

PCSOs had emptied all the adjacent buildings and were looking after their flocks on the wide pavement by the museum. There were too many people about, Daf observed – fifty-odd members of the public were of no use at all to the emergency services as they went about their work. He walked up to the nearest PCSO.

'Time everyone went home, Ted,' he announced. 'Take those who live here over to the Flash, OK?'

As he examined the crowd, Daf noticed John Neuadd standing very uneasily beside a smart woman in her late thirties. Batting way above his average, perhaps, but there were those countless acres to take into account. Daf was surprised at first that John had managed to attract a woman like that, then he noted the narrow, hard expression on her face. A succession of emotions ran through Daf's head in seconds: guilt, annoyance, sympathy. John's date had clearly overheard Daf speaking to the PCSO and she marched over to confront him.

'What's going on here? Are you going to arrest them?'

She pointed her finger in the direction of two tall men, one of whom was bald. Their clothes and uneasy air declared at once that they were the Poles Steve had spoken of.

'I've just arrived,' Daf explained, succeeding in hiding the tremble which ran through him on hearing a voice so like that of his ex-wife. 'You'd better move to a safer place.'

'I have a business here,' she continued. 'I'm not moving a step until I know there's no risk of looting.'

Looting! Daf hadn't heard the word since his A level History lessons.

'We're in Welshpool, not Stalingrad.'

'I'm not so sure of that these days,' she retorted, scowling at the tall men.

'There's no need for any concern. Everything is under control,' answered Daf, not believing his own words.

Darren stepped up and John's companion retreated, muttering.

'These lads live in the flat above the office,' Darren began. 'They want to go in to get their stuff.'

'The place is on fire, for God's sake.'

'Looks like that doesn't bother them. It's pretty clear they don't trust anyone.'

Only odd flashes of light could be seen through the windows by now; the flames had mainly been extinguished. The bald man pointed to the door of the building.

'Fire is over. Now we go in.'

'No, sir. I'm afraid the building is still very dangerous,' Daf replied.

'My place. I pay rent. I go in.'

'No, that is not allowed,' insisted Daf, thinking how peculiar it was that they were communicating in the Thin Language, with both of them having to translate.

After over twenty years in the police, Daf had learnt to assess a risk pretty quickly. Looking at the two men in front of him, he was more concerned by the quiet one. He was a very strong man, with shoulders like a bull and great, hard hands like wooden mallets. His face reminded Daf of pictures he had seen of the famous baseball player, Babe Ruth, his nose spread across his face. An accident, fight or genetic problem? That was not the sort of nose Daf had ever seen on a primary school teacher or minister of religion. The owner of a nose like that was used to trouble, and in the deep grey eyes of the man standing in front of him, Daf saw restraint. It was as though the man knew that he had to keep himself in check. He didn't say a word but Daf had the uneasy impression that his eyes were capturing images of everything and storing them in his memory to be used when required. Daf was very glad to see the familiar form of Joe Hogan approaching through the smoke. The arrival of the priest had an impact on the two Poles as well; they even stood in a less confrontational manner and the bald man stared at the pavement like a naughty boy caught out by a teacher.

'O *co chodzi, chlopcy*?' Hogan began.

'*A Ojciec*,' answered the bald man, but the priest interrupted him.

'These lads will stay with me in the parish house tonight, Daf. I know them well.'

'I never knew you spoke Polish, Joe.'

'Oh, we're very cosmopolitan in Wrexham. My father, Lech, came over in the war as an army doctor, and after 1945 he came to Maelor, to the Polish hospital.'

Daf would have loved to hear more about this but, with a large building on fire in front of him, he decided not to ask any questions for the moment.

'Thanks a lot, Joe. These boys are very keen to go in to get their stuff but the place is still on fire. Besides, the site will have to be preserved so we can investigate the cause of it.'

'I understand.'

The quiet man started to speak to Joe and there was an anxious look on his face. Daf had to admire the comfort Joe seemed able to provide his parishioners: under his care, the man's grey eyes grew calmer.

'Milek is concerned about his sister,' Joe explained. 'She lives in the flat as well.'

'Where is she now?' Suddenly, the nature of the event had changed. As a policeman, Daf was well aware of his duty to protect property, but to him, helping people was the point of his job. A fire like this was nothing but a nuisance, but if someone was trapped in the building, nuisance turned into tragedy. Joe picked up on his friend's concern.

'No, don't worry, Daf. Basia has gone out for the evening but her brother wants her to know where they are, if she gets here before they've had a chance to speak to her.'

'Hasn't she got a mobile?'

Joe smiled for a moment. 'Her phone is switched off. I get the impression that Milek is not overly fond of the boyfriend.'

'Well, if she turns up here, I'll tell her, of course.'

For some reason, perhaps the look in Milek's eyes, Daf was

curious and very keen to meet his sister. But before that, there was plenty to do.

Five yards ahead of Daf was Fire Officer Chubb Evans, talking on his mobile phone. Chubb had been in school with Daf and was, in his opinion, a thorough pain in the neck. With his wavy hair and fat face, he reminded Daf of a self-satisfied hamster.

'Oh. Daf,' he said, in a disappointed tone, as if he had anticipated an officer of higher status.

'Sorry, Chubb, the Chief Constable's on holiday.'

'And please stop calling me Chubb. I am Fire Officer Lewis John Evans.'

'Delighted to meet you,' joked Daf, shaking his hand, though he was perfectly well aware that Chubb had no sense of humour of any kind. 'What have we got here then, mate?'

'I would say that we have a rather suspicious fire. I've checked the HMO register and the HHSRS status and there are no reported problems with the flats upstairs.'

'What the hell is the HHSRS and ... whatever the other thing is?'

Daf watched the fat face of the fire officer puff up with pleasure as his technical knowledge gave him the upper hand.

'Housing Health and Safety Rating System, and Houses in Multiple Occupation.'

'Who's the landlord?'

'Rhys Bowen, the butcher.'

'Our Assembly Member? That's very strange.'

'Why?'

'It's strange to think that a Tory is renting an office to Plaid Cymru.'

'Ah, so that's what was on the ground floor. I don't have any specific information about the office but the whole building was rewired three years ago. We definitely know that the fire started in the office.'

'How do you know that?'

'Because, Daf Dafis, I am a fire officer.'

Daf sighed under his breath. A suspicious fire like this probably meant weeks of close collaboration between the police and the fire brigade, and if Chubb was going to be like this, Daf was not looking forward to the partnership at all.

Four men emerged from the front door of the building, and when the first of them pulled off his mask, Daf knew what team it was: the Llanfair Caereinion retained firemen.

Daf wasn't at all sentimental about his home patch, but when he thought about the Llanfair firemen, everyday heroes willing to risk their lives for their neighbours, he couldn't help feeling pretty damn proud. Time after time, Daf had worked with them in dangerous situations and seen their professionalism, their courage and, above all, their humour. In their number were three farmers, a quarryman, the warehouseman from Wynnstay Agriculture, a contractor, a caravan site owner, one of the mechanics from Top Garage, a tree surgeon and Roly the odd-job man. A gossip-addicted bachelor in his late thirties, Roly was the first to come over to have a laugh with Daf.

'Here he is, lads,' he cried, loosening the strap of his oxygen tank. 'The policeman who does a bit of thieving.'

'Go scratch, Roly. I don't steal.'

'You stole John Neuadd's wife!'

By now, they had gathered to receive the latest order from the Hamster but he was too busy with his mobile to pay attention.

'How's things inside?' Daf asked, ignoring the joke with a smile which made it clear that he hadn't taken offence.

'We got the flames extinguished pretty handy, because we got here in good time,' answered Mart, the tree surgeon. As the bravest of them all, Mart was always at the front, inspiring others.

'Old buildings like this are heckish strong,' added Roly. 'Old beams like concrete.'

'And you're sure there's no one inside?' Daf asked.

'We haven't been right through the place yet,' Mart explained. 'Behind the office, there's a second room, with a locked door.'

'But there's no reason for anyone to be in an office at that time of night anyway,' added Roly. 'These office types are nine to fivers.'

'This locked door,' Daf insisted, 'How much of a door is it? Because we ought to go through the whole place.'

'I wouldn't fancy putting my shoulder to it,' Mart replied. 'Even though the structure looks pretty sound, it's never a good idea to start forcing things in a building that's been on fire.'

'Fair enough. What about the lock? Do you reckon we could open it up if the key comes to light?'

Mart shrugged his wide shoulders.

'Worth a try.'

'Where did the fire start? On the ground floor, do you reckon?'

Chubb interrupted. 'I will not tolerate any theorising in a case like this, you understand, Fireman Parry?'

Mart gave Daf a sidewise glance before replying, 'Fine, boss. It's way too hot to open up the back room, anyway.'

Over the years, without developing any expert knowledge in the field, Daf had learnt something about the ways firemen work. One thing which always worried them was sudden draughts within a building or from outside: embers can roar into flame in seconds if fed with oxygen. Chubb raised his voice, 'Well done, Team Llanfair.'

'What about the others?' asked Roly, pointing at the other two fire tenders.

'Everyone has done very well,' added Chubb, clearly struggling to retain his patience.

Daf was very pleased to notice that the team had a new member, a young farmer who had run into a fair bit of trouble when the National Eisteddfod was in Meifod. At the time, Daf had considered charging him with possession with intent to supply but a strong warning proved enough for Ed Mills to change direction. After all, Daf considered, those who have never succumbed to some form of temptation during the

Eisteddfod are pretty few and far between. When Ed approached, Daf noticed that his face, beneath the soot, was rather pale.

'Can I have a word, Mr Dafis?' he asked.

'Of course you can, lad.'

Daf stepped into the shadows between the Cats Protection shop and the stylish ladies' outfitters, and waited for Ed to follow him.

'My first big fire, Mr. Dafis. Bit of an experience, I can tell you.'

'And how does the new job suit you?'

'This job, or farming at Dolau, do you mean?'

'Both.'

Ed grimaced. 'You know the missus at Dolau, Mr Dafis. She's some bit of a hard woman. But there's plenty of work to do there, and I've told her flat out that if she complains too much, she can look for someone else to do it.'

'Fair play.'

'But the fire business, that's grand. You get two thousand a year just for being on call and the training ... well, talk about an eye-opener.'

'And this is your first big fire?'

'House fire, yes, but there was a helluva show down Berriew a fortnight ago. Four engines needed for a big barn full of straw.'

'And you're coping with the job at Dolau, the work at home and being a part-time Fireman Sam?'

'The YFC are on their lambing break, which helps. I'd rather be busy, anyway. But I don't really have much of a clue about this job, you know.'

'You look to me like you're on the right track, lad.'

'Maybe, but ... Well, I don't want to sound like a novice ... You know we have to wear our masks when we go into places like this?'

'Of course.'

'Well, my mask wasn't quite comfortable so I waited a minute, getting it sorted, before going in through the door.'

'And?'

'When I pulled my mask off for a moment, just to adjust it, I smelt something.'

'What?'

'Like roasting meat, pork maybe, or beef, but there was a strong tang of iron in it. I remembered something some teacher said in school one time, that the smell of flesh ... the flesh of people burning, was like ... pork roasting.'

Daf widened his nostrils as a reflex but smelt nothing but smoke.

'Are you suggesting there's someone inside, lad?'

'No idea. I just know what I smelt.'

'OK, boy, fair play to you. Go get yourself a drink now and try not to say anything for a bit. This smoke can make you hoarse.'

When Ed was out of earshot, Daf pulled his phone out of his pocket with a trembling hand.

'Joe, can you ask that lad for his sister's phone number? And her chap's number as well, if that's possible.'

'What's up, Daf?'

'Nothing. Just trying to make one hundred per cent sure there was no one in the building, that's all.'

Less than three minutes later, Daf received a text from Joe. Two names: Phil and Basia, and the numbers. At least Milek was prepared to co-operate. There was also a note from Joe, 'Milek is certain Basia has gone out for a meal with her "boyfriend".'

Within ten seconds, Daf had imagined the story from start to finish. An argument between brother and sister over her relationship, a blow, perhaps one blow was all that was necessary. Then, a fire to hide the evidence. As a synopsis for an episode of one of those trendy noir programmes, it would work perfectly, everything fitting so neatly into place. But somehow, real life was never like that. Daf had certainly seen danger in Milek's eyes, but danger to whom?

Daf rang the first number. No reply. The second went straight through to answer machine.

'*Helo Phil Evans sy'ma.* This is Phil Evans. Please leave a message after the tone and I'll reply when I can.'

The voice was well known to Daf. Not many people scratched at their letter 'r' as much as Phil Evans, a farmer from Dyffryn Banw. It was a family thing, according to his neighbours, which was made more obvious by nervousness. And, Daf considered, Phil Evans had plenty of reasons to be nervous. Apart from the fact that Milek was not his number one fan if he was indeed Basia's boyfriend, there was the little matter of his matrimonial status. Phil Evans was the husband of Heulwen Breeze-Evans, Plaid Cymru candidate for Montgomeryshire in the Welsh Assembly election.

# Chapter 2

## *Monday evening, April 12, 2016 – later*

Daf hurried over to Chubb, who was talking to a tall man in fire service uniform. From Chubb's body language, it was obvious who the boss was.

'Mr Richards, here's Daf Dafis, from the police.'

The man nodded, but Daf stuck his hand out to be shaken. 'Inspector Daf Dafis.'

'Quentin Richards. Head of Response, North Powys.'

There was no for time for politeness so Daf asked, abruptly, 'Chubb, are you sure there was no one in the building?'

'Of course. The office was closed and when I asked the ... the men from Poland, they said the only residents upstairs were themselves and a girl. And don't call me Chubb.'

Daf was pretty sure Chubb had been on the verge of using a racist term but had reined himself in in the nick of time.

'Did you check?'

'The place was ablaze, Dafis. There was no point standing outside yelling, "Anybody there?" We went through the place with great care, as we always do.'

Daf ran off full pelt in the direction of the bridge. Just before he reached the canal, he turned up the narrow lane which ran behind the buildings, parallel to the street. He took his torch out of his pocket; it was dark in the smoke and the shadow of the high brick walls. Far behind him, he heard Chubb's voice, out of breath, trying to shout. 'It's not safe there!'

He saw a wooden door in the wall which was flecked with ash and soot, falling like black snow around him. It was locked. Daf threw his shoulder against it, hard enough to break the bolt loose, and fell into a small yard containing nothing but recycling bins. There was broken glass everywhere from the windows which had shattered in the heat. Daf paused to fill his lungs and, amid the smells of the fire, he detected something else. He had smelt burning flesh many times, mainly after car accidents. He approached the only ground floor window which faced the yard and raised his torch. Given that little glass remained in the frame, it was relatively easy to look into the room. There was a table large enough to hold a meeting, several filing cabinets and a wide desk. In a chair by the desk, there was a body.

Daf stepped back from the building to get his breath back before phoning the station. He saw Chubb standing in the door between the yard and the lane, a seriously angry expression on his face.

'What do you think you're doing, Dafydd Dafis? I've been shouting after you till I'm hoarse. This building is dangerous; no one is authorised to go into it.'

'But there's already someone inside actually.'

'What?'

'In the back room. There's a body.'

'Impossible. The boys have been through the place.'

'Martin told me that the door to the back office was locked. He was concerned about the structure of the building, so he didn't attempt to break in.'

'A wise decision, in the circumstances.'

'Oh, shut your face for a moment, will you, Chubb?' Daf exploded, unwilling to use the small amount of breath he had to talk crap with a man who seemed interested in nothing but covering his own back. 'I'm not blaming anyone, but this totally changes the nature of the case. Someone has been killed. If the fire was intentional, we're looking at manslaughter, if not, murder.'

Daf coughed and for a moment thought he was going to throw up, but the moment passed and he spat onto the ground. He felt filthy. He phoned the station and heard an unexpected voice: Sheila.

'What's up, *lodes*? You're not on duty.'

'No more than Nia; we've all been called in.'

'But Nia isn't newly married. What did Tom have to say about it?'

Sheila laughed. 'Tom's a very lucky man and he knows it. He married a policewoman and so he can expect me to be called in on an emergency every now and then.'

'Well, it's a real emergency now, *lodes*, there was someone in the building.'

'Who?'

'I'm not sure but I think it's a woman called Basia Bartoshyn.'

'Tall woman, blonde hair, big grey eyes?'

'Very likely. Do you know her?'

'I know her now. She just walked in through the door here, with Phil Dolfadog, believe it or not.'

Daf had two reasons to smile. He had to give maximum respect to Sheila: since starting courting Tom Francis, she had got to know every farmer in the district, as well as where and how they farmed. The second reason for smiling was his own over-confidence. After his conversation with Ed Mills, Daf had created a complete, convenient story which explained the fire, the body and the offender, all details present and correct. Unfortunately, the suspected corpse had just walked into the police station so he would need to get himself another theory.

'I want to talk to them.'

'She's concerned about her brother, who lives in the flat above the fire. She says he drinks too much sometimes.'

'You can tell her that Milek is safe and that he's staying the night at the priest's house.'

'I'll tell her now; she'll be very glad to hear it.'

'And after that, Sheila, you'd better phone HQ and give them some version of "Houston, we have a problem". Because Derek Bright from Newtown is on annual leave and Simon Harris from Aber hasn't come back from sick, so they're going to have to send one of the big chiefs up here to be Senior Investigating Officer. And given that the fire was in the Plaid Cymru office, that SIO had better be a Welsh speaker.'

'Can't you be in charge, boss? You're a good policeman.'

'You have to be a Chief Inspector to deal with a case like this, Sheila, you know that.'

'What nonsense.'

'Their problem, anyway.'

Daf's update produced a significant change in attitude amongst the firemen. No one fancied a joke anymore, or spoke above a whisper. Daf noticed that Ed Mills's face was as white as chalk.

'You were right, lad. Someone *had* died in there,' Daf said to him in a low voice.

'Shit, shit, shit, Mr Dafis. We couldn't have done any more – the fire had got a hold before we arrived.'

'You've all done grand, the whole team. I won't tell you not to think about it but don't feel guilty, right? There was nothing more you could have done.'

'Thanks, sir. But, well, you know how we all are. Up to now, it's been a good laugh, but now, thinking how we were joking on the way over here, well, it feels like we were insulting the person who died.'

'You're wrong there, lad. The joking is important to people like us, people who choose to spend their time dealing with crap situations like this. It helps us survive. Without a bit of banter, we would have all gone crazy years ago, which wouldn't have helped anyone.'

'OK.'

On his way over to speak to Nev, Daf encountered Martin.

'Can you keep an eye on the lad, Mart?' he asked.

'Of course I will. We all struggle a bit with our first stiff. Who was it?'

'No idea yet.'

'Was it an office, that back room?'

'Yes.'

'Bit late for someone to be working, wasn't it?'

'But it wasn't exactly a normal office, Mart. This was the headquarters of the Plaid Cymru election campaign.'

'Oh. I never follow that stuff. I just vote for Rhys Bowen because he's a good chap, that's all.'

Daf had to hide his disappointment. He was starting to think that the electors of Montgomeryshire needed some kind of major political consciousness-raising exercise but there were more pressing matters to hand.

'Hey, Nev, have you heard?'

'Yeah, boss. I've started with the tape barriers, front and back. Who's going to log people in and out?'

'You till midnight, if that's OK?'

'No worries. SOCOs on their way?'

'I'm not expecting to see any of them until morning. The place has to be safe before they get in.' And Daf knew perfectly well that the Scene of Crime officers weren't likely to drive up from Carmarthen in the middle of the night unless there was a very special reason indeed.

'What about the Crime Scene Manager? We're not going to get lumbered with that girl from Tregaron again, are we?'

Daf had to smile. He had been pretty sure Nev had taken a fancy to that CSM. She was a good-looking girl but Nev was spot on about her being annoying: she spoke as if she'd spent too much time in New Zealand with her voice rising at the end of every sentence like she were asking a question.

'I haven't thought about it yet.'

'You know what, boss? Steve has just finished that course, hasn't he? Forensics and Operational Policing or something like that? We've heard enough about it over the last two years, anyway.'

'Good thinking, Nev. You going to be OK here if I nip back to the station?'

'No worries. What if the press turn up?'

'Get real, lad, it's way past their bedtime. Unless it was Prince Charles in that back room, we won't hear a peep from them till at least ten o'clock tomorrow morning.'

Nev laughed, but there was a hint of disappointment in his voice: he was very fond of Warhol's idea about five minutes of fame and his seemed to be a very long time coming.

'I'll send Steve up anyway, CSM or not, OK?'

'Fair enough, boss. What do I do with the woman from the jewellery shop? She's a heck of a nuisance, her over there with your ... with your...'

'With my ex brother-in-law? Tell her she's got to go because she's within the outer perimeter of the crime scene and when the testing gets started, if there is any trace of her DNA, she'll find herself under suspicion.'

'And she'll swallow that?'

'Give her the choice between making herself scarce or coming down to the station for loads of tests. She'll disappear like snow off a bank, I bet.'

Daf had to leave his contact details with the fire officers. By now, the Llanfair engine had gone, leaving only the Welshpool crew and the Head of Response.

'Do you think the site will be safe by morning, Mr Richards?' Daf asked.

'In terms of fire risk or internal structure?'

'Both.'

'We'll have team members here through the night to monitor for hotspots, and the fact that the windows are out means the risk of compartment blowback is reduced. A building surveyor from the County Council will be over in the morning to assess the damage.'

'Of course, but first thing, the experts will be arriving: SOCOs, pathologist, forensic photographer, the lot, and it's vital that they get cracking as soon as possible.'

'I am perfectly well aware of the pressures, Inspector Dafis. If I were you, I'd get the carbon dogs in.'

'Carbon dogs?'

'Dogs which have been specially trained to detect various catalysts, or accelerants, as we call them.'

'Accelerants?' repeated Daf, uncomfortably aware that he sounded like a parrot.

'Anything used to make a non-accidental fire burn more rapidly or with increased intensity. Very effective, those dogs.'

'Thank you for the suggestion. Here's my card and I'll be sending your details on to the Chief Investigating Officer.'

'Thank you, Inspector Dafis.'

Perhaps it was paranoia but Daf detected a sneer in Richards's voice, as if he was using Daf's rank ironically. He was rather surprised, therefore, by the next question.

'Why do you call Fire Officer Evans "Chubb"?'

'It's his school nickname. He always had a tendency to be a bit of a chunky monkey and he liked his fishing. Hence, Chubb.'

Richards nodded without the slightest trace of a smile.

'Very witty, Inspector Dafis, very witty. No wonder you are often described as one of the most amusing officers in the Central Wales Emergency Services.'

Daf couldn't find a reply to this patronising remark. He made a resolution to never again crack a joke within earshot of the Head of Response.

On his way down to the station, Daf considered the identity of the body in the back office. He wasn't a member of any political party but in his time at college in Aber he had taken part in a number of protests, against Tony Blair and his war in Iraq and in support of the Welsh language. He shocked himself when he realised that, by now, he couldn't really recall the reasons for getting up so early on so many Saturday mornings and catching so many minibuses to go somewhere or another to oppose or support something. He also realised that he hadn't got the slightest idea about the process of an electoral campaign so he would have to speak to the candidate herself, but before that, he needed to talk to the candidate's husband, who was waiting in the police station, accompanied by a Polish woman.

Daf tried to recollect what he knew about Phil Evans. Older than Daf, a farmer, not one of the local big shots, not notable for anything in particular. No, that wasn't quite true. Daf remembered how, many years ago, Falmai and her friends had been discussing the attributes of local men and Phil Evans was at the top of every list as the most fanciable. One of the women had said, laughing, 'Who cares if there's nothing behind that pretty face of his? The pretty face is enough.'

After marrying, Phil hadn't settled. He still came down to the Goat on a Friday night and disappeared pretty regularly with some girl or another. Plenty like Phil about, good husbands during the week turning into Friday adulterers, and plenty of women willing to play their part in the game. Daf knew a fair number of them and they worried him less than those whose misdemeanours involved drinking ten pints and driving home. Daf tried to recall any of Phil's pick-ups in particular but couldn't.

The scene which faced Daf when he arrived at the station did not accord easily with his assumptions. Phil Evans was sitting with his arm around the waist of a woman a fair bit younger than himself, and the look in his eyes seemed to say that this was quite different from his usual run of flings. Until that moment, Daf had never really understood the enthusiasm all the women in the area seemed to have for Phil Dolfadog but tonight, with love reflected on his face, he was a very attractive man. The years had been kind to him, leaving not much grey in his generous fair hair and when he opened his mouth to speak, his teeth were still straight and white.

But if Phil ranked as attractive, the woman by his side was a real beauty: tall and slender with gleaming golden hair. She had enough of the colour of the sun on her cheeks to look healthy without make-up, while the shape of her lips forced Daf to think of kissing, but more than anything, it was her eyes which defined her beauty. Deep, wide grey eyes with a touch of anxiety in them, enough to suggest that she was awaiting a knight in shining armour to defend her from danger. Daf understood her brother's concern. Basia was worth defending, from everything and everyone in the world.

'Bloody hell, Daf Dafis, am I glad to see you,' Phil began. 'Basia's heckish worried about her brother.'

'Milek's safe. He's staying the night with the priest.'

'Thank goodness,' Basia breathed. 'He ... he does drink too much sometimes and sleeps very heavily. Is Wiktor safe as well?'

Her exotic accent and good Welsh enchanted Daf: he was glad that he was settled in a loving relationship because there was something very appealing about Basia, witness or not.

'You can speak Welsh?' he asked, without thinking.

'Well, I have tried to learn,' she replied with a wide smile. 'It's not polite to live somewhere without learning the language, is it?'

'Very much so. I wish everyone who came here agreed with you.'

'Ah, but do remember,' Basia responded, 'most have a grave disadvantage. Those who have been raised speaking world languages like English, or Mandarin, or Russian, they never value the pearls they could find in the small languages. They tend to be lazy because everyone speaks their languages.'

Phil squeezed her tight in a gesture of pride as well as ownership. 'Basia speaks seven languages fluently,' he boasted.

'But I have only learnt six of them,' Basia corrected him, modestly. 'We can't count Polish.'

'Come through and sit down for a minute, please,' Daf asked them. 'I have to learn a bit more about the building.'

A glance passed between Phil and Basia, and Daf tried very hard not to think that a girl like this deserved better than to be a notch on the bedpost of Phil Dolfadog.

'I'd rather speak to my brother as soon as possible,' Basia protested.

'Sorry, but this is a very serious matter.'

Phil noticed the expression in Daf's eyes and clearly decided to co-operate.

'We're in no great hurry, Daf,' he declared. 'But could Basia just make a quick phone call before we start?'

'Of course.'

While Basia was speaking to Milek, Daf took the opportunity to find Nia and arrange for her to take notes.

'I was about to go home for the night, boss,' she protested.

'No one else has got good enough Welsh to follow the conversation, *lodes*.'

'Welsh? Don't you mean Polish? Gosh, that little miss has got her claws pretty deep into Phil Dolfadog.'

'Looks to me like Phil is the lucky one there.'

Nia made a sceptical noise in her throat and Daf was glad of the warning. He would have to hide his admiration of Basia to avoid unfavourable comments from members of his team, particularly Nia and Sheila. They were of the opinion that Daf had a tendency to be too soft with women, especially if they just happened to be good-looking. Daf opened the door to Steve's office.

'I know you only did that forensics course because you're a sad weirdo with no life, Steve, but do you fancy being CSM on this one? We've got a body in the building.'

'If you reckon I could, boss...'

'No worries at all, lad. You know the drill, keep the paperwork sharp and don't take any shit from experts or the press.'

Daf was very glad to see the smile on Steve's face. He was a good officer but life in Montgomeryshire could sometimes be a bit quiet for an ambitious young man. 'Oh, and Steve?'

'Yes, boss?'

'Now you're not doing that forensics course, there's no excuse to avoid your Welsh lessons. We've got a witness in the case who puts you to shame.'

Steve sighed as he heard the familiar complaint, and Daf shut the door. Basia was just behind him.

'A body?' she asked, her eyes wider than ever.

'Yes. That's why it's so important to find out who was in the building tonight. Come in and sit down so we can have a proper chat.'

Daf noticed how often Basia's eyes turned in Phil's direction and, contrary to his expectations, Phil's attitude was caring and supportive. Given that he was a good twenty years older than Basia, there was something paternal in his attitude but there was nothing paternal in the way he ran his eyes over her body. Somehow, she didn't come across as a woman who was having an affair with a married man, but it was obvious that they had been out on a date that night.

'Right, here we go. WPC Owen is here to take a few notes but this is not a formal interview, OK?'

'Fine,' responded Basia, drawing her chair a little closer to Phil's before sitting down. Nia was clearly startled.

'And you're perfectly happy speaking in Welsh?'

'I am,' Basia answered with a smile. 'Unless you're fluent in Polish. By now, my Welsh is better than my English. I only seem to use English in the shops.'

'That's fine then, we'll continue in Welsh. How about starting with who you are?'

'I am Basia Bartoshyn. I'm thirty years old and I live in the flat above the Plaid Cymru office in Welshpool with my brother Milek. I was born in Czestochowa in Poland and I've lived in Wales for five years. I clean the Plaid office, the offices of the solicitors Bebb, Jones, Hamer, the infants school at Oldford and also at Mid Wales Meats, but only the offices there, not the factory.'

Fair play to her, Daf observed, she had learnt the irregular plural of the word 'office'.

'And you know me well enough,' Phil added. 'I'm Phil Evans and I've been farming at Dolfadog since I was twenty.'

'Is Dolfadog your farm?'

'Hell no, Daf, it's the wife's inheritance. And by now, my lad is more of a boss there than I am.'

'Looks to me like you've got other interests in life besides farming, Phil.' Daf had to admit that he did feel a flicker of jealousy towards a man who seemed to have achieved so little in his life and yet had managed to attract a woman like Basia. 'Anyway, who lives in the flat?' he addressed Basia again.

'Only Milek and I. But there is another room upstairs, not a proper flat but just a room, with a fridge beside the bed, and an oven almost in the shower, and that's where Wiktor sleeps, but he comes down to us to eat, or watch TV, or play cards.'

'And who is Wiktor?'

Basia sighed.

'I don't know. If you live like we live, as strangers, you tend to cling to anyone who is at all like you. He comes from the Białystok area originally, not far from Belarus. Milek met him at work.'

Daf saw a look on her face that suggested she was only telling half of the truth.

'And how do the three of you get on?'

'Wiktor is a bad influence. He always wants to be wasting money in the pubs and he persuades Milek to go with him. We get on alright, living together, but I wouldn't call him a friend.'

Perhaps Daf was imagining it but he thought there was some trace of pride in Phil's eyes.

'Is Wiktor a nuisance to you, Basia?'

She thought for a while before replying. 'He can be, but not usually.'

'Does he fancy you?'

Phil squeezed her hand for a moment. 'Is this relevant, Daf?' he asked.

'Someone died in the fire and it's very possible that they were killed. So, I am interested in everything that went on under that roof.'

'It's fine, Phil,' Basia declared, with a brave little smile. 'It's old news by now. Milek wasn't happy ... well, he thinks I need a husband. So, between them, Wiktor and Milek tried to put a bit of pressure on me. I tried to sort it out myself but in the end, I had to get a bit of help.'

'From Phil?' Daf asked, trying to imagine what use Phil Dolfadog might be against two large and stubborn men.

'Phil? Why would I do that? Milek doesn't like Phil so he'd never listen to him. No, I called Father Hogan in. Everything's been fine since then.'

'Father Hogan?'

Phil offered an explanation. 'You need to understand, Daf, religion is very important to them,' Phil explained. 'The church isn't just a place for funerals and so on. The priest is a big man for them, with a fair bit of influence, even over men like Milek and Wiktor.'

'Why didn't you move out, Basia, if your brother and his friend were making things awkward for you?'

'Milek's still my brother. And in fact, he is right. I would love to be married and have a family, only not with Wiktor.'

'You two hadn't thought of living together? You look pretty close.'

Basia reddened. 'Phil already has a wife. Whatever he feels about me, he still has a wife.'

'And, speaking frankly, it's your wife who has all the money, eh, Phil?'

It was Phil's turn to blush. 'This has got nothing to do with money, Daf. I'd sleep in the chip shop doorway if it meant I could be with Basia, get over the barriers between us. Money doesn't count for anything.'

Normally, when people denied any interest in money, Daf was pretty sceptical but there was a sincere tone in Phil's voice.

'Why not get divorced then? It's only a matter of filling in a few forms if money's not a big issue.'

'Mr Dafis,' Basia declared, her voice full of dignity, 'I don't know what you think about me, but I can guess. On this side of the desk, you can see a foreign cleaner in a relationship with an older man who happens to be well off. It's an old story. You think I was looking for an easy life, that I used my looks, if they could be used for such a thing, to make a move on Phil before I realised that every penny he has belongs to his wife.'

'Hey, *lodes*, I don't make assumptions. I just try to fit everything together, like doing a jigsaw.'

'It was me who chased after her, Daf. You know ... you know I like a bit of female company.'

'Everyone round here knows that, Phil.'

'I can't...' Basia paused and cleared her throat, blushing again. 'I can't love a man outside of marriage, Mr Dafis. Nor can I marry a man who has a wife already. That's it.'

Daf prided himself on his mature attitude towards women but the knowledge that a woman as attractive as Basia was still a virgin was intoxicating. He found himself starting to think of how privileged a man might feel if Basia decided to give herself to him. Then he recalled a discussion with Joe Hogan about the ridiculous rules of the Catholic Church. Daf always thought that any rules which stood between people and their chance at happiness were both stupid and cruel but according to Joe, they laid proper emphasis on important matters, expecting people to make their sexual choices with more consideration than choosing a brand of yoghurt from the chill cabinet of the supermarket.

In front of him, Daf saw a woman willing to sacrifice her happiness to follow the rules of her faith, old-fashioned or not. Then he recalled how many women had been in sexual relationships of various kinds with Phil over the years. Perhaps, from Basia's point of view, there was some advantage to be gained from the rules. Whatever else happened, she wasn't going to end up as another episode in Phil Dolfadog's history of hump and dump.

'OK, back to practical matters. There's a room at the back on the first floor, with the door locked.'

'Heulwen's office,' Phil confirmed.

'Who's got a key?'

'Well, I have, of course,' answered Basia. 'Heulwen herself,

Milek, because he does little jobs for her every now and then, things too small to bother the landlord about, the girl who's helping with the campaign, and the landlord himself, Mr Bowen.'

'It's an odd thing, isn't it, for a Tory Assembly Member to be renting an office to Plaid Cymru?'

Phil shrugged. 'He's a businessman, is Rhys Bowen, and as long as the rent gets paid, it doesn't matter to him.'

'The place has only been an office for three years,' Basia contributed. 'Before Plaid took it, Menter Maldwyn were there for a year and before that, it was a clothes shop.'

'I remember. How long have you been in the flat?'

'Since we came from Czestochowa. Over five years, now. Milek was offered the flat because he works in Mr Bowen's factory.'

'You mentioned a girl who works in the office.'

Phil cleared his throat. 'Her name's Anwen.' There was no interest in his voice.

'Anwen who?'

'I don't know. I've got no interest in this politics lark, to tell the truth. Montgomeryshire is a target seat, so they say, so Plaid have sent some girl to help Heulwen.'

'Local girl?'

'No, no, from way over by Mach somewhere.'

Daf managed to stop himself laughing aloud. Phil Dolfadog was parochial enough to describe a girl from Mach as though she came from another planet, but had fallen head over heels in love with a girl from Eastern Europe with a history, language and culture completely different to his own.

'Have you got a phone number for her?'

'Anwen's phone number? No, sorry. Listen, Daf, I think it's high time you spoke to Heulwen, I can't give you any more help.'

'Where is she?'

'No idea. Home, perhaps, or in some meeting.'

Daf noted the distance and boredom in Phil's eyes as he

spoke about his wife. As if he could read Daf's thoughts, Phil expanded.

'I'd better be honest, Daf. Heulwen decided she wanted a husband when I was twenty years old: she's eight years older than me. Of course, I was flattered. I was a labourer and she was the boss's daughter. Then Hywel died, her brother, so when the old man went as well, I was in charge at Dolfadog before I was twenty-five. But I wasn't master of the place; she was in charge of the lot. I didn't mind it so much until the kids were old enough to notice the disrespect in her voice and the scorn in her eyes. We've been living apart under one roof for ten years. We meet up in the kitchen every now and again. She gets on with her own things and I carry on from day to day.'

'And the children?'

'Gone. Well, Jac converted the old calf shed and he lives there with his wife.'

Daf saw Basia's eyes fill with weariness. He sympathised with her once more and couldn't see any pressing reason to keep her at the station any longer.

'Where will you stay tonight, Basia?' he asked.

'With my brother, I hope. There are two spare rooms at the presbytery.'

'Well, I think you've contributed enough for tonight. Make sure you leave your contact details at the desk.'

'If you have anything more to ask, can you do it now, please? I start work around five tomorrow morning.'

'No, that's fine, Basia. What about your things ... clothes and so on?'

'There's always a few spare things at the presbytery. I'll pop into Tesco's tomorrow some time.'

Phil cut across. 'I can't bear to think of you wearing second-hand clothes, or rubbish from the supermarket.'

It sounded like the latest round in a long-term argument.

'I'm poor, Phil, so I buy my clothes from charity shops and supermarkets. And you have no right to use your wife's money to buy me anything. I'm not your whore, Philip Evans, you remember that.'

For the first time, Daf saw the same flash in Basia's eye that he had seen in her brother's, a spark of strength and risk. Basia Bartoshyn was a woman and a half, Daf thought, and it was clear that Phil agreed, as he responded to her outburst with nothing more than an admiring sigh.

On the wall in his office, Daf had a clock which had once hung above the counter in his father's shop. It was large, with the slogan 'Nearly Horlicks o'Clock' running across its broad white face. Every time Daf looked at it, he was back in the shop, reaching for a little box of mustard from a top shelf and opening up a big package containing Benson and Hedges. Daf loathed the influence of all types of religion but at the same time respected the beauty of the language of the Bible. The clock reminded him of the verse from Isaiah: 'Forget not the rock from which you are hewn.' For him, the family shop was that rock.

Twenty past eleven. He thought of his bed, of Gaenor's welcoming arms, of the smell of Mali's skin on the pillow, but before turning for home, he had to discover the identity of the body in that back room. And having crossed Basia's name off the list of potential victims, one name was obvious.

'Nia,' he called, 'have you got the phone number for Dolfadog?'

'Yes,' she replied, 'and Mr Rhys Bowen is on his way to see you and it's pretty clear he's had himself a good supper somewhere.'

Nia came through with a Post-it note in her hand with three numbers on it, mobiles for Phil and Heulwen and the house phone. Daf rang the house. The phone rang for ages before he heard the answer machine.

'Dolfadog, Heulwen Breeze-Evans. Please leave a message after the tone.'

No answer on her mobile either; it didn't so much as ring.

'Sheila, can you check out the details on Heulwen Breeze-Evans's car, please? And ask the CPSOs to check the town car parks and the on-street parking. She could be the body in the office.'

He pulled out his phone: a text from Gaenor. 'If you need a lift home, I'll come down for you. Mals will be fine with Rhodri for half an hour whilst she's sleeping.'

He smiled to think of how she cared for him, cared for them all. Under her kindly influence, even Sion was growing up into a decent young man. He answered her text: 'Don't worry, *cariad*. I've still got a couple of things to do here. One of the troops will give me a lift. You deserve every second of sleep you can get xxx.'

He rang Dolfadog again, and, after some time, Phil picked up the phone.

'Is your wife there, Phil?'

'No. I haven't seen her since this morning.' There was a silence and when Phil spoke again there was a new note in his voice, a lightness. 'Do you want me to check her diary?'

'Please.'

Daf was angry with himself. If he had suggested to Phil that it could be his wife's body in the back office while he was at the police station, his reaction would have been obvious on his face. A chance had been wasted. And why? Because of Basia. Her presence had had such an effect on Daf that he'd failed to think clearly about Phil's situation: the man who admitted how things were between himself and his wife; the man who could not possess Basia, and who had been belittled by Heulwen for decades.

'Nothing after five o'clock. She was meeting the teaching unions at that time to discuss the county's school budgets, in her office, nothing after that.'

'Thanks for that. We're not sure yet but you'd better get ready for bad news. I'll come over to Dolfadog in the morning.'

'Not tomorrow, sorry, Daf. We've got new hens coming in tomorrow.'

'New hens?'

'Yes. Jac put up a laying unit three years back and tomorrow we're expecting sixteen thousand new hens.'

'Sorry, Phil, I thought you just said sixteen thousand hens.'

'That's exactly how many we're expecting here tomorrow. It'll be some heck of a busy day.'

'You don't get it, Phil – this won't be a social call. If Heulwen has died, we have to speak to her family, even if sixteen million hens are arriving, OK?

'OK.'

After putting the phone down, Daf tried again to recall all he knew about Phil Evans. Sociable, generous enough and on the edge between flirty and lustful with every girl he met, but never threatening. Superficial, lazy, teasing, the kind of man who took everything in life as a joke. From Daf's experience, murder was triggered from the depths of feelings, from uneasy characters, not shallow chaps like Phil Dolfadog. But because he had obviously changed under Basia's influence, Daf resolved to try to forget what he knew about Phil and treat him as he would any stranger under suspicion.

A man who hadn't changed enough, in Daf's opinion, came through the office door next: Rhys Bowen AM. He was a big man who always seemed to be wearing clothes which were rather too tight for him, as if he were unwilling to admit quite how much flesh was on his bones. His cheeks were red as a result of high living, plenty of steak, plenty of red wine. His hands were like spades and the bulky signet ring on his little finger looked delicate on such a paw. There was usually a broad smile on his face and the wrinkles at the corners of his port-coloured eyes were evidence of a jovial nature or, as Daf cynically thought, one who wanted to be seen to have a jovial nature. For a big man, he was light on his feet, and whenever he joined a group, he soon got the upper hand. The sort of man, Daf considered, who was inclined to enjoy giving orders to those whose labour brought him his profits. The sourness on his breath told of a good supper involving wine and garlic, and Daf struggled with the idea that Gaenor had ever had a crush on such a creature in school, no matter how many years had gone by since then.

'Inspector Dafis?' Rhys Bowen extended his hand over the desk before sitting down, not waiting to be asked. 'So this is what happens if you rent your place out to bloody nashies, eh? What happened? Sons of Glyndŵr training session, or what?'

'We don't have any theories at present but it is a serious case, especially since we've discovered a body in the back room.'

Bowen whistled through lips which were rather pale in comparison with his ruddy face.

'Fucking hell,' he hissed. 'Heulwen?'

'Very possible.'

'It was her place, that back room. The girl's not allowed in, that Anwen. A woman for keeping secrets, is Heulwen. Or she was. Fucking hell.' Little pearls of sweat appeared on Bowen's broad forehead.

'How well did you know Heulwen Breeze-Evans, Mr Bowen?'

'Oh, don't call me "Mister", *lanc*, I'm Rhys to everyone.' He took a deep breath before asking, 'Are you the policeman who pinched John Neuadd's wife? A right smart little piece was Gaenor Morris at school; I remember her well.'

Rage was almost choking Daf, so he couldn't say a word. Bowen licked his lips.

'Good taste, boy, good taste. Fair bit of a change for her, I'd say, but maybe what a man has in his bank account isn't so important to Gaenor as what he's got in his boxers.'

His patient nature had helped Daf time and again in his career, but he'd never been so close to punching a witness. The fact that Gaenor had once admired Bowen, even in her distant youth, made his words harder to ignore.

'Can we get back to the case, Mr. Bowen?'

'We had a school reunion just after Christmas, and there was hardly any talk about anything else. There were some couldn't understand it, given the farm he's got, but I said to them: a man like John Neuadd may be a big man at the Smithfield and still be a small man when he gets into bed.'

'Do you need a cup of coffee, Mr Bowen?' Daf asked, using up the last of his store of politeness. 'To clear your head a bit?'

'My head's fine, thanks, Inspector,' Bowen answered, pulling a little flask from his jacket pocket and taking a swig. 'You're not allowed a little brandy when you're on duty, Inspector?'

'No thanks. I hope you weren't thinking of driving home, Mr Bowen?'

'No, no. I've got some Tory boy hanging about somewhere to help.'

Daf had some sympathy for the Tory boy.

'So, did you know Mrs Breeze-Evans well, Mr Bowen?'

'I've known her for twenty years and more. I know Phil, of course, from the Smithfield, and I've been on a couple of committees with Heulwen.'

'What committees?'

'Business Development, Chamber of Commerce, things like that. And every now and again, she'd ask me to give a talk to Merched y Wawr and so on.'

'On what topic?'

Bowen laughed aloud.

'Well, no one's going to ask me to give a talk on democracy in Wales: meat is my trade. "Snout to tail" is my most popular topic, 'specially if I throw a couple of packets of scratchings into the deal.'

For the first time, Daf began to see what drew people to Bowen. For a man of some status, he kept his feet on the ground. And he was ready to laugh at himself: always a good sign.

'And since the campaign began?'

'Pure bollocks!' Bowen exploded, taking another swig of his

brandy. 'She's not a party woman, any party. She's just interested in her own patch.'

'And you, Mr Bowen?'

'You've heard the story, must have. Seven years back, I bought myself a right fine house up above the Meifod Valley and I hadn't been there a year when I got a letter on my doormat from those bastards in National Grid. I'm telling you, Inspector, I'm not paying the north side of two million to look out over a row of fucking pylons.'

'I remember, you were one of the leaders of the protest.'

'Of course I was. And the Tories were the only party to back us so when they asked me if I'd think of standing, I thought, why not?'

A stroke of luck for the Conservatives, Daf thought, but his opinion was immaterial.

'And you'd never done anything like that before?'

'No. I support the Tories of course, because I'm a businessman and I'm not fond of paying any more tax than I can help but I didn't have any interest in the process itself until the pylons business. To tell you the truth, I have heard that Heulwen had been expecting a phone call from the Tories, to ask her if she fancied standing for them.'

'But she's a member of Plaid Cymru.'

'Only since I got picked for the Conservatives. What's that English saying...? "Hell hath no fury like a woman scorned." A week after she heard that I'd been given the chance, and you've got to remember that she'd been an Independent county councillor for fifteen years by then, our dear Heulwen decided to ring Plaid Cymru, but she was too late to stand against me that time because they'd already chosen their candidate.'

'Is that how the system works?'

'Not everywhere but in Montgomeryshire, it's really important to find a well-known face to represent any party. Jesus Christ himself could stand here and he wouldn't get elected because he's a man from away.'

'Are we really as parochial as that?' asked Daf, finding himself interested in the conversation, despite himself.

'I reckon things have got worse round here since this bloody devolution lark. I'm a Welshman through and through, Inspector, but I'm a Montgomeryshire man first and we never get any fair play from the pinkos and *hwntws* down in the Bay. We need a strong voice from our area to oppose that Cardiff lot.'

This was easy pub philosophy and Daf began to see how Bowen had managed to persuade people to back him.

'So, there was a bit of bad feeling between you and Mrs Breeze-Evans, then?'

Daf observed that there was a pattern to Rhys Bowen's laughter. At the start, he hissed through his teeth, then a little puff of air escaped his lips as if he were trying not to laugh but failing. Eventually, a loud noise burst out and he would roar for half a minute or more, his eyes filling with tears. If it was an act, it was an effective one; after a quarter of an hour in Bowen's company, Daf had relaxed, even forgiving him for speaking about Gaenor. Yes, he was a Tory. Yes, he was a businessman who looked as if he'd been stuffed into one of his own sausage skins, but he was also an easy-going, open character without a trace of pomposity.

'No, no, I'm everybody's friend, me. But it was tough for Heulwen, I think, to get used to the idea that someone like me could go down to Cardiff to represent the area. She thinks I'm heckish common and she could be right. She always likes the big jobs, the grand titles. I remember running into her when she was chairman of the County Council, always dressed up to the nines, and I said to her: "Hey, Heul, you're smart, I haven't seen so many chains since the sale in Bogs-R-Us!" She didn't see the funny side at all.'

As the tempest of laughter died away and Bowen refuelled, Daf decided it was worth asking at least one more question to the Assembly Member, to see if the booze might have any influence on his response.

'But you rented her an office.'

Bowen reached his heavy hand over the desk to pat Daf's arm as if he'd been a pet dog.

'We understand each other very well, Inspector,' he declared. 'I know enough of your history to know that you've got an eye for the girls, and smart ones at that. I can't think of two smarter girls around here than Gaenor Morris and Chrissie Berllan, fair play to you. I bought the building to give a lady friend of mine the chance to start a little shop but as they say, it's never a good idea to mix business and pleasure and before too long, the place was empty. The tenant from the flat, another very nice piece of goods, wants to open a Polish shop there but some of the neighbours went mental at that, as if she was opening a knocking shop, not selling a few Jeżyki biscuits.'

'This tenant you're speaking of, it's Basia Bartoshyn, I take it?'

'Yes indeed and I feel right downhearted about little Basia. I heard there was no point running after her because she had some fancy moral standards, then I hear she's carrying on with Phil Dolfadog. Bloody unfair, that's what I call it.'

Daf had to say something.

'I don't think you've misunderstood Ms Bartoshyn at all, Mr Bowen. She strikes me as a very principled woman.'

'Then it's a serious shame she's got such a nice arse. Anyway, I didn't want to keep the place empty. Menter Maldwyn came in for a bit but then, of course, they lost their grant, so I took up the offer from Plaid Cymru. Fair play, they are prompt payers even if they are nutters.'

'I understand. Listen, Mr Bowen,' Daf began, trying to find appropriate polite words to explain that there wasn't much point in continuing the discussion when one party was so far under the influence, but the door opened suddenly.

'We've found Heulwen Breeze-Evans's car, boss,' Nia declared. 'It's in the canal, by Arddleen.'

For almost a decade, Dyfed Powys Police policy had

forbidden any kind of seating in the reception area of their police stations but Daf thought this ruling was both impractical and discourteous. Not long after being expressly told to do no such thing, Daf had nipped over to the garden centre in Guilsfield and bought a solid oak bench. Sheila's mother had run up three cushions to make it more comfortable. If any member of the top brass called in, Sheila would hide the cushions in the boot of her car whilst Daf and Steve moved the bench out onto the square of grass outside. Now, on the night of the fire, a young man was glad to avail himself of the bench, sitting quietly with a book in his hand and a cup of tea beside him. From the title of his book *Sex, Lies and the Ballot Box* and from his red chinos, Daf guessed that this was Tory Boy. On seeing Daf, he rose to his feet and extended his hand.

'Inspector Dafis? Is Mr Bowen with you?'

'Just gone to the Gents. You're driving him, I take it?'

'Yes. I'm his electoral assistant.'

'A fair old job, I would say?'

To Daf, there was something endearing about the polite young man. He was modest and his manner of speaking was rather shy. With his long neck sticking out above the collar of a shirt which was a little too big for him, he reminded Daf of a young giraffe. As a father, Daf wished he had a scarf to offer him before he went out into the fresh spring evening. He was a total contrast to his boss who came bouncing through the door.

'It's a very interesting job,' the lad replied, lowering his eyelids a little to avoid Daf's eye.

'Aha, you've met Tory Boy, Inspector,' Bowen said. 'There's not much to him and he comes in very handy at times.'

He added, in a lower voice which was still loud enough to be heard across an acre of ground, 'He's really a spy, Inspector. Central Office have sent him to keep an eye on me during the campaign.'

'You know that's not true, Mr Bowen,' the young man

protested. 'I need to learn from a candidate who really knows how to make contact with the electorate, that's why I'm here.' Bowen laughed again.

'Well, at any rate, you've learnt where some of the best-looking voters live. It's right handy to have a chauffeur if you're doing a bit of late night canvassing and fancy a glass or two after.'

Daf decided he would need a private word with the electoral assistant before long. As the old saying goes, no man is a hero to his valet.

'What's your name, lad?'

'Einion Vaughan, sir.'

'Make sure Mr Bowen doesn't drive home after a good supper, won't you, Einion?'

'I'm not stupid, Dafis,' exclaimed Bowen. 'I enjoy being in the Assembly no end and I've done a good job for the people of Montgomeryshire as well. I'm not going to risk my chance of going back for a glass of Shiraz, no way!'

Daf wasn't so sure of that, because Bowen looked to him like a member of a large group in the area: big drinkers who didn't think they had a problem. It was a familiar enough pattern; a small whisky with the luck money in the market, a pint or two at dinner time, a drop of brandy to warm the coffee after coming in from the yard, a couple of glasses of wine with the wife over supper, then down to the pub for a bit of a session. They were like sleepwalkers and some of them had no idea of the hold the drink had on them. One of the most important tasks of the police in the area was to try to ensure that they didn't do major harm to themselves or others before they realised the reality of their situation.

'I'll be in touch tomorrow, Mr Bowen. There'll be a bit of work to do with the insurance, bound to be, but for the moment, the building is a crime scene, OK?'

'I understand that, Inspector. You don't want some assessor marching his big boots through your evidence. Till tomorrow, then?'

Sheila was waiting, car keys in hand. Bowen paused for a moment by the door.

'Are you Tom Glantanat's new missus?'

'That's right,' Sheila answered.

Daf was delighted to note that her confidence was such that she was happy to speak Welsh even with a stranger. Daf expected some off-colour remarks but Bowen was too wise to annoy the wife of a significant business contact.

'That Charlie cross bullock we got from him killed real lovely. One of the best carcasses I've seen in a good while.'

'Glad to hear it, Mr Bowen,' Sheila replied with a broad smile. 'We've got a fair bit of faith in the bull we got at Ballymena last year.'

Daf saw the temptation in Bowen's eyes, the chance to make a joke about a bull to a woman recently married, but he restrained himself. He shook Sheila's hand and followed Einion through the door.

'Would you mind giving me a lift home after, Sheila?' Daf asked. 'I haven't got the car with me tonight.'

'No worries. I thought about popping over to check Mrs Breeze-Evans's car and go home after.'

'That would be grand, Sheila.' On their way out, he felt compelled to ask her opinion.

'What do you think of our Assembly Member, Sheila?'

'I don't rightly know. He's obviously done well for himself and people say he does a good job in Cardiff but...'

'But what?'

'I know I'm a bit old-fashioned, but I do prefer men who manage to keep their flies done up.'

Daf had to seize the chance to correct her: her Welsh was getting way too good.

'You used the word 'flies' like insects in that sentence, Sheila. We would say *copis* in Welsh.'

'Doesn't sound very Welsh.'

'It's one of those old English words preserved in Welsh, like '*twrnai*' for lawyer, from attorney or '*fferins*' for sweets, from fairings. Codpiece. Like Henry VIII had.'

'Whatever. Still, I suppose it's his own business.'

'Well, you've got a vote.'

'I know but I haven't decided who I'm going to back this time.'

'Bowen is definitely heavily involved in this case, Sheila. He said Heulwen Breeze-Evans had hoped to be nominated for the Tories last time but they picked him instead.'

'I wouldn't be a bit surprised. She was always hobnobbing with the local bigwigs.'

'Not sure about your use of 'hobnob' as a verb there, Sheila. Not what I'd call quality Welsh.'

'Go home and get your dictionary off the shelf, boss. It's a word. I checked.'

When they reached the canal, they saw two cars from Highway Patrol whose headlights revealed a silver car half in, half out of the still, dark waters.

'Well, what have we got here?' Daf asked Colin Traffic.

'You said to look out for a silver Discovery and we found it for you in no time, Inspector. It's just a shame we found it in the canal.'

The tailgate moved a little.

'Whoever drove it in got out through the back, we reckon. Don't normally see that with kids joyriding.'

'Whatever else this is, Colin,' Daf declared, 'it isn't any kind of joyride.'

He turned to see Sheila ending a phone call.

'I've just spoke to Newtown. They can send a couple of lads over to secure the site until morning. Nev needs everyone he's got to keep an eye on the location of the fire.'

'Thanks, Sheila. This is going to put a hell of a strain on our resources.'

'Definitely.'

After asking Colin to ensure the integrity of the soft banks of the canal, Daf was glad to relax in Sheila's car for twenty minutes.

'I forgot to say, boss, HQ rang. They said the Deputy Chief Constable would be glad of a word, first thing in the morning.'

'Fine.' He had to try to not appear tired, given that the investigation was only just beginning.

'And, they've decided to give the case a name: 'Operation Green Fuse'.

'Why, for God's sake?'

'From what I hear, they've got a list of names.'

' "The force that through the green fuse drives the flower" – it's a line of poetry from Dylan Thomas. Personally, I think R S Thomas is the far better poet.'

'I don't suppose for a moment they thought about your personal taste when they were drawing up the list, boss.'

'I don't see the point of those names anyway.'

'That's because you never do any paperwork. Suppose, and God forbid, another person lost their life in suspicious circumstances tonight in Welshpool, totally unrelated to this case. How can we sort out the resources if we don't know what has been spent on each case?'

She was right, of course. Daf yawned.

'How is Mali sleeping these days?'

'It's very odd. During the day, she can sleep for four or five hours. At night, twenty minutes max.'

'Is Gaenor ... is she feeding her herself?'

There was a mixture of interest and shyness in her voice. For the first time, Daf wondered what Tom and Sheila were planning. The Francis family would be expecting an heir before too long, especially from a bride who wouldn't see thirty-five again.

'She is, and the little creature is growing like I don't know what. You should call by and see us on Sunday, have a cup of tea and take a look at her.'

'Well, we don't want to disturb any plans, you know...'

The situation wasn't exactly easy. Sheila's new husband was a close friend of Gaenor's ex, John Neuadd, and, for a while, Sheila and Falmai had been close. But, as happened to all of Falmai's friends, the time came when Sheila was dropped from favour.

'Can't wait to introduce you to her, Sheila, and perhaps it's high time you and Tom had a bit of practice with babies, eh?'

Sheila went red and Daf knew his hunch was right: they were trying for a baby. For a moment, Daf's heart sank. Sheila was one of his most valued colleagues, but when he thought of the support network she could call upon, especially the two capable and competitive grandmothers who both lived locally, he felt confident that he could schedule a shift for Sheila the moment the cord was cut.

Daf was very eager to see the lights of Llanfair grow nearer; that whisky had made him sleepy. He stumbled out of the car, hardly saying goodbye to Sheila. When he entered the house, Gaenor was sitting on the sofa, pale but smiling, and in her lap, wide awake, eyes as bright as a robin's, was Mali Haf. Once again, Daf marvelled at the physical impact on him of the presence of his baby. Every ounce of tiredness vanished and he was more than ready to do his share.

'Hello, *cariad*. And how is Daddy's little angel tonight?'

Gaenor's eyes were so full of tenderness, he had to kiss her as he picked the baby up.

'She's doing fine, for a total insomniac.'

'You ought to follow her pattern for a while, Gae. When she sleeps during the day, you should get to bed. Every time.'

'Couple of snags with that plan. First, who's going to clean, cook or do the washing? And more importantly, it would mean I was never in bed at the same time as you, Daf.'

'I'm sure I could manage to pop back every now and then for a little "rest",' Daf replied with a wink. 'But you have to get some sleep now, you look shattered.'

'What about you? What's going on down in Welshpool? Sion rang to say it was a hell of a fire.'

'It was, and there was someone inside the building, unfortunately.'

'No! Were they hurt?'

'Dead. Now we're trying to work out if the fire was intentional.'

'Shit, Daf, you need to get up to bed right now. You've got to be on top form tomorrow.'

'I'm way too full of adrenaline to sleep, *cariad*. I'll be fine for a bit and if little miss here decides to doze off, the two of us will come right up.'

Daf saw the appreciation in her eyes. He realised yet again how lucky he was to share his life with a person like her. She rose slowly to her feet. She was still in some pain after a difficult labour and thirty stitches but she never complained.

'You OK?' he asked.

'I'd better keep the packet of frozen peas in my knickers for a bit longer, I reckon.'

'Do remind me not to ask for a Spanish omelette for a bit then.'

As so often happened between them, a feeble enough joke released a storm of laughter. Even under the strain of caring for a new baby, they were happy with one another. Daf managed to hug her even though he had Mali flopped over his shoulder. He was about to say something about how blessed he felt but decided not to in case he was tempting fate. He kissed her, which said it all. As they were kissing, Mali stretched out her tiny hand to stroke her mother's face.

For half an hour after Gaenor had gone to bed, Daf did nothing but admire his perfect little daughter. Because so much time had passed since Carys and Rhodri were born, he'd forgotten how perfect were every tiny fingernail, every soft hair, every inch of baby skin. He buried his face in the collar of her Babygro and drank in the sweet milky scent of her skin. He sang to her, walked her around the room, told her things he thought she should know, like how much he loved her. She didn't look as if she planned to sleep, even in the distant future. He went to the shelf and pulled down a book he'd been promising himself to start; he knew he was imagining it, but he thought her bright eyes widened when she saw the books. Daf remembered the old-fashioned word Chrissie Berllan used to describe him, because of his liking for books.

'Maybe they'll call you a real scholar too when you're older, Mals. And now, Dadi's going to read for a while so you can settle down for a rest.'

He managed three pages before he felt the little body in the crook of his elbow relax. She was sleeping and he dared not move so he tugged the throw from the back of the sofa over them both and that was how Rhodri found them when he came downstairs at half past six the next morning.

# Chapter 3

## *Morning, April 12, 2016*

After topping up the car in Londis, Daf started down towards Welshpool, assessing the case as he drove. The most important thing was the appointment of the Senior Investigating Officer, then it was vital to make sure Steve was totally comfortable in his new role. Taking responsibility for a crime scene for the first time was bound to be a challenge, whatever paper qualifications an officer might have. Daf considered how much difficulty might be caused by Steve's attitude to fire and hoped that his role in taking care of the site might help him come to terms with his fear as he dealt with consequences of such an incident. Working with the backing of a good team, even amidst the dust and ashes, might help to distance the old memories which troubled him. That was Daf's hope at least; but in reality there wasn't anyone else to do the job. Daf himself was hopeless at anything technical and he remembered Sheila admitting that she'd failed her GCSE Biology, while if they had to send for that girl from Tregaron, there would be precious little shape on Nev.

Nev was a bad one for workplace romances. Two probation officers, the custody sergeant from Oswestry, an unknown quantity of PCSOs and a lovely girl from the Youth Justice Service. Nev had had his heart broken a fair number of times and that was just the tally since the Eisteddfod in Meifod the previous year. Daf did try to give him a bit of advice but it was often neither deep nor especially wise. In fact, it often went no deeper that the song in *Frozen*. Daf had to restrain himself from actually singing 'Let it Go, Let it Go...', which really wasn't much help. Way too keen, that was Nev's trouble. After two dates, he started to think about deposits for houses. Keeping that bit of cardboard in his wallet for measuring ring sizes was a real giveaway too.

'You come over as desperate,' Daf said to him, time after time, at the monthly team-building pizza night in the Smithfield Bell. 'Just take one step at a time.' And every time Daf shared these pearls of wisdom, either Nia or Sheila would butt in with an unhelpful observation, such as, 'Nev, don't pay him any attention. You don't have to take lessons in one step at a time from a man who ran off with his sister-in-law.' That would lead on to Daf himself becoming the target of the banter, which he never minded. He did hope, though, that Steve would manage to overcome his anxiety around fire because the alternative would be a broken-hearted Nev. Again.

He was over halfway to Welshpool when his phone rang. Luckily he was close to a layby. He pulled over and parked.

'Daf Dafis.'

'Daf, it's Dilwyn Puw here.'

'Good morning, sir.' The Deputy Chief Constable had never phoned Daf before.

'As they say in the films, "Houston, we have a problem".'

Odd, Daf thought, that the Deputy had chosen exactly the same words as he had.

'I've got a fair number of problems on my plate at the moment, sir, do you mean one of them in particular?'

'Do you think that the corpse in the office in Welshpool is that of Heulwen Breeze-Evans?'

'Almost certain, sir.'

'So we'll need a Welsh-speaking SIO.'

'Definitely. She was the Plaid Cymru candidate in the election.'

'Derek's Welsh isn't good enough and Simon is still off. Comes down to a choice between you and me, Daf.'

'And I'm not a Chief Inspector, sir.'

'You're acting Chief Inspector, Daf, since the emergency HR meeting first thing this morning. I've got faith in your skill set but you will keep me in the loop, yes?'

'Of course, sir, and thank you.'

'Don't thank me too soon, Daf, it looks like a hell of a task. And, could I just say a word to the wise?'

'Knock yourself out, sir.'

'Heulwen Breeze-Evans was a woman with a lot of powerful friends. I know that you can be as diplomatic as anyone else when you put your mind to it, Daf...'

'I get it, sir.'

'And I know you were a bit of a hothead in your day, but keep it all level, eh?'

'I do appreciate it's a sensitive case, sir.'

'Fair play to you. Who's doing the CSO role?'

'Steve. He's just done that course, Forensics and Operational Policing.'

'Good to hear that. Keep everything in-house if you can. You know how we're placed, in terms of resources.'

'Appreciate that, sir. I think we may need some carbon dogs though.'

'Damn it, our carbon dogs are busy with a complicated incident at Milford Haven, in the Refinery. There's a company up in the north somewhere...'

'Our carbon dogs, sir?'

'Well, they're not really ours, they belong to the fire brigade. Loopy and Mr Smot are such lovely dogs. I'm their contact officer.'

Daf had never heard such warmth in the Deputy Chief Constable's voice. Evidently, he was a dog lover.

'Would it be OK for me to sort myself some private sector carbon dogs then, sir?' Daf asked, aware of how weird that sentence sounded.

'No problem. Keep in touch, remember?'

'I will, sir.'

'Good luck, Dafydd.'

'Thank you, sir.'

'Sorry, I forgot to ask HR, you have got your OSPRE Part 2, haven't you?'

'Yes, sir.'

'That makes things a lot easier at this end. OK, Daf, once more unto the breach!'

Daf was glad that, eighteen months ago, in a 'pictures no sound' phase of his relationship with Falmai, he'd decided to sit the next exam in the police promotion structure. Acting up! Bloody hell! There wouldn't be anyone to depend upon because everyone would be depending on him as SIO. He opened the window. Even so early in the morning and so early in the year, the particular scent of the Sylfaen lay-by filled his nostrils: tar, creosote and old coal smoke from the steam train track, diesel from the road, meadows of silage which would be ready to be cut by the end of the month, and slurry from the farm on the opposite side of the road. Every element was familiar to Daf and perhaps that was his advantage as SIO in this case. He might not be an experienced senior officer, but he knew his patch through and through.

Two messages on his phone: Gaenor asking him to pick up another pack of Pampers on his way home and Sheila telling him that there was a girl waiting to see him at the station. 'What girl?' he wondered aloud.

When he arrived at the station, his tèam looked confident and energetic. Darren extended his hand to him.

'Congratulations, Chief. HQ are asking if you're free for a press conference later on? The Public Engagement Officer is on her way.'

'Not that baggage who caused us so much hassle during the Plasmawr case?'

'Unfortunately, yes, boss. On the plus side, she's such a pain in the arse that Nev won't fall for her like a ton of bricks and that doesn't happen too often.'

'Good point, PC Morgan. Sheila said there was someone waiting to see me?'

'Yes. A girl called Anwen Smith. She works with Heulwen Breeze-Evans.'

'Right. A cup of tea would go down grand.'

Darren gave Daf a look of mild surprise but there was a big smile on Nia's face. Daf had a little policy of working against the sexist canteen culture which developed in so many police stations: if both male and female members of the team were present, he always asked the males to make the tea. This wasn't known to everyone, though Nia and Sheila had worked it out. Somehow or other, Nia still made most of the tea but she was well pleased by the attempts to get Darren, Nev and Steve to do their bit.

In the station, there were three interview rooms, one formal with all the tapes set up ready to go, one small and claustrophobic which Daf always chose to talk to anyone who needed to be warned about the difficulty of their situation, and one which was comfortable, with a box of toys in the corner, a sofa and a picture of Powis Castle on the wall. That was where Anwen was waiting for him. She was busy on her phone when he opened the door, which gave Daf the opportunity to gather his first impressions. She was a young woman, not much over twenty, with clear skin, no make-up and brown hair cut into a shape which didn't suit her face at all. She was dressed like a student who was making a bit of an effort: jeans and a clean sweatshirt with a slogan on it. Daf expected the slogan to be Welsh and political, the sort of sweatshirt people buy at the Eisteddfod, but instead, her breast proclaimed her support for 'Free Syria'. When she raised her head, it was obvious that she'd been crying: the skin was red around her large brown eyes.

'Anwen, I'm Daf Dafis. Don't get up, you look pretty shattered. Have you had your breakfast?'

She shook her head. She didn't look like the kind of girl who missed her breakfast very often. As the father of a teenage daughter, Daf hated the idea that a woman had to be stick thin to be attractive and Anwen was both well covered and appealing. Had it not been for her lack of confidence, she might have been the embodiment of 'all the right junk in all the right places'.

'How about a Danish pastry, eh?'

'No thanks. I'm on a diet.'

Daf's heart sank. Why did all these great girls berate themselves for not being a size six?

'Well, I'm going to order three and if I have to eat them all myself, I'll get diabetes and it'll be all your fault.'

Anwen giggled a little and Daf knew that he'd read the situation right.

'Right then, Anwen,' he began, sitting down in the chair opposite her. 'You've heard about the fire in Mrs Breeze-Evans's office?'

She nodded her head and her tears started to flow again. Daf offered her a handkerchief.

'Are you going to be OK to talk to me, Anwen? Would you like someone with you, your mum or dad, perhaps?'

'No, I'm fine. Sorry, I've never had to deal with anything like this before.'

'Nor me. We're almost certain that Mrs Breeze-Evans died in the fire but we can't open the door until we're certain that the structure of the building is safe, OK?'

'If there is someone in the back office, it'll be Heulwen. We meet people and hold meetings in the front room: that's where my desk is.'

'How well did you know Mrs Breeze-Evans?'

'Before the campaign, not at all. I'd seen her from a distance at various Plaid meetings, of course, but that's all. But since she was nominated, we've worked very closely together.'

'And what sort of woman was she?'

The girl blushed and hesitated for a moment, selecting appropriate words.

'A very able woman, I'd say. Very good on policy.'

'But?'

'But what?'

'There was a "but" in your voice, *lodes*. I'm not asking you to betray anyone or anything but there is a chance that Mrs

Breeze-Evans was killed deliberately. If that's the case, I have to collect every bit of information about her, in order to catch the person who did it.'

Anwen didn't say a word. It was clear that she was unwilling to run Heulwen down but it was also obvious that she had much more to say. Daf had to try a different approach.

'I've heard some people describe her as a bit of a bossyboots and, after being on a couple of committees with her, I'd be inclined to agree with them. What do you think, Anwen?'

For half a second, a weak smile appeared on Anwen's pale face, but it quickly disappeared.

'You've been working very closely with her over the last couple of months. How was she on the doorstep, chatting to people?'

The girl frowned and Daf realised that if he spoke about the campaign, he'd be likely to learn much more about Heulwen than via a direct approach.

'In terms of facts and party policy, she was great, Mr Dafis. But sometimes...'

'Sometimes what, *lodes*?'

'Well, a fortnight ago, we happened to be in Newtown at the same time as the Tories, knocking doors on a housing estate in an area of high deprivation. The people there would benefit from our policies more than anyone else but when we spoke to the residents, they'd almost all been charmed by Rhys Bowen. I decided to have a go at a bit of spying: Bowen was talking to a group of young mums outside the chip shop. He was talking about their policies on free childcare, helping people to buy their own homes and so on, but more than that, he was praising their babies, chatting really well with the primary age kids and pretty near flirting with the mothers. After ten minutes, he'd collected five firm supporters and another dozen very likely to back him. I went back to find Heulwen to see what she'd achieved in the same time: all she'd done was give a telling-off to an elderly woman who didn't agree with her about education.

She wasn't trying to persuade her, just giving her a lecture. Heulwen was never willing to listen to anyone at all and that turned lots of people against her, Mr Dafis. I was pretty frustrated with her, to tell the truth. Because of her personal shortcomings, people weren't able to see the difference a Plaid administration could make to their lives, turning instead to that snake Bowen.'

Daf managed not to smile at her description of the AM. He resolved to stay quiet, to give Anwen a chance to offload.

'An election is all about people, Mr Dafis. Of course, it's important to persuade people with strong arguments but it also matters to be likeable. Bowen is a millionaire who lives in a great big mansion, but he comes over as the friend of the common man. For decades, Heulwen has been doing her best for this community but she's seen as a stubborn snob. We're not prepared to play dirty, but everyone knows that Bowen will go after anything in a skirt and they're still willing to support him.'

Daf saw the disappointment in her honest, principled face and he felt guilty for his own reaction to Rhys Bowen. Somehow, despite everything, Bowen was likeable, a familiar face, the sort of man who is always first to buy a round in a pub.

'And how was Heulwen as a boss?'

'She was very demanding, but that was why I volunteered, to help, to secure a better future for Wales, to make a difference.' Her eyes were shining and for the first time in their conversation, she was full of energy.

'You should stand yourself, *lodes*.'

'No ... well, not yet, anyway.'

'What's the name of that girl from Scotland? Mhairi Black? Isn't she the same age as you, Anwen?'

From her wide smile, Daf realised that he'd succeeded in winning her trust.

'Don't even say it, Mr Dafis. But I do know that we won't

70

break through, here or anywhere, without an appealing candidate.'

'So, Mrs Breeze-Evans wasn't the ideal candidate?'

'Oh, I don't know. She was very hardworking, and a familiar face, which is really important in an area like this, but she was a cold woman, and manipulative.'

'In what way?'

'She was used to getting her own way all the time and she could be very clever in the ways she used to get people to follow her orders.'

Suddenly, fear clouded Anwen's eyes.

'Don't tell anyone, Mr Dafis, but she made me nervous. If people know that I was struggling to work in a place as quiet as the Plaid office in Welshpool, they'd never offer me another job. There was something very cold about her, and from time to time, she made some very peculiar suggestions.'

'What sort of suggestions? And remember, anything you say to me is totally confidential, OK?'

Unfortunately, just before Anwen began to discuss the nature of her unease, the door opened and Darren popped his head in to offer them both a cup of tea.

'Yes please, Dar, and while the kettle's boiling, nip over to Tescos and get a Pecan Plait, an Apricot Crown and whatever they call that vanilla one with the flaked almonds on.'

'I'm a policeman, not a waiter, boss.'

'Which is why I don't have to offer you a tip. Shift yourself.'

Usually, Daf enjoyed the way a bit of banter with his team lightened the atmosphere but on this occasion, Darren's interruption had a negative effect on Anwen who retreated back into her shell.

'You were talking about the strange things Mrs Breeze-Evans suggested.'

'We shouldn't be discussing her like this. We're not even sure if she's dead or alive and here we are picking over her, like, well, like ravens.'

'Listen, *lodes*, if she was killed, someone round here is a murderer, someone willing to start a very dangerous fire. What about the people who lived in the flat? What about the family who live next door, in the flat above the jewellery shop? They've got four children. You've got to help me understand what sort of woman she was, under the surface, because we need that information if we're going to catch the person who killed her.'

Anwen coughed, then mumbled, 'You know Bowen runs after girls all the time? Well, Mrs Breeze-Evans suggested ... she asked me ... well, she wanted me to put myself in his way, if you see what I mean.'

'And what did you do?'

'Nothing. That's not the way I expected to support Plaid Cymru.'

'And what was her response?'

'Oh, I didn't directly go against her, Mr Dafis, no one is allowed to do that. But after a while, she remarked that Bowen would never look twice at a ... at a fat, shabby girl like me.'

It was a cruel description and Daf could see the pain it had caused still lingering in Anwen's eyes. It was obvious that she had been brooding on the remark.

'Then she talked about how much Bowen drank, wondering if he could be caught driving home after five pints. I reminded her that he's got that lad, Tory Boy...'

'Einion,' Daf put in, irritated by the way she used the dismissive description about a young man who was very similar to her but working for another party.

'Him, yes. Well then Mrs Breeze-Evans suggested that if I distracted that Einion, Bowen was bound to jump into a car after a session and then the campaign would be won. That's not how we should conduct ourselves, Mr Dafis. I haven't given up a year of my life to act as a distraction to Tories, that's for certain.'

'Fair play to you, *lodes*. I've got no idea how an election is won but that doesn't sound right to me.'

'I'm not some naïve little fool, Mr Dafis but where's the vision? This isn't just about catching some boozed-up butcher in a pub car park; I'm trying to persuade people to work together to create a better Wales; not just to win, but to win fairly.'

'You really ought to stand yourself, *lodes*. You've inspired me, anyway.'

Anwen blushed right to the roots of her hair.

'I'm not ambitious that way at all,' she muttered, but Daf didn't believe that for a moment.

'Who was close to Mrs Breeze-Evans?'

'Close to her? Well, definitely not her husband, nor her children. Car Wat, I suppose, but he was more of a sidekick than a friend.'

'Carwyn Watkin ... sidekick?'

'Yes. He's a fellow County Councillor and from what I've seen, if Heulwen told him to jump...'

'I know Mr Watkin. Who are her friends in Plaid?'

Whilst Anwen was considering her reply, Daf noticed how they kept swapping tenses from the present to the past and back again as they discussed Heulwen, reflecting their uncertainty as to whether she was dead or still living.

'Jan Cilgwyn, the Assembly Member. They did a bit together. I think Heulwen stayed in Cardiff with Jan, after she had that row with her daughter.'

'She'd had a row with her daughter?'

'Oh, she was always rowing with someone, Mr Dafis. To tell you the truth, I've never seen her look relaxed, except sometimes when she was with Jan.'

'What did they quarrel about?'

'No idea. But Mrs Breeze-Evans did say something pretty nasty about her daughter's husband, using very unsuitable language, racist language, and that he was a homophobe.'

'Racist language?'

'She was referring to the fact that he comes from the Gambia.'

'And why call him a homophobe?'

'Well,' Anwen answered, uncertainly, 'I could be way off the mark with this, but her daughter does live in Cardiff. Which is where Jan lives, with her partner.'

Something in Anwen's tone of voice made Daf ask, 'Is Jan Cilgwyn gay?'

'It's no secret.'

Daf recalled seeing Jan Cilgwyn's face on current affairs programmes on TV: she was a very unremarkable looking woman. Daf was totally without prejudice but had never, to his knowledge, met a lesbian, even at college. He had been uncertain of the sexuality of one of Falmai's friends, because of her short hair and enthusiasm for netball but he had certainly learnt his lesson there – he'd offered her a lift back to Aber once and she'd leapt on him before they'd reached Dinas Mawddwy. Since then, Daf had never questioned anyone's sexuality. He had been on a course on preventing hate crimes and since then, he'd tried to stop Darren calling Nev a WilJil, but up to now, that was the sum total of his experience of the complexities of modern sexuality.

'What about her enemies or rivals? Anyone jealous of her?'

'How much time have you got, Mr Dafis?'

'Anyone in particular?'

'No, I can't think of anyone in particular.'

Policemen need to be able to tell the difference between truth and lies and Daf didn't break sweat in this case. Anwen was displaying a full set of 'tells', moving her head rapidly, breathing shallowly, raising her hand to hide her face. Daf wondered who it was she was trying to protect.

'What's happened to the computers in the office?' Anwen asked. By now, she was looking seriously tired.

'We haven't had the chance to go through the place yet but there's not a lot of hope; I would say that everything will have been destroyed.'

'But what about my database? Our area sheets and canvass returns, they can't be all gone. It's so unfair.'

With that last, childish sentence, her voice broke. She was only a young woman, Daf remembered, just a couple of years older than Carys.

'Go home and get some rest, *lodes*. We can talk again later, OK?'

Anwen nodded. As she rose to her feet, she clearly decided to make a statement.

'You probably think I'm off my head to waste my time with this politics lark. But, Mr Dafis, I want to raise my children in a better Wales, a fairer Wales. And if I was disappointed in this candidate, that doesn't matter at all. I'm still up for fighting for a better future.'

There was a bit of dignity in her walk as she left the room but, after she closed the door, Daf had to shake his head a little. Anwen frittering her time away on one campaign after another. Basia turning her back on love in order to conform to some stupid rules. Thank heavens for people who lived in the real world. He sent a message to Gaenor, reminding her that he loved her: when no immediate reply came, he hoped she was sticking to her promise to get some sleep while Mali was sleeping. A clear image came to Daf, he saw Mali in her basket and Gaenor beside her, sleeping soundly, her hair spread out smooth on the pillow. Daf had started to get used to the sound Gaenor made when she was asleep, not snoring but a low noise as if she were chewing a toffee. When Daf conjured up this vision of his family, the toffee-chewing noise was a part of it as well as the murmuring from the cradle; the sound of real life which had formed from the ashes of his marriage, not a dream. He thought about Phil Evans and his second chance at happiness, a chance which could never be fulfilled if Heulwen were still alive.

When he reached the door of his office, he saw that someone had stuck a piece of paper marked 'Chief' by the name plaque. Daf pulled a biro out of his jacket pocket and tried to add to the label but, of course, the biro wouldn't work at an angle so it was in pencil that he added the words 'Acting' and '*Dros Dro*'.

Three Danish pastries were waiting for him on his desk next to the phone, whose message light was flashing. As he enjoyed the apricot crown, he pressed the button to listen.

'Daf Dafis! What in the name of reason is going on in Canal Street? I can't reach my office. Phone me back at once.' Councillor Gwilym Bebb, important solicitor, one of the worthies who held respectable society together and, in Daf's opinion, a serious pain in the arse.

'Got the structural engineers in now: they reckon we can get it acrow-propped up by dinner time so the SOCOs can get in then and we can recover the body. I was just wondering if we could get the hydrocarbon dogs in, save a lot of time in the long run if we're looking for accelerants.' Steve, sounding as if he was relishing his new role as crime scene manager. Pretty promising, Daf thought.

'Good morning, Inspector Dafis, Diane Rhydderch here, Communications and Public Affairs department, Dyfed Powys Police. I'm on my way up to Welshpool to discuss your media strategy, including social media. I'll need to know which member of your team, for example, is going to take responsibility for tweeting during the investigation.'

The hands of the Horlicks clock on the wall told Daf that he had no time to spare for discussing twitter strategies with Diane Rhydderch. He picked up the phone.

'Nia, can you get in touch with that bloody woman who's coming up from HQ and tell her that I'm not going to be here when she arrives. Then get on to Gwilym Bebb and tell him that the road will be closed until tomorrow morning at the earliest, later, possibly. Any news on the car?'

'Nev's gone to Arddleen with the recovery team just now.'

'OK – I'll stop by on my way up to Dolfadog. I want

someone to get over to Rhys Bowen's factory, see what we can find out about Milek Bartoshyn and his sister as well.'

'I'll go, Sheila's trying to sort stuff out for Steve. That lad's gone off his head. There were at least fifteen messages on the system this morning, asking for better wi-fi to upload the evidence bag numbers straight up to the cloud and God knows what else besides.'

'Looks like I might have to have a quiet word. Being keen is one thing but we have to keep an eye on how much all of this is costing.'

'And the press have started to get in touch. We'll have to think about a press conference, boss.'

'I know. Is there anyone from the Fire Brigade to give Steve a bit of advice? Can you check and also make sure he knows that the moment they're ready to open up that back room, I want to be there. Oh, and having the key to that door would be a great help, so if you happen to see Rhys Bowen himself, could you ask him, yeah?'

'Sure. And I hear congratulations are in order.'

'It's only temporary.'

But, even as he said those dismissive words, Daf was secretly just a bit proud. Over the years, he had come across so many senior officers who were utter wankers, and one of the reasons he had such a name for being a rebel was that he couldn't respect those who hadn't deserved their step up on the ladder. He was determined to keep the respect of his team through his work, not the temporary pip on his shoulder.

Heulwen Breeze-Evans's car was standing on the bank of the canal in Arddleen. To Daf, there was something sad about how clean the rear of the car was, as if the effort of keeping it smart had been a total waste of time.

'What's occurring, Nev?' he asked.

'Pretty obvious that the car was stolen last night.'

'Hot-wired?'

'No, the keys were still in it. Someone drove straight into the water then climbed out through the back. I haven't had time to do the detail yet but there are a couple of footprints on the upholstery and when I looked on the canal bank over there, I saw pretty similar marks in the mud.'

'Grand job, lad. What time did you clock off last night?'

'Oh, before three,' answered the young man as if it were a perfectly normal thing for a shift to finish at three o'clock in the morning. 'She was from a farm, the woman who owned this car, yeah?'

'Yes, but she did a fair bit of politics as well.'

'Because there were a couple of little bottles in the car, the sort you get from the vet's.'

'Well, you know what it's like on farms, they always ask whoever's going to town to pick stuff up from the vet's.'

'I get that, boss, but these are empty bottles.'

'Get onto the vet and check it out, OK?'

'Sure. I've taken pictures of the footprints and sent them in.'

'Fair play to you, Nev, no one would ever guess that you've lost almost a full night's sleep.'

'We've all got to put the old best foot forward for the new chief.'

'Acting chief, remember, but thanks. Wouldn't be a bad idea to take the car back to the station then we can ask the SOCOs to give it the once over when they're up on the site.'

'Will do, boss.'

Daf reached into his pocket.

'Danish pastry for you, *cog*. Keep up the good work.'

When Daf had wrapped the pecan plait in a paper napkin it had looked very attractive, but after a four-mile journey in Daf's pocket, it was little more than a mess of crumbs. Kind gestures of this kind often didn't really work out in Daf's experience, but Nev was starving and therefore very grateful, despite the mess. The remaining Danish pastry was on the passenger seat of Daf's car and its scent filled his nostrils all the way up to Dyffryn Banw.

Daf parked in the lay-by near the Cae Bachau turning, to enjoy the last pastry from the assorted pack. He opened the window to feel the fresh air and heard the cry of the curlew, a rarity these days. He remembered the old saying that, after hearing the curlew for the first time, a farmer wouldn't lose any stock over a year old. Somehow, everything was doing what it was supposed to do: the birds were singing, the distant mountains were turning green and the lambs were gambolling flat out. He didn't need a map because almost all the local farms used to order their groceries from his father's shop, and Daf's job on Saturday had been to help his Uncle Mal deliver the goods in the van. Daf could still remember that the Dolfadog order was always the same, summer or winter, year in, year out. Most people rang in to change the order from time to time, a box of biscuits at Christmas or salad cream in the summer but Daf's father never received a call like that from Dolfadog. Daf fired the engine and turned down the lane, thinking of the family who ate the same meals week after week, month after month, year after year.

Dolfadog was a large house or, as Daf had described it as a child, two houses which had grown into each other. At the front stood a substantial brick house with three rows of sash windows and in the centre, above a wide threshold of pale stone, a broad green-painted door with a brass knob: the perfect film location for a Jane Austen adaption. But behind the brick house, a row of old oak-framed farm buildings had evolved until they'd not only joined together but also linked to the formal front part. Standing on a little hill above the river, facing south, Dolfadog enjoyed a favourable site, but to Daf, there was something missing. He compared Dolfadog with Neuadd under Gaenor's stewardship, when she used to spend hours in the garden, and he realised that what was missing at Dolfadog was care.

He rapped on the front door and pulled the chain of the brass bell which hung by the frame. No answer. He walked around the house, and as he turned the corner to the back, he realised why no one was answering the door. On the other side of a wicket gate, a flight of steep steps led down from the garden to the yard. From his vantage point at the top of these steps, Daf could see frenetic activity, a dozen people swarming like ants around a huge lorry. From the back, they were unloading great towers of cages containing hens. A forklift was going to and fro to the biggest shed Daf had ever seen. To Daf, it seemed like chaos, but it was clear that the workers knew what they were doing. Through the vast door of the shed, Daf caught a glimpse of a sea of hens: sixteen thousand of them, if he had remembered accurately what Phil had said the previous night, some clucking, some screeching and the rest starting to explore their new home.

By the time Daf had reached the rear of the wagon, the last cages had been unloaded. He spotted Phil amongst the team who were releasing the hens, and by his side was a man who must be his son. Both men were tall, wide-shouldered, with plenty of thick yellow hair, wearing boiler suits and wellingtons, but Daf observed a certain sharpness in the son, and also, a seriousness. Daf decided he wouldn't like to get on the wrong side of Jac Dolfadog. Every movement of his body betrayed his impatient nature, and after watching the busy scene for less than three minutes, Daf knew who the master of the farm was. The workers, full-time and casual, turned to Jac for the next command while Phil obeyed orders like everyone else. Jac noticed Daf and marched towards him across the concrete, head in the air.

'Inspector Dafis? What are you doing here? Didn't Dad tell you that today was a busy day for us?'

'And what about your mother?'

'Didn't come home last night. Dad says you think she's the body in the office.'

'Yes. We're almost certain your mother was killed in the fire.' Daf didn't see a trace of shock or grief in the young man's face.

'We weren't close, Mr Dafis. And, as you can see, it's a busy day for us here.'

From what he had heard of Heulwen's nature, Daf hadn't been expecting a loving family, but her son's coldness was alarming.

'I'm not sure you quite appreciate the nature of the situation, Mr Breeze-Evans.'

'Evans. The "Breeze" is long gone. Another bit of Mum's bullshit.'

'OK, Mr Evans. I'm investigating a very suspicious fire and the death of your mother. In a serious case like this, it's essential that I speak to the family without delay.'

'Are you a hundred per cent sure it's her?'

'It was her office on fire. We've found her car in the canal by Arddleen and if that isn't her body in the back room, where is she now?'

The young man shrugged his broad shoulders. 'I've got no idea. She never tells me where she's going. She's down in Cardiff a fair bit, especially since she started on this Plaid bollocks.'

'You don't support your mother's ambitions, I take it?'

Jac gave a faint smile. 'Anything that keeps her out of my way is fine by me and the farm. But I don't support her; I'll be backing a party that lets me keep hold of the money I work hard to earn.'

'I have to talk to the family, Mr Evans.'

'We haven't any time to spare. It could be someone else who's died, in any case.'

The tailgate of the wagon had been closed now and the fork-lift loaded onto the little shelf like a bike rack. The driver shouted across to Jac in a strong north of England accent.

'That's us, then, Mr Evans.'

For the first time, Daf noticed a young woman with long fair hair emerging from the shed. She glanced over at Jac and Daf before calling after the lorry driver, 'Aren't you stopping to have your dinner with us, Kev?'

She must be Jac's wife to issue such an invitation.

'Mr Dafis can get a bite to eat with us, eh, Low?' Phil suggested.

Daf saw the whole picture in Lowri's eyes: she loved her husband but he alarmed her as well. A fine-looking man, heir to a big farm, he was definitely a good catch, but after catching him, she had to live with him. Phil shared a glance with his daughter-in-law as if they were both anxious as to how Jac would respond. The lorry driver had clearly not seen much of a welcome in Jac's face.

'I'll get back up the road, thanks, Missus. I'll be back while it's still light if I get off now.'

The yard was filled with the sound of the powerful engine. Jac went to the cab to sign the paperwork and, after a friendly beep of the horn, the lorry began its journey. The vast door of the shed was shut with a clang which reverberated around the yard. Jac folded back the cuff of his boiler suit to look at his watch.

'We can get them settled this afternoon. Dinner in ten minutes, right?' he yelled.

Daf hoped that poor Lowri had found enough time to prepare a meal for a dozen people. She'd been the first of the group up to the house, but by the time Daf stepped through the door, she'd taken off her boilers and put on an apron, and there was a delicious smell wafting from the kitchen. The image of the perfect farm wife, Daf thought. He was feeling rather uneasy as Jac had not given formal consent for his presence, but he sat down beside Phil towards the far end of the long table. A large casserole emerged from the oven and there was clearly no 'ladies first' rule at Dolfadog: Jac was served first, then Phil, followed by Daf and so on right down to the teenage girl who was sitting opposite Phil. As with their hens, there was clearly a pecking order at Dolfadog.

'No dumpling for me, Mrs Evans,' said the girl, in a small, shy voice.

'Don't tell me you're on a diet, Ems,' Phil teased.

'No, I'm going gluten free.'

'Gluten free? What's this nonsense now, Emm? Give her a big dumpling, Low. No one's going gluten free under this roof.' Jac's voice was the voice of a bully, one used to getting his own way. The girl took her food, but it was clear to Daf from the look on Lowri's face that she was unhappy to be complicit in this bullying. Lowri had managed things exceptionally well, especially to think that she'd done her share on the yard as well. Her face softened a little as she settled into the seat beside her husband, and Daf thought how strange it must be to live like this, with no privacy or separation between work and home.

'Have you confirmed that it was Heulwen?' Phil asked in a low voice.

'We're going into the building this afternoon, got to make sure the structure is safe first.'

'Mr Dafis?' called Jac down the table, 'what if we eat our pudding in the study? We can have a bit of a talk then.'

So, with a bowl of apple pie and custard in his hand, Daf followed the young man through the maze of rooms in the older part of the building into a corner room of the brick house. Daf looked about him at the high ceiling, original sash windows, vast marble fireplace and rich velvet curtains. Bit of a waste of a fantastic room, he thought. Plain desks, computers and rows of filing cabinets, exactly as if the place had been requisitioned by the army for some military campaign.

'We need a room big enough for four of us to be working in at the same time,' Jac explained, settling himself down behind the largest desk. 'Me, Low, Marion – who keeps the books straight – and Dad, not that he's a big man for paperwork.

We've never used this room anyway, except once or twice for parties at Christmas, perhaps.'

'Did your mother approve of the change?'

'You don't understand. She always had some reason or another to get away from here, to do something more interesting. She had a couple of parties here when county council was her big thing but by now she entertains the big shots down in Cardiff. I'm glad, to tell the truth, she made us go around with nibbles on big plates, and I'm not fond of acting like a servant, not to anybody.'

'Did your dad like the parties?'

'Not much, not enough chance to flirt for him. But anyway, she hasn't bothered for – must be ten years now. Since she realised she didn't stand a chance of being leader of the Council. Always wanted to be boss, that's Mum for you.'

'Were they close, your mum and dad?'

'She wasn't close to anyone. She was a cold bitch, and if she's been burnt to death, I'll be glad.'

'Why?'

'She hasn't ever taken a bit of interest in us. As things are now, Gruff's gone and Nansi's gone and here I am, stuck here forever, working my balls off.'

'But this is a good business, isn't it?'

'Not too bad now, but who made the farm what it is today? No one had given a shit about Dolfadog since my Uncle Hywel died and that was before I was born. Who put up the laying unit? Me. Who decided to give up dairy and move into beef? Me. And who had to ask the bank manager for a loan of half a million to get the place back on its feet? Mum was always pretending to be the perfect farm wife in front of her friends on some committee or another but who was feeding the cade lambs? And when the lambing assistant left because she was getting too much harassment from Dad, who missed a month of school to sort the shit out? I'm telling you, Mr Dafis, Low and I are fair desperate to have kids but we're not going to have any until we've got time to raise them right. I never had any time to be young, Mr Dafis, no chance of going to college or to make any mistakes. I was raised by a bitch and a weak fool and I drag a great burden of debt behind me every fucking day. And now, I've got sixteen thousand hens to settle to get them laying right to pay the mortgage on the shed so the unit can invest in the rest of the farm.'

Daf changed his mind: Jac Evans wasn't a bully, just a young man at the end of his tether.

'When did you see your mother last?'

'Before the weekend. Thursday, I think, because the vet came round to see the calves. They were scouring something serious.'

'Did she go to the vet to pick up the prescription?'

'Her? No bloody chance. Anyway, they only needed rehydration in the end and we'd got plenty of Elanco to give them. We had to get some tests done, just to rule out anything more serious, but I got the all clear on Monday, when I was in Welshpool.'

'Did you stop by to see your mum at all?'

The young man rose to his feet. 'I haven't got time to go through everything. I saw her last on Thursday.'

'But you did go to the office?'

'Yes but the young girl there hadn't seen her and I hadn't got any time to waste, not with a trailer of stores bawling their heads off outside.'

Daf got up as well and he happened to be standing between Jac and the door.

'Why did you want to see her?'

'I needed her to sign a document, that's all. She's still a partner in the business, even if she never shows the least bit of interest.'

'What document was that, then, Jac?'

'Nothing important. To do with a lease we've got, over by Llangadfan. We've got two hundred acres there on tack and the lease is up. All the partners have to sign the document, the new lease, that's all.'

'But you were in a hurry?'

'It's a good bit of ground, Mr Dafis. I don't want to lose it. Other people will be after it, definite.'

'I understand.'

'This place is a good farm but Christ alive, the costs are high. You've got to keep the turnover high enough and there are too many passengers in this business. So, like a jigsaw, every venture we have depends on the other parts of the farm.' Jac stepped closer to the door. 'Do you really reckon it's her in the office, that she's dead?'

'It looks like it, I'm afraid.'

Jac was silent for a long moment, as if he needed time to think.

'Hmm,' he said at last. 'Low and I live over in the *helm* and it's a tidy little place but if she's gone, we can move in here. We can rent the *helm* out for holidays and the profit from that can pay for fifteen more suckler calves.'

Daf had seen similar situations before – people responding to sudden loss by concentrating on practical matters – but there was something very cold in the young man's voice.

'What about your dad?'

'He'll suit himself. I can't imagine he'll stay single for very long.'

'Do you know Basia Bartoshyn?'

'Dad's latest tart? I have met her a couple of times.'

'Did you know your dad had offered to leave your mum for her?'

Jac raised his eyebrows. 'Well, there's always something new under the sun. Why did he ever consider such a thing?'

'Because he thinks the world of Basia.'

Jac's laugh was bitter. 'He's always thinking the world of some girl or another. I got used to that when I was in primary.'

'Sorry, *cog*, this isn't me being nosey, you understand that?'

'I know that, but you need to learn what kind of family the Evanses of Dolfadog are. No one has the least bit of respect or liking for each other and we're only under the same roof because we have no choice. Nans and Gruff have gone but I'm determined to stay. I deserve this farm after all the work I've put in. And now, I've got to get on.'

On his way down the lane, car window open in the sunshine, Daf heard Jac's voice from behind him, yelling: 'Switch the fucking fan on, can't you, Dad? They'll roast before they lay in this heat.'

Daf recalled the pictures in the *papur bro* over the years: 'Generous donation by the Dolfadog family', 'The Breeze-Evans family enjoying Llanerfyl Fair' and so on. The pictures were all the same, a wide smile on Heulwen's face, her husband clearly bored stiff, but what about the children? Nothing, just empty eyes facing the world, young actors walking through the roles directed by their mother. Daf looked at the clock in his car which showed it was almost two o'clock: high time Steve opened that back room. Daf hurried down the main road to Welshpool, his head full of the many faces of Heulwen Breeze-Evans.

# Chapter 4

## *Afternoon, April 12, 2016*

Fair play to Steve, the crime scene looked very orderly. There was a large tarpaulin on the pavement, ready to put over the building in case of rain, and a number of acrow props had been placed to strengthen the structure of the building. Four SOCOs, in their white suits, were ready to go in. Steve was on the phone, so it was Nev who approached Daf to give him an update.

'We've got the key for that door, boss,' he started eagerly. 'Nia picked one up from Rhys Bowen at the factory this morning. And looking at it, there was one, very similar or identical, on the key ring we found in the Discovery this morning.'

'High time to go in then. Is there a white suit anywhere?'

Nia appeared with a box of the appropriate clothing and started to rummage through it.

'You're in luck, boss, there's just the one left in the chubster size range.'

Daf smiled in reply but he had to admit that it was a bit of a struggle to pull the thin fabric over his body without ripping it. He pulled on the plastic overshoes but waited until the last possible moment to pull up the hood. He overheard part of Steve's phone conversation.

'If you could get your team with the 360 degree camera over here first thing in the morning...'

Daf could feel his phone ringing in his pocket but without pulling off the suit, there was no way he could reach to answer it. Wearing two pairs of gloves, he clumsily took the key from Nev's hand and stepped towards the building. Steve hurried after him. 'Make sure you stick to the common approach path, won't you, boss? And do you want a mask?'

'I'm good for a mask, thanks Steve. You come right behind me with the tape and we'll mark out the path in that back room.'

Behind the front door, which had been warped by the heat, there was a narrow corridor with a flight of stairs and two doors, one to the left and the other straight ahead.

'Tread very carefully here, boss,' Steve warned.

Daf put the key in the lock and heard a click. The wood of the door was blackened, but evidently, the fire hadn't melted the metal of the lock. He pushed the door gingerly and opened it, releasing a thick cloud of dust and smoke. Daf stepped in carefully, glad to see that an acrow prop had been fitted from outside to strengthen the beam above the window. The familiar smell wasn't as strong as it would have been if the glass in the window had not shattered, and Daf was surprised to see how much of the body remained: there would be something for the pathologist to work on. There were even traces of clothing still visible. He coughed and turned to see Steve's pale face.

'OK, *cog*?'

'Yeah, boss, I told you ... about the fire thing.'

'And you're coping grand, aren't you?'

Steve nodded his head uneasily. They both heard a click and turned to see that the photographer had followed them into the office. Daf looked around. He was glad to see that the filing cabinets had survived the fire: he was very keen to see if they held any secrets. Perhaps some of the documents might be legible but he wasn't holding his breath, given that paper is so much more flammable. He looked again at the body. She was sitting in the chair by the desk. The effect of the smoke must have worked quickly because she hadn't even had the chance to get to her feet. Daf trod on something: in the quiet room, the cracking sound was like a gun shot.

'Perhaps we'd better leave the SOCOs to it,' Steve suggested tactfully.

Daf bent to see what he had destroyed and found a small glass bottle similar to those which had been found in the Discovery. 'We'd better find out where this came from,' Daf suggested to the nearest SOCO.

'Certainly, Inspector Dafis,' she answered with a smile. 'Do you mind not destroying all of our evidence?'

'Carry on, *lodes*.'

He was glad to get out into the fresh air. He unzipped his white suit and reached for his phone.

'Anwen, it's Daf Dafis.'

'Oh. Hello.' Her voice was sleepy as if she had just woken.

'Anwen, what was Mrs Breeze-Evans wearing yesterday?'

'Grey trousers, brown shoes and a green jumper. Dark green, I think.'

'Thank you very much, *lodes*. Until what time were you in the office last night?'

'About seven. There was a bit of coming and going but nothing for me to do so I left about seven.'

'Coming and going, you said?'

'Yes. People to see Mrs Breeze-Evans.'

'People you knew?'

'Well, I know her son, of course, and Rhys Bowen. The boys from upstairs came down for some reason, then there was a woman I didn't know. And, which was rather embarrassing for me, she had a bit of a row with Heulwen. Then a lad came in, another person I didn't know, a strange young man. Beautiful Welsh but he had a sort of trampish look.'

'OK, Anwen, I'm certain now that Mrs Breeze-Evans was in the back room so you're going to have to make a formal statement. Can you come in to the station tomorrow?'

'Do I have to?'

'You do. Sorry to be a pain.'

'It's OK. Have you heard when they'll be choosing a new candidate for the election?'

'Hold your horses, *lodes*, this candidate isn't in her grave yet. See you soon.'

Normally, Daf was very patient but one thing which always wound him up was people trying to get his attention whilst he was speaking on the phone. Nev and Sheila knew all his weaknesses so there was no excuse for their pulling faces or waving hands. As a result, when he finished his conversation with Anwen, Daf was very annoyed.

'What are you chimps playing at? I was talking to a witness and you were larking about like extras from Mary bloody Poppins! You were doing everything but singing Chim Chim Cher-bloody-ee!'

'We've got to have a word with you, boss,' Sheila said. 'We've had a phone call from HQ and they're getting very concerned...'

Daf didn't want to listen, and the perfect excuse to ignore everything else came over the canal bridge. She was a woman of around thirty with short dark hair, and she was walking purposefully towards them. She stepped over the security tape as if she'd done this many times before and, as she crossed the barrier, Daf understood the reason Lycra was invented, because he'd never before seen such a shapely bottom. He remembered reading at some point about a campaign in Montana to outlaw tight leggings: before now, Daf had never seen a reason for such a rule but now he knew exactly how dangerous such a garment could be. If he'd been driving and she had walked past ... He swore under his breath. She walked on the balls of her feet like a boxer and a sudden fantasy raced through Daf's mind, of her boxing in a gym against another girl, in her tight kit, glistening with sweat. Lack of sleep was his excuse, but the truth was, however much he loved Gaenor, this girl would still have been bound to catch his eye, if only in the abstract sense: he admired her as he would admire a beautiful sunset.

'Inspector Dafis?' she asked, extending her hand to Daf.

'I'm Daf Dafis,' Daf replied, aware that the eyes of his team were on him and obscurely relieved that, nice as they were, her breasts weren't quite as remarkable as her backside.

'Belle Pashley. I've come with the carbon dogs.'

Daf had a reason to look at her T-shirt: there was a picture of a dog on it and a logo, a cartoon showing a dog listening carefully and the name JS Bark.

'Very nice to meet you, Belle. We've just opened up the rear room in the building. We had to ensure the structure was safe before proceeding further.'

'Mr Dafis, I do four big fires a week. I know the score.'

'Have you got a team with you?'

'Of course. Myself, DJ, Saunders and Valentine.'

In the course of his career, Daf had been obliged to sample drugs on numerous occasions and he knew that even tiny quantities of strong acid can trigger later flashbacks. The situation facing him now was one of those moments when he wondered if he were paying the price for the unwise testing of some hallucinogen. There she was, the girl in the leggings which ought to be illegal, declaring that she was going to investigate a case of arson with the help of the Penyberth Three, the pre-War language activists who set fire to the bombing school in Llŷn. He tried to prevent his face revealing his confusion but he totally failed to form any kind of sensible response.

'The dogs, Mr Dafis. The three most intelligent springer spaniels you'll ever meet.'

'Of course. I'm not sure the site is quite ready for you yet, if the four of you fancy a quick coffee, or, of course, a bowl of Wynngold for the troops?' Daf knew perfectly well that he had a tendency to bollocks on when he was in deep water, and the look in Sheila's eyes bore witness to the fact that she had seen him do this once or twice before.

'We've only just arrived so we'll need to stretch our legs before starting anyway. Is there a park nearby?'

'Powis Castle Park. There are big gates in the centre of town.'

She wrinkled up her well-shaped nose as if Daf had suggested something disgusting.

'Are there deer?'

'Oh yes, any amount of top quality deer.'

'Valentine hates deer; they drive him off his head. We'd be

better off with a little turn along the towpath.' Belle turned on her heel and went to fetch the dogs from her van.

Throughout this conversation, Sheila had, once again, been desperately trying to attract Daf's attention. When Belle had gone, she tugged at Daf's sleeve.

'Boss, HQ say we can't spend another penny on external resources, including those carbon dogs.'

'What are you talking about?'

'The way Steve's spending, he'll break the bank.'

'On what? The SOCOs are in-house, and apart from them, I've only seen a photographer.'

'But he's ordered a 'Virtual Reality Crime Scene' from some company in Oxford who are coming up with 360 degree cameras which they use to create images which are uploaded onto an interactive platform...'

'And,' Nev cut in, 'it costs a bomb.'

'Dilwyn Puw has promised us the carbon dogs,' Daf clarified, conscious, once again, of how weird that sentence sounded.

'Then you better phone him, boss, because the moment Miss Tight Trousers starts her work, we're going to have to pay her for it. And Nev, don't even think twice about it, she puts lads like you in her blender every morning and drinks them as a smoothie.'

Daf tried to ring Puw: answer machine.

'How good would this Virtual Reality system be, do you reckon, Sheila?'

Sheila sighed like an experienced mother describing the familiar behaviour of a child.

'Steve's just finished that course, boss, and he describes the system as "state of the art" but nobody in Carmarthen has ever used anything like it. From what I heard at dinner time, the whole budget for the investigation could go like that.' She clicked her fingers.

Steve emerged from the front door, pulling off his mask. Daf knew how hard he was working to fulfil his new responsibilities and to master his fears. It would be a great pity to undermine his status in his new role. Daf phoned Dilwyn Puw again, without luck.

'You've got to persuade him to cancel the VR thing, boss,' Sheila advised. 'Or the carbon dogs, one or the other.'

'But he's set his heart on it, Shelia. It's his first go at managing a crime scene...'

Steve had pulled the tape from his right glove to free his hand in order to be able to enter the latest notes on his tablet. One of the SOCOs approached him with a question, and after receiving a prompt answer, she returned to the building. Steve was definitely doing a good job.

Belle Pashley came back into sight, her dogs on leads. Daf, after twenty years of avoiding his brother-in-law's psychotic sheepdogs, was not overly fond of dogs but he had to admit that these were lovely creatures. Two of them were black and white and the other had chocolate-coloured markings: their coats were thick and well kept. Daf started to feel stupid in comparison with how clever they seemed. As Mrs Thatcher once said about Gorbachev, Daf felt he could do business with these dogs, and with their mistress.

'Are you the CSM, Inspector?' asked Belle.

'No. That's DS Steve James.'

'OK then. If the photographer's finished, can we go in?'

Daf decided to play for time. 'I'll just have to check with the photographer. Nev, can you just ask Steve how the pictures are coming on?'

Belle smiled for the first time, showing a row of white teeth which contrasted with the light brown of her face. It was colour which came from the sun, rather than a fake bake, Daf guessed. She looked like someone who enjoyed spending time outdoors.

'It's great to hear so much Welsh in the workplace, I must say. I do a fair bit of work over the border, mainly in the Merseyside area but even when I am in Wales, I don't hear Welsh spoken like this very often.'

'The thing is, the boss always speaks Welsh to us, whether we understand him or not,' Sheila explained. 'In the long run, it's easier to learn, because we won't change him.'

'Fair play to you all.'

'And,' Sheila added, 'it's quite a clever tactic: Welsh speakers feel happy in this team so there's not many people who ask for a transfer.'

'My sister's an Urdd organiser,' Belle declared. 'She's going to love hearing about you lot.'

'Do excuse me for a moment, I have to make a phone call,' Daf apologised.

'I fully appreciate that it's a busy day. I always give priority to a case with a corpse. The lads and I were heading down to Kington today, but that's nothing earth-shattering, just the old, old story, the same thing you always get with thatched houses.'

'Thatched houses?' Daf asked as he pressed the redial button.

'After fifty years, a new roof is needed and it's not a cheap job. A lot of owners think they've been very clever by putting a match in the straw and claiming on insurance. These boys are great in situations like that; Saunders here can pretty well smell meths through a brick wall.'

Yet again, the Deputy Chief Constable didn't answer his phone. The photographer was making his way out through the front door and Daf had no further excuse for not confronting Steve.

'I just need a quick word with DS James for a moment,' he explained to Belle, unaccountably nervous. She did not strike him as a particularly patient person.

'Steve, we need to have a word,' he ventured.

It wasn't an easy discussion. Describing the advantages of the VR system, Steve succeeded in persuading Daf, but when he heard what it would cost, Daf felt that he wasn't far from a heart attack.

'It's a budget-buster, Steve – we just can't justify it.'

Steve resumed his praise for the system so convincingly that, a minute later, Daf himself was firmly convinced that no complex case could be solved without an interactive digital platform. He struggled to get a grip on reality.

'But we can't afford that and the dogs, Steve, and the dogs are here.'

Daf knew very well that this was a weak argument. By now, it was colder and the afternoon was wasting away at an alarming rate. Belle was pacing to and fro, her patience visibly eroding step by step. Before Daf could think of a better argument to give Steve, Huw Mansell arrived.

'I hear one of my patients is dead,' he said to Daf.

'Indeed, Dr Mansell, but you won't be able to do very much for her now,' answered Steve.

'I'm here for the ROLE,' Mansell responded, first in Welsh, then in English for Steve's benefit.

Even if the corpse was burnt to a cinder, the protocol still had to be followed. By law, a doctor or paramedic had to declare that the person was actually dead: the Recognition of Life Extinct. Until the ROLE procedure was completed, the body could not be moved.

'You know DS James, he's in charge,' Daf said to Dr Mansell, in English so that Steve would understand the faith he had in him.

Whilst the doctor was putting on his protective suit, Daf approached Belle.

'So sorry about this but the doctor's only just arrived for the...'

'Hell's bells, you guys are trying my patience. We're losing the best of the daylight and I will tell you this, I am not having DJ, Saunders and Valentine injure themselves by working into the twilight.'

Belle squatted down to talk to the dogs, stroking them. Daf could not help feeling slightly jealous; he wouldn't mind a bit if Belle chose to tickle his tummy, but he thought of the hardness in her eyes and the generous kindness of Gaenor, so he counted his blessings.

Eventually, Dilwyn Puw rang back. 'What's the problem, Daf?' he asked, with an edge to his voice.

'Well, I have tried to get hold of you a couple of times, sir...'

'I'm perfectly well aware of that. My phone rang halfway through the tribute I was giving to my father's best friend. We've been burying him today.'

Daf blushed. This was certainly not the best beginning to the conversation. 'It is important, sir.'

'The congregation in Bethania wouldn't agree but fire away anyway.'

'We ordered the carbon dogs as you suggested this morning, sir, but in the meantime, the CSM has contacted some company who...'

'I know the story. Do you want me to make a decision? You can have either the carbon dogs or this Sims game, not both. Do you understand?'

'Thank you sir, and I am so sorry about the disturbance, in the middle of the funeral...'

'I should have switched my phone off. He was a good man, my dad's best friend.'

Even over the phone, Daf could hear the tears in Puw's voice. The man didn't deserve any more hassle. By now, Belle had opened her bag, a bag similar to the one Carys had used for PE in the sixth form, and she was setting about fixing hi-vis bands on the dogs and little red boots on their paws.

'I have never seen anything so cute in my entire life,' breathed Sheila in a voice much quieter than usual.

'They have to be protected against broken glass and so on,' Belle answered abruptly. 'They aren't pets but assets of my business.'

A large drop of rain fell. Daf raised his head: the clouds had fattened and the sky above was dark. He heard Steve's voice from the building, 'Get the tarp over. We need to make this place watertight.'

Luckily, a member of the team who had put up the props was still nearby and under his supervision, the place was protected from water in a quarter of an hour. The ambulance arrived to move the body, which meant more delay for Belle. Daf seized his chance to speak again to Steve.

'We're not going to be able to afford the virtual crime scene, *cog*, very sorry.'

'If it's either or, boss, I reckon we can do without the dogs.'

Unfortunately, Belle overheard this remark and went off at the deep end.

'You know what, Mr Dafis? Dyfed Powys Police are going to meet my invoice, whatever the fuck else happens. I've been hanging round here like a spare prick at an orgy and I've got plenty of other clients waiting for me.'

'It's just a misunderstanding, that's all.'

'Do you want me to start working or not?'

At that moment, everyone grew quiet. Two ambulance men came out of the door, pushing a trolley. Daf stepped over to look at what was left of Heulwen Breeze-Evans. He lifted the blanket for a moment and immediately regretted it – it wasn't a person on the stretcher but a lump of carbon. He paused by the door of the ambulance until it closed and when he re-joined Steve, Belle was nowhere to be seen.

'She's gone in, boss. Wouldn't fancy crossing her. Are you one hundred per cent about the VR?'

'Sorry, lad, it's too expensive. Even if we cut the dogs, it would still be too expensive, HQ say.'

'OK, OK.'

The disappointment was visible in his face. After learning so much on his course, Steve's expectations were totally unreal: after a few years, these systems might be in common use but today, it had to be just a dream. Daf pulled his white suit back on hastily and followed Belle into the building. He realised at once how dark it was in there. From the door of the back room, Daf watched the dogs wandering through the chaos, heads down, sniffing. One of them raised his head as if something new had reached his nostrils and he galloped past Daf, up the stairs.

'What are you doing, DJ?'

There was no carpet on the stairs, so DJ's claws were loud on the bare wood.

'Can you go after him, Mr Dafis?' Belle asked, her expression much more relaxed now she had started on her work. 'I've got to stay with these boys.'

'Of course.'

Daf had reached the second step before she called out a warning.

'It's going to be slippery as hell underfoot; you take care.'

She was right, of course. The stairs were very slippery, and blackish water was gathering in the corridor. Daf was glad he had a torch in his jacket pocket to find his way through the gloom. At the top of the stairs there was a little landing, one closed door and another narrow flight of stairs, and from the sound, it was clear that DJ had climbed up to the attic. Daf followed the dog, slipping on every step as the plastic soles of his overshoes found no grip on the wet wood of the treads. There was a white door at the top of the stairs which had been forced by the firemen. Daf stepped in – there was water and the smell of smoke everywhere but it was obvious that the firemen had been able to control the fire before it took hold on the second floor. He looked about. It wasn't a flat he saw but one room: there was space for a bed but little else. Instead of a bedside cabinet, there was a small fridge and, in the corner, without door or curtain, a shower and toilet. To reach the shower, you would have to climb over the bed, and Daf wasn't surprised that Wiktor spent so much time with Milek and Basia, if this was his home.

The lack of space caused no difficulties to the dog: DJ had squeezed himself under the bed and appeared on the other side, barking loudly. His nose was near the wall by the shower but Daf could see no reason for his excitement. He climbed carefully over the bed and tripped over a pile of magazines. Daf could remember the days when there was a similar pile under the beds of many single men; these days, they could get all the porn they wanted on their mobile phones. But when he bent to see what sort of magazines they were, he discovered that it wasn't *Razzle* or *Hustler* which occupied Wiktor at night but hunting magazines, *Lowiec Polski*, full of pictures of dogs and guns. Daf was made a little anxious by the nature of this collection: this interest in guns was rather more sinister than admiration for women's bodies. He felt rather foolish to be putting so much faith in a dog, but this was a specially trained animal, he reasoned, so he turned his attention to DJ, whose nose was now right by the wall. Daf struck the wall with his fist. An empty sound. He noticed a narrow gap between the beam and the plasterboard.

'Is there something behind there, do you reckon, boy?' he asked, reaching in his pocket for the Swiss Army knife Carys had given him last Christmas.

It only took two minutes to pry open the joint in the plasterboard and Daf immediately saw what had drawn the dog to that particular spot. Behind the wall, in the triangular space between the room and the eaves, there was a storage area filled with Polish goods – bottles of vodka and beer, a great pile of sausages in vacuum packs and a number of large boxes without labels. He pulled out one of the boxes and opened it: two hundred packets of cigarettes of an unfamiliar brand, Fajrant, a golden eagle on every pack. He opened another: red packs, this time, with the name Jan III Sobieski on them.

Daf now knew why Wiktor and Milek were so anxious to rush into the building the moment the flames were extinguished: they weren't risking their lives for the chance to get their clothes but to avoid a charge of smuggling, which made a lot more sense. He stroked the dog.

'Well done you, DJ,' he said aloud, before noticing that Belle was standing in the doorway.

'When you start congratulating them, Mr Dafis, you're halfway to being as big a nutter as I am.'

In the darkness, by torchlight, her teeth shone very white, which together with her white-suited body, made her look like a character in a sci-fi film.

'A real Aladdin's cave we've got here, eh? DJ spent a lot of time in Holyhead last year, helping the Customs: he's damn good at finding cigarettes.'

'How are things looking downstairs?'

Belle frowned.

'I'm just sorry we wasted so much time. We haven't even started on the flat below. Saunders found the seat of the fire without any difficulty but there are a few things, both in the back room and the corridor, which don't make any sense.'

'It's going to be pitch dark in an hour.'

'I know and I've got at least three hours' more work to do. It's not fair to the boys to keep them working until nine o'clock at night, to say nothing of the lack of light.'

'What about tomorrow?'

The girl hissed through her teeth. 'I've committed to going to the site in Kington tomorrow. I do a fair bit of work with the insurance company there, Thatchkeepers. I put them off once and I have no intention of letting them down again.'

'What if you stopped by here first then then went down to Kington after? Where's your base?'

'Hawarden. It's at least a two-hour drive and if I leave early in the morning...'

'What if you stay the night here?'

Belle stepped in through the door. In the weak light, he saw a suspicious look on her face as she raised her well-shaped eyebrows.

'You're a sudden one, I must say, Dafis,' she answered with humour in her voice but also in a tone which made it perfectly clear that she was seriously considering spending the night with Daf.

'No, no, *lodes*,' Daf answered hastily, hoping that his admiration of her bottom hadn't been that obvious. 'We've got a spare room if you can put up with the chaos which goes with a six-week-old baby in the house.'

She delayed for a moment before replying, 'Well, it would definitely save four hours in the van.'

'Is it OK for the dogs to sleep in the van? Because...' Daf failed to even begin to describe how hard it would be to find a place for three boisterous dogs in a house which was already full to bursting point.

'Yes, the boys are fine; I'm the problem. I have thought of adapting a camper van to suit the dogs and me but, very often, I don't fancy staying in the places where we've been working. I don't like the idea of waking up to find the van on breeze blocks, Mr Dafis.'

'Not much fear of that in Llanfair Caereinion. We could call by the Indian on the way.'

'OK ... and thanks. Sorry I was a ... bit naggy before. This is my livelihood, you see. I'm not on a salary and I have to make sure I earn enough to cover my overheads.'

'And I'm sorry we were so all over the place, this is the first time Steve has managed a crime scene. I didn't want to be too hard on him, but he has got to keep his eye on how much he spends.'

Belle looked straight into Daf's eyes as she said, 'I'm expensive but I'm worth every penny.'

Usually, Daf was a champion flirt. He wasn't shy, he enjoyed female company without any hidden agenda, and after spending decades studying and reading literature of all kinds in both languages, he was seldom lost for words. But there was something very unexpected about Belle's way of communicating, as if she were issuing a challenge rather than seeking attention. He felt a cold shudder down his backbone and thanked fate that he wasn't in the slightest bit tempted to chase her: she triggered desire and fear in equal measure, and Daf was way too old for such complications.

'I don't doubt it,' he replied, glad to have the opportunity to present his happy little family to her. Belle started to lead the way down the stairs, still talking over her shoulder.

'I should have finished here in about an hour. I want to speak to the SOCOs because there are a couple of specific tests I want them to do, to make sure I'm on the right track.'

The torchlight was enough to give Daf an excellent view of her backside: it was clear that she was well used to moving safely through sites like this without slipping or tripping.

'How many times have you been in situations like this?'

'I'm on a fire site pretty well every day. But when there's a body? Only half a dozen times, over here, anyway.'

'So you've worked abroad?'

'Ten years in the army, Mr Dafis. I've been everywhere, Brunei, Afghan, SL...'

'SL?'

'Sierra Leone.' She stood for a moment outside the door of the flat on the first floor. 'I'll have to check in here tomorrow as well, in case there's any more of the stuff you and DJ found.'

'Thanks. We've got to understand as much as we can about what's been going on under this roof.'

'Of course.' She suddenly smiled and stretched her hand out towards Daf. She pulled off the glove on her left hand and held her wrist out in front of him. 'Check my pulse, Mr Dafis: I'm full of adrenaline.'

Daf took her wrist between his finger and thumb but didn't manage to count properly. Her flesh was warm but somehow full of tension, like a bow string. He was glad to release her.

'Running a bit fast, I'd say.'

'I haven't done a murder for ages. Is it a domestic?'

'Not sure yet. Mrs Breeze-Evans seemed to live a pretty complicated life.'

'I've been involved in a couple of cases where the father of the family has gone off his head and torched the lot, even the children. I don't understand women sometimes: if someone realises they've married a psycho, why don't they get shot of the bastard before they do any real damage?'

'Love is a strange sort of thing, I suppose.'

'It's not love, it's weakness. If any man even thought of threatening me, I'd slit his throat.' She drew her finger across her throat and a smile of satanic satisfaction came over her beautiful face. For a moment, Daf regretted inviting a person like this into his home but then Belle bent over to pet the dogs, showing the tender side of her nature. Daf felt relief as the fresh air outside met his skin as he stepped out of the building.

'Hey, Steve!' he called, pulling the plastic off himself. 'Right little Aladdin's cave on the top floor – cigarettes, vodka, all sorts. It'll need cataloguing.'

'OK. How's Ms Pashley getting on?'

'I reckon she knows what she's doing but she'll have to finish up in about an hour because of the light.'

'I could sort some arc lights...'

'Not without a lot of upheaval to the crime scene. She'll be back in the morning, first thing.'

'She's a cracking-looking woman, boss.'

'Don't you dare, Steve.'

'Only saying.'

A sulky look came over Steve's face and Daf recalled all the effort the lad was putting in.

'You're doing a grand job. Coping with the fire thing?'

Steve nodded, clearly unwilling to discuss this sensitive subject.

'OK. You know where to find me.'

Back at the station, there was a lot going on. Outside the building, Heulwen's car was being examined by Nev and one of the SOCOs. A big white BBC van with a satellite dish on the top was parked untidily by the pavement and there was a group of journos by the door.

'Inspector Davies.'

'Mr Dafis!'

'Sorry, friends, I've got work to do.'

'Will you be making a statement later?' asked the correspondent from the *County Times*.

'A statement will be released later.'

'And have you just come from the site of the fire, Mr Dafis?'

'Yes. I have to go.'

He was halfway through the door when he heard a question which startled him.

'Was it a hate crime, Mr Dafis?'

'What?'

'It's a valid question to ask, given the sexuality of the victim.'

Daf felt very confused as he closed the door behind him. Sheila was standing in the reception area, and the moment she saw Daf, she reached into her bag for a packet of baby wipes.

'You're covered in soot. You were going on about Mary Poppins earlier but you look like one of Dick Van Dyke's friends. You're going to look a right mess on the news tonight.'

'Do we have to speak to them, Sheila?'

'Well, Diane Rhydderch arrived an hour ago: that's her call, I suppose.'

'Where is she now?'

'In your office. She needed a quiet place to make a few phone calls,' Sheila explained, noting Daf's disapproval from his expression.

'Never again, *lodes*,' Daf growled, rubbing his face with a baby wipe. 'My office is not for general use, OK?'

Daf could smell her before he opened the door. He was annoyed to start with but the fact that she was wearing the same perfume Gaenor used made the trespass worse, more personal. Romance by Ralph Lauren, the perfume he'd bought Gaenor for Christmas, the one he'd massaged onto the underside of her wrists in the labour ward, the perfume which lingered in the soft collar of her coat on the hook inside the front door. He threw the door open and Diane Rhydderch raised her head to give him one of her fake smiles.

'Inspector Dafis. Very pleased to see you.'

'I'm not pleased to see you in my office. High time you picked up your pack and were gone.'

She smiled again but began to gather her papers into a file.

'Have you prepared anything for our friends in the press yet, Inspector Dafis?'

'Do forgive me but I've been too busy trying to actually solve the crime.'

'Of course, of course. I can see that a complex and large-scale investigation like this would be a challenge for any inexperienced officer.'

'HQ have got enough faith in me to give me the responsibility, which means...'

Diane chuckled scornfully. 'Oh, Inspector Dafis, what choice did they have? Anyway, it's important to us as a force to see things are all in order. Especially when there's talk of a homophobic hate crime.'

'Heulwen Breeze-Evans is the corpse, a local farmer's wife in her sixties.'

The Communications Officer had a laugh as cold as ice. 'Please don't tell me that you've got some stereotypical view of homosexuals, Inspector Dafis? Not every lesbian wears dungarees, you know.'

'But she had a family. A husband and three children.'

Ms Rhydderch shrugged her shoulders in her well-tailored jacket. 'People change. But one of the things which makes this case so sensitive is the identity of her partner.'

'You mean Jan Cilgwyn, the Assembly Member?'

'You knew about Ms Breeze-Evans' sexuality then?'

'I had heard something, yes, but I wasn't inclined to believe it.'

'Oh, you men, you always find it so hard to believe that we should have any interest at all in anything except keeping you happy.'

In the bitter tone of her voice Daf heard an old pain, a scar which hadn't healed. He began to feel some sympathy for her but on the other hand, he could also find a lot of time for any lover who had chosen to leave Diane Rhydderch.

'What if we arrange to meet the press in the morning?' Daf suggested, conscious that he had a number of tasks to finish before Belle completed her work.

'Fair enough, but don't expect Jan Cilgwyn to keep quiet in the meantime. I'll be staying in the Oak tonight. Why not call by so we can discuss our strategy?'

'I haven't a minute to spare tonight. The investigation is developing in all directions and I have got to try and keep a handle on it.'

'Shame.' Daf wasn't sure if she was flirting or simply trying to fill the time on a dull night in a strange town. It seemed as if flirting was her default mode when dealing with men but whatever her intention was, Daf had not the slightest interest.

'First thing tomorrow, then?'

'Sure.' Diane turned sharply on her high heels and stalked to the door. 'I'm only doing my job, you know. And I know perfectly well what gentlemen like you, with all your practical skills, think about a silly girl like me who spends her days talking to the media, but I am telling you, Inspector Dafis, if there was no one here to keep those wolves off your back, you'd know all about it.'

Daf sighed a little after she had gone as he settled back in what was, after all, his chair. He knew perfectly well that they did need someone to deal with the media but did that person have to be so patronising? Daf had no pretensions to sophistication but neither did he particularly enjoy people speaking to him as if he was the ultimate hick from the sticks. He rang home.

'Hi, Dad.'

'How are you, *cog*? How was school?'

'Alright. How's the big investigation? Everyone's talking about it.'

'Early days yet, Rhod. Gaenor about?'

'She's asleep, and Mals. I went up to see them, they're well cute.'

'Can you do a favour for me, then? Can you change the bedclothes in Carys's room?'

'OK. Why?'

'There's a woman who's been working with us and she's staying the night with us so she can get onto the site first thing in the morning.'

'I'd better run the hoover over the carpet as well then.'

'Thanks a lot, *cog*. I'd do it myself but I'm that short of time.'

'No probs. See you later.'

Good lad, that, he thought to himself as he put the phone down. As things were, every contact with home had the effect of raising Daf's spirits; in total contrast to the sense of sour failure he'd experienced when he lived with Falmai. He sent a text to Gaenor to warn her about Belle and to explain that there was no need to cook. He felt a moment of guilt as he recalled his admiration of Belle's backside before consoling himself with the idea that there was little to be done about human nature. He didn't totally succeed in shutting his conscience down, however.

There were nearly twenty emails waiting for him but he could deal with them at home. Half an hour. Time to nip up and arrange a translator for his conversations with Milek and Wiktor. Through the glass panel in the front door, he saw the silhouette of Ms Rhydderch talking to the press so he decided to slip out through the back door. There he encountered Nev who was busily making notes on his tablet.

'We've just heard back about the footprints you saw last night on the canal bank, boss. We're looking for a pair of Nike Air Huaraches, size six.'

'Small feet for a man.'

'Could be a boy.'

'Not many boys know how to get a car like that into the water and escape through the back.'

'Nothing back from the vet yet. I'll phone them again in the morning.'

'Well done, you. Don't stop too late tonight, mind, we're all going to need to be fresh in the morning.'

'OK, boss.'

As he was pulling his car out of its parking space, Daf caught a glimpse of Nev in the mirror. He was concentrating so hard that he'd stuck his tongue out between his teeth. Daf smiled: it was good to see his team making such an effort.

There were a fair few cars in the parking area in front of the ugly 1960s eyesore which served as Welshpool's Catholic Church. Daf assumed it was a meeting rather than a church service, given that it was half past five on a Tuesday. A slight young man sat on the wall opposite the church, oblivious to the rain. His grey skin and empty eyes were enough for Daf to assume that he was a user of some kind. Daf supposed he was there to seek help from Joe Hogan, who was a magnet for people with problems of all kinds, a process he described as 'being Christ in the world'. At least this time the priest wouldn't be giving up his shoes, the young man had a pair of nearly new trainers. He lowered his head as if he were unwilling to meet Daf's eyes, but whether that was through shyness or guilt, there was no time to discover.

Daf knocked on the door of the house beside the church. No answer. He rang Joe: no reply, so he left a message on the answerphone. The young man rose to his feet and ambled over to Daf.

'He's in the church,' he declared.

'Thanks, *lanc*,' Daf replied, hoping to hide his surprise, because not many of the recipients of Joe's charity spoke Welsh.

'No worries.' It was a local accent but with a flavour of Wrexham.

Daf pushed open the church door. In the foyer, he saw a large trilingual poster, Polish alongside the Welsh and English. It was a timetable of services but Daf had to admit that he didn't really understand it in any language. For Tuesday at five o'clock, the poster proclaimed Veneration of the Blessed Sacrament, whatever that was.

The church was in perfect silence. Daf opened the inner door carefully. In candlelight, about twenty people were kneeling, all eyes on the altar on which stood an object rather like a candlestick with the shape of a golden sun, well furnished with rays, on the top of it. In the centre was a large white disc. In the front row, still and silent, Joe was kneeling. If this was a church service, Daf thought, it was totally different from any he had ever attended. He recognised several faces: the old man who was grandfather to most of the tinkers in the town, the family from the Chinese takeaway, a tall old lady in an expensive coat who was the mother of the MP, and the single mother of a couple of lads in their mid-teens who had been wreaking a fair bit of havoc lately. There were three Filipino care workers in the uniform of the old people's home and the new doctor from the hospital, an elegant West African. In the second row, her back as straight as any soldier, Basia was kneeling. Joe cleared his voice and began to sing without accompaniment, though the song was more of a chant than a hymn. Gradually, the congregation joined in:

*Tantum ergo Sacramentum*
*Veneremur cernui:*
*Et antiquum documentum*
*Novo cedat ritui.*

Latin. A language no one speaks and yet these people, from every corner of the world, sang the words without book or hymn sheet. Even though the scene was very strange to Daf, it was, in its own way, representative of how life was in Welshpool. Some small part of Daf was secretly glad that they weren't singing in English – the language which seemed to have the power to make all other languages retreat. They became quiet and Joe rose to his feet. He knelt briefly in front of the altar then raised the object of their gaze. The congregation bowed their heads and Joe opened the little cupboard at the back of the altar. He placed the host in it and locked it before covering it with an embroidered cloth. He knelt again and disappeared through a narrow door beside the altar. Daf had no idea if the service was over or not: some members of the congregation were getting to their feet whilst others remained on their knees.

After a few minutes Joe emerged, having taken off the green silk vestments which had concealed his usual shabby black T-shirt.

'Daf!' Joe greeted him in a voice sufficiently loud to assure Daf that the peculiar service had come to an end. 'Looking for a bit of tranquillity at the end of a busy day?'

'I was looking for you, Joe. I didn't expect you to have a service on, not on a Tuesday.'

'We worship the Lord every day, Daf.'

'Shut up, you weirdo. I've got a favour to ask you.'

'What?'

'I need to speak to Milek, and Wiktor as well. I don't want to do things formally, not yet, and if I apply for a translator through the proper channels, I lose the chance to have a quiet word. To tell you the truth, Joe, I've got good reason to suspect that they were doing a bit of smuggling but at the moment, I'm a lot more interested in who killed Heulwen Breeze-Evans, not how much duty was paid on a packet of fags, so...'

'For a man in a hurry, you're heckish long-winded at times. Of course I'll translate for you, if it'll help.'

'Great. And ... can you keep an eye on them as well? I don't fancy turning up to work tomorrow only to hear that they've decided to take a little trip back to Poland.'

Daf hadn't noticed Basia approaching them. There was a look of intelligent tranquillity on her face and Daf thought yet again how fortunate Heulwen's husband was to secure the attention, let alone the love, of a woman like her.

'Don't worry, Mr Dafis,' she cut across. 'They're staying here, I can guarantee that.' She stepped out through the church door but didn't get wet in the rain; Phil was waiting for her with a large NFU promotional umbrella.

'Don't forget, Phil, eight o'clock tomorrow, OK?' Joe called after them.

Phil raised his hand in confirmation.

'You're meeting Phil tomorrow evening?' Daf asked, unable to mask his curiosity.

'Yes, and Basia of course, for what the Americans call the Pre-Cana.'

'And what on earth is that?'

'Marriage is a serious and important step, especially in traditions like ours which don't sanction divorce. The priest has to meet with the bride and groom, to ensure they fully understand what they're doing.'

'You're preparing Basia and Phil for marriage? His wife isn't cold yet!'

'Just because I'm meeting them, that doesn't mean they'll be getting married next week, by any means. I have to be sure that they are in a fit condition to accept the sacrament of marriage and those discussions can continue for months. Sometimes, people have to wade through a tide of sin to reach the altar but there is forgiveness available for everyone.'

Daf recalled the ten minutes he and Falmai had spent with the vicar before their wedding and he was grateful no one had tried to persuade him to think again. Yes, they had been too young and it had ended unhappily but they'd created two cracking children along the way. He tried to imagine

Phil Dolfadog, always happiest with a pint of Worthy in his hand, discussing the nature of marriage with the priest. If Phil was prepared to be as out of character as that to please Basia, what else might he do? Would he even consider killing his inconvenient wife?

'I have seen situations like this before,' Joe added, 'though not in such horrific circumstances. Man and wife can no longer tolerate one another, one of them meets someone else but can't leave the marriage. Feelings like that aren't a good foundation for a new relationship, let alone a marriage.'

'Are you saying that you'd consider refusing to marry them?'

'I don't know enough about the circumstances yet, Daf, and besides, it's confidential.'

They were standing in the foyer and the members of the congregation were passing them one by one. The old tinker stopped and shook Daf's hand warmly.

'I didn't think ya was a Catholic, Inspector,' he said, in a County Westmeath accent which gave no hint of the fact that he'd lived in Welshpool for the last fifty years.

'Indeed I'm not, Mr MacAleese. Father Hogan is just helping me with a case.'

The old man laughed as he pumped Daf's hand up and down. For a small man in his seventies, his grip was strong.

'Ah, you want to watch him, Inspector, he's a cunning fella, is Father Joe. He'll be helping ya, then he'll be chatting to ya and before you know where you are, you'll be being Received. I'll stand godfather for you right willing when that time comes.'

'Thanks for the offer, Mr MacAleese, but I'm a confirmed heathen.'

MacAleese crammed his old felt hat down over his ears.

'As were many of the saints in heaven before they turned, Inspector. Grand to see ya.' He walked away into the rain like a little clockwork toy and Joe and Daf shared a smile as they watched him go: they were both fond of MacAleese, who worked unceasingly to keep some sort of order amongst his numerous and quarrelsome family. Joe noticed the young man standing by the door of the house.

'Hey, what are you doing out in all this rain, son?' he called.

It was clear to Daf that the priest knew the young man and it was also obvious that he'd carefully avoided using his name in the presence of a policeman. Although they were physically totally dissimilar, there was something about the stranger which reminded Daf of Jac Dolfadog; perhaps that was how young men looked when there was no one taking care of them. Or, as often happened with complex cases, it might just be that Daf was seeing everything through the filter of the matter filling his thoughts.

'Waiting for you, Joe,' was the answer.

'Get inside,' Joe invited him. 'I'll see you tomorrow sometime, Daf.'

'What time suits you?'

'You know what, Daf? At the moment, I'm something of a gentleman of leisure on Wednesdays. I used to spend all day at the prison in Shrewsbury but since it closed, the bishop's asked me to keep a bit of slack in my timetable until the new prison in Wrexham opens, because I'll be the chaplain there.'

'How much of a job is it, being prison chaplain?' Daf asked, surprised that he hadn't discussed this with Joe before. 'Can't imagine that many of the inmates are exactly godly types.'

Joe laughed.

'I wonder what you think faith is all about, Daf. We throw ropes to drowning men in the hope of saving a few sinners, so prison is a very good place for our work. Plus, there's often a good refectory which is a bonus for a single man who can't cook.'

'I'll ring you first thing,' Daf said, eager to bring the

conversation to a close. Joe was one of his greatest friends but, almost as if he had married a woman Daf loathed, they had to tread carefully, and that was why they seldom discussed religion.

Back on Canal Street, things had quietened down. The last of the SOCOs was pulling off his protective suit, Steve was busy entering the reference numbers from evidence bags onto his tablet and Nev was chatting to one of the CPSOs underneath a Wynnstay Farmers umbrella. Before he could greet his colleagues, Daf spotted a depressingly familiar figure marching up from the direction of the canal. When the man reached the police tape, Nev went over to speak to him.

'Sorry, Councillor Bebb, but we can't allow anyone to enter the site without permission.'

Feeling suddenly very tired, Daf walked over in time to hear the end of the tirade.

'... I have a perfect right to enter my own office. I have no connection with this fire and I have several pieces of urgent work to complete. I take it you do know who I am?'

Daf interrupted his torrent of words. 'At the moment, Mr Bebb, the whole area is closed. We are in the process of collecting evidence and therefore it is imperative that the site is undisturbed. Your office is virtually next door to the building which was on fire.'

'But I had cases needing attention. A lease, for example, which comes to an end tomorrow. I need to complete the paperwork.'

'What lease would that be, Mr Bebb?'

'Why are you asking impertinent questions, Deifi Siop?'

'Would it be the Dolfadog lease?'

'All such matters are confidential.'

Daf waited for a moment and filled his lungs before uttering a sentence he'd waited twenty years to say. 'If I have to, Councillor Bebb, I'll arrest you for obstructing an officer in the course of his duties. You can answer that question here, or at the police station.'

A moment of the purest pleasure. In his head, Daf was pumping his fist in triumph but he stood perfectly still as he waited for the answer.

'Every director has to sign the lease. There was another bid on the table. I told Jac that if he didn't get the document back to me completed last night, I would recommend the proprietor accept the other offer.'

'How important was the lease for Dolfadog?'

Bebb considered before replying.

'Have you heard the English expression: 'money pit', Deifi Siop? That was what Dolfadog was before Jac took up the reins. It was a big farm but expensive to maintain. Any number of workers doing very little work and Phil wasn't sharp enough to make it pay. Heulwen was too busy with her public life. It's Jac who's sorted the place, built the laying unit, got out of dairy when the going was good and so on. He raised a mortgage of half a million when he was twenty years old.'

'Did you get the document?'

'I haven't had a chance to check but I can listen to the office answerphone remotely. Jac Evans phoned on Monday night to say that he'd put the papers through the door.'

'With all the directors' signatures on it?'

'Yes.'

'Were you expecting that call?'

Bebb shrugged.

'We'd had a conversation earlier when he'd called by at the office straight from the Smithfield, shit on his boots. He asked me if I'd accept the lease without his mother's signature but I refused.'

'Do you know why Mrs Breeze-Evans wasn't willing to sign the lease?'

Gwilym Bebb's laughter wasn't an attractive sound. It was

both cold and harsh, and Daf couldn't help comparing the sound with the boozy merriment of Rhys Bowen.

'I've been a member of Powys County Council for twenty years and they are the most stubborn group of people on earth. And who is the most stubborn of the lot? Heulwen. I've never known anything which could change her mind about anything.'

'I've heard something similar from several people, but was there any special reason for her refusal?'

'I have no idea. Perhaps she wasn't happy with the direction the business was taking: I do remember her creating a bit of a fuss when Jac sold the dairy cattle, telling anyone who would listen about the dreadful loss of the great tradition of milking at Dolfadog and blaming Jac for being idle.'

'I wouldn't have thought laziness was one of that young man's weaknesses.'

'Heulwen was forever talking about Dolfadog in its glory and that was how she remembered it. One of the best farms of the area it was, until her brother died young.'

'We may have to ask for a formal interview later, Councillor Bebb. In the meantime, I'll give you a ring as soon as we can allow you back into your office.'

Bebb wasn't willing to give a single word of thanks or even acknowledgement to Daf so there was an awkward silence which was broken by Belle and her dogs emerging from the building.

'What in the name of heaven...?' Bebb began.

'Hydrocarbon dogs,' Daf explained. 'To help in the investigation.'

'So this is how you spend the public's money, is it, Deifi Siop?' Bebb complained. 'I'll say this much for you, you've got good taste: that piece looks like she's got a fair bit of go in her. Have you got tired of John Neuadd's wife already? From what I hear, he'd be very glad to get her back, used goods or not.'

'I don't know this woman at all, Councillor Bebb,' Daf

answered abruptly. Unfortunately, Belle's first words totally undermined this statement.

'Did you say Indian or Chinese?' she asked with a broad smile. Bebb raised his eyebrows as he left and Daf hoped the old bastard didn't take his chance to do a bit of shit-stirring. He was enough of a busybody to take the story back to Neuadd, and the last thing Daf wanted was to give John some hope that he might be able to win Gaenor back. It had taken six months to get John out of the habit of ringing every day with some feeble excuse like asking where the mustard was or when Sion's passport needed renewing, when the agenda of every conversation was obvious: his attempt to persuade her to return to the great black-and-white barn of a house. Sometimes, whenever their little house was as full as a tin of sardines, Daf would recall seeing Gaenor arranging flowers on the wide oak table which stood at the foot of the massive staircase at Neuadd. Gaenor had given up her lifestyle and social status by coming to live with him so the very least he could do was avoid creating any reason for her to be jealous.

'Your call, both are good.'

'I'd rather go for an Indian. Very partial to a bit of spice, I am.'

Daf couldn't make her out. Some of her lines sounded as if they came straight out of a *Carry On* film but she delivered them with a totally straight face.

'How much parking is there at your place?' she asked him. 'Do you want a lift in the van?'

'I'll take my car as well, in case.'

In the Shilam, Daf spotted Phil and Basia enjoying a meal together. Before going over to speak to them, Daf wanted to observe them for a few moments: they were deep in conversation, their eyes sparkling. Phil was eating naan bread with his fingers and when Basia saw a bit of chutney on his fingers, she took his hand. She licked each of his fingers in turn before sucking his thumb. Even from the other side of the room, Daf saw the shudder run through Phil's body. He offered her a piece of the bread and she leant forward to nibble it from his fingers. If Carys had been there, Daf knew exactly what she would have said: 'Get a room.' For the first time, Daf witnessed the passionate side of Basia's nature and, for all the restrictions she observed, it was obvious that her relationship with Phil was sexual – consummated or not – as well as romantic.

After ordering the food, jalfrezi for himself, chicken mughal for Gaenor, korma for Rhodri and a very hot tandoori for Belle, he went over to speak to them.

'Congratulations,' he began, seeing that Basia had a costly new ring very much in evidence. Phil reddened a little.

'There's no reason to wait any longer,' Basia declared. 'But there will be a fair bit of organising to do. I'll want my family to come over and, of course, Phil will have to receive instruction.'

'Instruction in how to do what?' Daf asked, thinking to himself that one thing Phil Dolfadog did not need was any lessons in how to deal with women.

Basia laughed and Daf could see that the sound gave Phil a thrill of pleasure.

'We do try not to marry pagans if we can help it, Mr Dafis,' she said. 'Phil will have to be received into the Church before we can create a new family together.'

If you analysed it, Daf thought, it was a pretty familiar situation: a man in over his head and ears willing to do anything to please a beautiful girl. No doubt about it, men do think with their middle leg at times, he mused, including himself in that group. He couldn't foresee Joe having any trouble at all with Phil: he'd be willing to swear there were unicorns grazing on the top of Moel Bentyrch if that was the way to get Basia on her back.

'Good luck, anyway. Have you had a phone call to confirm that the body in the back office was Heulwen, Phil?'

'Yes. From a girl called Nia, I think. She described herself as the family liaison officer and asked me for contact details for Nans and Gruff.'

Usually, the role of family liaison officer was a very challenging one, helping a grieving family through the process of the investigation. The last time Sheila had undertaken that role, Daf had given her an extra week's holiday after she described the process as being like walking through a dark tunnel. Daf tried to imagine how the other children might react to their loss – up to now, the family at Dolfadog had shown no sign whatsoever of being heartbroken.

'Mr Davies,' Amrit called. 'Your food.'

'Do they come here often?' Daf asked the waiter quietly, indicating Phil and Basia.

'Mr Evans and his lady? Oh yes, very often, twice most weeks. They were here on Monday but they left in a bit of a hurry.'

Which could well be their alibi, Daf thought, though he needed to be clear of the time of death before coming to that conclusion. And they'd been in a hurry after getting Milek's phone call, no doubt.

Daf hurried to the car. God, there was some heck of a good smell coming from the plastic bag on the passenger seat. He could see Belle following him; but for her presence, he would have yielded to the temptation to pull in at the lay-by by Heniarth corner to check that the food tasted OK. He smiled as he remembered how worked up Carys got every time she opened up the food to find a poppadum missing.

'You're like a locust, Dad,' she would say every time. 'It's as if we'd sent a rat down to the Shilam.'

Then, on his iPad, Rhods had drawn a cartoon showing a rat with a strong resemblance to Daf in the uniform of Dyfed Powys Police at the counter in the Shilam, sniffing at the bags of food. The lad had a real talent for things of that kind; maybe he could make a living in animation, Daf thought, as he drove along. At least with animation, he had some idea what the job entailed. The last time he'd asked Carys what her job was, she'd described herself as an interactive events organiser, and Daf was none the wiser.

# Chapter 5

## *Tuesday night, April 12, 2016*

As luck would have it, there were two parking spaces right by the house, room for Daf's car and Belle's van. When Daf noticed the Neuadd Land Rover, he had a momentary guilty panic: what if Gwilym Bebb had already reported to John Neuadd that Daf had been flirting with Belle? He recovered himself by considering that it was far more likely to be Sion.

Gaenor came out to greet their guest and there, on the doorstep of their little house in Llanfair Caereinion, Daf fell in love with her all over again, which did happen from time to time. His emotions overcame him somewhat, meaning that he had to stand still for a few moments, silently admiring the amazing woman who had, for some reason, agreed to share her life with a fool like him. Every word she said was welcoming and friendly and it seemed to him that there was grace in her smallest movement.

Gaenor tried to persuade Belle to show her the dogs but when Belle explained that they were resting, Gaenor evidently noticed the weariness in Belle's face.

'Belle, do you fancy popping over the road for a quick gin while the boys sort out the food?'

'I'd love to. It's been a bit of a long day, taking everything into account.'

Daf was nowhere near foolish enough to mention anything about alcohol and breast feeding but it was clear that Gaenor had guessed his thoughts without their being spoken.

'A tiny gin drowning in a pint of tonic will not make any difference to Mals,' she laughed.

'I never said...'

'But you thought it, Daf! Come on, Belle.'

Rhod was busy laying the table and emptying the bags, and

the plates were warming in the oven. He began to put the food into ovenproof dishes.

'Everything should be warm enough to eat in ten to fifteen minutes,' he declared, waving the food probe in his father's face like a sword.

'I don't know why we need a thermometer to tell us whether our food is ready to eat or not. It's just common sense.'

'And that, Dad, is the reason why so many people of your generation suffer from food poisoning. We learnt how to use these in Food Tech in school and Gae agrees with me that it's better to be safe than sorry. But while we're waiting, why don't you follow them over to the pub?'

'OK, and thanks for all the help.'

'The only clean bedclothes were Power Rangers but she doesn't look like the kind of woman who minds that sort of thing, does she?'

'Shouldn't think so. She doesn't strike me as the sort of woman who spends her free time in Dunelm. See you later, *cog*.'

It was usually quiet in the Goat until nine on Tuesdays unless the dominoes team were playing at home but tonight, there was plenty of life in the place. Daf had to squeeze past a gang by the front door to reach the bar where Gaenor and Belle were perched on high stools chatting easily to one another. Daf saw half a dozen familiar faces, including Sion who was playing pool in the back room. There had been a great change in the boy over the winter, whether because he'd given up on the idea of going to college or because he was getting less daily care from his mother, but Daf was glad to see that he was a young man now, not a lad, and a decent young man at that. These days, he hardly ever looked for an excuse to avoid doing something. He seemed to have accepted, before the age of twenty, that he had a lifetime of hard work on the farm before him. The fat had disappeared from his cheeks and he'd recently boasted to his mother that he hadn't been asked for ID for months. Perhaps I did Sion a favour by taking his mother from

Neuadd, Daf considered, because he isn't such a wanker these days.

'You're not allowed to interrupt ladies on their first gin, Daf,' Gaenor protested. 'It's unfair.'

'I'm on the run from that bloody food probe. Ever since the kids learnt about bacteria, every takeaway has become some sort of biohazard.'

'You haven't got time for a bout of salmonella, Dad; you've got a murder to solve.' Carys's voice, emerging up into the bar from the cellar steps, wearing her T-shirt with 'The Goat' on it.

'What are you doing here?' Daf asked, startled.

'Thanks for the lovely welcome, Daddy dear. I've got a masterclass tomorrow so when I got offered a shift tonight, I decided to stay overnight.'

'But...'

There was only one 'spare' bed in the house and if Carys was intending to sleep in it, where would Belle go?

'Don't worry, Daf,' Gaenor responded, reading his thoughts yet again. 'There's a spare room here.'

'I'll pay, of course.'

'You'll get mates' rates, naturally, Dad,' Carys explained, 'but there's only the annexe available and someone damaged the lock at the weekend and we're still waiting for the carpenter.' She turned to Belle. 'The door closes but it doesn't lock so if you've got any valuables, you can put them in the safe overnight. The boss is very fussy about these things and wouldn't normally rent out a room in that condition, but I can persuade him.'

'Valuables?' Belle laughed. 'I don't often wear my tiara when I'm working with the dogs; I find the light glinting off the diamonds puts them off their work.'

Sion appeared from the pool room and smiled broadly as he caught sight of his mother. There was a small plate in his hands piled high with food: chips and gammon cut up into pieces. He was eating with his fingers like a small child and Daf recollected the root of this. In Neuadd, the children had had to eat formally very early: no marks were permitted on the wide white tablecloths and everything, even chicken wings, had to be eaten with a knife and fork, except at a barbeque. Therefore, when John was absent, Sion reverted, with Gaenor's blessing, to eating like a little pig and Gaenor rejoiced in the transgression.

Sion had slapped his plate down on the bar before Gaenor had a chance to introduce him to her new companion. Daf saw the lust in Sion's eyes as he looked at Belle, blended with a touch of sadness at the remoteness of his chances of making any progress with her, but he had no opportunity to note Belle's response to Sion's less-than-romantic opening sentence. 'Fancy a chip? They're fairly fresh,' because, cutting across everything, like a hurricane blowing in from the pool room, Rhys Bowen bounded into the bar.

'Bloody hell, Gaenor Morris!' he yelled. 'No, no, you must be Gaenor's daughter.'

'Don't talk rubbish, Rhys,' Gaenor responded, but she started to blush like a girl of fifteen.

'Well, you're a sight for sore eyes, *lodes*,' Bowen continued, lifting his big hand to touch her cheek as if he was judging the skin condition of some heifer. 'And you, Inspector, I'm going to phone the Police Commissioner to complain: if you can afford to get your girlfriend Botox this good, you're getting too big a wage from the public purse, by God!'

'It's not Botox, Rhys,' answered Gaenor, light-heartedly, 'it's hormones. I've only just had a baby.'

'Well, that explains the cracking tits at any rate. And who's your gorgeous friend, Gae? I haven't seen her before.'

'I'm not local. I've come here for work.'

It was clear to Daf that Bowen's flattery was having no effect at all on Belle but he couldn't say the same for Gaenor. Of course, he reasoned, she hadn't ventured out for a while and she deserved a nice evening, but he was starting to feel annoyed. Annoyed with Bowen for his cheek and inappropriate flirting but also with himself: what was the difference between his admiration of Belle's bottom and Gaenor's enjoying being the recipient of a bit of flirting from an old friend? No difference at all, apart from his own double standards.

The phone rang behind the bar and, after a short conversation, Carys said, 'The curry has reached an ideal temperature, so, according to Rhods, you've got four and a half minutes to get over there before it turns into a biological weapon.'

Daf was very pleased to have a reason to escape but in leaving, Gaenor had to push past Rhys Bowen in the doorway and, worse than the fact that he was evidently relishing having her body so close to his, Bowen bent and whispered something in her ear. Daf was furious. After opening the house front door for Belle, he grabbed Gaenor's arm.

'What did he say to you, Gae?'

'Who?'

'That fucking Tory pig. What did he say to you?'

'You're hurting me, Daf,' she answered in a low, calm voice. 'Don't act like a total fuckwit. You know perfectly well that I was friendly with Rhys Bowen before I knew you existed, Daf Dafis, and you know perfectly well what I feel about you.'

His heart filled with guilt and shame. Gaenor had done nothing to draw Bowen to her except be attractive which wasn't anything she could be blamed for. The blame lay with Bowen but instead of grabbing him by the collar of his expensive tweed jacket and throwing him out into the rain, Daf had turned on Gaenor.

'Sorry, Gae, I'm so sorry,' he mumbled.

'We'll discuss it later. In the meantime, Rhodri is being a better host than you.'

Perhaps surprisingly, the meal went well, due to Gaenor's courtesy and Belle's sociable nature.

'I'm so sorry about the room,' Daf began. 'Carys is only at home every now and again these days.'

'I'll be fine, no worries. I've done the same thing myself, turning up without notice and expecting Mum and Dad to kill the fatted calf, especially when I was coming back from overseas.'

'Have you been to a lot of different places, miss?' Rhodri asked, his eyes wide as they usually were when he had the opportunity to discuss anywhere more exotic than Llanfair.

'Yes, I went to plenty of interesting places when I was in the army and I've worked abroad on a fair few contracts since.'

'What's your favourite country?'

'In terms of people or landscape?'

'Both.'

'Now then, Rhods,' Gaenor interrupted. 'Give Belle a chance to eat her supper.'

'Don't worry, its fine,' Belle answered. 'Usually, when I start talking about my travels, I notice people's eyelids start drooping pretty quickly.'

'I love hearing about random places,' Rhodri added. Daf was glad of the opportunity to sit quietly, thinking of strategies to prevent himself behaving like a total wanker.

'In terms of the landscape, I'll never forget the mountains of Afghanistan, no matter how terrible things were there, but the best people I ever met were in Sierra Leone. I was working on a project looking after child soldiers. Lads younger than you, Rhodri, who have seen and done indescribable things: killing, burning, cutting people's heads off; but if you throw a ball to them, they enjoy a kickabout like anyone else. Maybe they came from a terrible past, but they certainly believed in a better future.'

'Did you always want to be in the army?' Rhodri asked, avoiding Gaenor's eye.

'I'm not sure. My mum wanted me to go to college then be a teacher, just like her.'

'My mum thinks just the same!'

Belle glanced over in Gaenor's direction for a moment.

'No, Gaenor's not my mother,' Rhodri explained, with the honesty of youth. 'She was married to my uncle, Mum's brother, but she and Dad ran away together because the others, Mum's family, are too boring. And now, they've had a lovely little baby and here we are.'

Daf had to laugh at the simplicity of Rhodri's story but Gaenor gently corrected him:

'It wasn't quite like that, *cog*.'

But the description was accurate enough, if a touch blunt. On cue, Mali raised her little voice from upstairs. As everyone had finished eating, Gaenor settled on the sofa to feed her. Belle remained at the table, looking a trifle uneasy.

'Would you like a coffee, Belle?' Gaenor called over to her. 'Or you and Daf could nip over to the Goat to talk shop, if you like?'

Was she trying to score a point, Daf wondered, encouraging him to go for a drink with such an attractive girl? No, she wasn't, he decided: she was just being kind, and that was exactly why he'd turned his world upside down to be with her.

'You know what, Gaenor, I'm not that good with babies,' Belle admitted. 'I get on a lot better with dogs! So, I'll pop over the road but there's no need for Daf to come with me.'

'No, I'll come with you, Belle. The dominoes lads don't often get to see unfamiliar females and a friendly face will help them with the shock,' Daf said mischievously, pulling his oilskin coat over his shoulders.

'I hope I'm not that alarming,' laughed Belle.

After Belle stepped out into the stormy night, Daf turned back for a moment.

'Can you light the stove, Rhods? It just needs a match put to it.' But Daf had a more important reason for returning: he bent down to give Gaenor a passionate kiss.

'Thanks; that's a big help with the milk. Does the world of good to get the hormones flowing!' she called after him just before he shut the door.

Daf wasn't surprised to see Sion still by the bar: there wasn't much to lure him back to the big, empty house, or the big house with his father in it, which was pretty much the same thing. But he was surprised to see another young man in the pub, reading his book quietly on the sofa by the fire. Einion Vaughan, or, as his boss described him, Tory Boy.

'Wild old night, Einion.'

The young man blew on his coffee before answering. 'Merched y Wawr don't bother about a little thing like a tornado, Inspector Dafis. Mr Bowen's giving them his popular talk tonight: "Everything But The Squeak: Getting the best out of a Whole Pig." And, of course, it's a great chance to meet people.'

'Is that quite fair? Shouldn't they invite the other parties as well?'

'According to rumour, they did offer a night to the Lib Dem but they weren't best pleased with the topic he chose.'

'What was his theme, then?'

'"Elder Women and their Role in the Prevention of Female Genital Mutilation." The talk didn't go down too well.'

'And I bet it was just in English?'

'Spot on. Plus, these ladies don't take kindly to being described as 'elders'. And, if I'm honest, I'm not sure how much of a worry FGM is in Llanfair Caereinion.'

'GM, perhaps, but not necessarily limited to the F – I do recall one local woman using a steak hammer on her husband's important little places after he'd eaten her cherry bakewell slice the night before she was due to enter it in Llanfair Show.'

'They're much happier chatting about scratchings with Mr Bowen.'

Sharp work, Daf thought. Thirty members of Merched y Wawr, women with a fair bit of influence in their community and the precise demographic most likely to vote. Daf hoped he could return to the comfort of his home before Bowen reappeared in the pub.

There was a pint awaiting him on the bar, from Sion, who had also bought Belle a pretty hefty G & T.

'You didn't even think of offering your sister a drink,' Belle teased him.

'I haven't got a sister,' Sion replied. 'Except the baby, of course.'

'I thought the girl behind the bar was your sister.'

'No, no. Carys is my cousin, and her dad is my uncle, Daf. But, now, to keep it cosy, he's some sort of stepfather to me as well.'

'Hang on a minute,' said Belle, smiling in mock confusion. She pointed one finger at Sion, the other in the direction of Carys. 'Now then, who's who?'

'Sion's my stepbrother,' declared Carys at the exact moment that Sion stated that he was her cousin.

'Inspector Dafis, please, the next time you run away with someone, could you choose someone who isn't a relation? It would make matters so much simpler for your new colleagues like me.'

As they were laughing, a gust of wind blew the window open. There was another sound plaited into the sound of the storm: a dog howling.

'Damn this bloody wind. Saunders hates being in the van in weather like this.' The light-heartedness left Belle immediately. 'You haven't got a dog kennel out the back?' she asked Carys.

'No, sorry. And if you moved the van, the car park is, if anything, worse for catching the wind.'

Sion cleared his throat and did his best to sound natural.

'We've got a spare kennel up at home,' he offered. 'Hasn't been used for three years. We used to do a bit of puppy walking, for the hunt, but we haven't done that for a bit now. It's right sheltered in the corner of the yard and I can put a bit of fresh straw down for you in a minute.'

'How far is it?' Belle asked hopefully.

'Only up the *boncyn*. Maybe a mile. Why don't we nip up

and see if it's suitable and if the kennel's no good, you could park the van in the shelter of the barn. It's handy enough.'

'Nothing to lose. Keep an eye on my drink, Mr Dafis, I'll need it when I get back.'

Sion opened the door for her with stiff courtesy, Neuadd manners. Daf tried not to laugh but failed.

'Full marks for effort,' Carys said, patronisingly.

'He doesn't understand the whole girl thing yet, does he, poor little beggar? It's one thing to aim at something out of your league but this is taking it to a whole new level. Where does he get the nerve, do you think?'

Carys looked straight into her father's eyes. 'You, above all, should understand that, Dadi. Sion may be a bit of a loser but he's still Sion Neuadd. When we were in school, there were always any number of girls after him, because of the farm he's got coming to him.'

'But a woman like Belle won't be interested in his bloody farm.'

'But, innocent little Dadi, at least she's had a chance to see the place. Sion's not a fool: he's got his own tactics.'

Daf was rather surprised to see Huw Mansell; the doctor didn't often come out on two successive nights.

'Wow,' he said, 'someone's on a long leash.'

'Zumbalates tonight. A new class.' His wife Dana was a big fan of fitness classes and usually followed the latest craze. 'A blend of Zumba and Pilates: rhythmic music like Zumba but does as much good to your core as Pilates, so I am reliably informed. It was Piyo last night, a mongrel of Pilates and Yoga.'

'Gae was talking about doing something to shift the baby fat but it's too early for her to start any of that, isn't it?'

'I would say so, especially since she had such a rough time of it. She's not like Chrissie Berllan: give birth to twins on a Monday and do six hours on the chain harrow Wednesday. Gae needs plenty of time before she starts worrying about that kind of stuff.'

'Is that official advice?'

'Definitely. Gaenor's had a shock to the system, especially with her history. She needs to get stronger before she puts any more pressure on herself.'

'Very glad to hear it. I couldn't give a flying fuck what size jeans she wears.'

'They don't go to all that effort for us, Daf. Yes, everyone wants to be attractive, but looking good compared to other women is more of a priority than we think.'

Carys put their pints on the bar in front of them.

'Wow!' she exclaimed, scornfully. 'Two middle-aged men who know exactly how we girls think! It's a total privilege to be in the presence of such experts.'

'Aren't we allowed to try to make sense of the world around us, Carys? Do you keep fit for boys or for your friends?'

'Oh dear little Dr Mansell, I have friends who are boys; the world has totally changed since you were in your twenties. Garmon and I enjoy keeping fit together; I don't do it to please him but because I want to.'

Carys was perhaps a little sensitive on this subject: she'd little interest in sport until she met Garmon, who had been the world Mountain Bike champion until a fall severed nerves in his spine. Garmon might use a wheelchair but he was fitter and stronger than most men of his age, and determinedly so.

Huw Mansell decided to steer the conversation in a safer direction.

'Just nipped home to do a shift here, have you, Carys?'

'No, I've got a singing lesson tomorrow and if I'm going to try and get into the Conservatoire next year, I've got to be on track.'

Daf couldn't hide the delight on his face. 'What does Garmon always say: "Be the best you can be",' he quoted. 'You'd regret it all your life if you didn't try.'

'I know that, but I have to clear Mum's voice out of my head before I come to any decision about it.'

Daf remembered so many discussions about Carys's future;

Falmai was determined that, whatever else she did, Carys needed an academic qualification. Carys fancied having a go at operatic training, no matter how competitive or difficult the process might prove to be. In the meantime, Carys had started to work in Garmon's business and therefore wasn't spending much time at home. She was avoiding her mother whenever possible and, in an attempt to be diplomatic, Daf had been carefully avoiding mentioning future plans. He was itching to ask questions, like when was her audition and when would she hear the outcome; had she considered the Welsh College of Music and Drama or even the Guildhall? But he decided to let her tell her story in her own time. Falmai's attitude, including what they described as her pushiness, had damaged her relationship with her children and Daf was determined not to go down that route.

When Carys had popped down to the cellar to get a fresh bottle of gin for the optic, Huw changed the subject. 'Intentional fire?'

'That's what we think.'

'To kill her?'

'Don't know. Early days. How well did you know her?'

'Hardly at all until perhaps four years ago. When you have a patient with a chronic condition, especially ... Well, you get to know them in those circumstances.'

'Was she ill? She always looked so well.'

'Depression. Got a file six inches thick in the surgery. We've tried a variety of things – Prozac, Tamazepan, all kinds of therapy. In the end, I suggested a psychoanalyst, a really thorough one, private, of course. She normally went every week but she hadn't turned up for a while. Dr Martinez rang the day before yesterday, asking what had happened to her. She was disappointed that Heulwen seemed to have given up, she said, because things were starting to improve. She was convinced there was a deep problem there, with a sexual root, which makes sense.'

'What do you mean, a "sexual root"?'

'Very often, if we have a patient presenting with enduring depression, we look to their past to explain their present. We have to ask, what stands between that person and their happiness, their self-esteem?'

'Abuse, you mean?'

'Sometimes, but in my experience an unhappy marriage is more often to blame, something which can wreck a patient's relationship with their children. And can leave them with a persistent sense that everyone else is enjoying something they can't access.'

'But she came across as ... well, as an organised woman with a perfect life.'

'Thanks to Astra Zeneca, and Pfizer. You've heard of "Mother's Little Helpers", Daf? That's what kept Mrs Breeze-Evans on her feet – a cocktail of chemicals. I tried to persuade her to cut down on the pills but she insisted that I give her a prescription. She reminded me that it was safer for her to get her pills that way but that she would buy what she needed through the Internet if she had to.'

'Hell's bells, Huw, I would never have thought it. She gave the impression...'

'Those are the ones, very often, with something missing deep down; the ones who pretend to be living perfect lives but can't face their own reflection in the mirror.' The doctor pulled an old-fashioned watch out of his pocket. 'High time I was getting a report on the Zumbalates. Pick up the phone if there's anything more you need to know.'

'Huw, could you sort out a bit of a report for me, please? Her condition, treatment, medication and so on?'

'No worries. Good luck.'

Another person checking his watch was Einion Vaughan. Daf was about to leave in order to be gone before Bowen came back but Belle appeared in the doorway.

'Well, talk about a handy little place!' she declared, cheerfully. 'And talk about a handy little chap as well.'

'Not so sure about the "little" business,' Sion protested, following her in.

'Well, we may see about that later,' was her astonishing response.

'Why don't we open a bottle of Cava?' Sion suggested, following the family tradition which reminded Daf of so many leaden celebrations at Neuadd, with John explaining how much a bottle the fizz had cost and Gaenor desperately trying to stay cheerful.

'We sell it by the bottle not the glass, you know,' Carys warned him.

'I don't foresee any difficulty with that,' Belle replied. 'But what are we celebrating?'

'A handy home, convenient for the carbon dogs,' Sion said. For some reason, Belle laughed loudly.

'Are you OK if I go home?' Daf asked her. 'I've promised Gaenor to help out with that little owl in a Babygro.'

'Of course,' Belle answered, 'but you'll miss the fizz.'

'I'm good for fizz, thanks.'

'Can you leave the door on the latch, Daf?' Sion asked. 'I won't be driving back up the *boncyn* tonight.'

'No,' Belle responded, holding Sion's eyes in her own steady gaze, 'you definitely won't be driving home tonight.'

She was definitely pretending to fancy Sion, for some reason of her own, and Daf didn't think this was a particularly pleasant trick to play on a relatively innocent lad ten years younger than her. Still, Sion needed to learn a lot and the quickest lessons are those from our own experience.

Rhodri had gone upstairs to *potsh* about with his iPad.

'Said he was trying to create a meme, whatever that means,' Gaenor explained. 'Is Belle ok? I heard the van move.'

'The dogs are spending the night up at Neuadd, out of this wind. Sion's suggestion.'

'Oh dear. Has he taken a fancy to her?' There was a note of

disappointment in her voice which hinted that this wasn't the first time such a thing had happened.

'Well, they're sharing a bottle of Cava, anyway.'

'She's nearly old enough to be his mother!' Gaenor declared defensively.

'But she's not nearly good-looking enough to be his mother, is she?' Daf responded. 'And listen, I'm so sorry about being such a knob earlier. I'm not one for jealousy, Gae, but the truth of it is, I just can't get used to how I feel about you, about little Mali, about this new family of ours. Sometimes, I can't believe how lucky I've been and then I start to fret about losing you.'

'You're not going to lose me, Daf Dafis, but there is no reason on earth for you to be prickly like that, right? Rhys is an old friend of mine and that's it.'

'I get it.'

Daf managed to keep his mouth shut for almost a minute, before he had to ask, 'So, you and Rhys Bowen weren't king and queen of the Llanfyllin Prom, then?'

Gaenor sighed as she passed him the baby.

'I'm not dumb, Daf, you're asking if Rhys and I used to shag when we were young?'

'No, nothing of the sort ... well, yes.' He couldn't lie to her, ever.

'I'm going to make a cup of tea. You change Mali and I'll tell you the whole story, you nosey bastard.'

Her tone made it clear that she'd decided to treat his unnatural and potentially damaging curiosity as a joke. Daf promised himself that he would never be such a fool again.

When she came back, Gaenor was ready to have her say.

'Like I said yesterday, I had a heck of a crush on Rhys when we were young. Especially after he left school, when he'd passed his test and got his own van, then his own business as well. He did suggest a couple of times in his joking way ... but unfortunately, my best friend thought the same. We were out one night, which just happened to be the first night out my friend had been on since losing her dad, so when Rhys offered to take me home, I asked him to drive Meinir home instead, just to raise her spirits a bit. But he wanted to know if I was being nice to my friend or whether it was just a brush-off because I didn't fancy him.'

'And how did you answer?'

'With the truth: I thought the world of him, but Meinir really needed a bit of distraction from her troubles at home. And to make sure he believed me, I gave him a heck of a snog and until you came along, that was far and away the best kiss I'd ever had. And, fair play to him, he took Meinir about for six months, till she went off to college.'

'Then?'

'Then nothing. I had a fling with my boss in the Forestry Commission but ended up having a very nasty shock when he turned up at the Christmas party with a pregnant wife. Not long after that I met John.'

'So, you missed your chance with Rhys Bowen, then?'

'It didn't feel quite like that. But there's something very nice about him, under all his bullshit. Meinir was so fragile, nearly off her head, and he looked after her without thinking twice.'

'He must have fancied her.'

'I'm not so sure of that. During her dad's illness, she went very thin, almost anorexic, which isn't at all the sort of girl he likes. And she was behaving in a very odd way at that time, but he never complained. She needed someone to cheer her up and he was prepared to do it.'

'He was playing the long game, making sure he kept your high regard.'

'Very likely, but it did Meinir the world of good. And when I heard that he'd gone and sold himself to some Saxon madam who's got a face as long as one of her bloody horses, I was disappointed. He deserves more than that.'

Suddenly, Daf remembered how narrow and empty Gaenor's life had been for years. No career, a dull and distant husband

and the heartbreak of losing babies almost annually. No wonder that she had thought about other possibilities.

'It's right odd, Gae,' he said, without any trace of jealousy. 'You know what I think about him as a public figure, but last night, when I was talking to him, I have to admit that there was something very likeable about him.'

'There is. Everything bad about him is right on the surface: it's easy enough to see that he's noisy and likes to be top dog and, of course, he's as randy as an August tup, but on the other hand...' Gaenor stopped in the middle of her sentence as if she'd suddenly remembered the context. 'But how is he involved in the case? Heulwen was in Plaid Cymru, so...?'

'Bowen owns the building.'

'Don't tell me, there's a smart little flat upstairs with a smart-looking girl living in it?' She smiled indulgently.

'Two big Polish lads live upstairs.'

'Not some fine-looking female?'

'Well, yes, one of them has a sister.'

'She's not the stranger who's nicked Phil Dolfadog, is she?'

'Gaenor, where do you get all this information from?'

'Oh, the jungle drums, Inspector. There's a fair bit of bad feeling towards her, for pinching him.'

'Really?'

'Well, Phil was very handy for lots of the local ladies.' Daf saw a bit of a sparkle in her eyes. 'It's perfectly possible for a woman to be married and still to feel that ... that she isn't getting everything she's got a right to get. What's required in those circumstances is a convenient man, no complications, with a performance guarantee: overnight fun and no funny stuff in the morning. You men think we're just your dear little ladies, but sometimes, the only thing that'll do the job is a decent fuck.'

'What do you mean by performance guarantee?'

'You've heard the expression "It's not the size of the boat but the motion in the ocean?" But there's a fair bit of motion in the ocean when the QEII is docking, and that's what Phil has to offer. Or so I hear.'

They were both laughing like fools when Rhodri put his head around the door.

'You're a right pair of idiots, you two. Is it OK if I stay after school for cricket tomorrow, if the weather clears?'

'Fine by me,' answered Gaenor, still giggling under her breath.

'Cricket?' Daf asked. 'This is a new thing, isn't it?'

'It's actually a very historical game, Dad, and I really like it. Anything with a bit of tactics required.'

'High time you were in bed, Blofeld!'

'No, Dad, not to bed, but to my hidden HQ where I can plan to dominate the world!' As his son went up to his room, Daf felt very glad to have raised children with a bit of humour about them.

There was a knock on the door. Daf expected to see Belle, but instead, Falmai was standing on the doorstep in a smart coat and new shoes.

'Come in, Fal,' he offered, noticing the anxiety in Gaenor's eyes.

'I can't stop,' she declared, clearly taking pleasure in every word. 'Jonas is waiting for me.'

Daf stepped out of the warmth of the room to speak to Falmai and over her shoulder he saw a large black Mercedes, a car that was pretty well known in Llanfair; it belonged to Jonas Roberts, Bitfel, successful builder. In the three years since Jonas had lost his wife to cancer, Daf had needed to have a word with him on several occasions about the behaviour of his sons, who were good lads at heart but running a bit wild. Jonas was, as they say, loaded, and lonely: a perfect mark for Falmai.

'Is Carys here? Jonas said he saw her car earlier.'

'No, she's working a shift over the road.'

Falmai made a noise in her throat: working in pubs was not a very Neuadd thing to do.

'It would be better for her to concentrate a bit more on her future instead of wasting her time like this. What's the latest on her plans?'

'I think you'd better speak to Carys herself, Fal. I don't want to be in the middle of this.'

Falmai laughed sarcastically. 'So sorry, Daf. I just thought for a moment that you were going to take your responsibilities seriously, then I remembered that you wouldn't be living in this house if that was the case.'

'You don't need to worry, Fal. Carys has got her head screwed on.'

'I do know that, Daf,' Falmai replied, her voice softening with the love she had for her daughter. 'I couldn't dream of a better daughter.'

'Listen, Fal, I'm not trying to avoid anything, except maybe misunderstanding. Why not give her a ring and arrange to meet up tomorrow?'

'I'm teaching all day but I will ring her.'

'Grand. You know what, Fal, we may have failed as husband and wife but we could still succeed as parents.'

Falmai gave her ex an unusually friendly smile and Daf recalled good times, when they had spent their days, and their nights, enclosed in a bubble of love, not worried about money or family or the world around them. Then Jonas pressed the horn of the Mercedes and Falmai turned on her heel and ran from the shelter of the eaves to the sleek car. She was as light on her feet as a girl of twenty and Daf had to admit that he found it hard to believe that a man like Jonas had brought about this change in her. Then again, even if Jonas was a bit vulgar, he was bound to be better than another lonely night in the bungalow.

He went back into the house and sat down on the sofa.

'What did she want?' Gaenor asked, her voice full of uncertainty.

'She'd heard Carys was about and wanted a word with her.

But I also think she wanted me to see her out on a date with Jonas Bitfel.'

'The builder? Bit of a difference between you and him, I would have said.'

'He's made a fair old fortune.'

'And you think Fal fancies helping him spend it? His wife Nicky was a lovely woman, very down-to-earth.'

'Whatever. Before she knocked the door, you were talking about Phil Dolfadog's … endowments, and you sounded like you had a bit of inside information.' Daf wanted to turn the conversation away from Falmai because the guilt, buried beneath the surface of his thoughts, was far from comfortable; he hated to dwell on the harm he had done her by leaving. Gaenor was also quite happy to change the subject.

'I've never been with Phil but he did make me an offer one time.'

'Oh yes? And when was this, may I ask?'

After a bit of jiggling about and a good back rub, Mali opened her mouth and burped loudly. Gaenor was shifting her from one knee to another which was one of the reasons why she didn't look Daf straight in the eye as she told the story.

'Do you remember the Farmers' Ball, the year after Rhodri was born?'

Daf remembered it very well, for a particular reason. Falmai was supposed to be babysitting Sion so her brother John could take his wife out, but Rhodri'd developed a touch of colic so Daf had crossed the yard in her place. He was watching 'Dennis the Menace' with Sion in the sitting room when Gaenor came in, ready for the Ball, wearing a silk dress the colour of a wild rose. She was more than pretty, she was perfect, and Daf would never forget that moment because that was precisely when he began to desire his sister-in-law. There was a sad history behind the new frock: four months earlier, Gaenor had lost a baby, a late miscarriage, and she'd haemorrhaged badly afterwards. John had, with his characteristic lack of finer feeling, offered her seven hundred pounds: 'to get yourself something right smart to show the world there's nothing much wrong with you.' And that 'something right smart' was the dress she had worn to the Farmers' Ball.

'We hadn't been out for a fair while, if you remember, and I suppose I was hitting the wine a bit fast. John was discussing the price of cattle feed, honest to God, so I went back to our table by myself. Who came over but Phil, a glass of wine for me in his hand and a big smile on his face. We chatted a bit about nothing in particular then, out of nowhere, he offered to call by to see for me some time. I declined the offer but do you know what was odd about it?'

'The fact that you turned him down?'

'No. What was odd was the timing. John and I hadn't ... well, we hadn't got back to it since losing the baby and somehow, Phil could sense that.'

'Well, thanks for that new perspective on Phil Dolfadog. He'd be a chap worth keeping, then?'

'That's what's so peculiar about the Dolfadog situation, Daf. None of us can understand Heulwen at all. With a man like Phil at home, who would *potsh* about with stupid committees or the County Council? I wouldn't let him out of the bedroom to make a cup of tea, let alone choose to go to some stupid meeting. And they've got a lovely family as well.'

'It could be possible, missus, that not every woman is a nymphomaniac like you.'

'That's what we want you chaps to think, that we're innocent little girls talking about what washes whiter, Ariel or Persil.'

As so often happened, talking to Gaenor had made Daf see things from a different perspective. He considered his opinion of the Belle and Sion situation. If a thirty-year-old man was staying in a hotel for work and met a young local girl, Daf wouldn't have thought twice about it.

'Do you reckon Phil broke Heulwen's heart with his carrying on, Gae?'

'No, and that's the really odd thing. What's that expression: 'You don't go out for a hamburger when you've got steak at home.' From what I hear, Phil didn't start to wander until it was clear that Heulwen had no interest in him.'

'So, there was some deep problem in their relationship?'

'Please don't use the word 'deep' in the same sentence as Phil Dolfadog; I've just had stitches in a very sensitive place.'

Daf could never remember things being like this with Falmai, sharing sexy jokes until laughter was mixed with the loving. He gave Gaenor a long kiss.

'I can't wait for these bloody stitches to be gone, Daf,' she whispered.

Mali decided to raise her little voice at this point and Daf got to his feet, floorwalking her from one side of the room to the other.

'I'm going to bed, Daf. Are you coming?'

'Nice invitation but I think this little lady may have other ideas.'

'Well, you know where to find me.'

Even though she was in her father's arms, Mali still bawled until her face was red. Gaenor rose carefully from the sofa but before she'd reached the foot of the stairs, the house phone rang. Gaenor saw the number on the caller display screen and frowned.

'Neuadd,' she said, her voice tired.

'It's probably Sion. He asked me to leave the door on the latch for him – perhaps he's gone home earlier than he expected.'

Gaenor lifted the phone and the smile on her face vanished as she heard the voice at the other end.

'John. You'd better speak to Daf.'

She passed the phone to Daf and took Mali, who had replaced her bawling with a penetrative moaning, from his arms.

'A bit late for a chat, John.'

'There are strange dogs in the kennel.'

'They belong to a woman who's working for the police. Sion suggested it was a good place for them; she's staying at the Goat.'

'Why on earth did he do such a thing, Daf? What a stupid thing to offer.'

'He's a polite young man.'

'Where is he now? I want to speak to him.'

'Over in the Goat, more than likely.'

'I've tried his phone any number of times.'

'I'll pop over and see if he's there, if you like.'

'I don't like him being mixed up in things like this.'

'He's only offering overnight accommodation to three spaniels, John, not spending his whole life in witness protection.'

'He shouldn't have offered without discussing it with me anyway.'

'Oh, fair enough. I'll just go over there now.'

Daf didn't have to repeat the conversation to Gaenor, she'd got the gist of it.

'What's Rhodri's latest expression? Oh yes, "batshit crazy". That's how John was, just over three little dogs. I'll be back in a minute.'

'That's John, never good with anything unexpected.'

The bar was quiet. three pairs of domino players still at their fives and threes in the pool room, Carys setting the tables for breakfast and two old men drinking quietly. But on the bar was evidence of a fair spree; two empty Cava bottles, an empty packet of pork scratchings and three wired corks. Daf stepped into the dining room.

'Seen Sion, Car?'

Carys raised her eyebrows. 'Where do you think by now? They've taken the third bottle upstairs.'

'I've got to speak to him.'

'Don't be stupid, Dadi. They're only having a bit of fun together.'

'He'd be better speaking to me than to his dad. In the annexe, are they?'

'Yes, but...'

Daf climbed the wooden stairs outside the back door, half expecting to hear sounds of talking or laughing. He paused outside the door for a moment: silence. Perhaps the Cava had hit them and they were sleeping. Daf knocked on the door, having totally forgotten the lock was broken. The door swung open and Daf saw a scene he would never be able to erase from his memory.

Sion lay across the wide bed, stark naked apart from a black silk mask fastened over his eyes. His wrists and ankles were fastened tightly to the bed with thick straps of black leather. There was a broad smile on his face but what disturbed Daf most, having changed his nappy countless times, was the remarkable size of his erection. Belle's voice was heard clearly from the en suite: 'You're a bad boy, Sion Jones and bad boys always get punished.'

The handle of the door to the ensuite began to turn and Daf turned on his heel and tried to creep silently down the slippery steps. He paused in the shadows by the back door of the pub to get his breath back. Belle appeared for a moment, silhouetted in the bedroom doorway. The wind caught her voice.

'Damn this wind. I'll just put a chair by the door, we don't want to be disturbed, do we?'

As she turned to close the door, Daf was certain that he saw something in her hand, something very like a whip. He staggered to the bar and called for Carys. By now, the bar was empty.

'Get me a big whisky, please, *cariad*.'

'You look like you've seen a ghost, Dadi.'

'I remember Rhods talking about mind bleach once. That's what I need now, mind bleach.'

Carys went red before she began to laugh. 'I told you about the door not fastening properly.'

'The wind caught the door. I'm in shock.'

'Oh dear, innocent little Dadi. It's only natural.'

Daf was about to say that there was nothing natural about leather straps and blindfolds and whips, but he just about managed to keep his mouth shut.

'But I've got to calm your Uncle John down. Those dogs are important. I don't want him getting the huff and letting them out, out of spite. They could be eaten by badgers or something.'

On cue, the door opened and John came in. Daf tried to imagine a more awkward situation but failed. Here he was, his former brother-in-law, looking for his only son, who just happened to be upstairs playing Cava-fuelled S&M games with one of Daf's colleagues. Some sort of a start to conversation had to be made.

'The weather's turned right sudden, John,' he ventured. 'Be hard for those new lambs of yours, I bet.'

'I didn't come down here at this time of night to chat about the weather, Dafydd. Where's Sion?'

'Well...'

'It's all my fault, Uncle John,' Carys began, giving him her most innocent and appealing smile. 'Can I get you a pint to begin to say sorry?'

'You've done nothing wrong, *lodes* I'm sure of that. I'll buy you a drink.'

'I've got any number in,' Carys explained, pointing to a small whiteboard behind the bar with names and tally marks clearly displayed. 'The girl who owns the dogs, Belle, she's helping Dadi discover what happened in Canal Street on Monday night.'

'I was there,' John put in. 'I've got a ... a friend who owns the jewellery shop there.'

'The dogs can help us work out what caused the fire and if it was intentional or not,' Daf added.

'The dogs? How?'

'They've been trained to find things like oil and petrol. They were late starting, then the rain began, so they didn't get their work finished before is started to get dark. So Belle's staying here.'

'But,' Carys added, 'the wind was upsetting the dogs and Belle is absolutely gorgeous, so Sion thought he'd make a good impression on her by offering somewhere sheltered for them to stay overnight.'

'So, where is Sion now, then?'

Daf could scarcely believe, even after knowing John well for decades, that any human being could be so slow on the uptake. Carys was doing a good job of explaining things; she was far more patient with her uncle than Daf could ever be.

'Well, don't be cross with Sioni, Uncle John, but the two of them were getting on champion and they decided to drink the third bottle up in her room.' Carys could wind her uncle round her little finger: she'd always been a great favourite of his.

John opened his eyes so wide that his forehead vanished beneath the peak of his cap.

'Sion ... Sion went upstairs with a woman he'd only just met?'

'She seems like a lovely girl to me,' Carys persisted. 'She's lively and confident and, of course, she's a total stunner.'

Daf was about to launch into a lecture about how courting practices had changed since their youth but then he remembered that it was John's sister he was courting in those days, the sister he had since abandoned to live with John's wife, so it was better for him to keep his mouth firmly shut.

'These dogs, are they worth a lot of money?' John said, in a dry, hoarse voice.

'I would imagine so,' Daf replied.

'You don't happen to know if Sion had discussed occupier's liability with this girl at all?'

'She's working under contract to Dyfed Powys Police so the paperwork will be fine, wherever the dogs are.' Somehow or another, Daf couldn't imagine that the terms of his father's insurance policies would have been much of a conversational priority for Sion.

John hid his face in his pint and Daf saw an opportunity to escape.

'I'd better go. I'm on the nightshift with Mali.' He wondered, as soon as he had spoken, if it was exactly tactful of him to mention the child who had been conceived when John and Gaenor were still living together, but he was too tired to care.

'OK then, Daf,' John replied. He paused and Daf couldn't help thinking that, although John was only six years older than he was, he seemed to be on the threshold of old age at times. John added, in a small and rather sad voice, 'Remember me to Gae, won't you?'

Daf dashed across the road and closed the door behind him, resting his back against it for a moment to shut out the outside world. The room was quiet, and he could smell Mali and Gaenor. Milk, Sudacrem and Ralph Lauren Romance. He pulled his shoes off and crept up the stairs to the bedroom. He undressed in the dark, not certain where Mali might be, but when he pulled the duvet over himself, he could hear her gentle breathing on the pillow.

'She's not quite ready for her basket yet,' Gaenor mumbled. '*Cwtch* round my back. Did you find Sion?'

'I certainly did,' Daf replied, hiding his face in her hair. 'I knocked the door and...'

Gaenor couldn't laugh aloud after hearing the story in case she woke Mali but her whole body was shaking.

'Oh, poor old you.'

'You've got no idea. It's not as if they were just ... well, on the job.'

'What do you mean?'

'Have you read *Fifty Shades of Grey*, Gae?'

'Of course I have. I wasn't going to be the only person in Friends of the School who hadn't read it.'

'And, what do you think about ... that sort of stuff?'

'I suppose everyone suits themselves in that department. I'm pretty vanilla myself but you'd be surprised how many people round here enjoy getting their little parcels from Lovehoney.'

'What's Lovehoney?'

'The sort of stuff which makes Ann Summers looks as innocent as Sali Mali. I had a look at the catalogue once but all it did for me was make my eyes water.'

'Well, when I opened the door, and saw Sion tied to the bed like that...'

'That's not an easy thing for a mother to hear, Daf.'

'It wasn't an easy thing for me to see, I'm telling you. But he was obviously happy as a lark.'

'And where was Belle?'

'In the en suite. I had the idea she might have been changing into something, some costume maybe, but I disappeared before she could see me.'

'Bloody hell. My little Sion.'

'Whatever else he is, he's certainly not little, honestly, Gaenor.'

Very gingerly, she turned her head to face him without disturbing the baby.

'Well,' she concluded, in her warm and gentle voice, 'at least he's a passionate and adventurous lad and he doesn't get that from the Neuadd side of the family.'

They managed, with some considerable effort, to kiss.

'What page of the Kama Sutra is this contortion?' Daf asked. 'I'm going to have some heck of a crick in my neck in the morning.'

'Never mind your neck, just keep those hands of yours a safe distance from my stitches.'

'Those damned stitches.'

# Chapter 6

## *Wednesday morning, April 13, 2016*

Daf woke on the floor by the Moses basket, his head in his shoes and his feet under the bed. Gaenor was looking down at him, laughing, a mug of coffee in her hand.

'You said she'd sleep soundly in her basket if you rocked it a bit for her, and promised me a proper *cwtch* after. Instead, you spent the night on the floor, rocking an empty basket.'

'Where is she, then?'

'After your trick didn't work and you went off to sleep, I took her back into bed with me. She didn't sleep a wink and she needed feeding again about two, then Carys took her upstairs in her little chair. I did try to wake you but you were snoring like a hog.'

Daf rose slowly to his knees and hid his head under the duvet.

'I'm that creaky, I feel like I've been through the mangle,' he said, muffled.

'Don't you dare think about going back to bed, it's almost eight.' Gaenor set the coffee down on the bedside cabinet and gave Daf a fearsome slap on his backside.

'Don't tell me a taste for that kind of thing runs in the family!' he exclaimed, recalling Sion's situation in the annexe bedroom of the Goat.

'Into the shower – now!'

Daf decided it was wise to try and put the events of the previous night out of his mind. The Neuadd Land Rover was no longer parked outside the pub. Whatever he'd been up to under cover of darkness, Sion would have to be in the milking parlour at half past five, as he was every day. There was a message from Belle on Daf's phone: 'Gone straight down to the site. OK if I call by for a word before I go?' He replied with a thumbs-up emoticon and also sent a text to Nia: 'Put the kettle on, *da lodes*'.

He felt like a man in his nineties as he walked across the car park. Some representatives of the press were there already, including some faces unfamiliar to Daf, correspondents drawn up from Cardiff, even from London, by the story. Daf was painfully aware of how rough he looked: a button hanged by a thread from the front of his jacket and his hair badly needed a cut and, as he had said to Gaenor, he was walking as if he'd been through a mangle. Maybe Ms Rhydderch was right, he should leave the press to her.

'Don't tell me you played football last night,' Nia observed. 'That's just how Barry walks after his first session back at training after the summer break.'

'It's a long story about a small baby, Nia. *Duwcs*, that tea looks good!'

'Had I better make one for the woman who's waiting to speak to you?'

'Who is she?'

'Some Lisa Powell, from Cardiff. In a big hurry, said it was very important.'

'To do with the investigation?'

'She made it pretty clear that talking to her was above my paygrade so I'm not really sure of the details, but yes, so she said.'

'Well, I'm sure she'd appreciate a cup of tea anyway.'

Yesterday, it had been Anwen waiting to see him; the woman on the small sofa was a total contrast to her. In her expensive work clothes and spotless patent leather shoes, she looked formal, even official. Daf admired the colour of her hair. As the father of a girl, he knew very well the difference between hair like that and the effect of two packets of Nice'n Easy from Superdrug. Her face was attractive enough to start with but she'd succeeded in painting every part of it with such artistry, using all kinds of make-up to create the image of perfection.

The only thing which detracted from her image was a small tattoo in the shape of a star in front of her ear. Daf wondered what she had been like as a girl. A weekend rebel, perhaps?

'Ms Powell? Inspector Dafis, Dyfed Powys Police.'

She rose to her feet and extended her hand to him, in a most professional manner. 'I was a friend of Heulwen Breeze-Evans.'

'I'm sorry for your loss.'

'When I say that I was a friend of Heulwen's, that's not strictly true. She was a friend of my partner.'

'And your partner's name is...'

'Jan Cilgwyn. And that's the reason I've come all the way up here to see you. I need to protect Janet.'

'Protect her from what?'

'From herself. From stupid notions. You do know that she's been in touch with the police suggesting that this was a hate crime?'

'I did hear something about that last night.'

'It's utter nonsense. And it won't help with her election campaign, either.'

'Because there are so many ... narrow-minded people in south-west Wales?'

'Not at all. Jan has never concealed anything about herself from her electorate. But with this business about Heulwen, she's gone rather hysterical. I don't think there was any connection between Heulwen's death and her sexuality. Not many people knew she was gay, in any case.'

'Was she gay? She was married and...'

'Well, there are many theories about sexuality, Mr Dafis. Perhaps you've come across the research which indicates that heterosexual women don't exist?'

Daf felt considerable unease as he formed his reply. 'I'm pretty certain I've met one or two,' he ventured.

Ms Powell gave him a patronising smile.

'I'm sure you've met some women who were going through

a heterosexual phase. That doesn't mean that they didn't have experiences with women before meeting you, or at the same time.'

Somehow, Daf couldn't imagine Falmai having any such adventures, but Gaenor? He shook his head a little to dismiss the image of Gaenor and one of her school friends: Ruth, perhaps, or Charlotte or maybe Hawys from the Forestry Commission...

'And, of course, there are many women who follow a conventional pattern without achieving any satisfaction and who discover an important part of their nature in later life.'

'I'll never be able to look at Merched y Wawr in the same way again.'

'Mr Dafis, we are discussing important matters here and I'm getting the impression that your understanding of the complexities of sexuality seems to be based on old *Noson Lawen* sketches from the 1970s.'

'Very sorry. So, what is it that you're saying about Heulwen? That she'd discovered her ... her nature comparatively recently?'

'Or perhaps she was in search of some novelty. If you remember, she'd only recently discovered her true ambition, her true political party etc., etc.'

'You weren't a big fan of Heulwen, I take it?'

'She was the shallowest, most selfish and most superficial person I ever met. She charmed Jan with her stereotypical, salt-of-the-earth, farming woman act. Bogus, that's what she was. She was pretending to be gay, just as she was pretending to support Plaid Cymru. Or pretending to be the perfect mother and farmer's wife. But poor old Jan was innocent enough to fall for it.'

The smooth shell surrounding Lisa had started to crack, revealing the burning anger inside.

'Was Jan having an affair with her?'

'I'm very sorry, Mr Dafis, but have you seen her? So old-fashioned, so dull, so...'

'I hate having to push you on this point but were Jan and Heulwen close?'

'Jan and I are close.'

'Ms Powell, please. A woman has died, in circumstances which raise serious concern. Someone has started a serious fire and we're lucky that half a dozen other people didn't lose their lives as well. In an hour, I'll be appealing to the public for any information anyone has about Heulwen Breeze-Evans. If she was having an affair, someone is sure to know. I take no interest in people's personal lives until they get killed but after that, it's my duty to find out all I can about them. And if you are determined to keep secrets, Ms Powell, I have to start asking why.'

'Is this homophobic bullying, Mr Dafis? Just so we all know where we stand.'

'No way. I'm talking to you just as I would talk to anyone else who has a connection with a victim which I need to explore. And if you think that you're going to be able to use your sexuality as a get-out-of-jail-free card, you're totally wrong. I'm going to ask the question again. Was your partner having an affair with Heulwen Breeze-Evans?'

Lisa lowered her head before answering. 'It was just a stupid fling. We've not long got engaged and we're planning to get married in Cardiff Castle next summer.'

'But?'

'The whole nonsense started up in the north, in Bala, I think, at the Plaid Spring conference. They had a bit of a sesh and ended up in bed. Jan confessed and described it all as a mistake. How could it be anything other than a mistake with a woman like that?'

Daf agreed but merely said: 'You weren't speaking about it as if it had just been a one night thing.'

'No. For three months, I didn't notice anything because Jan was often away at weekends anyway, doing things with Plaid. I always took the chance to catch up with the housework, cleaning and ironing and so on while she was away.'

Daf was about to say something about the way women used to live their lives back in the 50s, but decided against it.

'I'm sure you've noticed, Inspector Dafis, how ready your friends are to come to you with bad news? Someone was always telling me they'd seen the two of them somewhere, the Felinfach Griffin, the Bull in Beaumaris, the Polyn, nice places, fancy places. But do you know what the cherry on the bloody fairy cake was? Burger and Lobster. I'd been wanting to go since it opened but Jan's a vegetarian and always says places like that stink of blood. It's just so unfair.'

She was almost stamping her foot and Daf started to sympathise with her. It's a hard thing to admit the person you love doesn't return the love, at least not as much as you do. He suddenly remembered how he'd felt when he saw Rhys Bowen touching Gaenor's cheek. To be betrayed by someone so close could totally undermine anyone's self-respect.

'Have you thought of parting, you and Jan?'

'No. It's all very well for Jan. She comes from a modern middle-class English family; all she had to do was go to them and say that we were a couple. I come from Bedwas. My father started his working life underground and all they wanted for their only child was a husband, a nice house, foreign holidays and three children. It took ten years for them to get used to Jan and in the end, it's her they like, not the idea that I'm gay.'

'So how did you deal with the relationship between Jan and Heulwen?'

'I tried to ignore it, until Heulwen got thrown out of her daughter's house. Before that, she'd stay with her daughter and her family when she was staying the weekend in Cardiff. But Heulwen took advantage, pushed people too far. Her son-in-law came home early one Saturday afternoon and found her in bed with Jan.' Lisa sighed. 'Love is the problem, Mr Dafis. At work, I'm renowned for my common sense.'

'What is your job, Ms Powell?'

'I'm a senior manager in the Developing Effectiveness Team

in the Welsh Government Department for Fostering Self-disciplined Communities.'

'Interesting job?' asked Daf, eager to conceal the fact that he had no idea what she was talking about.

'Very interesting. Too much work to do and not enough budget to do it with, of course. But that's how it is these days for us in the public sector.'

Daf was rather irritated by her connecting her bureaucratic stuff with cuts to the emergency services.

'And how long have you been there?' he asked, politely.

'Only three years. Before that, I was working at the Promoting Developing Enterprise Project. Perhaps you remember what happened there?'

Daf noticed the new energy she showed when discussing her work, and decided to invest a little time in trying to understand her better.

'Sorry, no. I'm hopeless at following the news.'

Lisa gave him a rather pitying smile.

'The story was rather complex. Promoting Developing Enterprise Carew Castle invested three point seven million pounds in the Pig of the Future project.'

'What happened after that?'

'The pig died in the Three Counties Show after drinking seven gallons of pear cider.'

'Which was perry bad news for the project.'

Daf regretted the joke immediately and Lisa looked at him with puzzled disappointment.

'I see,' she said in a dry voice. 'Perry as in the drink. Very droll.'

'Sorry, I can never resist a pun. Anyway, back to the story.'

'There was hell to pay, especially as the pig died outside Wales. The Minister decided to totally restructure the department. Promoting Developing Enterprise ended up being lumped in with two other sections to create a grouping which was much tighter and more focused. We lost three hundred jobs, a hundred in Aber, a hundred in Llandudno and a hundred in

Abercrave, and they closed all the outreach offices in the Sea-ahead branch. How can we develop islands like Enlli and Caldey without any government presence there, I'd like to know? Talk about short-sighted.'

'Did you meet Jan through work?'

'Yes. I was on secondment in the west, on the Plwmp Peach Project. Jan gave the project a good deal of support.'

'What happened to the peaches?' Daf asked, glad that, at last, he had understood some part of Lisa's work.

'Worms,' she replied, abruptly.

'Shame. But at least you had the chance to meet Jan.'

'Yes. And when I received an invitation to attend the European Stone Fruit conference in Malmö, I asked her if she had any interest in attending. Next thing I knew, she was presenting a paper there: Damsons in Distress: Austerity and Women Fruit Entrepreneurs in south-west Wales.'

Daf tried, and failed, to think of anything more boring but Lisa's eyes were full of nostalgic love. She sighed deeply and pulled a tissue from her bag as if she were on the verge of tears. Daf reached for her hand and couldn't resist wondering where exactly she was on this spectrum of sexuality she described.

'I know exactly what you're thinking, Mr Dafis,' she said with a teary little smile. 'You're thinking that there's nothing really wrong with me but I just haven't met the right man yet.'

Daf was unprofessional enough to colour at having his mind read so easily.

'I didn't...'

'I don't take it as an insult, but please don't go anywhere near there with Jan. She's much more sensitive, and to her, everything personal is political, and that's why she's gone off at the deep end now. Heulwen Breeze-Evans may have been many things but she certainly wasn't a martyr for gay rights. She was still pretty deep in the closet or, in her case, perhaps that ought to be the oak corner cupboard. Jan believed that after all the fuss with the son-in-law there was a chance for

Heulwen to be a bit more open, but being honest never suited her. She told a lie with every breath.'

'Did Jan discuss Heulwen's situation with you?'

Lisa nodded her head sadly. 'She told me that Heulwen was non-negotiable. She gave me the choice: share her or lose her completely.'

Daf gave what he hoped was a sympathetic nod.

'How many people do you know in politics, Mr Dafis?'

'No one, really.'

'It's a very peculiar world. Full of people who come over as super confident but are damaged inside. They attack each other, knowing each other's weaknesses so well, and every blow leaves a scar. To Jan, who has never pretended to be anyone but herself, her background is a serious problem.'

'In what way?'

'She's too middle class. She's envious of my heritage in the coalfields because she's the child of two doctors from Usk and there's no mileage in that.'

'I see.'

'The Tories, especially, have been very cruel to her. They keep pretending to invite her to come over to them, referring to her father's membership of the Golf Club. Rhys Bowen is the worst. He presents himself as the voice of the common man and he's always undermining Jan in the Chamber. His latest trick is to keep on looking at her hands, to see, as he puts it, "if she's ever done a day's work in her fancy little life." Jan has complained to the Presiding Officer but then, of course, she gets accused of telling tales.'

'I can imagine.'

'The real truth is, Mr Dafis, Jan's met very few "ordinary folk" in her life. So when she met Heulwen, it was as if Heulwen could provide her with a bit of depth, a bit of meaning behind her statements. She could talk about the changes in subsidy regime, badgers and TB, fair funding for rural schools. And Heulwen promised her that she would depose that bastard

Rhys Bowen.' She drew a deep breath. 'I wasn't too confident about Heulwen's chances before coming up here but now I'm pretty certain that Bowen will get back in.'

'Could well be right. He's a familiar face and he made a bit of a name for himself fighting the windfarms.'

'Jan put her trust in Heulwen. She was looking forward to welcoming her to the Assembly.'

'If Jan goes back herself.'

'She's safe, she's on the List. But she's not so safe that it does her good to go about making wild accusations about hate crimes.'

'In a complex investigation like this, we always try to view things from every possible angle...'

'Mr Dafis, you're a busy man and I've got to get on. Can you give me your promise that Jan's name will be kept out of all this fuss?'

'But if she's determined to talk to the press...'

'You speak to the press. There's no evidence that Heulwen was gay. She was married, as you said. You could shut this story down.'

'But if Jan is...'

'We have to protect Jan. She doesn't always act in her own best interests.'

Daf glanced at the clock and exhaled. 'I've got no interest in gossip, Ms Powell, but if Jan intends to discuss her relationship with Heulwen openly, I can't silence her.'

'I understand,' Lisa replied in a surprisingly small, shy voice. She rose to her feet.

'Thank you for your co-operation, Ms Powell. Keep in touch, won't you?'

'Fine.'

Daf's phone rang.

'Good morning.' Joe Hogan. 'What time do you want to have this chat with Milek and Wiktor? They've got a bit of free time now because their shift doesn't start till midday.'

'How about now?'

'Give it a quarter of an hour so I can walk down; the car wouldn't start this morning.'

'Have you rung the RAC or AA or whatever?'

Joe laughed. 'I've got cover that works a bit better than that, Daf. I've phoned MacAleese and the car will either be sorted by dinner time or I'll have a new one in its place.'

'You can't walk down in all this rain. I'll nip up and get you.'

McAleese had reached the church car park ahead of Daf, accompanied by a young man with several piercings in his ear.

'Did ya ever see such a disgrace as this fella with all his ironmongery, Inspector?' he said to Daf in a conversational tone. 'I'm glad his grandmother, God rest her soul, never lived to see her flesh and blood run through like a heathen from the South Seas.'

'Granda, please,' muttered the lad, drying his hands on the seat of his trousers as he looked under the bonnet of Joe's car.

The door of the presbytery opened and Joe appeared, talking to the young man Daf had seen waiting for him the previous afternoon. Obviously, he'd enjoyed a decent meal and a good night's sleep. He was still pale but there was a new light in his eyes, a flash of personality, perhaps. Daf overheard the last sentence of their conversation.

'That's what you need, lad,' Joe said to him. 'Skills, a trade. Declan here's a fair bit younger than you but he's got a few pounds left in his pocket at the end of every week.'

There was a respectful look on the young man's face, as if he was really considering what Joe had said to him. He shook the priest's hand and walked off.

'Did I hear you say my name, Father?' Declan asked, having recognised his name in the Welsh conversation.

'I was just telling him to be like you, get a trade.'

'You may be right there, Father, but I haven't got myself a pair of trainers like that, Air Huarache, they are.'

'You'd best set about saving for them,' pronounced his grandfather, 'Though it's a powerful lot of money you young fellas are willing to lay out for a pair of runners.'

Daf recalled hearing something about that particular brand of shoes recently but couldn't remember in what context. Joe was happy to leave his car in the capable hands of the MacAleese clan and he got into Daf's car for the journey down to the station.

'Who was that young man, Joe?'

'Come on, Daf, you know me better than to ask for names. I met him in prison. The old, old story: junkie mother, lack of care, homeless, jobless, in and out of institutions.'

'You don't often come across Welsh speakers in those circumstances.'

'Don't show your prejudices, Daf.'

'But it's true. What did you recommend he should do?'

'He's got a home here and he knows it, but, and it's a big but, he's got to be clean to stay here. There are plenty of pretty fragile people who come to the presbytery expecting to be safe, which isn't something I can promise when there's an addict on the premises.'

'Fair play to you, Joe. He's a Catholic, I suppose.'

'No, but we're all children of God.'

Since getting to know Joe, Daf had got used to his religious language but it still got on his nerves. Although, if he was honest, Joe's obsession was not that different to Huw Mansell's attempt to bring football into every conversation.

'Thinking of all God's children, what kind of evening did you have last night?'

'I take it you're referring to my assorted house guests? Basia made us a lovely supper, then went out for a couple of hours without eating herself, to see Phil, I imagine, whilst the rest of us watched *Fast & Furious 5*. Good film.'

Daf had to admire Joe's relaxed attitude. A young addict and a couple of tough guys from Poland, who were at least smugglers and possibly murder suspects, had just settled down to watch whatever was on Netflix.

'How well do you know Milek and Wiktor?'

'They come to Mass every Sunday, even if they've had a heavy night the previous night, and they're always willing to lend a hand. Wiktor in particular is too fond of his vodka, I'd say, but then, they're men who spend a lot of their time feeling lonely, so they self-medicate, like most of us do. Both of them worship Basia, of course.'

'Basia told me you helped her when she was getting a bit of hassle from Wiktor.'

Joe raised his eyebrows. 'Hmm. That was a bit on the awkward side. Lonely men, without a proper social context, these things are likely to happen.'

'And Milek isn't best pleased that Basia spends so much time with a married man, is he?'

By this time, they'd reached the police station and they continued their conversation as they got out of the car.

'Basia does her best to follow the rules laid down by the Church, Daf, but she's a woman of flesh and blood, like everyone else. To Milek, a relationship between his sister and Wiktor would be an easy way to solve two problems at once: secure a future for his sister and find a wife for his friend. There's nothing sinister about it; I'm sure you've done a bit of matchmaking in your time.'

'Not guilty, your honour. Fal was always trying to fix people up and I saw how pointless it was.'

'I don't want you to run away with the idea that Milek controls his sister in any way. They're just a couple of young people who happen to live a long way from home.'

'You're talking as if you thought I was a racist, Joe. Surely you know me better than that.'

'Sorry, Daf, that wasn't what I meant, but it is sometimes hard to understand how people think when they come from a radically different background. In this country we tend to live as individuals so we don't get how extended families work. It's perfectly natural for a brother to worry about his sister if she loves a married man old enough to be her father.'

Daf couldn't help thinking of how he felt about Belle and Sion: fair play to Milek.

Milek and Wiktor had decided to stand as they waited for Daf and Joe, which Daf was glad about as he didn't reckon the bench would have withstood their combined weight. Nia was keeping a close, somewhat suspicious, eye on them. Daf formally shook hands with them.

'I'm Inspector Dafis and I need to have a bit of a talk with you. Father Hogan will translate and WPC Nia here will take a few notes.'

Wiktor came through first. Despite the language barrier, his nature was pretty clear to Daf. A bit of a lad, always with an eye to the main chance. Not afraid of hard work but a man who fancied himself as a wheeler-dealer. He admitted to owning the goods in the storage area under the eaves but denied any wrongdoing.

'The stuff, the food, the vodka, it's just stuff from home, that's all,' he explained via the translator.

According to Wiktor, he'd had the chance to go home in a Transit van three months back, to help a cousin move to Liverpool where he'd found work. After loading the cousin's belongings, the bits of furniture and half a dozen boxes, the van was still half empty. Wiktor had filled the space with the sort of stuff he'd missed since leaving home. Daf asked him for a cigarette. Without thinking twice, Wiktor pulled a packet of Fajrant from the pocket of his fleece and offered one to Daf.

'Why have you got so many Jan III Sobieski cigarettes if you smoke another brand?' Daf asked.

'For my mates,' came the answer, a bit too pat. Daf decided to wait until the formal interview before putting further pressure on Wiktor; it wouldn't do any harm for him to sweat a bit about the severity of punishment given to smugglers in Britain.

Looking at the rather self-satisfied smile on Wiktor's face as he was dismissed, Daf gave him a bit of a warning.

'Joe, can you make sure our friend here knows that I'm expecting him to stay in Welshpool until the inquiry is completed? No little trips, OK?'

Wiktor left the room with a spring in his step, in total contrast to Milek, who dragged himself through the door as if he were on his way to the funeral of a close friend. His wide face had a sickly colour.

'Are you feeling OK, Milek?' Daf asked.

There was a brief exchange between Joe and Milek, then the priest grinned.

'He says my house is too warm for him. He's used to sleeping in a draughty house so he went to bed in his clothes, including socks, as usual but he couldn't settle all night.'

'I see. Could you ask him when he saw Heulwen last?'

'Friday afternoon,' came the answer. Milek folded his thick arms and stared at Daf, his eyes totally empty.

The process of asking questions via a translator was far from simple, especially when the person doing the translating was a friend to both the policeman and the person being interrogated. The strength and certainty of Daf's questions were filtered by Joe's kindly nature.

'Tell him to not bother telling lies. I know for a fact that he had a conversation with Heulwen on Monday night. I want to know what they discussed.'

There was a pause after the question, giving Milek time to think. Daf was certain that Milek could understand almost every word but chose to conceal himself behind the curtain of language.

'They were discussing a couple of little jobs that needed doing,' Joe repeated. 'Mrs Evans was always wanting little running repairs done, and it would seem that her husband isn't much of a handyman.'

'What jobs, exactly?'

'Little things.'

'Such as?'

Once again, there was plenty of time for Milek to think.

'The weather's been so nice, she wanted to open the window but it was hard to open. She said if it needed a new sash she'd nag Bowen to get it done, but if it was just a bit swollen after the winter, she'd let Milek deal with it.'

'How did she pay for the work?'

It was a simple question but also a trap for Milek. If he said she paid in cash, Daf could ask about his tax status. He didn't expect the answer he got.

'She paid cash and Milek says he's got a record of everything. He'll pay everything he owes in tax, the moment Google and Starbucks pay what they owe.'

Daf managed not to laugh. He didn't believe for a moment that Milek intended to pay but he admired his attitude.

'What did he think of Mrs Evans?'

For a few moments, language didn't matter. Milek turned his head, Daf raised his eyebrows and Milek nodded his head.

'Nia does need to have something to write down...'

'She was an old bitch. Gave no respect to anyone, always wanting a shilling's worth of work for a penny's worth of pay, collecting information about everybody in case it could be something she might use to her advantage one day. Milek also describes her as a racist, always calling them "Polacks". She would always talk as if they were about to leave overnight. Milek wants you to know, Daf, that there's no reason for him to go back to Poland and that for him, and for Basia, Wales is their home now. He hates it when people speak as if he's on the verge of moving off somewhere.'

'But there are things they miss about home, right? Things like food, even the brand of cigarettes?'

Daf saw the tension in Milek's face which he supposed came

from guilt about the goods stored under the eaves, but when he started to speak, Daf didn't have to wait for the translation to know that it was anger, not guilt.

'They should have had the opportunity to open a shop. Basia's a bright girl: she deserves better than to be a cleaner all her life, and Rhys Bowen offered them the ground floor to use as a shop and said they needn't pay rent for the first six months, to get the business off the ground.'

Daf clearly didn't manage to keep his opinion of Bowen's motives from his face because Milek rose to his feet, towering above Daf.

'Not as you think,' he declared in English. 'Basia good and Mr Bowen knows this. Mr Bowen wants shop for Polish people and he knows Basia is clever and honest. Not for bad reason, like you think. Like Phil, no. When we first in Welshpool, Mr Bowen ask Basia will she go with him but she say no and he is not on and on to say again.'

Joe said something to Milek which sounded to Daf like an order and he sat down abruptly, the chair squeaking under the strain. Hundreds of words flowed out of his mouth in a torrent, and Daf caught the names of Basia, Phil and Bowen. Joe pulled a notebook from the pocket of his shabby black jacket and started to write quickly.

'Milek's asked me to tell you this, word for word, Daf, so here goes.' Joe cleared his throat before repeating Milek's words. 'We're poor, Basia and I. We work hard but the only jobs available for us are bad jobs. We were very keen to set up a shop for our friends from Poland but the old bitch from the jewellery shop and the old lawyer, they stopped us. Mr Bowen was very angry with them, for us. So Basia cleans for people though she is much more able than them and because she's poor, men like Phil Evans treat her like she is a whore. Wiktor and I, we have started a business of our own, to raise money to start another shop for her but then Mrs Evans said we had broken the terms of our lease by keeping the goods in the flat. She asked us to do something we were unwilling to do and when we said no, she tried to force us to do it, but I refused.'

For half a minute, Daf tried to guess what it was that Heulwen had tried to make them do. Nothing sexual, he was sure of that, but from what he had heard about Heulwen, perhaps she was in need of a couple of heavies. Then he forced himself to return to reality: she was a Plaid Cymru candidate, not Queen of the Mafia. Yet she had tried to persuade Anwen to set a trap for Bowen, and that was definitely blackmail. Before starting the investigation, Daf hadn't exactly been the greatest fan of Heulwen Breeze-Evans but by now, he had heard so many random things about her, he was prepared to believe almost anything.

'What did she want them to do?'

Milek seemed to have relaxed slightly after making his statement, and his answer came back promptly.

'Milek says Mrs Evans was very curious about Mr Bowen's business affairs. Wiktor agreed to let her see some of the documents from the business but she wanted more.'

'What kind of business affairs?'

Milek said not one word.

'Joe, does he understand that I'm investigating a serious offence? I don't give a stuff about a few bottles of vodka by Wiktor's bed, or whether or not the right duty's been paid on them. What happened to Heulwen and how the building came to be on fire, that's what interests me.'

Milek nodded when he heard this but he was clearly unwilling to say more. He repeated, like a mantra, 'Mr Bowen is good man.'

Given that the press conference had been arranged for noon, Daf had no time to delve any deeper into Rhys Bowen's business. He decided to take another tack.

'You're close to Basia?'

'Close? We are brother and sister.'

'But the two of you decided to come here together, leaving the rest of the family back in Poland?'

'There were only the two of them left there,' Joe explained. 'Their father died at forty, from the kind of illness which was very common under Communism, factory dust clogging up his lungs. Then, their eldest brother got a chance to go to America. After three years, he needed help with looking after the children he had over there, so their mother joined him. Milek found himself a job in Welshpool and as soon as he knew he had somewhere to stay, he knew Basia could come with him.'

'As simple as that? Didn't he leave a girl behind?'

Milek grinned, displaying a row of big brown teeth, the result of years of smoking.

'Milek says that he doesn't find it easy to come across girls,' Joe explained. 'He says that there's not a lot of call for big, poor, ugly men, especially if they also happen to be pretty shy.'

His honesty was appealing, and his words rang true: how many respectable parents in Montgomeryshire would be delighted if their daughters brought home a boyfriend like Milek?

'And Basia?'

Milek lowered his eyes.

'Milek isn't prepared to discuss private things,' Joe said.

'Can you please get it across to him that I have to find out about Heulwen and her family, and that naturally includes Phil.'

Milek made a noise in his throat, halfway between a growl and a hiss.

'Milek says that Phil isn't fit to come within a mile of Basia, and not just because he's married. He's way too old for her and he's an idle bastard who's lived on his wife his whole life through. He respects no one and doesn't even love his children.'

'But Basia loves him?'

'She's always had a lot of romantic dreams, and Phil has a good supply of old lines.'

'But Basia's life would be much easier if Phil had lost his wife, wouldn't it?' Daf pressed, watching Milek's face closely.

'Phil could never provide her with a good future, in Milek's opinion,' Joe answered. 'If Phil couldn't get what he wanted, which Basia wouldn't give without marriage, he would have drifted off soon enough.'

'So Heulwen's death was to Basia's advantage?' Daf persisted.

Milek gave a bitter laugh. 'You did not know Heulwen Evans,' he said in his halting English. 'Her to be dead is good thing for everyone.'

# Chapter 7

## *Wednesday morning, April 13, 2016 – later*

Daf had to give Diane Rhydderch her due, the press conference was well organised. Daf had been alarmed when he heard that the conference was to take place in the Town Hall; his idea had been closer to a quick chat in the station reception area with the familiar faces from the local papers. And when he walked into the upper room of the Town Hall, he hadn't expected to see fifty people. Some were known to him, of course: the local senior reporter from the *Montgomeryshire County Times and Express*, the red-headed girl from the *Shropshire Star* and so on. Daf was surprised that so many other faces were familiar from their TV roles. For some reason, he'd assumed that all of these front men would have teams of supporters to do the legwork like press conferences in Welshpool on damp Wednesday mornings. Some had a Londony look, the sort of people who considered white Converses sensible footwear for Montgomeryshire at lambing time. At the back, exercise book in hand, was a man from Bettws Cedewain, and Daf was very surprised to see him there.

'Carwyn Watkin, what brings you here?'

The man raised his head to face Daf. His cheeks had been whipped by the spring winds until they were almost purple, and a faint aroma of manure surrounded him.

'I want to get the murder story, for *Plu'r Gweunydd*.'

Hearing the title of the local *papur bro* in such an unexpected context was enough to give Daf a moment of total perplexity. Watkin was just being nosey, of course, but Daf saw no particular reason to throw him out; the man who had been described as Heulwen Breeze-Evans's sidekick was an innocent enough creature. And to be totally fair to him, he did write a column for the *Plu* faithfully every month, a collection of old sayings from the past and trite observations on the news of the day. Such a column was hardly a suitable platform to discuss the tragic outcome of arson, infidelity, violence and hatred.

Daf was very fond of the Watkin family of Brynybiswal. For years, Brynybiswal had been the last farm on his round in the van with his Uncle Mal, and old Mrs Watkin always offered them a cup of tea. Mal would fret about the tea break making them late, but old Mr Watkin always rang Daf's dad in the shop to check that they were allowed to stay. Daf loved the old-fashioned kitchen with a great hunk of bacon hanging from the beam and religious prints on the walls, the Good Shepherd or David singing for King Saul. They always had more than the cup of tea: ham sandwiches, salad with home-grown vegetables, especially the deep green, tough lettuce, and Daf's favourite, caraway cake full of scented seeds. When everyone was seated around the table, Mr Watkin always asked the same question. 'Are you two in a hurry today?'

'No hurry at all, Mr Watkin.'

Then Mr Watkin would open the drawer in the kitchen table and pull out a little cardboard packet with the logo 'Players Navy Cut' on it. They were playing cards: the pack Mr Watkin had bought as a present for his new wife to pass the time on their train journey to Llandudno for their honeymoon. Thirty years on, not as much as a joker had been lost. The family at Brynybiswal were great whist players, and since they had a daughter and a son, they had a ready-made foursome to play the game. Unfortunately, in terms of their domestic playing, their daughter Christine had fallen for a Kiwi shearer and followed him back to New Zealand making them a lady short, so they were delighted to take the opportunity of teaching Daf how to play. After five sessions, he was good enough to play without help and he recalled how he would play hand after hand with them whilst Mal sat in the big chair by the stove, amusing himself with their cheeky Jack Russells. Even when he was at college, Daf would call by to see them pretty often and he recalled a visit when he'd noticed a bluish hue on old Mr Watkin's skin. Daf wasn't surprised when he heard, a month or so later, that the old boy had had a stroke. Things were never the same at Brynybiswal after that. Mrs Watkin outlived her husband by more than a decade, leaving Carwyn on his own, as he had been ever since.

Daf walked to the platform. Diane Rhydderch was sitting there already, as was Nia, with an empty chair between them. Daf considered a joke along the lines of a rose between two thorns but decided, from the focused look on their faces, that this was unlikely to go down well. There was a brown envelope on the table in front of Daf. He opened it to find a note from Steve: 'Path lab confirm positive ID from dental records. Deceased is Heulwen Breeze-Evans. Jarman on the case with cause of death etc.'

As Diane Rhydderch was presenting him to the press, Daf was regretting his attitude towards her the previous day. The whole superficial system, with its emphasis on Twitter and empty words, was certainly not her creation, and she was only doing her job, no matter how much she got on his nerves. He would have to make more of an effort to be civil to her, he resolved. The presentation had reached its conclusion.

'Dyfed Powys Police are confident that this case will be resolved very soon. The senior investigating officer, Chief Inspector Dafydd Dafis, is one of our most able and experienced officers. Therefore, if you have any questions, Mr Dafis will be happy to answer them.'

Daf's mouth had gone dry and he remembered standing on a very similar stage when he was five years old, reciting in Eisteddfod Seilo.

'Good morning, friends. We were investigating a suspicious fire in the first case, then we discovered the body of Mrs Heulwen Breeze-Evans in the back office. We have received confirmation that it was her body, but we are still awaiting reports on how she died and how the fire started. Therefore, we're asking for the help of the public, anyone who knew Mrs Breeze-Evans and anyone who happened to be in the vicinity of Canal Street in Welshpool between six and nine on Monday night. Please contact us on the number which WPC Nia Owen here will provide.'

He took a deep breath and awaited the questions.

'Are we talking about a hate crime here, given the sexuality of the victim?' asked a woman from ITV Cymru.

'It seems pretty clear that Mrs Breeze-Evans had a rather complicated personal life. At the moment, we don't have any evidence which specifically connects the victim's sexuality with the crime, but it is early days as yet.'

'Have you had experience in dealing with homophobic hate crime, Chief Inspector Dafis?'

Daf felt Diane Rhydderch's eyes on him, waiting for him to make a mistake, perhaps. He saw the trap in the question and tried to avoid it.

'We don't have a lot of hate crime in this area, *lodes*,' he ventured. 'We're right tidy people here, by and large, like the old saying goes, mellow Maldwyn.'

'So you don't prosecute homophobic people in this area, then, Chief Inspector?'

'Listen, *lodes*, I prosecute every crime in my patch which warrants prosecution.'

'So, just how many hate crimes did you prosecute last year then, Chief Inspector Dafis?'

On the envelope in front of Daf, Nia had written a number. That number was zero.

'None.'

There was a look of triumph on the young woman's face, as if she'd discovered some significant secret.

'Would that be because of your attitude towards the local LGBT community, do you think?'

'More likely, it's because of the attitude people have around here towards their neighbours, giving them a bit of peace, no matter who they choose to love.' The annoyance audible in his voice wasn't going to help the situation, but he couldn't help himself. Nia broke in.

'We can provide you with a list of the activities we have undertaken in the last year, in schools, youth clubs and so on, to raise awareness of the rights of LGBT people. In addition, we have received a full training programme from Stonewall Cymru and I attend the monthly meetings of Rainbow Powys.'

The smile on Diane Rhydderch's face said it all. One of the unknown journalists rose to his feet, a man of the same age as Daf, rather fat with expensive glasses and a smile which was rather close to a sneer.

'Gavin Porter, *Mail*. So, what we have here, Inspector, is a suspicious fire in which a nationalist politician is killed. So, obviously, everyone is linking this to the Sons of Glyndŵr outrages in the 1980s. I was struck too by the attitude you have shown this morning, speaking in Welsh to exclude people: to what extent is this area a hotbed of extremism?'

His father had always advised Daf to count to ten before speaking; he had reached eight before replying.

'I spoke in Welsh first, Mr Porter, as a mark of respect for the deceased and her family. I have no interest in excluding anyone but as Welsh is one of the two official languages of our nation, our policy is to give priority to whichever language is most suitable for any given occasion. And as for this area being extremist, that is nonsense. There is no connection whatsoever between this case and the historical arson cases of the 1980s.'

'Are you an extremist yourself, Chief Inspector?'

'No.'

'Yet you took part in a number of nationalist protests in the 1990s, I believe?'

'Like most students. Together with protests against the war in Iraq and I do think I may have tried to save the odd whale.' Daf would have liked to give Mr Porter of the *Daily Mail* a good shaking.

'Dyfed Powys Police have every faith in Chief Inspector Dafis, who is one of our most capable officers. Next question.'

Fair play to Ms Rhydderch, she was professional enough to brush creatures of that type to one side without thinking twice. By the end of the conference, Daf was bubbling with fury.

'Thank you indeed, Ms Rhydderch. People like that get right up my nose.'

'Inspector Dafis, dear Inspector Dafis, that's what they are trained to do, it's intentional. The idea is that they scratch at you until you rather lose the plot and blurt out things you shouldn't have said.'

'Of course. But whatever, I do apologise for my attitude yesterday. I was blaming you for doing your job, which is always a pretty stupid thing to do.'

'I understand very well, Inspector Dafis,' she replied, giving Daf the most insincere smile he had ever seen. He managed to swallow down a sigh, noting that she only used his temporary rank in public.

The police station was a haven to him, busy as always but running like clockwork. There were three documents on his desk waiting for his attention: the report from the canal where the car had been found, a list of phone calls received overnight and a note from Janet Cilgwyn, on official paper from the Assembly, asking to speak with him urgently. He picked up the phone.

'Darren, who's about?'

'Only us two at the moment, boss. Nev hasn't arrived in yet, after doing three shifts on the trot; Nia said she was going straight from the press conference to see the Breeze-Evans family; Steve's at the site, of course, and Sheila's gone to the doctor.'

'Sheila? She never gets ill.'

'She said it was only a check-up but that it had been arranged for ages.'

'OK. Can you phone Jan Cilgwyn and tell her I'm available till one o'clock today, yeah?'

'I will, boss. What about Councillor Gwilym Bebb? Is he allowed back into his office yet?'

'If Steve is cool with that, yes.'

Daf's mobile began to ring. He finished his conversation with Darren as quickly as possible but that clearly wasn't good enough for the pathologist.

'I realise you're busy, Mr Acting Chief Inspector, but I've got half a dozen corpses here requiring my attention including a lad of Muslim extraction who needs his PM done before sunset to allow his family to bury him and, of course, there is your little problem.'

'Sorry, Dr Jarman, I was on the other line.'

'That's what they all say. However, I have just started work on Mrs Breeze-Evans and there is something which doesn't add up.'

'In what way, Dr Jarman?'

'Did she have any health problems?'

'I haven't heard of anything specific. She was taking tablets for depression.'

'Can you check? We'll speak later, and kindly remember that I do expect you to answer the phone on the first ring, understand?'

'Of course, Dr Jarman.'

The pathologist was only some ten years older than Daf but ever since they had first worked together eight years back, Jarman had always treated Daf like a naughty schoolboy. Daf had no idea why but because of the respect he had for the old bastard, he accepted it, even though there would have been hell to pay if anyone else dared to speak to him in that tone. Obediently, he picked up the phone and rang Dr Mansell: no answer. There was a knock on the door.

'Come in.'

Belle was standing framed in the doorway, and for an

instant, Daf was alarmed. Since seeing Sion tied to her bed, he'd somehow managed to forget just how good-looking she was. She stepped across the room and, for some reason, she turned the chair around before sitting on it, her face and shoulders visible above the back of the chair. Daf was uncomfortably reminded of the famous picture of Christine Keeler from the days of the Profumo scandal.

'How's tricks, Inspector? Up all night with that baby of yours?'

While you were up all night with my partner's other child, Daf thought, quickly remembering how much there was that he wasn't supposed to know.

'I spent hours lying on the floor rocking an empty cradle,' he admitted. 'How were the dogs?'

'Champion.'

'Did you meet Sion's dad this morning?'

'Yes. I popped up this morning just as they were finishing milking.'

'Because he was looking for Sion last night. He needed an explanation for the "strange dogs in his kit" as he put it.'

There was a hint of a smile on Belle's face but she didn't say a word. Daf decided to get onto safer territory by discussing work.

'How's the site this morning?'

'Good. I've just finished. Nothing of note in the flat upstairs, apart from a drawer full of very fancy underwear, but in terms of the fire, there is definitely something a bit weird.'

'What do you mean, *lodes*?'

'To start with, there were two fires: one just inside the front door and the other, which is definitely odd, inside the door between the back office and the passageway.'

'Are you sure?'

'Different accelerants. I've had a word with DC Steve "my face is up here, hello" James and they'll do a few more tests to confirm it but I know what I saw: two-stroke in the office and meths by the front door. Whoever set the fire by the front door couldn't have done a crappier job if they'd tried: pushing a durex full of meths through the letterbox is great in theory but how do you light it after? Flick a match through the letterbox after it? I reckon what finally set the meths off was the other fire, which must be the definition of a crap arsonist, one who needs the whole place to be on fire before his accelerant catches.'

'Forgive an old man who didn't get much sleep but if you are saying that the fire in the office was started from the inner side of the door, are you saying that it's possible for Heulwen to have started that fire herself?'

'Either that or she sat quietly in her chair while someone chucked a fair bit of two-stroke about.'

'Two-stroke?'

'Definitely. It burns differently to ordinary petrol.'

'Got time for a cup of tea, *lodes*?'

'A quick one. How far is Kington?'

'If you go over Cider House after Newtown, you'll take half an hour off your journey.'

She gave him a warm smile. 'You're like a dad to everyone, aren't you, Daf?' she said in a low voice. 'Always trying to sort out everyone else's troubles. I understand what Sion means.'

'And what exactly does Sion say about me?'

'That you look after them all, even his dad. Sion thinks the world of you, you know.'

'And I think the world of him too. Fair play to Sion, he's always been a...'

'*Cog bêch clên?*'

'I do not talk like that, miss,' Daf responded, bristling a little at her mimicking of his dialect and accent.

'Not as much as Mr Jones Neuadd, that's for certain. My sister did her dissertation at college on the dialects of north-east Wales – she'd be very sorry to miss such a rich source of material. *Wtra, sietin, bing* – I've never heard these words before.'

'Don't you laugh at us.'

'I'm learning, not laughing.'

Nev opened the door and had a very good view of Belle's bottom which caused him to shake so much that a lake of tea spread over the tray. His voice was trembling as well.

'Tea for you, boss, miss.'

As the door was shutting, Daf concentrated on cleaning up the tray and steered the talk back to official topics.

'Would it be possible for someone to start a fire like that as a means of committing suicide?'

'It does happen but not often. I've only seen one case like that in this country, and that was a fireman. Heck of a nice lad too, I'd met him a fair few times with work.'

'Can it be a way of killing yourself without damaging the family? To conceal the suicide?'

'Possible, but anyone who thinks their family will get the insurance just because they've set a fire had better think again. As far as insurers are concerned, every fire is a suspicious fire.'

'But if Heulwen was sitting in the chair, why didn't she move when the two-stroke was being splashed about?'

'Do we know for certain that she was killed by the smoke?' Belle asked.

'What do you mean? That someone might have, say, strangled her, then set the place on fire?'

'It's possible, isn't it?'

Daf drank his tea as he thought.

'You've learnt a lot about this Heulwen in the last couple of days. Does she come across to you like a heartbroken woman, a woman at the end of her tether?'

'Far from it. Very self-satisfied. But it's worth remembering, she was receiving treatment for depression.'

'There we are then. What does the path lab say?'

'Nothing definite yet, apart from the ID.'

Belle finished her tea and rose to her feet. 'You'll have my full report by the weekend. If it isn't ready by Friday, I'll bring it down with me.'

'With you?'

Belle paused for a moment by the door. 'Yes, with me. I'm staying in the Goat for the weekend. You can buy me a drink if you like.'

And off she went. Daf was sweating. He rang Gaenor.

'What's up, Daf?'

'She's coming back on Friday.'

'Who, Heulwen Breeze-Evans, like a zombie?'

'No, no, Belle. Arranged to meet Sion, I bet. You'd better have a word with him.'

'To say what? We had the condom talk years ago. Honestly Daf, I'm surprised at you, it's lovely for Sion to have a girlfriend.'

'Exactly. It's a girlfriend he needs, not a dominatrix.'

'They'll have to have their Sunday dinner with us.'

'How can you be so reasonable?'

'Because you going off on one won't help anyone. If you hadn't opened that door, you'd be congratulating Sion.'

'Fair enough. You are right, as ever. But what about inviting them for tea, not dinner? I can buy a couple of cakes from the WI stall in the market and you won't have to slave over the stove half the day.'

'Great. See you later. Pizza for supper.'

'Rhod's favourite. Bye.'

Before he could catch his breath, there was another knock on the door.

'*Tyrd i mewn,*' Daf called, expecting Jan Cilgwyn.

'English for me, I'm afraid.'

A tall man entered, neat as a pin in paper in his tweed suit, and Daf could have shaved in the reflection of himself in his highly polished but not shiny shoes. He extended long, thin fingers in Daf's direction and Daf was obliged to shake his hand to avoid being discourteous. Mostyn Gwydyr-Gwynne, the local Member of Parliament.

'Just thought I would pop in, Inspector Davies, for two reasons, actually. First to congratulate you on your promotion; I am certain you know very well that you are very highly regarded in many quarters. The second is rather a social thing. I was wondering if you and your ... your partner would do Haf and I the honour of coming to a bit of a party we're having on the last Friday of this month, to celebrate our engagement?'

'Be a pleasure,' Daf answered at once, thinking of how much Gae would relish a chance to see inside Plas Gwynne, their big house. Then he thought of Haf. What on earth was a campaigning, radical, left-wing lawyer doing marrying that? The MP's motivation was pretty clear: Haf was attractive and clever and he needed an heir for the name, the great house, the estate. But even if he was made of money, would she be happy? She and Daf had worked very closely together on a complex case a couple of years ago and they'd been friends ever since. Daf thought he knew Haf pretty well and the MP was near enough the last sort of person he would have though suitable for her. But that wasn't Daf's call.

'There will be a card in the post, of course but...' Gwydyr-Gwynne failed to complete his excuse. 'And, while I'm here, I just wanted to say that I'm sure this unfortunate business of Mrs Breeze-Evans hasn't got anything to do with politics. I know our friend Bowen is a rough diamond but I'm sure he would never be mixed up in anything sinister.'

'Early days.'

'I did hear that she was,' and he coughed before continuing as if the subject was deeply distasteful to him, 'that she was having a relationship with another woman. That will be your best line of inquiry, Inspector. Very tempestuous, some of these types, I'm given to understand.'

'And what types would those be, Mr Gwydyr-Gwynne?'

The tall man laughed as he turned on his heel.

'We will so look forward to seeing you and ... and...'

'Gaenor. I live tally with a woman called Gaenor.'

'Haf often mentions your sense of humour, Inspector, and she is a good judge,' he said, without so much as the shadow of a smile on his face. He strode out like a heron and Daf was furious. Who did he think he was, marching into Daf's office as if he owned the place? Handing out advice about the investigation! That was the reason for the visit, of course, to keep Bowen out of deep water. A night sipping sherry in Plas Gwynne was not going to succeed in suborning Daf from his duty: if Bowen was in the shit, Daf would treat him just like anyone else. Not to mention the 'tempestuous' comment...

The phone rang.

'Ready to see Ms Cilgwyn, boss?' Darren asked.

'Send her in.'

Jan Cilgwyn looked like an amenable little woman, on the surface, at least, and a good deal more homely than her partner. In contrast to Lisa Powell, she was rather scruffy, more like a mature student than a legislator. If it took Lisa most of the weekend to do her partner's ironing, she must be pretty slow at her work, Daf thought.

'Ms Cilgwyn, do take a seat. Cup of tea?'

'I'm fine, thanks.'

Her face was white and a tiny muscle under her eye was pulsing repeatedly.

'Are you sure? A cup of tea would be...'

'Why do men always think that bloody tea is the answer?' she cried, before immediately regretting her temper. 'Sorry for the bad language.'

'I've heard worse. You're under a fair bit of strain. You were close to Heulwen Breeze-Evans, I understand?'

'She,' announced the little woman, with unexpected dignity, 'was the love of my life.' Even though she had a handkerchief in her hand, she tried to hold back her tears. 'But because of our hypocritical society, I don't get to mourn. The, the blond pig, he'll be sitting in the front of the chapel with any number of his floozies turning up to see her buried. He'll choose who does the tribute, he'll even choose her coffin. Totally stupid, Mr Dafis, and totally unfair.'

'If you want to take part in the arrangements, I can suggest something to the family.'

'You don't know them, Mr Dafis. The girl is vile, describing people like me as suffering from some sickness. They weren't prepared to admit that Heulwen and I loved each other.'

'I can see it's a difficult situation. And, of course, your partner, Lisa...'

The tic under her eye increased its frequency.

'What did she say?'

'She came to see me yesterday, to discuss your relationship with Heulwen.'

'And what did she say?' Her voice was very quiet, so low that Daf could scarcely hear it.

'That you were in a relationship with each other but that you had met Heulwen. She was trying to protect you, as I understood it, from the press, from any hassle.'

'She's always trying to keep me safe, making sure I don't make mistakes.' There were obvious speech marks around the word 'safe'.

'Lisa suggested that your relationship with Heulwen wouldn't last.'

'How could she say a thing like that? What business of hers was it?'

'But,' Daf ventured, 'she was talking about marriage.'

'She was always talking about marriage but I'm not Prince Charming, providing the happy ending for all her Disney fantasies.'

'I'm sorry to have to ask this, but who did you see yourself sharing the future with – Lisa or Heulwen? Or with them both, perhaps?'

'Heulwen was uncertain about living together. She didn't want it to have an impact on her chances of winning the election, if everyone was discussing her sexuality instead of the policies.'

'The inhabitants of Montgomeryshire don't live in the Stone Age, you know, Ms Cilgwyn,' Daf responded. 'We're pretty fair, on the whole.'

'But imagine how much fun Rhys Bowen could have with the information. That bastard would turn the election into a referendum on sexuality.'

'Some people say that Mr Bowen has secrets of his own.'

'They aren't secrets. He's proud of the fact that he's such a ... Sorry, I am a learner, you know. What Welsh word should I use to describe him?'

'We'd tend to use the word for 'bull', that would suit right well.'

'You understand, Mr Dafis, someone has to beat Bowen. I don't know that I can put up with another five years of his unacceptable behaviour.'

'But you're a professional woman. Surely you can put up with a bit of name-calling from the likes of Rhys Bowen?'

'I've never come across anything like it before. He's a total bully and he seems to have absolutely no boundaries.' Her cheeks blazed red. 'Bowen is undermining everything I've worked for. I very often leave the chamber shaking from head to toe.'

'What if you turned on him? He's bound to be sensitive about something: his weight, perhaps?'

'I won't stoop to his tactics. I'd rather leave the Assembly than turn into a thug like him.'

'So, if you felt you needed to keep your relationship with Heulwen out of the spotlight, for a while at least, where did that leave Lisa?'

Jan dropped her eyes.

'We can all be selfish when we're in love, Inspector. I suggested to Lisa that it might be better if I moved out to live on my own for a while, but she started to talk about how lonely she would become and how much she'd supported me over the years. I offered her the house entirely if she was willing to walk out of my life completely but she is stubborn. In the end, it was easier to just let things drift on, until after the election at any rate.' She paused for a moment and Daf noticed a self-satisfied little smile on her face, as if she were rather enjoying being at the apex of the love triangle. 'I'm certain it was a member of her family who killed Heulwen, Inspector, to prevent her from coming out. I did think it might be the blond pig but he can never hold an idea in his head for half an hour. A conspiracy between Jac and Nansi, the daughter, with the help of her husband, the Reverend Righteous. Perhaps he killed her.'

'Why do you say that?'

'Because he's a homophobe. If someone doesn't believe we are equal, they don't respect us. And if you don't respect gay people, then you're well on the way to Auschwitz.'

Daf remembered the caring face of Joe Hogan as he said goodbye to the young addict that morning and he made up his mind to challenge the Assembly Member a little, on Joe's behalf.

'Not everyone who follows a traditional moral code is a Nazi,' he ventured. 'I've got a friend who is a kind and decent man who belongs to a tradition which only permits sex between married men and women.'

'There's no place in Wales for people who think like that. I hope you don't share your friend's views. We need to get rid of them all, the narrow-minded people like that.'

Daf managed to keep his mouth shut. For the first time, he seriously considered giving his vote to Bowen, or to anyone else who stuck two fingers up to this perfect example of bigotry who sat opposite him.

'Ms Cilgwyn, are you really suggesting that Heulwen's family would kill her?'

'If only you knew everything they'd done to her over the years. The pressure Phil put on her only six months after the first baby was born, the lack of respect from that bully Jac; Nansi's shocking behaviour which destroyed her mother's greatest charitable project...'

'What about Gruff?'

'He ran away as soon as he could, breaking his mother's heart. You don't know the half of it, Mr Dafis.'

Tears started to flow and Jan started to sniff loudly. Without warning, Rhys Bowen marched in with Darren scampering behind him, like a Chihuahua trying to steer a St Bernard.

'Mr Bowen,' Darren was saying, 'Inspector Dafis has someone with him at the moment...'

'Bloody hell! The baby of the National Assembly's crying again. Got enough Kleenex, Daf? If not, ask this chap here, he's got the look on him of a lad who uses a fair few tissues.'

Fortunately, Darren wasn't quick enough to grasp the point of Bowen's insult.

'Mr Bowen,' Daf began. 'If you could just wait for a moment, Ms Cilgwyn's just about to leave.'

'Cilgwyn!' dismissed Bowen, his nostrils as wide as a bull's. 'Her name's not Cilgwyn. Her name is Wilkes.'

Jan rose to her feet, a little shakily.

'I changed my name by deed poll, Mr Bowen, so it's totally legal.'

'Oh, listen to her, Inspector Dafis, with her sixth-form arguments. I never said it was illegal to change your name, but it is stupid, which is a hell of a lot worse. What if I started asking people to call me Rhys Rissole from now on, because I make the best rissoles in Wales? Spell it in Welsh, if you like, with one "s". People would laugh behind my back about that, and they'd be quite right to do so.'

'The system of nomenclature we use today is a direct result of the oppression we Welsh have suffered at the hands of the English for centuries. And it represents patriarchy, which I utterly reject, so I have decided to create a name for myself which symbolises my self-actualisation.'

Bowen caught Daf's eye and raised his eyebrow.

'Did you follow a single word of that shit, Inspector? No,

nor me. "We Welsh" she says, "we Welsh", by Hell, when there's not a single drop of Welsh blood running in her veins, for certain. I'm amazed you can find enough people pigshit thick enough to vote for you, Miss, I really am. Oh, hang on a minute; you're on the List, aren't you, *lodes*? You didn't win a real vote anywhere, did you now?'

'Now then, everyone, we're not in the Assembly now. If you two want to stay here and argue, be my guests, but I'm off, I've got plenty of work to do.'

'Bowen, I'm watching you,' Jan said, curtly, turning for the door. 'Keep in touch, Inspector Dafis.'

Daf was glad to see the back of her but felt that he needed to have a strict word with Bowen.

'Listen here, Mr Bowen, I have gathered that you and Ms Cilgwyn aren't the greatest of friends, but don't bring your quarrels into my office, right?'

'OK, OK.' The anger on his broad face had turned to laughter. 'But that little bitch represents everything I hate. Vegetarian, townie, green in every sense of the word, phoney nationalist, leftie from a well-off family. And to crown it all, she's a lesbian.'

'What she does in bed is none of your business at all, Mr Bowen,' Daf responded.

'You've got a head on your shoulders, Inspector. Education coming out of your ears. I'm the opposite, you ask Gae. I've made my way with my body: strong back, big hands. Yes, I'm sharp enough to see I get the best of a fair few bargains but I'm a craftsman, me. Round here, everyone knows me and takes me as I am and if I have to communicate with any man, there's always one way of settling the argument; I can throw a punch and stand a fair good chance of winning. With a girl, now, there's another way to win an argument, and since I've been down the Bay, there's a fair few political ladies have had their minds and their legs opened at the same time. But what do I do with Jan whatever she calls herself?

She's too much of a girl for me to give her a punch but not enough of a girl for me to have a go at fucking some sense into her.'

Daf could not believe what he was hearing. He thought about Diane Rhydderch and her communication strategies. How would she manage if she had to spin Bowen's unorthodox methods of winning a debate?

'You shouldn't speak like that these days,' Daf chided him, disappointed at his own feelings of sneaking admiration for the butcher's honesty.

'Don't talk to me about "these days". I had a hell of a shock last week: I've got an apprentice training up to the butchery trade and he uses moisturiser. Not just on his hands to stop them cracking up in the cold but on his bloody face! I'm glad I'm not young these days: too bloody complicated.' He smiled as he shook his head. 'You've got a lad at home, haven't you? Apart from Gaenor's boy, I mean.'

'Yes. Nearly fifteen.'

'Oh.' Daf remembered that there were no children in Bowen's mansion in the Meifod valley. 'If he fancies coming to me for his work experience, in the business up this end or down in the Bay, he'd be right welcome.' He paused for a moment or two. 'I came to see you for a reason. Has Mr Poker-up-his-arse Gwydyr-Gwynne called by?'

'He has, this place has been bedlam this morning.'

Bowen smashed his huge fist down on the desk in front of him.

'What the fuck is he playing at? I'm big enough to take care of myself without him, the patronising bastard!'

'He came to invite me to his engagement party, but he did want to discuss the investigation, of course.'

'Engagement? What the fuck is the matter with the girl? Yes, he does shit sovereigns but she'll be longing for something a bit hotter than that wanker by the time a month's up. Bloody waste too, she's a right smart bit of goods.'

Daf frowned to hear his own sentiments coming out of the mouth of Rhys Bowen.

'She's a friend of mine – we've worked together a fair bit. Hence the invitation.'

'Her as well, Daf? I always respect a man with a good eye, for beef or blondes. By the way,' he added, as he turned to go. 'It wasn't me who killed that sour bitch Heulwen, but I can't wait to shake the hand of whoever did it.'

Following his conversation with Belle, which chimed with the observations of the pathologist, it was high time Daf went back to the scene of the fire. Compared to the comings and goings of the previous day, the place was quiet, with only Nev there keeping an eye on things. Daf pulled his white suit on.

'Steve's gone down to the store with a van full of evidence, boss. He wasn't sure what to do with the stuff from the flat; are we going to be keeping everything?'

'If the photographer's made a full record, I don't see that we'll need to keep all the belongings upstairs. Not that there'll be much worth keeping, most things'll be spoiled by the smoke.'

'We don't mean the collection from the eaves, that's already gone off as evidence. Up to a bit of smuggling, were they, boss?'

'Looks likely.'

Twenty hours of rain and the fire brigade's hosepipes had changed the atmosphere in the building so that now it was as wet and malodorous as a cave. Daf pushed the front door shut carefully, looking for traces of the meths. Nobody uses meths these days, he thought to himself. He remembered his dad selling plastic bottles of the purple liquid in the shop but he never knew what the customers actually did with the stuff. He walked through to the back room. The filing cabinets had gone and the emptiness, together with the cold, created an atmosphere of sadness. Daf tried to organise all the facts he'd heard about Heulwen Breeze-Evans, and noted how few people were mourning her. He thought about Gaenor's puzzlement: how could any woman be unhappy with Phil Dolfadog? Much easier to understand her discontent if her taste lay in a totally different direction. Perhaps she'd tried to fill the gap in her life with respectability and activity. Without any doubt, she was a stubborn woman, difficult to deal with, but she didn't deserve to be killed like this, especially when, perhaps, she was coming close to happiness for the first time in her life. After all, however much of a pain she could be, she still deserved justice.

He considered what Belle had said about the two-stroke. That could point to someone who did a bit of garden work, whether with a strimmer or a fair-sized mower. He was glad he'd insisted on the carbon dogs instead of the new technology; Belle certainly knew her stuff. On the other hand, perhaps an IT company from Oxford was less likely to send a representative who would start an S&M relationship with a young member of Daf's family.

Upstairs in Basia and Milek's flat, Daf paused for a moment to register the mess which had been made of what must have been a tidy little home. On the corner of the curtains there was a little label which meant they had come from a charity shop, but they'd been carefully hemmed to fit the window. There was a clean cloth on the table and a picture of the Virgin Mary above the fireplace. A wave of sympathy and anger swept through Daf: why did Basia and Milek have to work so hard for every scrap of comfort when men like Mostyn Gwydyr-Gwynne had everything given them on a silver plate?

He noticed a bunch of keys on the table by the fire, each one neatly labelled: Mid Wales Meat; Bebb, Jones and Hamer, Solicitors; Infant School. The places where Basia worked. It was perfectly possible that the keys would be kept as evidence, in which case they'd be held for at least a week, and Daf imagined what kind of a fuss someone like Gwilym Bebb might make about that, maybe even sacking her for not taking care of the keys. Daf decided to do something highly unprofessional, and slipped the keys into his pocket to give to Basia later.

There were two bedrooms in the flat but only one bed; Milek slept on a mattress on the floor. On the walls of his bedroom were pictures of cars he had cut out of motoring magazines, the kind of cars he would never be able to afford. Daf opened several drawers which all contained neatly folded clothes. There was something else in the corner of one of the drawers; Daf reached for it and pulled it out. It was a change bag from the bank, full of twenty-pound notes. Daf counted out two thousand pounds and put the money in his pocket with the keys, in case it should be stolen. Perhaps Milek might get himself a smart car someday, even if it had to be second-hand.

Basia's was a pretty little room, with a view over the roofs of the town towards the castle. By her bed was a book in Polish and, from the illustration on the cover, Daf guessed that it was a romance. Just like in her brother's room, every drawer was full of cheap clothes neatly folded except the lowest one. In that drawer were several items of blue and white china, all carefully wrapped in brown paper. Was this her version of the old tradition of a girl collecting belongings for her wedding? Under the crockery was a collection which was rather more personal: a dozen boxes of expensive lingerie from shops in Chester. Each box was still sealed in the original cellophane. Though there was something rather creepy about the gifts, as if Phil had been attempting to seduce Basia with fancy underwear, the messages on the cards were loving: 'Forever, whatever may come, P.E.' in an old-fashioned, rather laboured but tidy script. 'Whatever may come.' What did that mean? 'Until I've killed my wife so I can get hold of you'?

In the kitchen, everything was neat as a pin. Daf opened the lid of a tin which was on the work surface: it contained a home-made Victoria sponge which smelt beautifully of vanilla. For the second time that day, Daf was reminded of the family at Brynybiswal. Mrs Watkin always told Carwyn that he should look out for a girl who smelt of vanilla as if she'd come straight out of the kitchen, but the sad fact was that Carwyn hadn't come across a girl who smelt of anything, and was still a bachelor.

As he was on his way back to the station, Daf was passed by a car like one of the pictures on Milek's wall, a top of the range Lexus, the sort of car Rhod would describe as 'no change from eighty grand'. There was a beep on the horn: Tom Francis, Sheila's husband, driving a car which was as flashy as he was homely. The car pulled up and Tom opened the window.

'How's it going, Daf?' he asked, as if he were enquiring about the price of fat lambs in the Smithfield instead of a murder investigation.

'Early days, Tom. Is Shelia OK? Darren said she'd been to see the doctor.'

Tom went brick red and Daf suddenly understood; they had been married for over six months and Sheila hadn't conceived yet.

'Only a check-up. Listen, Daf, I was in the Oak on Monday night: NFU meeting.'

Daf hoped to God he wasn't going to get all the details of the union meeting. Tom was a thoroughly decent man but dull.

'Oh, yes?' he replied, trying to be polite whilst at the same time ensuring that his tone didn't give Tom too much encouragement.

'There was a right odd woman there, thin, smart hair. She came into the bar round about half six, with a savage look on her face. Something odd happened then; she bought a drink and put her card on the bar to pay, you know, and I noticed the name on the card, Powell. Same name as the National Treasurer, who gave us a talk last year on running a sustainable County Branch.'

It crossed Daf's mind, rather spitefully, to wonder if Tom Francis had tried to sell the film rights for this gripping tale but he said nothing, managing an encouraging noise.

'Then she changed her mind and said she'd put the drink on her room tally.'

Tom paused again and Daf hoped he could manage to wrap the narrative up in less than half an hour.

'Yes?'

'And that was what was odd. The girl behind the bar said, and she's the only local girl there these days, you know, so she said to her, 'That's room 30, Mrs Wilkes.' And that was the odd thing, Powell on her card, Wilkes on the register. It so happened, half an hour later, I was standing in the reception area, right by the desk and the register was open. Only one guest in room 30, according to the register, under the name of L Wilkes. Address in Cardiff somewhere.'

'Many thanks, Tom.'

'I just thought, because of what happened to Heulwen Dolfadog, it might be important.'

'It's a right interesting piece of information, Tom.'

'I didn't say anything to Sheila. She torments me a fair bit if I go anywhere near police business, calls me Sergeant Francis and what have you.'

Looking at Tom's honest, cheerful face, Daf felt guilty about feeling dismissive towards him. Even if the story was a bit long-winded, the information was well worth having. Lisa Powell had said she had come to Mongtomeryshire on Tuesday but was she there in the Oak on Monday night, when Heulwen was killed? And what had made her, in Tom's words, 'savage'? And why had she decided to register at the hotel under the name of Wilkes, Jan's original name?

'You come straight to me if you get any other little gems like that, Tom. Really grateful.'

'Any time. Sheila tells me we're stopping by to see this baby of yours Sunday afternoon?'

'You are indeed, I hope. Let's hope she doesn't make too much noise for you!'

'I'm sure she's lovely, especially if she takes after her mother.'

By now, there were a dozen cars in a row behind the Lexus, and when Tom noticed this, he pulled out carefully and drove away. Daf walked quickly back to the station, where Sheila was waiting for him.

'Boss, Nia's having a hell of a time of it up at Dolfadog; they're fighting like cats in a sack, she says. Could you nip up there and see if you can get any sense out of them?'

'Sure.' Daf had intended to have a conversation with Phil before the news bulletins in case the coverage took the 'hate crime' line. Daf didn't want Phil to hear about his wife's sexuality via the TV. 'In the meantime, can you check up on the history of a woman called Lisa Powell, Jan Cilgwyn's partner? She works for the government down in Cardiff. I need to know where she was on Monday.' He handed Sheila the money bag from the flat. 'And can you put this in the safe, Sheila? Two thousand pounds in cash, belonging to Milek Bartoshyn.'

'Is it evidence?'

'Not sure. I don't think this money's connected to the investigation but it might just be. And after today, we won't be watching the site day and night: anyone could walk in and help themselves.'

'OK, boss.'

Daf had to ask. 'You OK, Sheila? You went to see the doctor.'

She went red, but a much paler shade than her husband. 'Only a check-up. I'm fine.'

# Chapter 8

## *Wednesday afternoon, April 13, 2016*

Daf didn't notice the beauty of the scenery or the scattering clouds as he drove back up to Dyffryn Banw. He skirted the foot of Moel Bentyrch without a single glance at the slice of heaven which was opening up in front of him. He was rehearsing, like an actor without a script, and he simply did not know where to start.

Heulwen and Phil had been married for over thirty years. They'd raised a family together and even if they weren't particularly happy, it was bound to be a shock for Phil to learn that his wife was gay. Or bisexual. How the hell was he going to broach the subject? 'Phil, Mr Evans ... I've got a bit of information to share...' Or, rather more chatty? 'Phil, you know when you said your marriage had a few difficulties? Well ... Maybe, super formal: 'In the course of this investigation, we have encountered at least two witnesses who have said that your wife was...' Every line was more lame than the previous one. Daf sighed as he drove over the first cattle grid.

A large blue car was parked by the back door of Dolfadog, a Dacia estate with an unmissable Christian Ichthus symbol in the rear window. Daf read the sticker on the rear bumper: 'He who kneels before God can stand before anyone'. There were two child seats in the back and it wasn't hard to guess that this car must belong to Heulwen's daughter Nansi, wife of the man Jan Cilgwyn had described as the Reverend Righteous.

Daf knocked on the door. There was no reply but perhaps that was unsurprising; his knock was unlikely to have been heard above the loud voice coming from inside. The door was open so Daf entered and followed the sound until he arrived in a large sitting room with no less than three sofas and a vast TV on the end wall. Through the open door, he saw the family, or almost all the family: Phil and Basia on one sofa, Jac and Lowri hand in hand opposite them, and on the largest sofa, under the window, a woman very like Jac, or a female version of Phil, with two little children on her lap. Standing with his back to the fireplace as if he were master of the house, was a dignified, tall man of African heritage, holding his hands outstretched, palms upwards, in supplication to heaven.

'Father God,' he said in a deep, resonant voice, 'Pour down your endless blessings upon this family in its time of desolation. We remember, Father God, how those You loved were put to the test and tried with sore afflictions.'

Nia was sitting in the corner on a footstool, looking thoroughly ill at ease. Daf noticed that Basia was wrapping something around her fingers, something like the chain of a necklace, and she was holding it tight.

'Let us take our lesson from Job and put our lives and our faith in Your hands, Father God, that we may come through this trial purified and cleansed for Thy holy service.'

'Amen,' repeated his wife and children, one after another.

Basia rose to her feet and Daf realised that it was a rosary she had in her hand. She walked over to the TV and switched it on, sound up high. She sat down beside Phil with a delightful smile.

'Ah, *Prynhawn Da!*' she declared, showing great enthusiasm for the afternoon magazine programme on S4C. 'Let's hope they've got a lovely recipe for us today.'

'Could we finish our conversation before watching the telly?' Nia asked in a shy voice, as if she knew she couldn't get her point across.

'We weren't having a conversation, we were listening to his rubbish,' answered Basia, indicating the Reverend.

'It wasn't rubbish,' Nansi responded, cheeks pink with annoyance, 'but the true word of God.'

Basia laughed scornfully. From his vantage point just outside the room, it looked to Daf as if Phil was enjoying the dispute.

'Father God,' the Reverend began again but Basia pulled the remote out of the depths of the sofa and drowned out his voice with an item of fashion: *When should we take off our opaque tights and welcome the Spring?* Nia made another attempt, but she was doomed to fail.

'Friends, if we could perhaps get back to...' The Reverend stepped forward from the fireplace and raised his voice to sing: 'Amazing Grace, how sweet the sound...'

His wife and children joined in and Daf thought that this was it, the definitive victory, but Basia turned the TV volume down and began to chant:

*'Ave Maria, gratia plena, Dominus tecum...'*

Her voice was as pure as moonlight on snow and she froze out Nansi, who slowed, stumbled over familiar words and grew silent. It was clear to Daf that Nia, who had been putting up with this sort of behaviour for some time, was at the end of her tether.

'*Dyna ddigon!* That's enough!' Daf called out. 'I'm Inspector Dafis, from Dyfed Powys Police, as some of you know already.'

The Reverend extended his arm in Daf's direction and, after shaking hands, he gripped Daf's hand for a long moment, placing his other hand on Daf's shoulder and looking straight into his eyes.

'Reverend Seth Bockarie. Delighted to meet you, Inspector. Even in such sad circumstances.'

His wife jumped to her feet to join him, to show the world a united family.

'I'm Nansi Bockarie and here are Nathan and Hope.'

The Reverend clearly didn't hang about: Nansi's breasts were still heavy with milk for Hope but her rounded belly showed that there would be another baby before the summer was over. The Evans family seemed to Daf not to be a group in any sense but a series of couples. Jac, who had seemed to be the master of Dolfadog, was now sitting beside Lowri as passive as his father.

'WPC Owen has come here to help you through the process, to explain the role of the coroner, help you to make arrangements...'

'When can we get her underground?' Jac asked. 'I want to see her buried.'

'We'll need to arrange her funeral service,' Seth said. 'I've already spoken to the Minister at Moriah and...'

'*Twt lol!*' exploded Jac. 'The old bitch worshipped nothing but herself.'

'It would be a great comfort to me to arrange a nice service for Mum,' Nansi declared, smoothing Hope's golden hair. 'To give thanks for her life and to state our hope that we will all be reunited in the Everlasting Life.' Seth smiled to show his approval.

'I'd rather burn in Hell than be with her forever,' Jac spat. His words alarmed Basia; she made the sign of the cross on her forehead. After a moment, she reached over to protect Phil with the same sign. When she finished by touching his shoulder, Phil picked up the hand and pressed a passionate kiss on her palm. This clearly displeased Seth who stared at Basia as if she were a serpent. She noticed his disapproval and placed her hand on Phil's thigh to make her status as his lover perfectly clear.

Daf tried again.

'While we've got the family together like this, WPC Owen can explain how we can help you, explain the way the investigation will go and so on, OK?'

'But the family isn't together,' Lowri insisted, in a soft voice. 'Gruff's not here and what about...?'

Jac interrupted her at once.

'I rang Gruff. He was too busy to come; he said the arrangements were our business, not his. He hadn't seen her for ages, anyway.'

'Where does he live?' Daf asked, expecting the answer to be Canada or New Zealand.

'Other side of the brook,' Jac answered, waving his hand in

an easterly direction. Daf was surprised. How could a man avoid his mother when he lived so close?

'Is he married?'

Jac gave a sour laugh.

'We're not exactly a good advertisement for marriage here at Dolfadog, Inspector. I took Lowri by the church one morning to please her nain and you can see what kind of a man Seth is: Nans wouldn't get a jump out of him without putting her white dress on.'

'Do you have to speak like that, Jac?' Nansi protested. 'Whatever you thought of Mum, Seth's never done you any harm.'

'Whatever *I* thought of Mummy dearest? It wasn't me who tried to slit her throat!'

'What?' Daf asked.

Nansi's eyes filled with tears and she dashed out of the room, closely followed by Seth.

'It was just kids playing about,' Phil explained hastily. 'They were playing a game, acting out something they'd seen on telly. Heulwen tried to take the knife from Nans but she tripped and fell on the blade. That's all.'

Daf watched the smile strengthen on Jac's face.

'Are you sure, Dadi? Fell on the blade, did she? I thought Father Christmas was responsible, it was Christmas morning after all. She had fifteen stitches for her Christmas present. Did you ever notice, Inspector, that she always wore polo necks or shirts with a high collar, or one of her fucking scarves? She wanted to be careful to avoid re-igniting the rumour in the area, the story that one of her family had tried to kill her as a Christmas present to the others. I didn't do it, Gruff was feeding the stock and the old bastard hasn't got half enough pluck for a job like that, so who's left? Oh, Mrs Amazing fucking Grace herself.'

'There's no reason to dig up old stories like that, Jac,' said Phil, with an attempt at authority. 'It was an accident which took place over ten years ago now, that's it.'

Daf looked from one to another. There was little chance of real communication in an atmosphere as hostile as this. He resolved to speak to Nansi by herself, as soon as possible.

'Lowri,' he asked, 'is there any chance of a cup of tea?'

She looked glad to have an opportunity to leave the room.

'Phil, can we have a private word?'

Basia gripped his hand. 'Phil and I share everything,' she declared defensively.

'I realise that, Basia, but I have my duties to fulfil. Come on, Phil, let's go.'

'I'll be back in a minute,' Phil said to Basia, clearly reluctant to contradict her. It didn't look as if the poor creature was going to get any of his own way in his second marriage either, Daf thought, but there was no denying the warmth in Basia's eyes as she watched Phil rise to leave.

'Fancy a bit of fresh air, Phil? It's nice now after all the rain.'

The garden had changed, even in a day. The lawn was freshly cut and someone had pulled up half of the weeds from the central bed; the appearance of neglect was fading.

'The press have started sniffing about, Phil,' Daf began.

'I couldn't care less. I've got nothing to hide.'

'They're looking for stories about Heulwen.'

Phil laughed. 'Plenty of those to find.'

'About her personal life?'

'What's anyone got to say about her personal life, except how frigid she was?'

'She wasn't always … cold with everyone, from what I'm given to understand.'

'Who'd run after her? She wasn't some juicy twenty-five year old, was she?'

'She was in a relationship with someone.'

'Fuck off!'

'Honest to God.'

'Not that saddo, Carwyn Watkin? I did wonder why he was always so true to her when she was so spiteful with him.'

'It wasn't a man. Do you know Jan Cilgwyn, the Assembly Member?'

'Little woman like a wren? She stopped here with us a couple of times.'

'Well, she tells me that she and Heulwen … loved one another.'

Phil sucked in a huge breath as if he needed all the oxygen possible to process such unexpected information. Then, he made a fist and pumped it in a gesture of victory.

'Result!' he yelled. 'Give me high five, Inspector.'

'I realise this must come as a shock to you, Phil…'

'Not at all. I'm so glad to hear it; things make sense now.'

'What do you mean?'

'Inspector, you're known as a clever man. Education, qualifications, successful career. Jac's another example, he's an excellent farmer, good with stock and solid on all kinds of business. You haven't met Gruff yet but he's got some heck of a flair for horses, he can do anything with 'em. Well, when I was fifteen, I didn't reckon I had anything special about me. Nothing I could do better at than the next man. But there was a woman living next door to us, heckish smart-looking woman with a couple of little kids, and she took a fancy to me. Before that summer was over, I'd learnt what my talent was, that is … well, I was going to say "loving", but "fucking" would be nearer the mark. Before Heulwen, I'd had twenty girls on their backs and got every one of them going right well but with her, the magic just didn't work. That was one reason why I agreed to marry her: I was sure I could make her less sour with a month of my special treatment. What Marvin Gaye would call "sexual healing", if you get my meaning. But I couldn't do it, Inspector. She stayed that cold, and that hateful, and nothing I could do made her happy. Of course, I wanted a bit more response, more of what I was used to, so to say, so I went out for my fun. I got the impression … but, no, that's stupid…'

'What impression?'

'Well that she felt relief, somehow, as if some other woman was willing to do some job about the place she didn't like to do herself, like having a cleaner. But it all makes sense now, and the blame doesn't stick with me.' Phil laughed under his breath. 'I'm so bloody fucking glad about this, Inspector, I'm telling you. Basia's a fair bit younger than me and she'd decided ... well, you know, they've got these rules. I don't want to disappoint her, not when she's waited this long.'

Daf concealed his boredom: he had no interest in Phil Dolfadog's sexual anxieties and he was disappointed by this superficial response. He had expected some reaction to this revelation, some passionate outpouring and instead, he'd reinforced Phil's already considerable self-satisfaction. Time to change the subject.

'What really happened between Nansi and her mum, Phil? I don't believe a word of the story you told just now.'

'The hospital accepted it.'

'Very likely but I've seen how things are under this roof. I've got no interest in raking through cold ashes but I will get to the truth, you understand that, don't you?'

Phil shifted uneasily, paused then shook his head a little as if he were reluctant to obey Daf but found himself obliged to do so.

'OK, but please remember, Nansi has changed completely since then. She's a brilliant mum to those kids and the parson back there keeps her right happy, though he does like the sound of his own voice a bit.'

'How badly was Heulwen hurt?'

'It was just a flesh wound but there was blood everywhere and the turkey damn near spoiled.'

'So Nansi tried to slit her mother's throat, on Christmas Day in the morning?'

For some reason, Phil found himself unable to resist humming the familiar carol tune, in a voice which was surprisingly strong and sweet. He coughed slightly and began the story.

'They'd got up very early to go to the Plygain in John Hughes's chapel, like they always did. No opening presents until after the Plygain. I had to milk, so I didn't go and there were plenty of mince pies for breakfast.'

'What sort of Christmas was it?'

'Same as ever. Jac had a bit of a thick head after a session in the Black, Gruff was out with the stock, as usual, and Heulwen was making a massive fuss over the cooking. Nans had been a bit low in spirits since the summer, like teenage girls can be. Nothing particular.'

'But?'

'I was having a bit of a snooze by the woodburner in the front room, because, back then, we used to eat there some Sundays and special times, like Christmas, up the other end of the house. The kitchen is that far away, I don't know if Heuls and Nans were quarrelling or what. Then I heard a scream and when I got there, I saw Heuls sitting by the table, where she'd been chopping up nuts for some fancy recipe. Chestnuts, I think, to go with the sprouts.' He coughed, as if the memory had caught in his throat.

'And where was Nansi?'

'Standing behind her, with Heulwen's hair held tight in her left hand. She'd pulled her mother's head back and ... and she had a knife in the other hand. She'd had one go already, I could see that, from the cut and ... and from the blood on the knife, and she was getting ready for another try. The red line across Heul's throat opened up before my eyes and the blood started to pour down her neck.'

'What did you do?'

'Took the knife off Nans and put my handkerchief on Heulwen's neck. Hell, but she was bleeding! There was an empty look in Nansi's eyes, like she was walking in her sleep. Someone had to look after her, because she was shaking like a leaf and crying like a little baby but ... but well, I suppose I thought I needed to save Heulwen's life. We found out later on that there wasn't any major damage done but the blood, Inspector, the fucking blood...'

His broad shoulders were shaking and his easy-going face was shadowed with remembered fear. This wasn't a violent man, Daf decided, but a weak man who had chosen to ignore the seriousness of the troubles in his family.

'I called Gruff in to go and see his sister, they've always been close, and I took Heuls to the hospital in Shrewsbury. Even though it was only a flesh wound, it left some hell of a scar.'

'But why did she do it, Phil? I've got family of my own and I know well how difficult girls in their teens can be but, God in Heaven, there's a difference between sulking and cutting your mother's throat.'

'There was someone, a friend of hers, who was a bit of a bad influence on her. This friend came from a rough family, and Heulwen had said they shouldn't be seeing each other. That was the root of the matter. And, to tell the truth, Inspector, she was in the middle of her teens, hormones all over the shop and at one time, I was right worried for her, but look at her now, as happy as Larry.'

Daf wasn't sure he completely agreed but saw no reason to argue. For the first time, he saw the trace of the passing years on Phil; he had the look of a man who'd been carrying a burden for a long, long time.

'Can I go now? I don't want Jac to start on Basia again.'

'I should think she can take care of herself.'

'She likes to give that impression but her nature, you know, is that kind and gentle...'

Daf thought of the religious argument between Seth and Basia but didn't say a word.

'I need to have a word with Nansi, Phil. Can you send her out to me, without Seth?'

'I'll give it a go.'

Daf looked at his watch; it was half past three and he was starving.

'Phil, I'm doing my best to be civil but every one of you needs to remember that I am a police officer, a policeman investigating a very serious crime. I'm going to sit here on this bench and you are going to send your daughter out to me, on her own, to have a chat.'

By now, apart from the griping of his empty stomach, Daf's mind was filled entirely with the peculiar family at Dolfadog, with all their secrets, anger and lies. From what he'd heard so far, the other son appeared to be less complicated, but where was he on the day when the family had all gathered to arrange his mother's funeral? Daf resolved to ask Nia to make contact with Gruff as soon as possible.

As she walked over the grass towards him, Daf noted again the similarity between Nansi and her father. She didn't look as if she coloured her hair but it was the colour of September hay, tied back in a maternal ponytail, and Daf could imagine the soft waves falling over her wide shoulders. Daf started to worry: of all the girls he had encountered in the course of this investigation, there were only two he hadn't fancied at all so far and they were lesbians. He began to wonder if he could ask Dr Mansell for some sort of HRT patch, then he remembered Diane Rhydderch and breathed a sigh of relief; for all her long legs and high heels, she didn't raise a flicker of lust in him so he clearly wasn't a total satyromaniac.

He tried to work Nansi out. Like her dad, she seemed to want to be a friend to everyone, but what was responsible for the dark smudges under her big blue eyes? A child who was unsettled at night, or something deeper?

'Dad said you wanted to speak to me.' Only the faintest traces of her original accent had remained.

'I do. Sit down here by me.'

'I'd rather stand, the moss on this old bench can leave a heck of a green stain.'

Daf jumped to his feet, cursing under his breath.

'Your wife'll get that sorted with a bit of Vanish,' Nansi

assured him. Somehow, the mess had created a homely atmosphere, which was helpful.

'I'd better sort my own Vanish,' Daf replied, starting to walk over the grass towards her. 'We've just had a baby so I shouldn't make any extra work.'

'Get it done right away,' she suggested. 'You look like a calf that's been scouring, all green.'

'I will.'

'I haven't got any idea who killed Mum, you know. But she did have some quite odd friends down in Cardiff. Women who pretended they were men, men who wore dresses...'

Daf didn't want to hear Nansi's prejudiced take on her mother's friends, so he interrupted her. 'Did you know your mother was gay?'

'She wasn't gay, she was just a pain. She just wanted a bit of attention. I remember all her little schemes, supporting the Welsh language, raising money for poor children in China or somewhere, developing the rural areas with European funding, *Plu'r Gweunydd*, the welfare of the elderly, *ysgol feithrin*, sustainable energy, renewable energy. I think the elderly were my favourite; they did stink but they usually had good biscuits. Oh, and she had "depression" to get a bit of attention from the doctor.'

'But she was having a relationship with another woman.'

'I know. Seth ... discovered them in our spare room.'

'Oh dear,' Daf said, considering whether finding your middle-aged mother-in-law in the throes of passion was possibly the only thing equal to opening the door on your stepson acting out his BDSM fantasies with one of your colleagues.

'I'm afraid "Oh dear" doesn't really cover it, Mr Dafis. Seth is a highly religious man and he has status in his faith community. He comes from a totally different tradition; to him, being gay isn't a lifestyle choice, it's a sign of Satan working in our midst.'

Daf struggled not to give her a piece of his mind. 'And you, Nansi? What do you think?'

'Love is my faith, and forgiveness. I can't judge anyone.'

'Because you tried to kill your mother?'

'Because of the many mistakes I've made. And I still sin every day, I need grace just to survive.'

'But *lodes*, that Christmas, on the day when every family at least pretends to be happy, you'd got to the end of your tether?'

She nodded. 'Seth doesn't know about that. I made a new start, left all the crap behind me, that was the thing.'

'*Lodes*, all I want to know is who torched that building on Monday. I need to understand the family.'

'I was at home with the children on Monday, after leading Messy Church until six.'

'Fair enough, but what happened that Christmas? Presents that bad, were they?'

It was a feeble joke but she raised her eyes for few seconds.

'Mum and I hadn't been getting on for a while. Like any number of mothers and daughters.'

'Your dad said you had a friend who was a bit of a bad influence and that your mum had stopped you seeing this person. Then, you flipped.'

'Yes, yes, that's just what happened,' she responded in a way which made it clear that this story needed to be filed under fiction.

'Boy or girl?'

'We never ask, we take each child as a gift from God.' Nansi stroked her swollen stomach.

'No, I was asking about your friend.'

'He was a boy, from a really rough family.'

'And was he your lover?'

'I was fourteen. Way too early for anything like that.'

'Fair enough. What happened to him?'

'He wrote a couple of times but he moved about a lot after leaving the area. I haven't heard anything about him for years. I've got no idea what happened to him.'

'It's a sad story but is it enough to make you try to kill your mum?'

'You didn't live under this roof, Inspector. I've lost count of the times Jac threatened to kill her. I lost hope when Gruff moved out, I was just counting the days until I could get away to college.'

'Fair enough.' Daf didn't feel inclined to believe what she said but he didn't have anything specific on which to build his disbelief. He knew well enough that adolescent girls could be fragile and unpredictable, but in his experience, they were more likely to use a knife on themselves than on anyone else.

'Have you finished with me, Mr Dafis? It's nearly time for Hope to have a feed.'

'Can we have a chat again?'

'Of course. And please get those trousers sorted out, won't you?'

Daf checked his phone before returning into the house: no messages. He went into the kitchen where Nia was explaining the process of the inquest to Jac, and beckoned her to come to him.

'I'm just borrowing WPC Owen for a moment, folks,' he explained. The two went out through the back door and Nia sighed as Daf shut it behind them.

'This place has been like bedlam, boss,' she exclaimed. 'The father's as much use as a wet fart, the brother's going out of his way to be foul and the bloody religious stuff is driving me crazy. And don't get me started on the children! I need danger money to stop here a moment longer, honest.'

'And no one's grieving?'

'Far from it. Every now and again, the brother reminds them of some occasion when Heulwen was hateful to them, as if he was trying to justify his feeling of relief at her death.'

'We need to get in touch with the other brother. They talk about him as if he'd emigrated but he only lives half a mile away.'

'He is the other side of the brook; perhaps that's abroad, as far as they're concerned.'

'Could well be. Hey, why didn't you tell me that Sheila and Tom were trying for a baby?'

'Because it's so obvious. I don't have to remind you that the sun gets up in the morning now, do I?'

'I've invited them round to see Mali Haf. Is that the right thing to do?'

'You can't hide your baby, boss. I think it's a nice thing to do.'

'Right, but let me know if you think I'm doing anything stupid or tactless, won't you?'

'What a great opportunity...'

Daf's home was quiet when he dropped in to change his trousers. Usually, the hours between four and six were hectic but tonight the sitting room was empty. Daf went up to the bedroom and saw them: Gaenor curled up like a hedgehog on the bed and Mali on her back in the Moses basket, her arms and legs thrown wide like a starfish. The contrast between this peaceful scene and all the hatred at Dolfadog was startling. He lay down beside Gaenor, gazed at her lovely face and couldn't prevent himself from putting the palm of his hand on her soft cheek. She stirred in her sleep and wrapped her arm around him.

He hadn't meant to sleep but when he woke, the streetlights were coming on through the undrawn curtains. He looked in panic for his phone, which was in the pocket of the stained trousers on the floor. Half past six. He'd missed four calls and there was a text from Steve:

'Opened up the safe – there's something here you need to see.'

'On my way,' Daf tapped back.

He decided to make a sandwich for himself before going back down to Welshpool, and he was trying to decide between a slice of ham which was older than Mali or a lump of cheese which had developed a skin like tree bark, when Rhodri came home.

'Hiya, *cog*, where have you been till now?'

'About.'

'About where?'

A number of images jumped into Daf's mind, most of them concerning drugs.

'Just with my mates, Dad.'

'What mates?'

'Josh, Morgan and Harri. We had chips.'

'Gae's making pizza later.'

'I can always find room for a bit of pizza.'

Daf finished his bread and butter and looked at his son. He'd grown suddenly but he'd also changed his hairstyle, brushing his long fringe over his forehead and shaving the back of his neck. To Daf's old-fashioned eyes, the effect was stupid, as if his hair had slipped over his eyes like a wig, but apart from calling him Donald Trump a couple of times, there was nothing he could do about it. Carys and Gaenor had voted in favour of the new hair, which was, in their opinion, a sign of Rhodri growing up. The next step would be a girlfriend, beer and choosing a college. And if Rhodri was growing up, of course, that meant that Daf himself was getting old.

Daf was surprised to see Sheila still at the station. She looked smart, as if she were about to go out somewhere.

'Tom's going to the Charolais Society meeting tonight and we're having supper in the Oak after,' she explained, without Daf having to ask. 'And there are a couple of things you need to know. HQ have been on to the police in Poland, and our friend Milek has a bit of a history.'

'I didn't think he was exactly an angel.'

'Perhaps the second thing will be a bit more of a surprise to you, then. Lisa Powell.'

'What about her?'

'To start with, HR in the Welsh Government think she has a degree in Public Administration from Swansea University. She did go to Swansea but she was excluded in her second year.'

'What for?'

'Stalking. She had a crush on a member of staff, that's what the file says, and in the end, after months of counselling and any number of warnings, the lecturer got an injunction preventing Lisa from coming anywhere near her.'

'Very interesting.'

'And, two years ago, she was questioned by South Wales Police.'

'About what?'

'Abusing her partner. Her partner's mother saw a mark on her wrist and contacted the police. Her partner didn't want to prosecute – the old, old story.'

'And the name of her partner was...?'

'Jan Cilgwyn.'

'Wow.'

'And here's another little gem for you, boss: Lisa hasn't been into the office at all this week. She rang in on Monday to say there was a family crisis and she'd have to take a week's annual leave at short notice. I got a picture of her sent up from the HR department there and when I took that picture over to the Oak, she was the Mrs Wilkes who stayed there on Monday night.'

'That's a good day at the office, Sheila!'

'Wait till you see what Steve has found,' Sheila boasted, with a grin.

'Is Steve about?'

'Gone home for the night. But just you come and see.'

On Steve's desk, standing on a thick, plastic sheet was a small safe, about the size of a microwave. It had been white but was now mainly brown in colour, with darker patches of soot; it had clearly been in the fire.

'Have we got the combination?'

'It's open, boss. Steve contacted the manufacturers and they gave him the emergency override code.'

'You lot have been cooking on gas.'

Thoughtfully, someone had left a pair of plastic gloves on the desk beside the safe. Daf carefully pulled out of it a thick A4 manila envelope. On it was written, in large letters, in careful handwriting: 'J Rh O (Rh B)'. In it were a pile of black-and-white photographs, obviously taken with either a long lens or a hidden camera. The pictures showed about two dozen different women performing a variety of different sexual activities in a number of different rooms: the common denominator was the man.

'He's quite flexible for such a bulky chap,' Daf remarked. 'I'm surprised he's got enough time to even cut up half a dozen chops, let alone be an Assembly Member and do all that anti-wind farm protesting.'

'I thought the same,' Sheila concurred, looking over Daf's shoulder at a photograph of Rhys Bowen enjoying the attentions of two girls similar enough to be identical twins.

'You don't have to look at these, *lodes*,' Daf said, defensively, trying to turn over a picture of a stark naked Bowen. 'There's doing your duty and then there's above and beyond.'

'I don't mind,' was her careless reply. 'They're very educational. Who is going to do what to who with that pink rubber thing, do you think?'

Daf pushed the pictures back into the envelope and pulled out another bearing the letters 'J Rh O (G B)'. The contents of that envelope might not have been so entertaining as the previous one's but they were every bit as interesting. Page after page of complex accounts, following the budget of some trust, which showed how much of the trust's assets seemed to fall into the hands of one of the trustees, Cllr Gwilym Bebb. They would need a forensic accountant to make full sense of it. Daf pulled out the rest of the envelopes from the safe, over twenty of them. They all had the letters 'J Rh O' on them, together with someone's initials. Inside were the records of their lapses, their conspiracies, their sins. The majority were local people, the area's big shots, but Heulwen's web had reached as far as Cardiff; various prominent members of all parties had caught her attention.

Daf turned his attention to the very last envelope, which was rather crisp, as if it had been in the safe for a long time. 'J Rh O (CW)' was the code, and inside was a rather sad little record of the crimes of Carwyn Watkin, Brynybiswal. A picture of him enjoying the hospitality of a house developer in the Millennium Stadium, pictures of him at Ludlow Races in the company of a family who had submitted a plan to build a mega-dairy, and Carwyn receiving a parcel in the shape of a bottle from a woman who was seeking to double the size of her caravan site. Fixed neatly to the back of each picture was a photocopy of his declaration of interest for the relevant meeting of the planning committee. Each time, Carwyn had declared that he had no interest in the case. Daf was angry. For one who could play a game of whist so strategically, Carwyn had made a right fool of himself. He wasn't selling his vote, the foolish son of Brynybiswal, Daf was sure of that, but he had put himself in an impossible position by trying to be popular. And the result of his effort was a thick file condemning him and no gain for himself at all.

'Right, Sheila,' Daf began at length. 'This is an archive for blackmail. I'll take the lot home with me and tomorrow morning we start working out who's who.'

'Boss, do you think they knew Heulwen had all this information about them?'

'Of course they did, that's the whole point of blackmail. Why do you ask?'

'She was a first language Welsh speaker, wasn't she?'

'Very much so. What's that got to do with anything?'

'What if the 'J Rh O' stood for *Jyst Rhag Ofn*', '*Just in case*'? Perhaps it wasn't so much blackmail as an insurance policy.'

'Very good point and well done you for guessing. So we'll just have to find out all we can about these people and their connections to Heulwen. And if you get a moment before that nice supper in the Oak, can you start the paperwork for a search warrant? I fancy having a sprot round Rhys Bowen's office, and his house as well, while you're about it.'

A lovely smell welcomed Daf home, even if it was rather late for supper on a school night. Rhodri was sitting at the kitchen table, his baby sister in his lap, talking to Gaenor. She hadn't combed her hair, which made Daf's thoughts immediately head in a bedroom direction. He went red, in case his libidinous thoughts were visible on his face.

'What happened to your trousers, Dad? The ones you left on the bedroom floor? Gae showed them to me and it looks like you sat down in a puddle of crap.'

'Damp moss on the bench in the garden at Dolfadog.'

Gaenor caught his eye for a moment before pulling out of the oven a freshly baked pizza which smelt of yeast, garlic and...

'Not bloody pineapple again!'

'You know the rules, Daf, whoever helps make the pizza gets to choose the toppings.'

Daf had a sudden memory of Carys perched on a high stool, swathed in one of Gaenor's vast linen aprons, making pizza in the four-oven Aga which stood at the heart of the kitchen at Neuadd. He recalled his own feelings so clearly at that moment: he had a revelation of how an attractive woman who just happened to love his children made him the prisoner of an irresistible desire. He chose to hide his sentiment behind irritation.

'Pineapple turns a pizza into a piece of nonsense. You never get pineapple on your pizza in Italy.'

'But you do get it in Pizza Express, which is nearer,' was

Rhodri's response. 'Mals, Dad knows jack shit about food, remember that.'

'I was going to suggest that we open that bottle of Sicilian Red we got from Tesco's,' Daf continued, in his fake sulk, 'but I've got no idea what to drink with that half-tropical bollocks.'

'Oh, we're doing "tropical bollocks" in Geography next term, straight after glaciation and the rain forest,' was Rhodri's joke in reply.

'We could have a pina colada,' suggested Gaenor, 'but I'm sleepy enough as it is.'

The pizza was delicious despite the pineapple. While Rhodri was loading the dishwasher, Daf sat down by the wood-burner with Mali on his knee.

'I've got a pile of papers to go through, Gae, so would you mind if we didn't put the telly on? I can just about cope with murder and Mali but not baby, blackmail and *Becws Beca*.'

'You must be seriously busy to turn your back on the Welsh Nigella. That's your favourite programme.'

'Normally, yes, but tonight, I've got to try to concentrate, and Beca's buns would be a distraction.'

'Of course.'

Gaenor took her baby daughter and settled on the sofa.

'You're too far over there, Daf, come over and *cwtch* by us.'

Daf sat down beside Gaenor on the sofa and opened the first envelope. Inside was the story of a company called Tir Taf. They'd purchased land from the government, often getting spectacular bargains, then sold the land a few months later for a fortune. It just so happened that the brother-in-law of one of the directors was high up in the Labour Party. Daf made a note of the basic facts of the case: more work for the forensic accountant. Mali had settled well to her supper and Gaenor really was sleepy. Her head dropped onto Daf's shoulder but Mals was as happy as a lark feeding as her mother dozed. Ten minutes passed and just as Daf was opening the third envelope, Mali released her mother's breast and Gaenor woke with a start. Daf turned the picture face down but not before Gaenor had caught a glimpse.

'Was that a picture of Rhys?'

'There's an envelope full of them. From the safe in Heulwen's office.'

'Blackmail, then?' Gaenor asked, moving Mali onto the other side.

'Looks like it. I'm not sure how much of a secret Bowen's antics are, mind you. His wife is bound to know by now.'

'Not sure she'd care, if the cheques keep clearing. And as for his mother, she always knew he was a bad lad, and made a joke of his behaviour.'

'Oh yeah, and there was me forgetting that you were the world's greatest expert on Rhys Bowen.'

'It's true. He was like his uncles, her brothers, so she said. I remember her giving him a lift over to our place one evening when he was the same age as Rhods is now, and her telling my mum how he was just like them.'

'And what was Bowen doing at your house? As if I needed to ask?' Daf was pleased with himself for keeping it light.

'He was big mates with Jeff. They still do a fair bit together.'

'That's an idea, I can ask your brother for a bit of the background.'

'Worth a try. I remember that night clearly; it was the first time I was allowed to stay up late with the grown-ups to feather the ducks. Rhys had necked them for us, a whole pen too, a dozen. We were on the damson gin from the year before and it was dead good stuff. After we pulled out the big feathers, Rhys started to deal with the down. He put an old Fray Bentos meat pie tin full of meths on the floor and he chucked a match into it. Then he stood over the flame with those long legs of his and swung the duck from one hand to the other until all the down was scorched away. We were killing ourselves laughing and my mum was screaming because she thought Rhys was going to set light to himself. His mum was laughing loudest of them all, encouraging him to be as wild as he liked.'

'I had no idea your family was so close to the Bowens,' Daf said.

'Well, you know what it's like in a small village: not that much choice. Oh no,' she added, dramatically, 'I forgot you grew up in downtown Llanfair so you're much more cosmopolitan! Mrs Bowen and Mum weren't especially close but they'd chat when they saw each other. And, of course, Rhys started butchering when he was younger than Rhodri so he was too busy for much socialising after that.'

'Talking about downtown Llanfair, do you know where Rhods was when you were having your little nap?'

'He was with his friends.'

'Yes, but what were they doing?'

Gaenor laughed. 'Eating chips. Looking for girls. Hanging about, like lads do.'

'Sion never hung about on street corners.'

'Because we lived in the countryside. It's different in town.'

'Hmm. When this case is sorted, we're going to start looking for a house, out in the middle of nowhere.'

'Rhods is a tidy lad. He's not about to start drinking White Lightning in the churchyard.'

'I know that.'

'And maybe it would have done Sion a bit of good to spend a bit more time away from home.'

'I don't know about that. How many lads of his age are getting themselves tied up and whipped by a girl as smart as Belle?'

The kitchen door opened.

'I'm going up to my room,' Rhodri announced.

'Fair enough. Homework?'

'Done. I want to go on the computer for a bit.'

'And how is the old "Minecraft" getting along?'

'Dad, please. I'm not in primary anymore.'

After he'd gone, Daf looked for advice. 'Since when was "Minecraft" classified as crap? And why didn't I notice?'

'Since he borrowed "Call of Duty: Black Ops 3" from Josh.'

'Is he allowed to play violent games?'

'Don't be a knob, Daf, of course he is, as long as he doesn't get onto a higher level than I do.'

'What?'

'I've already raised a boy in the modern world. Someone in the family had to get up to speed with those games, and John couldn't cope with first person shooters.'

'Bloody hell, Gaenor Morris, you amaze me every single day.'

'Like Shrek said, I've got layers.'

Gaenor turned her attention to Mali, and Daf pulled a couple more pictures out of the envelope. Gaenor abruptly turned her head.

'Hey, that's Miss Davies. Teaches the Foundation Phase in Tregynon school.'

'A teacher? One of Bowen's pick-ups?'

'Well, she certainly looks like she's having fun.'

Daf saw the pattern. Some of the pictures clearly showed Bowen with a prostitute in some hotel room but over half were taken in more domestic circumstances, on the sofa in a black-and-white cottage or on the carpet in a newly built house. And his partners weren't stick-thin girls with empty eyes but a cross-section of ladies between thirty and fifty with a tendency to being rather well endowed but still slender in comparison with him. Daf noticed another familiar face: Miss Beynon from the high school.

'Bloody hell, Gae, this one teaches R.E.!'

He made a list of the pictures, putting an asterisk beside those who looked as if they were prostitutes. It was a pretty long list but, Daf reasoned, the contents of the envelope were very possibly the fruit of years of research. If Heulwen had been building up her collection over, say, five years, then Bowen hadn't been unnaturally busy. But if Heulwen had been paying someone to tail Bowen for five years to collect evidence of his shocking behaviour, she must have spent a fortune. He needed to look at her bank accounts, or rather, get Nev to do so.

He pulled another envelope out of the bag and a picture fell onto the floor, a clipping from an old copy of *Plu'r Gweunydd*. 'The Dolfadog Family carol singing' was the caption above a picture of Heulwen and Phil, torches in their hands. In front of them were a row of children in their winter coats with colourful hats pulled down over their heads. Daf could recognise Jac, the tallest, his face betraying his deep boredom. There was a boy with dark hair, similar enough to his mother for Daf to guess he must be Gruff. Nansi was the little girl with long plaits escaping from her hat, and by her side was another boy with a pale face and shoulders too narrow for his heavy coat. The hat was similar, the coat was similar, the wellingtons were identical but he did not come from Dolfadog stock.

'Who do you reckon that lad is, Gae?' Daf asked.

'Some friend, bound to be.'

'But he's dressed just like the others.'

'Maybe Heulwen lent him a coat and hat.'

Somehow, the thought of a house full of friends lending stuff casually did not make sense to Daf, and, furthermore, he was almost certain that he'd seen that narrow face somewhere recently, but the question was, where?

# Chapter 9

## *Thursday morning, April 14, 2016*

After a comfortable night, with hardly any trouble from Mali, Daf was in good spirits but Gaenor did not look well at all. Her cheeks were too pink and Daf thought there was an unnatural shine in her eyes. Over breakfast, she seemed rather confused. Daf suggested that he ring the surgery but she refused.

'Don't worry, *cariad*,' she said, planting a hot kiss on his forehead. 'I'm a woman knocking on for forty with a baby just over a month old; I'm not going to be coping every day.'

'Have you got a temperature, Gae?'

'I'm fine, I'm telling you.'

Rhodri raised his head. As often happened, he'd been cuddling his little sister and paying no attention to anything else in the wide world.

'You look shattered, Gae,' he said. 'I've only got DT and Games today so why don't I stop at home and look after Mals while you have a rest?'

Daf interjected. 'Do you happen to remember which governor in your school has responsibility for attendance? Yes, me. You're not going to get away with taking a day off school just because you fancy cwtching the baby all day long.'

Red spots appeared on Rhodri's cheeks; he was loath to admit how much he doted on Mali.

'He was only offering a bit of help, Daf,' Gaenor insisted. 'Anyway, it's a big day today, I'm going out.'

'Where to?'

'Mali and I are venturing up to Ti a Fi.'

'She's way too young. It'll make no difference to her.'

'I know that but I'm determined to get into a better pattern this time. With Sion, I just brooded in Neuadd like an old hen, keeping my little chick safe under my wing pretty well until it was time for him to go to school.'

'High school,' added Rhodri, laughing.

'Very nearly,' agreed Gaenor with a wide smile. 'Anyway, I've promised Chrissie I'd go today.'

'Chrissie?' Daf asked, trying not to think about Chrissie Berllan. Last year, when he was imprisoned in an unhappy marriage, it had been natural for him to flirt with Chrissie, but now? As luck would have it, there was a bit of balance in the situation because Gaenor fancied Bryn, Chrissie's husband at least as much as Daf fancied Chrissie. They laughed about it often enough but even though they treated it as a game, it still made Daf feel guilty, especially in the middle of an investigation which seemed to present Daf with a new girl to admire every day.

'Yes. I saw her in the clinic with the twins last week. She said they'd been lambing flat out and she was dying to sit down for half an hour and have a chat.'

'Rob hasn't been in school since the start of term,' Rhodri added. As governor with responsibility for attendance Daf knew he ought to display some measure of disapproval but all he could think of was the gulf between Rhodri and his friend Rob, Chrissie's eldest son. Rob was a young man, with responsibilities, hands hardened and split from work, and a sex life, whilst Rhodri, thank God, was still a lad.

'Are you sure you feel well enough to go out, Gae?' Daf asked.

'For God's sake, Daf Dafis, I'm only going up Mount Road to the *ysgol feithrin*, not climbing Everest.'

And that was how they left it but as he was topping up the car in Londis, Daf felt uncertain. Sometimes he could feel the echo of his relationship with Falmai affecting the way things were between him and Gaenor. Falmai's complaining nature had been a major factor in the failure of their relationship and so, being a woman who had an instinctive understanding of relationships, Gaenor tended towards the other end of the spectrum, not allowing herself to admit to any suffering, even when she was patently not well. That bothered Daf, her bravery. Of course he felt like a shit for leaving her but he had no choice. He resolved to phone her a couple of times during the day, just in case.

With his head full of Gaenor, he walked out of the shop back to the car without having noticed who was filling up at the pump next to him, smart as ever in her work clothes. Falmai was holding her purse in one hand and squeezing the nozzle with the other, so, when her scarf was caught by a gust of wind and blown over her face, she couldn't move it. Daf stretched out his hand to free her but Falmai jumped back in alarm.

'What are you doing, Daf?' she asked abruptly.

'Your scarf...' Daf began but couldn't continue. What he wanted to say was unsayable: 'Once, I loved you so much I thought my heart would leap out of my chest like in the Meatloaf song, and even now, I can't let you stand like a dick by the pump in the Londis with a piece of violet-coloured silk over that face I once kissed for hours on end.'

'Oh. Yes. Thanks.'

Fal put the nozzle back in its place with a definitive click.

'Did you have a word with Carys in the end?'

'Yes, thanks.' They were speaking like strangers, which was what they had become. Daf could remember the bare facts of how he used to wait for her with a bottle of wine and a picnic blanket in her father's barn, but the smell of the hay, the sensation of touching her skin, the gagging sweetness of the warm white wine, all of those were gone.

'Nice evening Tuesday?'

'Very nice, thanks. Listen, Daf,' Fal said, cleaning her hands on the paper provided, which no one else did in the Londis from one week's end to the next, 'Jonas is worried about some woman who keeps a shop in Welshpool. She's got her claws in poor John, it seems. Do you know anything about her?'

'I've met her once, that's all.'

'And? What sort of person is she?'

'Looks very smart, expensive clothes and that. Doesn't come over as the most gentle and kind woman in the world.'

'That's exactly what Jonas said, though in language which was a bit more ... colourful.' A spark came into her eye as if she were relishing remembering the conversation. Daf tried and failed not to think about the light he'd once caused in her eye. He'd let her down, big time.

'You're seeing a bit of Jonas, then?'

Her eyes darkened and she turned her back to him. 'You've long since lost the right to ask questions like that, Daf Dafis.'

As he was parking in the police station car park, Daf saw the message light flashing on his phone. He was expecting a text from Gaenor, but it was from Falmai.

'Don't ever lay a finger on me again, ever, Dafydd.'

Thank God he had a murder to take his mind off his innocent mistake.


His team were there, waiting for him. Since coming back from her honeymoon before Christmas, Daf had noted a change in the way Sheila worked, and even after a couple of full-on days, she was still following the new pattern. To start with, she was now always very lively and cheerful first thing, as if she'd enjoyed a worthwhile night in bed. Daf found this hard to reconcile with a man as tedious as Tom Francis but he remembered Nia's observation: 'Lots of people say she's done a clever thing there, marrying a bachelor who's been longing for a wife for over thirty years. They're like pressure cookers, just about ready to boil over.' The other change was her work rate. Before meeting Tom, Sheila had put work before everything, and she'd spend any number of extra hours in the station, anything to avoid going home to her mother and their quiet home. Now she was a farmer's wife with an extended family and a network of social expectations but, instead of slacking, Sheila had resolved to do more work in less time. She'd always been a good officer but now her work was more precise, as if she needed to get everything right first time. She only took half a minute to greet Daf, handing him an incident report sheet.

'Someone's broken into a farm by Llanerfyl, the other side of the brook from Dolfadog,' she told him. 'Overnight, sometime.'

'Oh yes?'

Daf was inclined to be rather suspicious: since the previous autumn, a fair few quads, a fair few Land Rovers, even the odd tractor, had vanished. Every time, it was an old piece of kit which went missing and the vast majority were insured by what the NFU called an Aladdin policy: if a farmer lost something old, the union would pay for a new replacement. Dean in the NFU office in Newtown was pretty sure it was some kind of scam, especially since this pattern had developed since the price of fat lambs had dropped.

'Nothing mechanical this time,' added Sheila, reading his thoughts.

'No?'

'It's a woman who breeds cobs. Someone broke into their barn overnight and took a bit of ketamine from their medicine chest.'

Daf nodded: ket. Once again, the drug dealers had moved faster than the law; a strong painkiller for horses had become fashionable. Usually, the parents of the young people involved had no idea about the side effects or symptoms of using ket. Dr Mansell said that at least three times in the previous year, mothers had come to the surgery with sons complaining of blood in their urine or other bladder problems, oblivious to the fact that they were presenting with the classic signs of ketamine use. Daf sighed. Whatever he did to keep his area safe for young people, there was always some new threat. He thought about the scene in his kitchen at breakfast, his son cuddling the baby.

How in hell could he protect them in a world so full of ever-changing dangers?

'OK. What's the name of the place?'

'Tanyrallt.'

'Oh, I know who you've got. Margaret Tanyrallt is a big name in the world of cobs.'

'And she says some of them have been ... hurt, as well.'

'Hurt? How?'

'Manes and tails been cut, so she says.'

Before Daf had a chance to reply, Nia appeared with a thick brown file in her hand.

'This is Milek Bartoshyn's history, boss. Been a bit of a bad lad back in Poland, so it seems. Fair play, the team in Carmarthen have translated everything from Polish for us.'

Daf ran his eye quickly down the first few paragraphs. 'Nothing much here, nothing within a mile of murder.'

'Turn the page, boss.'

On the next page was a report from the police in Częstochowa. Seven years earlier, Milek had attacked a German man on the Jasna Gora hill in the town. The victim had had to spend a week in hospital. Milek was prosecuted but the judge decided to give him a relatively low sentence: six months in prison. According to the report, the German had threatened Milek's sister and had insulted her by offering her two hundred Euros if she spent the night with him. According to Basia's evidence, the German had expressed the opinion that all Polish girls were cheap and that he could get half a dozen for two hundred Euros. He hadn't noticed Milek, who was, as usual, following his sister home from her evening shift, to make sure she was safe, keeping his distance but always watching. Milek stepped out of the shadows and, after a conversation which included a discussion of the massacre which took place in the town in 1939, Milek beat and kicked the man. Basia ran for help but by this time, the German was already seriously injured.

'Ah,' Daf responded.

'So,' Nia concluded, 'if he was ready to break this man's ribs to defend Basia, perhaps he'd be ready to kill the woman who stood between her and her happiness.'

'Could be,' Daf responded. 'But there's a big difference between raising a fist against a man who's insulting your sister and planning, in cold blood, to kill a woman.'

Nia made a low sound in her throat. 'I've got no idea where your behaviour code springs from, boss, but the days of chivalry are long dead. Milek's not some knight from the Middle Ages but a rough bloke with tattoos and a violent history. The image you have in your head of the brave pilots who came over here to help us beat Hitler is just a fantasy now and the Poles who hang around drinking lager outside the pubs in Welshpool aren't saints by a long way, even if they do straggle in to see your friend Joe Hogan on Sunday morning.'

'Young men without family around them, that's all they are, nothing more sinister. And to be fair to Milek, he's only got two tattoos, which are the White Eagle, symbol of his country, and the Sacred Heart of Christ, which is a symbol of his Faith. Whatever, it looks like we'll have to have another chat with him later – can you sort it for me?'

'OK, boss. Are you planning on keeping him in this time?'

'Why?'

'Because he's got a reason to kill Mrs Breeze-Evans, he had plenty of opportunity and now we know about his background...'

'I don't need a file from Poland to tell me that Milek was handy enough with his fists but that doesn't make him a murderer. We'll need that talk with him in any case. Can you make sure it's at a time when Father Hogan is available to translate?'

'Fine. Dr Jarman says he'll want a word at some point in the afternoon if that's OK with you?' Nia asked.

'Is he going to release the body? The family are keen on getting on with the funeral arrangements.'

'He was talking about running additional tests,' Nia replied.

'What if they held a memorial service in the next few days then the funeral itself later?' Sheila suggested. 'A lot of people are asking when the service is going to be held.'

Daf considered that was very likely to be the case. There were plenty of people looking forward to seeing this woman buried, this ideal wife, this prominent member of every committee, including her family.

'Either you or me, Nia, can discuss it with them after I've spoken to Dr Jarman. I'll nip up to Tanyrallt now. Ring them to let them know I'm on my way, Sheila.'

There was some thinking time available on the run up to Llanerfyl. Before leaving Welshpool, Daf sent a text to Gaenor, without expecting an answer because there was no signal in the *ysgol feithrin*, but a reply came straightaway:

'On our way to *ysgol feithrin* – Mali Haf sleeping like a piglet. Please don't worry, Daf.'

After the words came four xs. He had to smile; since they had been living together, Gaenor had lost her shyness about displaying her feelings, another sign of the thaw she felt after leaving Neuadd. At times like this, she came across like a girl in her teens. Having been reassured by the message, Daf cleared his head to think of Heulwen Breeze-Evans and to prepare to hear what had happened at Tanyrallt.

A totally unexpected sight faced Daf as he turned the corner between the high hedges and crossed the cattle grid into the yard at Tanyrallt. A tall man in his twenties, wearing nothing but long black leather boots and a riding hat, was standing outside a loose box beside a large brown horse. Daf ran through what he knew of the history of Margaret Tanyrallt, a single woman in her sixties who'd devoted her life to breeding horses and who did the bare minimum of farming required to be able to meet the vets' bills. She was old-fashioned and stubborn, ready to share a joke with her friends in the world of cobs but ignoring everybody else. If Daf had had to name the yard in his patch where he was most unlikely to meet a young man stark naked, he would have said Tanyrallt. The man was standing perfectly still. His face, under the shadow of the hat, was pretty familiar to Daf and even if he couldn't put a name to the face out of context, he was certain it was one of the inhabitants of his patch. Daf tried to form a sentence to start a conversation in these peculiar circumstances but before he managed it, he heard the voice of a woman: 'Lovely, Griff, that's great.'

From the shadow of the stable stepped a young woman with a large camera. 'Griff', she'd called him, in an English accent. The young man was Gruff Breeze-Evans, Heulwen's younger son. A strange thing to do, Daf thought, posing for pictures of this kind so soon after your mother's death. Gruff took off his hat and moved it down to his groin which was just as well, since the girl was having quite an effect on him. At least Margaret herself wasn't on the yard: that would have made the awkwardness unbearable. Daf walked over to the two young people. The girl was showing Gruff some pictures on the screen of her camera, and to Daf, they looked tasteful enough. In Daf's opinion, the young man was better-looking from behind: his legs were long and his backside firm but there was a weakness in his face. His eyes had a sulky look, and he had what Carys would have described as a monobrow.

'Dafydd Dafis, Dyfed Powys Police. I'm looking for Margaret Hamer.'

'Mr Dafis, you've been at Dolfadog, Jac said.' There was plenty of embarrassment in Gruff's voice. 'She's in the big barn with the Section As.'

'Thanks.'

'Don't think I walk around like this all the time, Mr Dafis,' he began, turning into English for the benefit of the girl. 'Clara's come to take some pictures. It's for the "Slow Down for My Horse" campaign. Mr Davies is a policeman, Clara.'

The girl gave Daf a broad smile. 'So you must know how

some idiots drive past horses like maniacs. What we're doing is raising awareness, putting pictures of fit people naked on Facebook, and Twitter and Instagram, to try to make these mad drivers think twice.'

'And,' Daf said, turning back into Welsh as he addressed his question directly to Gruff, 'is Ms Hamer happy for you to use the yard in this way, *lanc*?'

'Actually, when the girls from the campaign got in touch,' the girl interjected, 'I thought of Margaret straightaway. She's always got some handsome creatures on her yard, and Griff's not too bad either.'

'Good luck with it,' Daf replied, very curious as to Gruff's status at Tanyrallt. The photographer talked about him as if he was Margaret's son.

In the barn, the weak light showed a rather sad scene. Feeding contentedly from a small bale of hay were four lovely ponies with large eyes, trim feet and a remarkable shine on their coats. Even in his state of profound ignorance, Daf knew he was in the presence of 'Section A' Welsh ponies of a high standard. But instead of the plentiful waves which should have cascaded down their necks, their manes were nothing but a few ragged tufts, and it was obvious that this vicious trim was both radical and deliberate. Their tails told the same story. They looked bald and somehow stupid. Looking at them, leaning on the gate, was a short woman in a ragged oilskin coat, its long-vanished closing studs replaced with loops of blue and orange baler twine.

'Ms Hamer?'

She looked around at once. Her dark hair was turning white and there was no sign that she had visited a hairdresser for many years. Deep-set black eyes examined Daf, glinting in a face as brown and wrinkled as a walnut. Daf remembered a remark his father had made about Margaret Tanyrallt many years ago, after she'd popped into the shop for a packet of loose tea and twenty Bensons: 'End of the day, she's one of Abraham

Wood's family.' Daf hadn't been sure if this meant that his family had thought Margaret had gypsy blood in her veins or whether it was a convenient way to describe her as an outsider in the valley she had lived in all her life. She was a strongly built, solid woman, with large dirty hands, and Daf was certain she could put most men on the floor with one blow of her heavy fist. A cigarette rested on her lower lip, and her false teeth gave a slightly slack shape to her mouth.

'Daf Dafis? I'm surprised you've found time to come up and help us. I saw you on the telly last night, talking about what happened to Heuls.'

'Your case is important too, Ms Hamer. Are these the ponies that have been...?'

'Spoilt? Yes.'

'Their manes and tails will grow back pretty quick, won't they?'

'Not before the Royal Welsh, no. Take a look at her: Tanyrallt Dancing Girl. The best chance we've had for a decade.'

'Do you think it's just some sort of vandalism, or something that was done with serious intent?'

'No idea, but whoever was responsible certainly knows something about horses. These ladies were outside, in the meadow by the brook, which is a pretty big field. Whoever cut their manes and tails knew exactly how to catch ponies with a head collar.'

'So did someone break into the stable and take the head collar with them down to the field?'

'Maybe, or Gruff could have left a halter on a nail in the shelter shed, which he does on times. Do you want a cup of tea, Daf Dafis, or will you take a small whisky?'

'A bit early for a whisky but a cup of tea would be grand.'

'Not too early for those of us who've been up and about at our work since five. Come along.'

Since living with Gaenor, Daf had become infected with her weakness for property programmes. *Homes under the Hammer*,

*Location, Location, Location* and repeats of *Pedair Wal* had opened Daf's eyes, and even though he dismissed such programmes as property porn, he still watched them. 'Potential' that was the word that leapt into Daf's mind as he walked up to the door of Tanyrallt. It was a Victorian house, exactly like Wil Cwac Cwac's home, with its stone walls and little green-painted porch. No one had painted the back door for fifty years but somehow, in the April sunshine which coloured everything with the promise of summer, the place looked quaint, an example of shabby chic rather than neglect. When Margaret opened the back door, three little dogs ran up to greet her, terriers with a very adventurous look about them as if they were forever hunting or battling mighty badgers, not snoozing by the Rayburn.

The heat of the Rayburn filled the kitchen completely. Above the stove, on a wooden rack, hung no less than seven pairs of cream-coloured jodhpurs, some with long legs, others the same shape as Margaret. Gruff's jodhpurs, perhaps. Margaret's eyes followed the direction of Daf's.

'Hunting clothes,' she explained. 'We won't go out again till the autumn, so everything gets put away till next season.'

Daf wasn't a big fan of hunting because of all the Saturdays he had wasted as a young officer trying to separate the sabs from the followers of the Tanatside and David Davies hunts. He still received a couple of phone calls every season from people accusing the hunt of catching foxes. As a result, it wasn't Margaret's hunting which interested him so much as who she meant when she spoke of 'we'. Whose were those jodhpurs?

'Who do you hunt with?' Daf asked, courteously.

'Tanatside, of course. Gruff's crazy about hunting, he goes out twice a week, when he can.'

'Does Gruff work here?'

Margaret pulled the big kettle on to the hottest plate of the Rayburn before replying. 'Gruff's my son. He lives here, he works here.'

She lit another cigarette before turning to Daf. Her fingers were yellow with nicotine and, as Daf looked at the cream walls, he wondered if they had been white once.

'Sorry if it's a stupid question, but I thought he was Phil and Heulwen's son.'

Margaret used her cigarette to indicate that he should look at the wall. Amidst the pictures of horses, many with rosettes pinned in their corners, was a large black-and-white portrait of a young man. His clothing and appearance declared him to be a youngish farmer from the 1970s, with his collar-length hair and dark sideburns. He wasn't completely good-looking; his nose was too big and his eyebrows met beneath his wide forehead. Yet his smile was appealing in its frankness, his eyes brimming with kindliness and humour.

'Do you know him, Daf Dafis?'

Daf shook his head.

'Hywel Dolfadog. Heulwen's brother. The best man in the world. Don't you see how alike he is to Gruff?'

'They are alike, yes,' Daf agreed, without adding that there was a stronger, less sulky look about the man in the picture.

'Like father and son, many people have said.'

She turned back to the Rayburn to pour the water for the tea and as she did so, Daf saw her eyes wet with unshed tears. Daf noticed for the first time that she wore an engagement ring but no wedding ring on her finger. Margaret heaved a deep sigh, as if she were trying to prevent the tears flowing.

'Anyway, you've come here to settle this case of theft, not ask all these daft questions.'

'Sorry, Ms Hamer but I've got a pretty big interest in the whole Dolfadog family after what happened to Mrs Breeze-Evans.'

Suddenly Margaret released a laugh which turned into a heavy cough.

'If I'd known the old sow was roasting, I would have nipped down to Pool with some apple sauce. How was the crackling, Daf Dafis? Plenty of fat under her skin, wasn't there?'

Daf chose to ignore the ghoulish question. 'I'm not trying to be nosey at all, Ms Hamer, but if we are going to find out who set the place on fire, I need to know as much as I can of the family history.'

Margaret set herself down in an old-fashioned wooden chair which was missing an arm.

'Gruff's not much of a carpenter and I'm no better.'

One of the dogs let loose a bark from the far corner of the kitchen where they were fighting over some leftover gravy in a Fray Bentos meat pie tin which they'd pulled out of the recycling box.

'All this recycling is a load of nonsense,' Margaret declared, carefully aiming a copy of *Horse and Rider* magazine in the direction of the dogs. 'I saw a programme showing how they just ship the whole lot out to China and bury it in the ground there.'

'You're lucky up here, you can use the purple bags. We've got one of those wheelie bins which is nearly bigger than our yard.'

Margaret sucked in a mouthful of smoke and looked at Daf as she released it slowly. 'Oh yes, you've left Neuadd, haven't you? Stole John Neuadd's wife on your way out, they say.'

'Life's complicated sometimes.'

'That's true. I remember you coming here with your Uncle Mal on the van. No more than a little *cog* at the time, you were. Always had nice manners. Do you recall coming up here?'

'I never forget a lane with three gates on it, Ms Hamer.'

'Margaret, please. I hate this Ms business, sounds like a buzzing bee. And Miss Hamer sounds like a teacher, which I'm certainly not. You remember my mother, then?'

'I do indeed. She always praised my maths.'

'I remember her saying very often: 'He's a tidy little chap, is the *cog* from the shop. He's got a head on his shoulders.' Mum wasn't wrong that often. So, *cog* from the shop, I will tell you a bit of the history of the Dolfadog family, if you like.'

'It would be a great help. I have to know all I can about Heulwen's background.'

Margaret opened the drawer in the kitchen table and pulled out a half bottle of whisky. 'Certain you won't take a drop with me?'

'I'm working, sorry.'

'Hmm.'

She poured a generous measure into a dirty glass.

'My mother was from Llanwddyn. Descended from the famous Abraham Wood, you know.'

'I recall my Dad saying something like that.'

'Yes, but mind you, everyone calls gypsies "the family of Abraham Wood" but he was my I-don't-know-how-many-greats grandfather. Don't think for a moment I'm not very proud indeed of my mother's heritage: up in Llanwddyn, almost everyone's got a drop or two of gypsy blood in them; that, or they're descended from the navvies from Liverpool who built the dam. It's very different down here, everyone's alike, no one's any different at all.'

She filled her mouth with whisky.

'Heulwen was the same age as me, and she was a spiteful little bitch from the very start, since I was a little four-year-old girl at school. She used to ask me every day where my pegs were, if I lived in a caravan, encouraging all the others to bully me.'

'Children can be right cruel at times.'

She emptied the glass.

'You don't have enough time to hear old stories from an old woman, I'm sure, Inspector.'

'Take your time, Margaret. And why not call me Daf, if you like? Everyone else does.'

'I will, then. And are you sure I can't tempt you to take a little drop of this Scotch?'

'I'm right out of practice, sorry. If I had a mouthful, I'd fall asleep at my desk after dinner.'

'Oh yes, I forgot, you've got a little baby now, haven't you?'

'Indeed, and since having the others, I've got old.'

'Don't talk about getting old, *lanc*. Anyway, I was fine in school in the end, because of How. Heulwen had been spoilt rotten but How was a very tidy chap: fair-minded, generous and honest through and through. He was two years older than me. When I was ten, he was my best friend and by the time I was fifteen, I was head over heels in love with him. He went to college in Llysfasi after he left school and when he came back, we decided we loved each other.'

She closed her eyes for a moment as if she could retreat into the past.

'Heuls was not happy, to say the least of it. She had tantrum after tantrum, saying How deserved a better girlfriend, saying that everyone was discussing how much of a disgrace it would be to have a gypsy sitting at the head of the table at Dolfadog. A year went by and then another one. There was no reason for us to be impatient when we had the whole of the rest of our lives to look forward to living together.'

Daf thought of the image that Heulwen projected in pictures in *Plu'r Gweunydd*, no hint of foul temper or ugly racism. He was struck by the way in which Margaret's impressions chimed with what he had heard from Anwen, Rhys Bowen and the Dolfadog family themselves.

'Don't start thinking that How was weak, but he had to obey his father, and the old man was very influenced by Heulwen. She'd been keeping house for them since their mother died when she was thirteen and she was definitely the mistress of Dolfadog.'

'So what you're saying is that Heulwen tried to prevent you from marrying her brother?'

'Mum said we could put a caravan here, up in the orchard, and I shouldn't have minded at all starting our life together under the old damson trees, but How thought it would play into Heulwen's hands. "If we give way, she'll work on Dad till in the end, she'll end up with all that should be mine, given the work I do. We'd best just wait a bit longer," was what he said. Don't forget how young we were. How's Dad said that Heuls should marry first, to give her a chance, so that she didn't have to lose what he called "her place" as lady of the house. Years went by, we lambed, we harvested, took the cattle in for the winter and nothing changed, but on the morning of my twenty-seventh birthday, How took me up to the top of the *boncyn*. From the top up there, you can see the ground all laid out like a carpet, and Dolfadog right there in the centre. "We should be in that house by now, Mags," he said to me. "High time we gave the old man a bit of a shock. To tell the truth, it's high time I was a dad myself, knocking on nine and twenty like as I am." I bet you're thinking that you're wasting your precious time on the ramblings of a sad old lush, aren't you, Daf?'

'Listen, Margaret, if you're prepared to share your story, even though it's a sad one, you deserve a bit of fuel to keep you going.'

Margaret raised her glass in a toast.

'Fair play to you, *cog* from the shop. People say you're right good at your job and I think I'm starting to see why.'

'If people are willing to rake through their memories, I've got to respect how hard that can be.'

'I know how people talk about me, you know. I may be odd but I'm not blind or deaf. I'm a figure of fun, I know, the old spinster who wastes her life on horses because no man was ever willing to marry her. And I've always been an outsider, despite being born in the parish. But once upon a time, I had a chance of another life, a life which would have been totally different.'

'I'm sure. Often, when we look back, we can see the turning points, the moments when everything changed through some little thing.'

'No, you're wrong there. It wasn't anything small which changed my life but an enormous thing, a great tragedy.'

'Hywel's death?'

'I'm not one for weeping. I don't cry. I'll tell you the story as best as I can but if I ask you to go outside for a while, you will, won't you?'

'Of course.'

A dangerous glint came into her eye, as if revenge rather than mourning was on her mind.

'We wanted to put a bit of pressure on How's dad. It was How's idea at first but I agreed, all the way. Just after lambing, we went down to see the old bastard, hand in hand, to tell him that, wedding or no wedding, a baby was on its way. Something like that was a fair old shock in the 70s, you know, especially to a respectable family like the Breezes. To tell you the truth, the old man was fine about it, almost as if the scandal was wiped out by his eagerness to be a grandfather. He talked about renting a house in the village whilst he set about putting up a bungalow, for him, not us. "This baby's to be born in Dolfadog, that's for certain," he declared, and he repeated that over and over. Then the bitch came in, screaming about disgrace, gypsy tricks and the good name of the family, but the old man laughed and gave her a choice: find a husband quick or move with him, her dad, to the house in the village. I've never seen such a storm of temper but the next morning, she set out in earnest to find a husband.'

'Wasn't she a bit of a good catch in those days?'

Again, a mixture of coughing and laughter emerged from Margaret's mouth.

'Her? No chance. Her face wasn't ugly but she almost never smiled. And she had a name as a terrible bossyboots: she nearly killed the YFC club in the year she was chairman. But Phil Evans was convenient and a little bit innocent, for all he was the Casanova of the council houses in Llanfair Caereinion. "Heulwen Dolfadog won't be so full of herself now," my mother said, "not now she's picked her husband up off the yard." But nothing could dent Heulwen's view of herself.'

'Phil was working at Dolfadog then?'

'He was. A farm servant, twenty years old, eight years younger than her. He didn't stand any more chance than a moth stands with a candle. Anyway, a wedding was quickly sorted but on the night before the wedding, How was killed.'

'How did it happen?'

'Some of Phil's friends were mucking about, the old tradition of making mischief. They'd raised the cover of the well because they thought it would be funny to drop some raddle in, so that when the bride took her morning bath, the water would run red. They were all drunk and some of them hardly more than children. Heulwen went off her head, naturally. She didn't want her big day spoiled so she sent How out to deal with them. As he was trying to get them to stand back from the edge of the well, he slipped and fell in. He drowned.'

Daf recalled the story, which had been a talking point in Llanfair for months, but he'd not remembered the name of the farm where the tragedy occurred and had never known the connection with Margaret Tanyrallt. The tradition of pre-nuptial pranking had mercifully subsided though Daf recalled a lecture on Thomas Hardy in which these practices were praised for their authenticity. For Daf, mischief-making meant late-night callouts on summer Fridays to adjudicate farm-based fights between the bride's family and the groom's companions. Before his own wedding, four of Falmai's cousins had chained the main gate at Neuadd shut. John had wisely set his alarm for 4 a.m. and had begun the great day with a tour of the perimeter, armed with bolt-cutters and a loaded twelve-bore. The death of Hywel Dolfadog had passed into legend but it wasn't his tragic death which calmed things down: CCTV and the decline in home-based weddings had pushed into abeyance the tradition which was now characterised only by the occasional theatrical stunts marking the weddings of well-known YFC characters.

'I'm so sorry.'

'There's no call for you to be sorry. The woman who

stopped those dull lads calling the police or the fire brigade, she's the woman should be sorry. No fuss or scandal before my wedding, she declared, while her brother's lungs were bursting as he tried to escape. His poor fingers were all bloody from trying to climb up the damp concrete.'

Margaret lifted one of the terriers onto her lap and, after a long silence, she finished her story.

'So, instead of living in comfort with the man I loved at Dolfadog, my baby was born here, with my mum's help. He was a lovely little chap, the living image of his father. I never expected a penny from them. Heulwen chose to make things pleasant for me in her own special way: she went around confiding in her fifty best friends that the baby wasn't How's and of course, we couldn't get a paternity test done with the father being dead. But we got along and every day he grew more like How, which was the best thing in my life then. I went down to the cob sale in Llanybydder as usual, just before he turned three; he was running a bit of a temperature but nothing out of the ordinary. We only had the one vehicle then, the Land Rover which I'd taken to the sale. I set off early, leaving him with Mum but at about three, she phoned the auctioneers' office, because that was in the days before mobiles, to say that he was very sick indeed. The doctor wouldn't come out to see him, Mum couldn't take him anywhere without a car and he died in the ambulance on the way to the Shrewsbury hospital. Meningitis. And that was us, then. Mum broke her heart with the guilt of him dying in her care and I will never forgive myself for going away when he needed me. Of course, stuck as she was without a vehicle, Mum had phoned everyone she could think of for help: no one came. Heulwen was at home but too busy, she said, getting a finger buffet ready for a fundraiser for the *ysgol feithrin* that night. So there's our story for you and now we'd better have a look around the tack room.'

Dat reached out his hand to take hold of Margaret's brown hand. It was a simple enough gesture but it had a significant effect on her. Her wide shoulders started to shake beneath her boiler suit and several tears rolled down her cheeks. Then, as if deciding not to waste another moment on emotion, she pulled a rag from her pocket and, when she managed to find a corner which wasn't saturated with hoof oil, she blew her nose on it.

'That's enough of that. You know what, *cog* from the shop, I don't blame John Neuadd's wife one bit. There's something right nice about you.'

'I often get to hear sad stories in my line of work but this one's nothing short of tragic.'

'But look at me! I still get up in the morning to care for my stock, I still buy and sell, and only now and then, when someone makes me smile, I think about the other life I could have had. And I paid Heulwen back a bit by stealing one of her sons.'

'I don't get it.'

'Well, she had three sons and never gave one of them a bit of love or care. So when I saw Gruff loved his horses, I asked him to come up here to live. He's my heir, partner in the farm and we get along right well between us. Heuls wasn't best pleased, kicked off about kidnapping and who knows what, but he'd turned sixteen, so he could suit himself. Tack room?'

She rose stiffly to her feet, releasing Daf's hand.

'One small question. I know Jac and Gruff, but who did you mean by the third son? Is that how they describe Nansi's husband?'

'No: Cai. Don't say that the respectable folk at Dolfadog have forgotten him entirely?'

'Cai?'

Margaret laughed again as she opened the door.

'Heulwen wasn't getting praised quite enough, in her mind. She was the perfect mother, of course, but not yet a saint, so she decided to adopt a lad from over Wrexham somewhere. His mother was a junkie, in total contrast to the blessed Mrs Breeze-Evans.'

'Where is he now?'

Margaret waited until the last dog had followed them out before shutting the door

'You never knew Heulwen, did you?'

'I've met her but couldn't say I knew her. We were on the Board of Governors together for a while.'

'She had no patience, no sticking power. After a couple of years, she'd got bored of Cai. What was the expression she used? Oh yes: "The adoption has broken down." And off he went.'

'Where to?'

'Back into the system.' She bent down to pick up a small stone to aim at a crow which was perched on a post in the corner of the yard. It cawed and flapped away into the branches of the pines behind the house. She had a very good eye for a woman of her age, Daf observed.

'Do you know the history of these old Scots pines?' she asked.

'No.'

'In the days of the old drovers, they were a sign of welcome. If you notice, there's not a single pine by Dolfadog and there's a cold welcome there, now as ever. Cai got a cold welcome in the end, when all's said and done.'

'Do you know what happened to him after?'

'No idea. If I'm honest with you, I don't like to think about what happened to the lad, not when you consider the things we hear were happening to young people in children's homes in north Wales then. I offered to ... but never mind about that.'

'What's his surname?'

'Breeze-Evans, of course.'

'Yes, of course.'

They had reached the yard. At the end of a row of loose boxes with their upper half doors open there was a larger door with a heavy bolt on it. Hanging from the bolt was a heavy padlock which had been cut open.

'Somebody knew exactly what they were doing,' remarked Margaret.

'Yes, it's a tidy job,' Daf agreed, 'but these days, that doesn't necessarily mean experience: there are plenty of YouTube videos around to teach anyone the basics of theft.'

Daf opened the door fully without touching the latch.

'Don't worry about the fingerprints, we've been in and out any number of times since six this morning without thinking. Shouldn't think there's any evidence left worth collecting.'

Daf was secretly rather glad to hear this. If Daf had had to add the cost of a forensics team for Tanyrallt to all the money already being spent on the main investigation, someone down at HQ in Carmarthen was likely to blow a fuse. He stepped out of the sunshine into the tack room and saw a shape in the darkness. By now, Daf had seen way too much of that lad's arse. This time, he was wearing jodhpurs but they were pulled down around his calves. In front of him, kneeling on the concrete floor, was Clara the photographer. Daf went red and tried to step in between Margaret and the sordid scene.

'Why don't we just stay outside in this sunshine for a minute?' Daf mumbled, not even convincing himself.

An expression of mild boredom came over Margaret's face as if she had seen such things many times too often in the past. She followed Daf but paused in the doorway for a moment. She reached into her boiler-suit pocket and pulled out a packet of chewing gum, then, with an aim as true as when she had hit the crow with the stone, she threw the packet at Clara. The missile landed on the girl's shoulder and she raised her head, her large eyes clearly visible through the gloom, like some fawn with a guilty conscience. Margaret walked to the other end of the yard.

Daf had to say something. 'Is that Gruff's girlfriend?'

Margaret made a scornful sound.

'Girlfriend? She's been after him since he won the Chase Me Charlie in Berriew Show last year.'

Daf realised that he'd been lucky in coming across someone

who could translate from Polish for him, but this horsey language was confusing on a whole new level. He decided not to ask for an explanation; if it mattered, he could always rely on Google. Margaret lit another cigarette.

'Gruff's not to have a proper girlfriend, not yet. I don't want him and some girl to be waiting for me to go. If I keep on with these cancer sticks, Gruff'll be able to suit himself in five years. And don't you worry, *cog* from the shop, you can't be a member of the Welsh Pony and Cob Society for over forty years without seeing someone getting a quick blow job. Horse Hill in the Royal Welsh is like Sodom and Gomorrah: plenty of things as hard as the hats, I'm telling you.'

Daf had to laugh but he also thought of the contrast between Margaret's lively personality and her heartbreaking story. Her joking created in his mind an image of her relationship with Hywel Dolfadog, and he could imagine how bitter that loss had been. The eccentric spinster described by the gossips in the village was a woman with the potential for real happiness which had been darkened by tragic fate. By fate, or by Heulwen Breeze-Evans?

Purposefully, Margaret was showing the yard gate to Daf when Gruff came out of the tack room. Given his height, he couldn't exactly sneak away without being noticed, but he tried his best. He vanished into the barn without a word and they heard the sound of Clara's car starting. Margaret yelled after Gruff, 'Have a go at tidying them a bit, can you, Gruff?'

'OK.' His voice echoed from the zinc sheeting of the roof high above him.

Daf couldn't tell whose relationship struck him as more peculiar, the one between Margaret and her adopted son, or that between Gruff and his pony-loving fan-girl. He followed Margaret back into the tack room. She didn't say a word, but picked up the packet of gum from the shelf where the hats were kept: there were two pieces missing. She slipped the gum back into her pocket.

'Here's the medicine chest.'

On a high shelf, Daf saw an old-fashioned heavy wooden chest with a cross on it.

'It's a right handy box; Taid used it in the Home Guard.'

Daf sighed. 'No lock on it?'

'We lock the whole tack room. There's some nice bits of kit in here we've collected over the years, would cost a fair bit to replace.'

'And what's missing?'

'I got a bit of Anesketin in to help Dancing Princess, Dancing Girl's mother. She picked up a thorn in her pastern, just above her hoof,' she added, seeing the confused expression on Daf's face, 'and by now, it's gone a bit nasty and she's gone lame. Normally, I could sort something like that out easily myself but Dancing Girl is a bit of a prima donna; she won't let anyone near her when she's in pain. If I give her a shot of Anesketin and Rompun she'll sleep right through the whole treatment. She's too young to run lame. I want to take her down to be served by a very smart stallion down in Pembrokeshire and she'll have to be on top form for the journey down.'

'How much did you have?'

'A small bottle, 50 ml, I think. The vet would know for certain.'

'And the Rompun's still there?'

'Yes.'

'Well, that probably rules out a thief of Puerto Rican origin, as they're the boys mad for Rompun,' Daf couldn't help saying, showing off rather.

Margaret narrowed her eyes for a moment. 'The thief is way more likely to come from Pontrobert than Puerto Rice so please don't talk shit, *cog* from the shop.'

'Fair enough.'

She'd seen through his instinctive desire to display his obscure knowledge and had called him out on it. She was a very observant woman, not to be underestimated.

'Have you seen enough? Because I've any amount of work to do, including getting down to the vet to sort out some more Anesketin, amongst other things.'

'Yes, thank you, I have. Did you hear anything in the night?'

'No, but I've gone a bit deaf lately. I went to bed about eleven and slept soundly till five: that's what you get if you've got a clear conscience.'

'Good. I want a word with Gruff, then I'll get back to the station to have a look through what data we have on file. Usually, we've got a pretty good idea which person in the area tends to take what drug but this Special K has come into fashion so recently that many people we've got down as users of coke or speed may well have turned to ketamine by now.'

'You really don't need to flash your jargon about to convince me that you know your business, Daf. What about the Section As?'

'They were the only ones damaged?'

'Yes. Gruff's hunter was in the same field but they didn't touch that ugly great bugger. He's a good weight bearer with some bit of go in him but he's got a head like a Tyrannosaurus Rex. It's as though whoever hurt them knew which were the best.'

'I hate to ask this question, Margaret, but was there anyone, in the horse world, maybe, who was jealous of you? Someone who resented your success, perhaps?'

Her solid body shook like a jelly as she doubled up with laughter. It took over a minute for her to get over her chuckling but to Daf's experienced ear, there was a slight note of hysteria in the sound.

'Are you asking if I've got any enemies? I've been breeding, showing and judging horses for over half a century: of course there are going to be some people who bear a grudge against me. Judges do get a bit of flak, every single time they refuse a red rosette to some boss-eyed monster who would shame a donkey class.'

'I understand that, but are there any names in particular which spring to mind?'

The humour vanished from Margaret's eyes.

'The only person nasty enough to hurt my Section As died in a fire in Welshpool on Monday night. If I have to name any particular enemy, the only one I can think of is Heulwen Breeze-Evans. I'd stolen something she thought belonged to her and she could never forget a thing like that.'

Under the weak light of the only working lightbulb in the barn, Gruff was doing his best with one of the ponies, a grey with huge, long-lashed eyes. His fingers were moving gently over the creature's soft skin and he was speaking to it in a low, tender voice.

'Don't you worry, *del*, you'll be fine in a couple of weeks, you just trust me.'

With little scissors and a metal comb, he was trying to improve the appearance of the ragged mane; her tail now looked short but not so untidy. Daf began to see why a girl like Clara might have some interest in him: Gruff might not be the most sparkling personality in the world but as he smoothed his hand over the pony's withers, there was something almost painstakingly tender about him. And his love for the animal was so obvious. In Daf's experience, some girls went for obsessional men in the hope that one day they might be the subject of their obsessional interest.

'Well, Gruff,' Daf began. 'What do you think?'

Gruff raised his head without pausing in his caressing of the pony. 'Well, Mr Dafis. Fucking stupid thing to do.'

'Any idea who did it?'

'Some nut job.'

'Anyone out there who doesn't like Margaret?'

'Apart from Heulwen, I can't think of anyone. And she's out of the picture by now.'

'I hate to say it, lad, but you don't sound too heartbroken when you speak about your mother. The rest of the family got together yesterday to talk about the investigations and about arrangements for the funeral, and you decided not to turn up, even though you only live over the brook.'

'I didn't do much with her, tell the truth, Mr Dafis. Dad comes up often enough with a six-pack of Carling to watch the telly with us but I only used to run into her by chance, Heulwen.'

'You call her Heulwen not Mum?'

Gruff closed his eyes for a moment.

'Margaret, she's been my Mum for ages, Mr Dafis. I've almost forgotten what it was like to live at Dolfadog.'

'Happy family?'

'Busy family.'

'What about Cai?'

Gruff spat. 'One of Heulwen's schemes, pulling that little fucker into our home, just so people could say how nice she was. And look how that worked out. The apple doesn't fall very far from the tree, Mr Dafis, not very often anyway.'

'What happened to him?'

'No idea. Prison, I should hope. He should have been killed for what he did to Nans.'

For the first time, Daf saw some strength in Gruff's eyes, something like the look in Milek's eyes when he was talking about Basia.

'What did Cai do to Nansi?' Daf asked.

'It's ancient history, Mr Dafis. It's not fair to Nans to discuss it, not after all this time.'

'Listen *cog*, your mum is dead and it looks as if it wasn't accidental. From what I hear, things weren't always easy in your family.'

'It's not *my* family, Mr Dafis. Tanyrallt's my home and Margaret is my family. I couldn't give a shit about the rest of them.'

'Even Nansi?'

Gruff folded his arms across his chest in a defensive

gesture. 'She's been gone a long time, down to Cardiff with that fucking God botherer.'

'Her husband?'

'Yes, him.'

'I take it you're not a big fan of his, Gruff?'

'I hate all that shit. Sunday School and Thou Shalt Not. Making people live their whole lives looking over their shoulders trying to please some fucking skyfairy.'

'But that's not how Nansi sees it?'

'She was escaping, Mr Dafis, like every one of us. I was lucky, I didn't have to go to the other end of Wales to make a new life for myself.'

'What would Nansi have been escaping from, *lanc*?'

'All the shit at Dolfadog. And that little bastard as well.'

'Cai?'

'His name wasn't Cai, Mr Dafis. He was Kyle but that wasn't Welsh enough for Heulwen so Kyle lost his 'l' and ended up totally losing the plot as well.'

'What went on between him and Nansi?'

'Nothing went on between them! How can anything happen between a tidy *lodes* and a lump of fucking shit?'

'It's clear you're still angry about it.'

'Of course I'm angry, but I'm not going to talk about it. You'll have to ask Nans if you want to hear about it but it's got fuck all to do with the fire on Monday night.'

'We'll see about that. Back to what happened last night. Do you know anyone who uses ket?'

Gruff laughed and resumed his brushing of the pony's neck.

'No, Mr Dafis, but every pothead in Llanfair has asked me lately if I've got a supply. We don't use it that often. Felicity says she could make more selling K than what she earns from being a vet.'

'Felicity?'

Gruff went rather red. 'Friend of mine. She's a vet. Some heck of a tidy girl.'

'As tidy as Clara?'

'Mr Dafis, the horses draw the women, and I'm too young to settle.'

'And these ladies, are they happy with the situation?'

'If the girl's got any romantic ideas, she can go elsewhere. If a bit of fun is on the agenda, they know where to find me.'

'Fair play. So you haven't broken any girl's heart? Any girl who would know exactly which of the Tanyrallt ponies were the best?'

Gruff shuffled from one foot to the other as he started to rub the other side of the pony's neck. Confusion rather than guilt seemed to be clouding his eyes.

'Mr Dafis, there isn't a girl on the face of this earth who would do anything at all because of her feelings for me. I'm like … well, like a climbing frame or a trampoline, something that stays in one place where they can go to for a bit of fun. Bounce, bounce and off they go.'

It was an unfortunate comparison. Daf admired his honesty but Gruff's ideas didn't quite ring true in the experience of the romantic policeman. As far as Daf had observed, women who could enjoy a man's body without any emotional link at all were thin on the ground. In fact, Daf had only ever met one woman with an attitude like that in his entire life: Chrissie Berllan. It might well be that Gruff had broken some girl's heart without realising.

'And you can't think of anyone with a reason to want to injure Margaret, you said?'

'No one in particular. The Gilchrists from Carmarthenshire are always bollocksing on about the bad bargain they got when Margaret bought Lady Fair off them. She's Dancing Girl's grand dam but if they weren't savvy enough to realise the potential of a filly like her, well, should've gone to Specsavers, as they say, Mr Dafis. They didn't like the set of her ears, the fuckwits.'

'Well, if anything crosses your mind, pick up the phone, will you?'

'I will, Mr Dafis.'

Driving down the lane, Daf realised how much he had learnt in just over an hour at Tanyrallt. Margaret's tragic history, an interesting depiction of the family at Dolfadog and the finer points of top quality 'Section A' Welsh Mountain Ponies. But he still had no idea about the Chase Me Charlie business. And he had learnt about the existence of Cai.

Like many farms in the area, there was no mobile phone signal at all at Tanyrallt so when Daf drove over the second cattle grid, several beeps were heard from his pocket. He had four missed phone calls and two texts, one from Huw Mansell and the other from Chrissie. He clicked on Dr Mansell's message first:

'Daf. Gaenor's got mastitis, she fainted in Ti a Fi. I've sent her home with some strong antibiotics but if she's not better later, we'll have to take her in for IV. Mrs Humphries is looking after her and little Mali.'

Daf instantly felt full of guilt. It had been obvious that morning that Gaenor was ill, even Rhodri had noticed. But he'd had to go off to work, being an important man, as if his job were more important than everything else in the world. Even more important than Gaenor's health. He had a strange feeling in his chest as if a cold hand were squeezing his heart. He read the second message:

'Mr Dafis. Gae was right poorly so I took her home. Call by when you're free.'

Daf drove back to Llanfair like a man in a deep sleep. Outside his house was the big black pick-up from Berllan, with three rolls of chain link fencing in the back. Daf opened his front door, totally unprepared for the scene before him. Sitting comfortably on the sofa, feet up and a large glass of water by her elbow, was Chrissie, her shirt open to her waist, feeding a baby in a white Babygro. But at her feet in their colourful little seats, sleeping deeply, were her twin boys.

'Chrissie!'

'Oh hello, Mr Dafis. Gae's sleeping.'

Ever since he'd first met Chrissie, Daf had entertained a number of fantasies involving her breasts but never in a context like this. He stared, unable to say a word, as Chrissie transferred his daughter to her other breast.

'What a nice-looking girl she is,' Chrissie remarked in a conversational tone. 'Just like her handsome dadi.'

Daf remembered the expression he'd often heard from people who had experimented with some new drug: 'It wrecked my head, Mr Davies.' That was a perfect description of his current condition, he thought. His head had been totally wrecked by the vision of Chrissie, who just happened to be the sexiest woman he had ever met, feeding his baby with those breasts which had so often preoccupied him. He wasn't just confused, he couldn't cope. Daf decided, as he often did, to hide behind humour.

'I know I'm no expert, Chrissie, but I think you're feeding the wrong baby.'

# Chapter 10

## *Thursday afternoon, April 14, 2016*

Daf attempted not to gaze at the creamy flesh above his little daughter's head but he couldn't manage that level of restraint.

'No, no, Mr Dafis, I can tell the difference between this little lady and those ruffians there. But that's the problem, Mr Dafis; Mali *fech* is too dainty to empty Gae and that's when the bloody milk fever kicks in.'

'But why are you feeding her, Chrissie?'

'Fair play to Doctor Mansell, he's been great and the health visitor came over with a little pump to help but it was heckish painful to use so then we had another idea. The *cogie* are always hungry, so after feeding Mals, Gaenor gave them their dinner a bit early. I'm telling you, Mr Dafis, they emptied her right out in five minutes and she felt grand after: she went straight to sleep. She needs a tidy rest so when little Miss *Fech* woke up early, I gave her a little snack so her mum can get herself better.'

Daf collapsed down in the armchair. By his feet, Chrissie's twin sons slept, two lumps of snuffling contentment.

'Don't say that I've given you a fright, Mr Dafis,' Chrissie commented as she buttoned up her shirt with a teasing and unnecessary slowness. 'I would have thought it was pretty hard to shock you, at least with my clothes on.'

Daf tried to laugh but nothing came out of his mouth.

'It's just a practical thing, Mr Dafis, that's all. You look as if you'd walked in and found Gae and me in bed together.'

'But,' Daf ventured, in an uncertain voice, trying to suppress the very interesting image Chrissie had just planted deliberately in his mind, 'it's such a personal thing...'

'Oh *twt lol*, Mr Dafis,' Chrissie dismissed as she lifted Mali onto her shoulder to efficiently dispose of her wind. 'The trouble with you men is that you can't understand that our boobs have a useful purpose: they're not just toys for you to play with – which is grand, of course, but you can't understand the other side.'

'I've never heard of such a thing.'

Chrissie did up her final button and Daf had to admit that he felt an almost physical shiver of disappointment.

'Not everything gets talked about, Mr Dafis. Forget about it. After dinner, you get yourself back to work; I'll stop here with Gae until teatime, whenever.'

'Thank you for being so kind, Chrissie.'

'Go up and see Gae, Mr Dafis, I'll get a bit of dinner for you.'

'There's no need for you to do any such thing, Chrissie. You're not a maid in this house, you know.'

Chrissie winked as she shoved Daf towards the stairs.

'What a shame, eh? Because the master always takes shocking advantage of the poor little maid, and I'd enjoy that no end.'

Upstairs, Gaenor was looking better, even in her sleep. The hectic colour had left her cheeks, and when Daf touched her hand, she was warm rather than hot. He sat on the bed to watch her sleep. He stroked her soft hair; her forehead was still rather damp. She turned over in her sleep and the duvet slipped off. As Daf pulled it back into place, she opened her eyes.

'Daf? What time is it?'

'Lunchtime. How are you?'

'Feeling a lot better, thanks to the antibiotics and Chrissie.'

Daf was very reluctant to broach the subject of the feeding but he didn't want there to be any conversational no-go areas.

'Hmm. I've heard about your ... strategy and seen it for myself as well.'

Gaenor grinned from ear to ear.

'I was fiddling about with that bloody little pump and it hurt like hell. The Health Visitor said Mali wasn't drinking all the milk I'm making and I need to be really empty if I'm going to shake this fever off. Those Berllan boys are like little Dysons: I fed Mali while Chrissie was feeding them, then I gave them a bit of a top-up.'

'Please stop talking about it, Gae, and when you're better, let's never ever mention it again.'

Gaenor started to laugh, and from the kitchen, the smell of cooking onions and bacon filled the little house.

'Don't be so ungrateful, Daf; Chrissie's making your dinner now and she's promised to stay until the children get home from school.'

'I'll ring Carys, she'll come and help.'

'Don't trouble her. At the rate things are going, I'll be better before she can get a chance to come here.'

'We'll see, shall we? And Gae, I'm so sorry I went into work today. I knew you weren't well but I still went. If you're prepared to forgive me this once, I promise that I'll never neglect you like that again.'

'Don't be daft, Daf, of course you had to go into work.'

'Mr Dafis!' Chrissie's voice was as loud as if she was calling over a fifty-acre field, which, of course, she often did.

'I won't be late back, I promise.'

'I've only got a touch of milk fever, Daf, not Ebola. Get a grip, please, especially in front of Chrissie.'

There was an omelette waiting for him on the kitchen table.

'There's not a lot of food in the house, Mr Dafis. No meat at all.' She reached for Daf's arm and squeezed it above the elbow. 'And not half enough meat on you, either,' she pronounced.

Daf had to compare himself then with Chrissie's husband Bryn, who had firm banks of muscle under his tight T-shirts and arms like the trunks of smooth, strong beech trees.

'I'll get that freezer filled for you if you like,' she offered.

'You're doing too much for us as it is, Chrissie. And don't worry about me wasting away: the opposite is true. I've put on half a stone since coming to live here.'

'And, fair play to you, you've made a right tidy little family here, and I get to scan at Neuadd.'

'What?'

'John Neuadd has booked me, right early, to scan all his ewes, and to do his cattle later on in the year.'

'Watch yourself, Chrissie: he's always fancied you and now that he's single...'

Chrissie laughed loudly.

'I don't think Bryn needs to lose any sleep in case I run off with John Neuadd. Anyway, how's the murder case going? Who killed the old bitch?'

'You didn't like her?'

'She and that ... that simpleton Car Wat tried to interfere in my planning application, saying that they didn't think Berllan was a suitable place for a garage, the fuckers. I got my permission in the end but no thanks to them.'

'Why did they oppose it? Heulwen was always talking about supporting rural business.'

'Oh dear Mr Dafis,' Chrissie said and Daf couldn't help watching her sharp little teeth as she finished her slice of bread and butter, 'she always said whatever suited her at the time and she'd very often actually do something totally different.'

Daf got to his feet. 'Thank you so much for all your help, Chrissie, you've been great.'

'You've never given me a chance to show you just how great I can be, Mr Dafis. You'll have a cup of tea before you go?'

'I've got to go, heckish busy down at the station.'

'Get off, then.' She put her hand in the small of his back to push him towards the front door, as if he had just said that he was reluctant to go, rather than the other way around. 'Oh, and I bet you Rhys Bowen didn't do it.'

'How can you be so sure?'

'Killing someone on the sly isn't Rhys's style. It'd be a different matter if he was being accused of thumping someone outside a pub or something like that, but nothing like this.'

'So you're a bit of a Bowen fan then?'

'Well, he's a fair-looking chap despite carrying so much timber, and you know what they say about it being handy to have a bit of cushion for pushing. And he's a butcher who always gives a good price for fat lambs being sold by a girl in a low-cut top. What's not to like, Mr Dafis?'

Daf was laughing all the way down to the station, delighted to be able to concentrate, knowing he had left Gaenor in safe hands.

Bad news awaited him in the station. Sheila stood in the reception area with a less than cheerful look on her face.

'Can you phone Puw straightaway, boss?'

'What's up?'

'He didn't say.'

The tone of the Deputy Chief Constable's voice made it all clear. 'Dafydd, I've had a good few favourable reports thus far.'

'Glad to hear it, sir, the team are working like I don't know what,' Daf replied, trying to avoid the 'but' he could hear in the senior officer's voice.

'But we haven't seen half enough evidence to justify a warrant to search Rhys Bowen's factory, let alone his home. He's a Welsh Assembly member, you know.'

'I know that, sir. I also know he had plenty of reasons to hate Heulwen Breeze-Evans.'

'Please, Dafydd, don't say anything about the old copper's hunch. What exactly were you looking for?'

'Evidence to confirm that Heulwen was blackmailing him.'

'Well, you can't get that evidence by warrant because we won't even start the process of applying. You've got no reason to suspect him of concealing anything: he's co-operated thus far. If you want something, ask him first. If he refuses, I would consider putting your application before of a magistrate.'

'Has Mostyn Gwydyr-Gwynne been in to see you, sir?'

'Since this investigation started, you could think I was

auditioning for a Cardiff edition of *Question Time*: I've had everybody short of Charlotte Church through my door. Yesterday, the Lib Dem leader rang to remind us to pay some attention to their candidate. I think they'd rather we arrested him than ignored him.'

'For God's sake! I haven't spoken to UKIP yet, or the Greens and...'

'I was joking, Dafydd. But if you reckon any Jack or Jill in a suit can come into my office and tell me how to run an investigation into a serious crime, you don't know me very well at all.'

'OK, sir, I get it.'

'Once more unto the breach, Dafydd.'

He put the phone down.

'Fuck.'

'Well, that's a very nice welcome!'

Inspector Meirion Martin from North Wales Police was standing in the doorway, a fat file in his hand.

'Mei? What are you doing down here?'

'Apart from checking that you are as ugly in life as you were on the news the other night, *cont*? I was passing through and wanted to catch up with the acting Chief. And I believe you may have tripped over a bit of information on a property fraud we've been working on. I'm more than happy to buy you something to eat, especially since I don't need to worry about you choosing anything too expensive, not in this tuppenny ha'penny little place.'

'Sori, Mei, but the sexiest woman in a fifty miles radius has just cooked me an omelette. Coffee?'

'Oh, there's a Montgomeryshire man's fantasy for you: hot stuff standing right by the stove. Come on, you can tell me how it's going, you look as though you might need to cry on your old uncle Mei's shoulder?'

'This politics lark is driving me off my head, I feel like I'm walking on eggshells all the time. And Gaenor's ill as well.'

'Nothing too serious, I hope?'

'No, but I just wish I could take a couple of days off to look after her.'

Ten minutes later, Meirion was sprawled over the sofa upstairs in the Bay Tree, trying to decide between a chicken sandwich and an afternoon tea.

'I'll make the effort to seem healthy and go for the sandwich. Come on, *washi*, I want to hear the whole story.'

An hour in Meirion's company was a tonic to Daf. He managed to get his perspective back: even if he couldn't see the big picture, he could at least follow Meirion's sensible advice. 'Don't try to understand everyone, get back to the old Cluedo methods: how, when and who.'

Back at the station, Daf surprised Sheila by his lack of ill-temper. 'Sheila, I found a picture in one of the envelopes. It's still in the bag, I think.'

'I saw it. It's from the *Plu*.'

'I want to know the history of the fourth child. He was adopted by the Dolfadog family but they sent him back into the care system.'

'What's his name?'

'Cai, or Kyle, Breeze-Evans. But it's highly possible that he's gone back to using his original name.'

'Sure. Gutted about the warrant.'

'Don't worry. Bowen's an odd man. Who knows, if I ask him straight out for the evidence, he may just hand it over to me.'

'Tom and I were chatting last night. Tom's done business with Bowen for decades and he says he's straight as a die. A good man at getting a bargain but he never deceives anyone.'

'Ah, but Tom doesn't know about the contents of the safe. We can say for certain that Bowen is straight but can we really say he never deceives anyone?'

Sheila went red. 'I did tell Tom and he asked a question which I thought was a heckish good point: did any one of those ladies expect anything more from Bowen than they got?'

'Mmm. Some of them were professionals, so to speak, but there were lots of women who might expect a bit more from a relationship than a bit of nocturnal gymnastics. There were a couple of teachers in that group.'

'And a woman I know from Rotary: she's an accountant. Shall I ask her what it means to be involved with Bowen?'

'If you can. But remember, she may not know about all the others. And send Nia over to Dolfadog to ask the family about Cai.'

'Right. I rang Father Hogan, he's not available until six tonight. He's doing something called "Preparing Children for their First Holy Communion".'

'OK. If you see Nev, can you ask him to pop in?'

Settled at his desk, Daf glanced at the clock. High time to ring the pathologist. With sweaty palms, Daf picked up the phone but he needn't have worried, Jarman was in an affable frame of mind.

'Good to hear from you, young Dafydd. It wasn't possible for me to contact you earlier: pressure of work, you know.'

'Of course, Dr Jarman.'

'And I have some significant information to share with you, Dafydd. Do you have a biro and a piece of paper?' The pathologist's tone was like that of a teacher preparing a Year Two pupil for a not terribly important test.

'Yes, Dr Jarman.'

'Cause of death, inhalation of smoke. No surprise there.'

'Oh, right.'

'But why did she sit still in her chair as the fire was strengthening? There's no evidence that she made any effort whatever to escape. Well, that passivity was caused by the ketamine in her bloodstream.'

'Ketamine?'

'Considering the condition of the body, it's difficult to be as exact as I would like but I would say that she'd taken between 1.5 and 2 grams of the drug. From the condition of her bladder, she was not a regular user. She took the ketamine intravenously by injection into a vein in the lower arm, not the action of someone who was unfamiliar with drug use. Her skin had deteriorated too much to reveal an entry point but it was visible in the subcutaneous flesh of her wrist.'

'So when the fire was being set, she was in the K-hole?'

'She would have been under significant influence, yes. Did she have a history of drug use?'

'Anti-depressants. Nothing else, as far as I know.'

'So why did she decide to take a shot of K? And to administer it in such a manner as to guarantee maximum influence? That is the puzzle for you, young Dafydd.'

'Thank you very much, Dr Jarman.'

'One other thing. I can't be one hundred per cent certain, because of the way in which the skin had burnt, but it's possible that she had an injury to her cheek, an injury which would be consistent with a slap to the face.'

'From what I hear, there were many people keen on giving her a slap.'

'That is your business, of course. My report will be on your desk by the weekend.'

'Thank you once again, Dr Jarman.'

'I'm doing my job. You make sure you fulfil your obligations as well, young Dafydd.'

'I'll try, sir.'

The K-hole. Sometimes users of ket reach a condition where they lose all control of their bodies, are unable to move or speak, yet remain fully conscious. No wonder Heulwen couldn't move. Injecting straight into a vein makes it more likely for a user to fall into the K-hole. How much had Heulwen known about the drug she used?

Daf rang Nev. 'You remember the little bottles you found in the car, Nev? Were they ketamine?'

'I've not been able to clear that with the vet. I've rung half a dozen times, left a good few messages.'

'Which surgery? Four Crosses or Welshpool?'

'Severnside, Welshpool.'

Daf was on his way out through the front door of the station when a short man pushed in past him, his pink face full of fury.

'You're the boss bloke?' he asked, in a flat, accentless type of English which sounded as though every trace of individuality had been squeezed out of it.

'I'm Inspector Dafis, yes.'

'And I'm Brian Clarke, UKIP candidate. Is it true that tonight's hustings is going to be cancelled?'

'I'm afraid I have no idea.'

'Obviously the Nash woman is dead, but why has Bowen pulled out?'

'Really not my department,' Daf replied, though he himself would have been able to understand Bowen's reasons.

'It should be here tonight, in the Town Hall, and with immigration being such an issue, we should get a good crowd.'

'Like I say, it's really not my department but live and let live is always a good rule, I find.'

'With migrants filling our towns? Making our own language a rarity in our schools?'

Daf had to respond to this, even though he knew the best thing would have been to keep his mouth firmly shut. 'Oh, don't worry, Mr Clarke, we're fine with you. We've got used to you, in fact. Some of you even make a contribution. I have to go now.'

Daf gave the candidate a courteous smile as he left him standing in the doorway, open-mouthed. A moment later, Clarke came scampering after him across the car park and stood between Daf and his car.

'What do you mean by that? I'm not an immigrant, my family have lived in Yorkshire for generations.'

'Yes, but you're not in Yorkshire now, are you, Mr Clarke?

And that makes you a newcomer here just like our friends from Poland and the Philippines. Live and let live, eh?'

Ten minutes later, Daf was sitting in the vet's waiting room with about ten other people with dogs, cats, hamsters and budgies in cages or carriers on their laps. Behind the desk was a familiar face, a woman from Meifod who had a girl the same age as Carys.

'Hello, Wendy. How's college suiting Mared by now?'

'She's got settled at last. It's a big change for them, isn't it? Oh, I forgot, Carys didn't go in the end, did she?'

There was a triumphant note in her voice, and, despite being the least competitive parent in the world, Daf took pure delight in saying, 'Well, you don't just wander into a conservatoire with a UCAS form, you know. It'll take her a good year to be properly trained for the auditions.'

'Of course, you must be so proud of her.'

'It's what she wants, which is the main thing. Wendy, I do need to see one of the vets as soon as possible, it's an urgent case.'

'Of course. Sit down here and I'll fetch one of them for you now.'

Daf sat by the desk, reading a poster on the effect of worms. He felt something by his foot and glanced down to see a little pug jumping onto it.

'He really likes you,' said the owner, a rather self-satisfied looking woman in her sixties.

Daf didn't really get this pet business. Here was this woman, for example, of perfectly respectable appearance, allowing her dog to hump the feet of perfect strangers. He considered raising his shoe and kicking the cheeky little bastard away but he knew from experience that such an action wouldn't go down all that well, so he tried to ignore it.

At length, one of the white doors opened and a man emerged with a python wrapped around his neck like a scarf.

The man appeared to be irritated, the python coolly indifferent.

'It's a fooking disgrace not to have a herpetological specialist in such a big practice.'

Following him out of the consulting room was a tall red-headed young woman in a white coat, her professional patience visible on her face.

'I'm sorry you've been disappointed with your consultation, Mr Harper. You're very welcome to seek a second opinion, of course, but it I were you, I would just try warming up Dolores's cage by, say, five degrees and see how she feeds then. And do give the frozen mice a try, most people find them very convenient.'

'You don't know fook all about pythons, you don't.'

Her smile did not fail her for a moment. As Mr Harper and Dolores the python left, Wendy approached the young vet to explain Daf's errand.

'Please come in for a moment, Mr Dafis.'

Daf smiled as he obeyed. As he passed her, he noticed her badge: 'Felicity Jones, Assistant Veterinary Surgeon'. Was this the friend of Gruff Dolfadog who had remarked that she could earn more selling ket than by being a vet? She was certainly attractive enough to arouse Gruff's interest. In Daf's opinion, Clara the photographer would be well out of her league if she were to consider herself to be in competition with the willowy young vet.

'How can I help you, Inspector?' she asked, in the kind of accent Daf associated with the children of families where not a word of Welsh was spoken at home but the children had, nonetheless, been educated though the medium of Welsh.

'I know you will have heard about the serious fire in the town on Monday night.'

'Yes, of course.'

'In the course of the investigation, we've come across three bottles of medicine which originally came from this surgery. The bottle numbers are here for you to check.'

Daf pushed a piece of paper over the desk towards her. She didn't glance at the piece of paper but gave her response in an uncertain voice, 'I know where this stuff came from. From my bag. On Monday night, I was on my way back home from a long day's TB testing down in Minsterley, and I bumped into a friend. We went to the bistro for a bit of tapas. I completely forgot about the three bottle of Anesketin in my bag. I don't always carry the stuff but I was expecting to go and see a mare first thing the following morning who might need a C-section to have her foal.'

'Did you lock your car and put the controlled drugs in the glove compartment?' Felicity went red, which Daf thought rather suited her. 'Oh dear. You know the rules. Substances like ketamine have to be in a secure, concealed place. Was there a sign in the window at all?'

'Vet on Call.'

'*Nefi blw, lodes*! You really haven't helped yourself, have you?'

'But I always feel so safe in Welshpool.'

'You've broken enough rules to warrant a prosecution, but you know that perfectly well. You could lose your licence to practise and this surgery could be banned from holding controlled drugs.'

She bowed her head in evident shame. 'I know.'

'Have you been in touch with the controlled drugs link officer?'

'No.'

Well, bloody hell, *lodes*, have you done anything at all about the matter? When the drugs register is checked, the thing will become obvious straightaway. Are you sure you lost this ket, rather than sold it?'

Her face by now was white, her green-blue eyes appearing to double in size with fear.

'I totally panicked. Meltdown, no idea what to do. A policeman rang, asking about the bottles, and I told Wendy to refer any questions like that straight to me and that I would get back to him, but I didn't. My friend suggested that I find out the next time the register was due to be checked so we knew how much time we'd got to make a plan.'

'I've got to ask, are you one hundred per cent sure it wasn't your friend who stole the stuff?'

'Positive. He was with me in the bistro and then, when we went to back to the car, I saw the bag was gone.'

'Why did he go to your car? Doesn't he have a car of his own?'

'It was a nice evening so we fancied going for a spin. And he's got a short-wheel-based Land Rover, an old Defender.'

Daf by now had no doubt as to the identity of Felicity's 'friend' and he doubted that sightseeing would be the intention of any car trip Gruff would have taken with the pretty young vet.

'And you can't get any courting done in a Defender, eh?'

'You can't get any talking done, it's so noisy.'

'Where do you live, Felicity?'

'I've got a flat in Glanmenial, the country house near Berriew. It's very nice.'

'Why didn't you take your boyfriend back to your flat?'

'There are three of us sharing, which is ideal if you want a game of Monopoly but it cuts down on the privacy.'

'Hmm. And did you manage, the two of you, to cook something up to explain the disappearance of the ket?'

'Not at once. But, total coincidence, someone broke into the tack room at my friend Gruff's home last night. He had a brainwave. If I wrote him a prescription for three extra bottles and backdated it, he could pretend that the ket had been stolen from them, not me.'

'Oh great! Conspiracy to pervert the course of justice now!'

Her pale face was wet with her streaming tears by now but she was managing to hold back her sobs and attempting to speak clearly. There was no double bluff in her distress, Daf judged.

'Please. I know how stupid I've been, but it was only a mistake.'

'I hope you've learnt your lesson, that's all, *lodes*. To turn to the other matter, when you were out and about in town on Monday night, did you notice anything strange or unusual?' Daf was certain he wouldn't be prosecuting Felicity for her carelessness but didn't want her to be too certain, not when he wanted her to rack her brains for information which might help him.

'When?'

'Anytime but especially when you were on your way to the bistro and while you were there.'

'Oh, sorry not to be able to help, sir. We were a bit caught up in each other.'

'I get it.'

'No you don't. We're not in a relationship, Gruff and I, we're friends. I was concerned about one of the other girls, one who didn't understand the rules.'

'What rules?'

'He's not supposed to settle yet so there's no point in him seriously courting, as you put it, with anyone. Most people we know, the cob people, understand that very well.'

Daf recalled his discussion with Margaret Tanyrallt and Gruff's description of himself as a trampoline.

'But?'

'Well, he agreed to let some girl take his picture and she's been running after him since...'

'Since the Chase Me Charlie at Berriew Show?'

'Yes. Were you there? He was just flying, wasn't he?'

'So I heard.'

'I just wanted to make sure that this photographer understood the game, in case she ended up getting hurt, so we needed to have a proper talk. But, now you mention it, there was one unusual thing I noticed.'

'What was that?'

'We were sitting in the window of the bistro and a man walked past, a little thin man with a dreadful colour to his face, like he was really ill, or taking something. He reminded me of the man who'd tried to sell us a copy of the *Big Issue* when we went to see a film in Wrexham last week. I'd been about to give him some money, because he did look so bad, but Gruff said, head in his phone as ever, that I'd make things worse by giving him money because he'd spend it all on drugs. I'm sure it was him who walked past the window of the bistro but there was something different about him from a week ago, he was wearing a very fancy pair of trainers.'

For two people who weren't together, Gruff and Felicity seemed to spend a lot of time in each other's company, Daf thought, trying not to think about the scene he had inadvertently witnessed in the tack room.

'I don't suppose you remember what kind of trainers?'

'I've got a teenage brother, Mr Dafis, and he's mad on his brands, worse than any girl I've ever known. High-end Nikes they were, at least a hundred pounds' worth, which is strange for a man selling the *Big Issue* the week before.'

Daf recalled the conversation outside the church when MacAleese's grandson had expressed his envy of the trainers worn by the young man who'd spent the night at the presbytery. And he suddenly recalled where he had seen that thin face before. In his imagination, Daf put a woolly hat on his head and hung a heavy coat over his narrow shoulders: Cai.

'Thank you for your co-operation, Ms Jones. Don't lose too much sleep about this ket: I can't see there's much reason at all for the authorities to go after you. We'll have another chat about that again and in the meantime, you can tell anyone who asks that I'm investigating the break-in at Tanyrallt, because I am, OK?'

'Right.'

She held out her hand for Daf to shake. It was cool and elegant with a touch of firmness which contrasted with her anxious, teary face. Unjustifiably, Daf felt that Gruff Tanyrallt, sulky and venal, didn't deserve to be touched by such fingers.

The look on Sheila's face told Daf that her investigations had been successful. She handed Daf a photograph and notes from the prison archive in Shrewsbury.

'Kyle Holland, also going by the name Cai Evans, twenty-seven years old. He went straight from the care system into a young offenders' institution and from there to adult prison. He's spent most of the last decade in prison, boss.'

'What for?'

'A bit of everything, but drugs are behind it all. Any number of thefts, a couple of dishonesty offences and one assault but mainly possession with intent to supply.'

'What's his drug of choice?'

'Started out on skunk, then acid. He did use heroin for a while but he went on a treatment programme and it seems that it worked.'

'Treatment? Who gets access to successful heroin treatment on the NHS?'

'It wasn't NHS, boss: some private clinic near Conwy. He's clear of heroin but he hasn't got a home, a job or a future. Since his treatment, he's been arrested for theft and possession, acid and ket.'

'Ket?'

'Yes. For eighteen months, that's what he's been doing, like a game. Breaking into a vet's car, a farm or stables or what have you, stealing the ket, getting caught, three months in prison, out, stealing ket again and so on.'

'Has he got family?'

'His mother was an addict. She could cope while her father was alive to support her but after his death, social services took the boy and he was fostered, then adopted. It isn't easy to find a place for a boy of ten, especially one who needs Welsh-medium education.'

'Hang on a minute, Sheila. I remember a call for more Welsh-speaking families to foster...'

'And in the end, to show leadership, one of the County Councillors decided to set a good example by fostering the boy herself...'

'Heulwen Breeze-Evans. But it wasn't a happy ending.'

'Far from it. When he was fifteen, Cai was accused of sexually abusing the girl of the family, Nansi. He denied the accusation, saying that they loved each other, but he was out, back into the care of the local authority.'

'So Cai was the friend Heulwen separated from Nansi? *Nefi blw*, Sheil! We need a whole pot of tea to process this lot.'

'You'll need a drop of whisky in it when you hear the next twist in the story, boss.'

'What more can happen? It's a horror show already.'

'Cai ended up in a place called Derwenlas, a residential home for boys with behavioural problems. Three years after Cai left, the manager killed himself after being charged with thirty-seven counts of abuse against boys in his care, including Cai Evans.'

Daf couldn't prevent tears springing to his eyes. 'No!' he exclaimed. He blew his nose to hide his emotion and took the picture from Sheila. The boy in the big coat had grown up into the ghost of an adult, his skin so delicate, his arms covered in scars and as thin as an old man's. Sheila had printed out the notes of a number of meetings with social services, which gave the bare bones of what had happened. 'Father wishing to work through the issue if firm guidelines are set: mother will not permit C's return, stating that protection of birth family comes first. Father suggests that C is family: mother does not agree.'

'We've got to find Cai. Send a copy of the picture to all the hostels and rough sleeper teams and phone Nia. Get her to bring Nansi in here at once, and Phil.'

'I've spoken to Father Hogan, he's got no means of reaching him. He just turns up out of the blue every now and then.'

'What was the name of the clinic where he had his treatment?'

'Hafod Recovery Centre.'

Though he felt he would need a week to absorb Cai's story, let alone assess what it meant for the inquiry, Daf went straight back to his desk and Googled the recovery centre. The website was attractive: it was clearly aimed at wealthy families with troubled children, people who would be willing to lay out thousands a month to secure a future for a young person gone off the rails. Cai had no such backers, so why did they accept him? Daf clicked through the pictures and paused at the image of a plump man with plentiful white hair, all in black except for his white collar. The caption read: 'Dr Fr Graham Parr founded Hafod ten years ago to provide a centre for whole-person recovery. Though Father Parr's own vocation is to the priestly life, he is a clinical psychologist with twenty-five years' experience in the treatment of addiction, and guests of all faiths and none are welcomed to Hafod.'

Well, Daf thought, a warm welcome for those whose parents had a big enough cheque book. He dialled the number on the website and, two minutes later, he was talking to Doctor Father Parr. His strong Birmingham accent came as a bit of a surprise. As soon as Parr knew Daf was phoning from Welshpool, he made the connection with Joe Hogan.

'Bane of my life, is Joe 'Ogan. Costs a fortune, keeping a place like this going, and Joe sends me 'is down an' outs.'

'Did you treat a young man called Cai Evans?'

'Oi did. 'e got the H licked, did that lad.'

'And the fees?'

'Oh, Joe got one of his rich ol' ladies to stump up for 'is keep an' I didn't charge nothin' else. He did a few jobs round the place, especially outside.'

In Parr's opinion, Cai was in a good physical condition to change his life, having managed to overcome the most dangerous of his addictions, but he needed a settled lifestyle and a chance to face down some of the demons of his past. He had no way of contacting him. He did have some suggestions as to places Cai might stay, on his recovery journey, as Parr put it, but only if he was clean and remained so.

Soon afterwards, he received a phone call from Belle. 'What the hell are you up to, Daf, keeping me in suspense like this?' In the background, Daf could hear the dogs. 'What did the pathologist have to say?'

'I've only just heard from him myself. He says there were significant traces of ketamine in her bloodstream.'

'Ket? I thought she was a respectable farmer's wife?'

'She's got a pretty complicated past.'

'Well, that theory pleases me no end, Daf, and do you know why that is?'

'Why?'

'In my experience, any theory, however crap it turns out to be in the long run, is better than no theory at all. Now you're cooking on gas.'

'How's the report shaping up?'

'Ooh, you're such a slave-driver, Daf.' The tone of her voice was nothing less than saucy and Daf wished, yet again, that he could unsee what he'd seen in the bedroom of the Goat. 'Valentine had to go to the dentist in Chester and that took up the whole morning. I've been at it since lunchtime.' Her nudge, nudge, wink, wink vocabulary was very hard to handle and Daf thought that if he had to deal with her on a daily basis, he would probably start to drink heavily.

'And you're sure there were two fires, and two different people who set them?'

'The SOCOs took a good few samples and even they shouldn't be able to bugger up tests as straightforward as that.'

'OK. Thanks for ringing, Belle.'

'See you on Sunday, if not before.'

'Yes, right, Sunday.'

'Daf, are you turning into a judgemental father on me? Or should that be a judgemental uncle?'

'Not at all. It just takes a bit of getting used to. I mean, there's a bit of a gap between the two of you and...'

'It's not quite a case of grab a granny, Daf; I won't be getting my pension for a good few years yet.' Belle was laughing.

'No, it's not just his age. You've seen the world and so on, Belle, and Sion's hardly out of nappies.'

'And do you know what I've learnt in the four far corners of the world, Daf Dafis?' Belle asked, with a hard note of certainty in her voice. 'Nothing is so rare as a decent, kindly man and when you trip over one, you're a fool not to reel him in.'

'Fair play to you, Belle,' muttered Daf in answer, rattled by her inexorable tone and serious words.

When Phil and Nansi appeared, it was clear they'd both been weeping. Nansi was grasping her father's hand tightly.

'They'd like to talk to you together, if that's OK, boss,' Nia explained. 'Talking about Cai has certainly stirred things up.'

'Let's start off together anyway, right?'

Phil nodded his head.

'I know how busy you are, Nia,' Daf ventured, 'but a cup of tea would do us all the world of good.'

'No worries, boss.' Nia seemed to be happier now the relatives were showing some appropriate emotion.

Phil sat down without releasing Nansi's hand, so his daughter was dragged down into the chair beside him.

'You think I'm a total bastard,' he began in a shaking voice. 'I had no idea what was going to happen to him.'

'Dadi, please don't carry on bullshitting, it's gone beyond that. I told you what kind of things went on in those places and she made the decision; you don't have to cover up for her any more now she's gone. We're free of the lies. We can find Cai and apologise, and I've got more to say sorry about than anyone else.'

'Why so, *lodes*?' Daf asked. 'You were only a young girl at the time.'

'Yes, but ... God, it's so hard to start talking about this.'

'It was a right quiet time in Dolfadog,' put in Phil, trying to help her out. 'Heuls had just been put on the board of the Council, Jac was spending a lot of time with Low and her family and Gruff was always up at Tanyrallt with the horses.'

'And you?'

'Well,' Phil admitted, 'I'd come across a right pleasant piece of goods over Dolanog way, and I was there a fair bit. Nans and Cai were always on their own together.'

'I'd always been close to Gruff,' Nansi continued. 'There's only a year between us and we'd always done everything together but that year, he stayed up on Horse Hill all through the Royal Welsh. Well, he started talking about girls and bloodlines and parties, leaving me behind. I ... I wanted to grow up, to be like Gruff.'

Nia came into the room and put the tray on the desk without a word. Waiting until Nia had shut the door behind her, Nansi started again.

'Cai wasn't like a brother to me. We hadn't been brought up together and when he first arrived, it was supposed to be a temporary thing. Dad told us to think about him the way Nain Maesgwastad thought about the evacuees who came to them during the war. No one talked about flesh and blood, brother and sister. I liked talking to him, he was full of plans. He wanted to be a lawyer and he used to talk about the way he would help each one of us when he was qualified.' Nansi started to weep quietly and her father tried to comfort her. 'I didn't feel ... No, I don't know what I felt. One night, we were watching a romantic film, something like *The Notebook*, and when the characters were kissing on the screen, I said to him: 'That looks like it could be fun.' So then, we kissed and that night, I slept in his bed.'

'And did you...?' Daf struggled for the sensitive way to ask his question.

'Love like a man and wife? We did. I'd had some condoms from the Youth Bus that came to school. I'm not proud of this, Mr Dafis, but for a while, we were right happy together, the two of us.'

'Until?'

'Until Gruff realised what was going on. It was the day of Llanfyllin Show. We went to the show together, Jac showing his Lleyn sheep, Mum judging the Arts and Crafts and Gruff competing in the Show Jumping. Gruff was very keen to get me to meet some friend of his, some Marcus from Penybontfawr but I wasn't interested. That night, when we were alone in the house as usual, we were cuddled up on the sofa watching telly when Gruff came in the back door like a whirlwind, cursing us both and saying that his friends all said I was a freak who slept with my own brother.'

'Then it all got a bit out of hand, Mr Dafis,' put in Phil, once more trying to take the pressure off his daughter. 'Heuls wasn't prepared to listen to anyone – I tried to tell her how bad it would look if Cai just disappeared but she ... None of the rest of us thought we'd actually end up losing him. I thought maybe that boarding might be a good idea, until things simmered down a bit, but no. He needed to be properly punished, she said.'

'Gruff didn't want things to go that far. He even persuaded Margaret to offer him a place at Tanyrallt but, according to the authorities, that would have been too close to me,' Nansi explained. 'Once Mum had started using that word, "abuse", it all escalated really quickly. That's why he was sent to that fucking place.' The swear word seemed to explode from her mouth. 'He rang, Christmas Eve, to tell me what that bastard was doing to him. He only managed to make that one phone call. And that's why, after being in chapel, hearing her sing songs about the Baby Jesus, I went for her. There she was sitting in her lovely kitchen, by her four-oven Aga, chopping up fancy nuts no one wanted to eat, singing "Teg Wawriodd" whilst one of us was...'

'I understand.' Daf interrupted to prevent her from having to say anything more. 'Have you spoken to him since then, Nansi?'

'Never. But I see him in my dreams, thin and hopeless, a great burden of pain on his back, all because of me.'

'And you, Phil?'

'I know it sounds right daft, but last night, no, Tuesday night, I went to pick up Basia from the house by the church where she's been stopping and I saw a face in the window, looking just like how Cai would look now.'

'It was him,' Daf explained. 'He stayed with Joe Hogan on Tuesday night. Before you go, one more question. Do you think that Cai would be capable of killing Heulwen?'

Phil considered for a few moments before replying.

'I can't really answer that question because I don't know him anymore, but he was a right tidy little *cog* at heart. I don't know what he'd be like now, after all that's happened.' Phil sighed deeply and squeezed Nansi's hand.

'I don't want Seth to hear about all this, Mr Dafis. For him, purity is a very important thing in a woman and he's been so kind to me.'

'I'm afraid that depends on the result of the investigation, Nans *fach*. If it's Cai who killed your mother, there will be a court case which leads to attention in the press.'

Nansi nodded her head sadly. There was a weary air about her.

'Sorry to keep you but there is just one more thing: was Heulwen using drugs at all, apart from what she got from the doctor?'

'No idea,' was Phil's reply. 'She was my wife and I didn't even know she slept with women, so who knows?'

Nansi hesitated before giving her answer.

'I wouldn't have thought so because she always wanted to be in control of everything, including herself. I've seen Dad totally hammered any number of times, but her? Never.'

As the door closed behind them, Daf felt a great empathy for any therapist – the storm of emotions across his desk had left him feeling exhausted and rather ill. He went out through the front door for a breath of air and saw Basia, standing strong between Nansi and Phil, one arm round the young woman's waist, the other reaching over Phil's back to draw him in. They were both weeping and Basia was saying, over and over, to comfort them, 'He can come home to us now, he can come home.'

Daf realised he wouldn't have time to ring Gaenor when he saw Joe approaching the station with Milek at his heels like an unwilling dog. He was swinging his large head from side to side like a lion in a cage. He snarled at Phil as he passed him and Daf hurried them inside.

'Nev still about?' he asked Nia.

'Think so.'

'Can you ask him to hang about until I've finished here?' Daf had seen the danger in Milek's eyes and was keen to have help within a call if it proved necessary. 'I don't want to take up too much of your time,' he said to Milek, who was bending his large body down onto the chair. 'I got your history through today, from Poland.'

'Milek says that all young men misbehave from time to time.'

'Not all young men put someone in hospital for a month.'

Milek pulled his upper lip back to show his long teeth. He spoke rapidly, and Joe paused for a while before translating, as if he were giving Milek a chance to change his statement. No change was made.

'He says that the German who insulted his sister was a ... a piece of human waste and that he would do the same again to protect her.'

Daf pushed the envelope which contained the pictures of Bowen over the desk.

'You said yesterday that Heulwen was interested in Bowen's business. Do you know anything about these?'

Milek opened the envelope and glanced at a couple of pictures, his face displaying his distaste.

'Stuff like this is nobody's business,' came the answer, via the priest. 'Bowen's business activities were what interested Heulwen.' Daf noticed the way in which Milek, as soon as he realised the nature of the contents of the envelope, attempted to conceal their nature from Joe, who showed no interest whatsoever.

'Where were you on Monday evening?'

'In the flat till eight, then in the Wellington until the police came and told people to leave.'

'Alone?'

'With Wiktor.'

'What were you doing before you went out?'

Milek shook his heavy head again.

'Business. Arranging to deliver some of the goods Wiktor had brought back from Poland.'

'Who to?'

'Polish friends. He won't say anything more.'

'I've got just one more question: do you know who killed Heulwen Breeze-Evans?'

'He has no idea but there were plenty of people coming and going to her office.'

'Did he see Cai on Monday evening?'

Milek dropped his eyes and said nothing.

'I'm asking for an answer from him, Joe.'

Like a dam bursting, words poured from Milek's mouth.

'To cut a long story short, Milek doesn't tell tales. He's got a complex story to tell, involving his great-grandfather's brother and a Russian soldier but it doesn't seem very relevant, but he also points out that he only met Cai for the first time on Tuesday night so he wouldn't have been likely to notice whether he'd seen him before that.'

Daf decided to give him a shock.

'Did you kill Heulwen Breeze-Evans, Milek?'

Milek laughed and the sound alarmed Daf.

'If he had killed her,' Joe explained in his patient voice, 'he would have moved all their goods from Wiktor's storage place first.'

It was difficult to dispute his reasoning. Daf shook Milek's hand to show that the interview was at an end and the big man stood up without releasing Daf's hand.

'You do your job, I know,' he mumbled in his halting English. 'I not know who burn our place. I know, I say, yes?' Then he waved his hand in the direction of the envelope on the desk. 'Welsh girls, they like fat men?'

'Not usually,' Daf replied, unable to suppress a laugh. 'But Mr Bowen is a bit different.'

'Yes. Bit different.'

Daf was feeling guilty. Apart from one text message, he hadn't contacted Gaenor all afternoon, despite his protestations of never neglecting her again. He was delighted to see the Berllan pick-up was still outside the house when he arrived home but was rather surprised to see a Land Rover as well, not the respectable blue one belonging to Neuadd but one with a flashy metallic red paint job and a large sticker on the door proclaiming the possession of a non-standard sound system: Animal. Bryn owned the pick-up: the Land Rover was Chrissie's pride and joy. Daf wondered if a vehicle swap was in process.

For half a moment after opening his front door, Daf felt that the scene inside was like something from the Arabian Nights, if the Sultan and his harem had been keen viewers of S4C. Monopolising the sofa with a cushion under each baby, Chrissie was feeding the twins. In the armchair, looking a good deal better, Gaenor was feeding Mali. And between them, lying full length on the floor, was Bryn, his long legs and well-muscled arms all over the place. Daf then noticed that there was a girl, about six years old, also lying on the floor, tucked under Bryn's arm.

'Well, hello all,' Daf began, feeling very unsociable, as if he had just finished a twenty-hour shift.

To be fair to Bryn, he did scramble straight to his feet.

'Sorry for the trespass, Mr Dafis,' he began.

'I tried to explain to him how to fend for himself and Anni at home but in the end, it was easier for me to cook for everyone here,' Chrissie explained. 'Your supper's keeping warm. Go fetch Mr Dafis his supper, Anni Mai.'

The little girl ran full pelt to the kitchen.

'Put it on a tray, tidy,' Chrissie called after her.

Daf perched on the arm of the chair beside Gaenor. From there, he could see that two boys of about nine and ten were sitting at the little table in the kitchen, playing tractor-themed Top Trumps.

'Massey Fergusson, that's a four,' said one.

'If she's red, best leave her in the shed,' retorted his older brother.

'Quiet there, *cogie*,' thundered Bryn: 'We're Mr Dafis's guests.'

After making this declaration, Bryn sank back to the floor, making himself comfortable like some vast cat. As dignified as if she were taking part in an Eisteddfod ceremony, Anni Mai came through the kitchen door, bearing a plate piled high with Chrissie's idea of a decent supper, which was, of course, a roast. There was a mountain of food on the plate, slabs of beef as thick as some of the slim volumes of poetry on Daf's shelves, no less than six roast potatoes, carrots, swede, cabbage, roast onions and over it all like a wave of tastiness, gravy.

'Chrissie, thank you so much: this is perfect.'

'Nonsense, Mr Dafis: it's just ordinary supper.'

Daf realised how hungry he was, and without thinking of his manners, started to fill his mouth, conscious of being watched by numerous pairs of eyes.

'Are you OK watching *Ffermio*, Mr Dafis?' Bryn asked, remote in his hand. '*Eastenders* on the other side.'

As Daf's mouth was full, he assented to the programme choice with a nod.

'You come through now, *cogie*,' Chrissie commanded. 'There's an item on Speckles.'

Bryn managed to make room for them and Daf realised that over three-quarters of his living room carpet was covered by the Humphries family. Watching *Ffermio* with them was like an agricultural episode of Gogglebox: one after another, the family members seemed obliged to make observations on what they saw on the screen and no detail passed them by.

'Needs a new tyre on that Isuzu.' Bryn.

'I don't like his leg. Not at all.' Chrissie criticising a ram.

'Can they get Wynnstay deliveries right down there?' The older boy.

'Bet they catch the rain so close to the sea.' The other.

'I was chatting with that girl in the Winter Fair.' Bryn, hoping to provoke Chrissie, given that the girl on screen was an attractive twenty-five-year-old.

'Next time you see her, why not explain to her what makes a good ram? She doesn't look like she's got a clue at the moment.' Chrissie, straight back at him.

'I wouldn't be so sure of that.' Bryn, in a lazy, self-satisfied voice.

Chrissie threw a cushion at Bryn's head. He laughed and Daf began to feel very middle-aged.

As he slipped into a food coma, Daf remembered something. 'Where's Rhodri?'

'Gone out, with Rob.'

'To do what?'

'Oh, looking for girls, of course, Mr Dafis,' answered Chrissie.

'I thought Rob had a girlfriend already?' Daf asked.

'Always a good idea to have something in reserve,' said

Bryn, slowly and deliberately, as if he were an expert on such matters, which, Daf ruefully admitted, he probably was. Chrissie threw the other cushion at him. He grinned.

'Anni Mai,' she chided, 'Mr Dafis has nearly finished, where are your manners?'

The girl jumped up and climbed over members of her family to stand beside Daf. Gaenor gave her a warm smile: she was blissfully feeding, in a bubble in this busy scene.

'Mr Dafis, would you like some more?' she asked courteously. 'There's plenty enough of everything.'

'I'm grand, thanks.'

'Go make the custard, *da lodes*,' her mother ordered, in a voice which displayed her satisfaction at her girl's helpfulness.

'Custard?' murmured Daf, feeling as if he were drowning in food.

'It's only crumble, Mr Dafis, no need to excite yourself. I didn't have time to do anything special.'

'Anything special, Chrissie?' Gaenor put in. 'You've made us all a wonderful meal. And thinking of meals...'

Mali had finished and Gaenor passed the baby to Daf, who was very glad to have Mali in his lap to draw his attention from what happened next. Chrissie buttoned up her shirt.

'I'm as empty as an eight-year-old Holstein,' she declared. 'Go get your pudding from Auntie Gae, *cogie*.'

If Daf had found if unacceptably strange to see Chrissie feeding Mali, the other way around was even worse, especially in the presence of Bryn, who appeared to take no notice at all of his sons nuzzling Gaenor's breasts. Daf managed to raise an explosion of wind from Mali which momentarily drowned the slurping sounds.

'Shall I change Mali for you, Mr Dafis?' Chrissie asked, sensing that Daf was out of his depth.

'Please. I've got some papers to get from the car.'

As Chrissie took Mali from Daf, Bryn beamed at them both.

'She's a right beauty, is Mali *fech*,' he pronounced. 'These lads will be fighting over her, no doubt.'

Daf felt rather sick: Chrissie had confided in him about the relationship she had enjoyed with both Bryn and his now dead twin brother and Bryn's chance remark raised the alarming prospect that his baby daughter might grow up to be the girl lying in the king-size bed between the handsome Humphries twins of her generation. He almost stumbled through the front door, gulping in fresh air.

On the street, the interior light of the Defender was on. In the front seats were Rhodri and Rob Berllan, listening to George Ezra on that superior sound system, almost loud enough to warrant a telling-off for disturbing the neighbours, but not quite. Between them sat a fair-haired girl of their own age. Through the windscreen, Daf could see that his son liked the girl but that she admired Rob, who was paying very little attention to her. Perhaps she was the inspiration for Rhodri's new haircut, Daf surmised, but he didn't see much chance of success for his son: just like his Uncle Bryn, there was a remarkable sheen on Rob's black curls, like the feathers of a raven. There was a cruel inevitability in Rhodri's situation. It's like a reading from the Gospel According to Disney, Daf thought. 'It's the Circle, the Circle of Life.'

# Chapter 11

## *Friday morning, April 15, 2016*

Daf hadn't been woken by the alarm since Mali's birth. The electronic sound was so unfamiliar that he felt as he did when waking up in a hotel on holiday, the strangeness contributing to a sense of relaxation. When he saw that Gaenor was still sleeping soundly, her skin no longer showing the damp flush of fever, he was grateful beyond words to Chrissie, even if she had shaken him to the core, as she tended to, and even if her family had invaded his house like Vikings the previous night. He would have to think of an appropriate way for this gratitude to be displayed but he had no headspace to think of that until the investigation was sorted, one way or another.

He opened the fridge door to see evidence of Chrissie's concern on every shelf. There were the remains of the vast joint of beef carefully wrapped in foil, a four-pack of Guinness he presumed was intended to build Gaenor's strength, and the largest quantity of bacon Daf had even seen in his life. He started to fry a few rashers and before long the smell woke Gaenor. It was delightful for Daf to see the change in her as she waited for her sandwich whilst giving Mali her breakfast.

'Did Chrissie get the bacon?' she asked.

'And heaven knows what else besides. She thinks I'm wasting away, seemingly, because you don't do me a roast every day.'

'Hmm.' Gaenor's scepticism was full of humour. 'And I just wonder what interest Chrissie has in your physical condition? Does she want to feed you up for some reason of her own?'

'All I can say is, if I ate a meal like that every night, I'd be going around on a mobility scooter in six months, too fat to walk. Bryn must have some hell of a metabolism.'

Gaenor's eyes were shining, as if this were a subject which interested her a good deal.

'I know she kicks him out of bed at five to start working,' she said, 'but I think he'd have to burn at least six hundred calories a day in bed not to be putting on the timber, which he certainly isn't.'

Daf passed her a bacon sandwich and bit into his. 'What would burning six hundred calories mean, in terms of activity, would you say?' he asked, putting his non-sandwich hand on her knee.

'Well, according to this calculator I read in a magazine once...'

'What sort of magazine?'

'Just *Cosmo*, I think, or something like. Nothing bad. Anyway, the article said a man could burn a hundred and twenty calories in half an hour, if he put his back into it.'

'That's over four hours of sex to make up for the roasts!' Daf exclaimed.

'Come on, Daf, be honest. Wouldn't you spend four hours a day in bed with Chrissie if it meant you could have a roast like that every night?'

They were both laughing as if they were in bed together and Gaenor had reached out to stroke Daf's hair. They'd completely forgotten about the existence of Rhodri, who was standing in the kitchen doorway.

'They just happen to be the parents of my best friend,' he said in a cold adult voice. 'If you have to fantasize about their sex life, don't do it in the kitchen.'

Daf was struck with remorse. He could only imagine how awkward it might be for Rhodri to overhear that kind of banter, and he remembered how generous and easy the boy had been throughout the upheaval which had brought them down to the little house. Daf mumbled an apology which was clearly not accepted. Gaenor used her grace to smooth things over.

'Oh, blame it on me feeling that much better, Rhods. We

were just being silly. Dad'll have to go straight to work so I'll do you a bacon sandwich.'

She was wise, Daf thought, as he closed the door; with her kindness and Rhodri's adoration of Mali, things would soon be made good between them, and their reconciliation would spread to him in a while, but Freud wouldn't need to break sweat to deduce that the father's presence in this situation was unlikely to help. Besides, Gaenor was right, there was plenty for Daf to do.

He received a phone call before reaching the station: they'd found Cai.

'He was sleeping in the doorway of the bookshop in Oswestry,' Nev explained. 'But he's not in a very good state, so they took him to Maelor Hospital for tests.'

'What's the matter with him?'

'He's got a hell of a cough, they think it could be bronchitis or even the white plague.'

Daf smiled to himself at Nev's archaic use of the term to describe TB.

'I'll go straight there. Anything else important?'

'The test results have come back from the lab: there was meths by the front door but a mixture of oil and petrol in the back office.'

'Two-stroke. The carbon dogs were spot on, then.'

'And Ms Rhydderch has heard, somehow or other, that you're just about to arrest someone. She's asking if she can arrange a press conference for this afternoon.'

'Can you make it clear to her that we haven't arrested anyone? And tell her, because she likes to feel important, that the moment I'm anywhere near an arrest, I'll phone her straightaway.'

'OK, boss.'

Daf turned left at the roundabout by the Raven, heading straight for Wrexham. Six miles further on, he reached the Vale of Meifod, in its glory in the spring sunshine. Just before turning towards Llansantffraid, Daf paused for a while to appreciate the place where Rhys Bowen had chosen to live. His large Victorian house stood on a shelf of land high above the valley, surrounded by parkland where mature oaks gave shelter to elegant horses. In total contrast to the energetic stock at Tanyrallt, there was an idle look about Bowen's horses as if their function was purely decorative.

On a whim, Daf decided to drive up the slope. Outside the house stood a brand new BMW X6 and, half hidden around the corner, a tatty Citroen Saxo. Daf stopped for a moment to enjoy the view; the river Vyrnwy was making its leisurely way through fertile fields, with nothing to disturb the tranquil loveliness. It was a landscape too beautiful to damage, Daf thought, beginning to understand Bowen's role in the battle against the pylons.

As he walked across the gravel to the broad wooden front door, Daf thought he might take a picture of the house for Gaenor, as she was always interested in property. But then he changed his mind, as he considered the alternative life such a picture might trigger in Gae's imagination. If she had, as she had wanted to, accepted Bowen's offer of a lift home from that dance, this would be her home now, not the little house opposite the Goat in Llanfair.

Daf rang the heavy brass bell and heard it echoing through the house, just like in a horror film. A young girl from Eastern Europe opened the door, explaining that only Mrs Bowen was at home.

She led Daf through into a formal room and, looking at the hand-blocked Chinese wallpaper and the dainty antique furniture, he experienced a wave of fierce socialism as he thought of Milek and Basia and their kind, whose sweat had bought this luxury. Yet there was something sad about the chairs whose spindly legs would never support their owner's weight, and Daf couldn't see a single item which would render a house a home: no family photos, no books or CDs and, of course, no toys.

Daf had been under the impression that Rhys Bowen's wife was a plain woman, the sort of girl who needed a dowry if she was ever to find a husband. Instead, the woman who came into the room was stunningly beautiful. She was no longer young – over fifty was Daf's guess – but her skin was perfect, stretched taut over high cheekbones. She was taller than Daf: over six foot, and she threw her hips forward when she walked, as if she were on a catwalk. And like many models Daf had seen in magazines, her eyes were totally empty.

'Yes?' she began, with no grace or welcome in her voice.

'I was looking for Mr Bowen.'

'He isn't here.'

'I'm Chief Inspector Daf Dafis, Dyfed Powys Police.' He used his rank, temporary though it was, as a shield against her scorn.

'Oh. I thought you might be one of those tiresome pylon people. They wear jackets like that.'

'I'm investigating a suspicious death. Do you know where your husband is?'

'No idea. Out canvassing?'

'Perhaps. Will he be home later?'

'Eventually. When there are no more throats to slit or legs to spread for the day. Unless he literally sleeps with one of the foolish sluts.'

A cold shiver went down Daf's spine. The contrast between her crude choice of words and the calm, leisurely tone of her voice, as if she'd grown tired of hating her husband, was chilling. He noticed the ring on her finger: a huge diamond and two sapphires.

'Was he at home on Monday night?'

'Eventually, I suppose.'

'At what time?'

'I have no idea. He ate his breakfast here, unless, of course, we were burgled by someone with very rudimentary table manners.'

Daf saw in her nothing of the grace he associated with the gentry ladies who had been customers in his father's shop, with their privileged courtesy, and he had no idea how to communicate with her.

'Ah. You didn't notice ... before breakfast, like?' he asked, aware how coarse and yokelish his voice must sound.

Mrs Bowen began to laugh in an unnatural tone, as if she had been trained to do so.

'You surely didn't...? Oh, but you did ... Poor Mr Policeman, I don't suppose for a moment that you live what one might call a varied life but still, you must have guessed that I would scarcely be likely to share my bed with something like him.'

Perhaps no one would have predicted his success, both financially and as an Assembly Member, but Daf was pretty certain no one could have foreseen that Rhys Bowen would have a wife like this. He didn't deserve this, either, for all his obvious weaknesses.

'But you married him,' Daf had to say, thinking of himself for the moment as the voice of romance.

'I was part of a business arrangement, like the leasing of the refrigerated lorries. I agreed because I was bored to tears at home. Now, I am bored to tears here.'

'I won't take up any more of your time, then.'

She was too rude to even say goodbye. He stood for several minutes on the broad step outside the front door, thinking about Rhys Bowen, a *cog* from the back end of Dyffryn Tanat with his grand mansion, his exquisitely beautiful wife and his successful career but with never a moment of company or comfort, alone in all this splendour. Daf mused on the words of Oscar Wilde, the thing about there being two tragedies in life: not to get your heart's desire being one, the other being to get it. He thought of the boisterous, hopeful young man Gaenor had described, singeing the down from a pen full of ducks, laughing, necking the damson gin. It seemed, all of a sudden, like a very long journey from there, and not necessarily in the right direction.

A young man who had never had his heart's desire was lying in a high bed in a side ward in Maelor Hospital, his face as white as his sheet. Every now and again, he turned to cough into a small plastic bowl.

'How are you, *cog*?' Daf asked, after introducing himself.

'Not bad, considering I slept out in the rain the last two nights.'

'I know who you are, *lanc*, and a bit of your history as well.'

'If you know who I am, you're doing better than I am: I've got no idea who I am. I half remember someone I once was, years back, but now, no clue.'

There was sweat on his grey forehead, and Daf offered him a towel.

'Fever, this is,' he said, drying his face. 'Not comedown. I haven't taken anything since Gruff and Margaret's ket.'

'You stole it?'

'I did, and trimmed their fucking ponies for them.'

'Why?'

'Ever dropped acid, Mr Policeman?'

'I can barely cope with romance and carbohydrates, let alone more complicated pleasures.'

The light-hearted answer seemed to please Cai, because he smiled.

'I've often had an acid dream that's a bit like a scene from *The Lord of the Rings*, or a 70s album cover: girls in long dresses, wild flowers and mountains in the distance, and the dream sticks with me after the acid's gone. And do you know why? Because I try not to think too much about my real life; it's none too pretty. About a fortnight ago, I was selling the *Big Issue* outside Debenhams in Wrexham, hoping no one would have nicked my tobacco or pissed on my bed when I got back to the hostel, when I saw out of the corner of my eye, a girl like the girls in my dream: long red hair, big blue eyes. When she came over to buy a magazine, she smiled as she pulled out her purse, and for just a moment, I though real life wasn't all shit. She was opening her purse when the boyfriend appeared, expensive leather jacket, dealer boots, sweatshirt with a foxhound on it and a slogan 'Fuck the Ban'. He turned his head to warn her not to give me any money because I'd spend it all on drugs. It was Gruff Tanyrallt.'

'Before that, when was the last time you saw him?'

'On the day when they dragged me, literally dragged me, from Dolfadog. To be totally fair to him, he and Dad were the only ones there that morning. Do you know how they do it, Mr Policeman?'

'I've been with the social workers a couple of times.'

'I'd said I wouldn't cry but when I saw the car, I was fucking close. Gruff was the only one who tried to stop it, Nans must have talked to him. "It's a mistake," he said. "Cai should stay with us." A bit late in the fucking day, big brother.'

There was a pause. Daf lifted Cai's notes from the end of the bed.

'You're not supposed to look at those, they're just for doctors and nurses.'

'Oh, I'm a bit of a rebel, me,' Daf answered. 'And I now know they're thinking of discharging you later today. Why don't you come down to Welshpool with me?'

'Why?'

'Because I've a fair bit to discuss with you. Where else were you going?' Cai frowned. 'Why don't we go see Joe Hogan and see if he's got any ideas?'

'Are they still there, the Poles?'

'Yes.'

'When I heard about Joe at first, I assumed he was one of *them*.'

'One of who?'

'Abusers. A lot of their priests are, you know. Plenty of people look very innocent and kindly but what they really want is a vulnerable young man to play with. Joe's not like that.'

'Where did you meet him?'

'In Shrewsbury, in prison. Quite often, he and I were the only Welsh speakers there.'

'Are you a Catholic?'

'No way. I've got no interest in a god who fucks over innocent people. But I heard from other people who live rough that Joe puts people up.'

'OK then, are you willing to come along with me now? We can talk as we go and that'll save time and hassle.'

Cai nodded.

It took half an hour to sort out the paperwork but when Daf met Cai again in the reception area, with his clothes covered in mud, his thin hand shaking as he held his carrier bag, Daf felt uncertain. Cai might get better care somewhere where there were specialists to help him, but Daf couldn't think of a suitable place anywhere in Wales, let alone anywhere convenient to Welshpool.

'Let's stop by the town and get you some dry clothes, eh Cai?'

'I've got no money.'

'Don't worry about that.'

Ten minutes in TK Maxx and he was kitted out. He grinned at Daf.

'Haven't had new clothes for a fair spell now. Some of the charity shops can be a right rip-off and I haven't got the time to be farting about with sizes.'

Back in the car, Cai asked, 'Are you allowed to buy clothes for me, Mr Policeman?'

'Daf Dafis is my name and I've got no idea what the rules are.'

'But what if you can't claim the cost back on your expenses?'

'Oh, it was only thirty pound.'

Cai was quiet for a while but as they were driving past the football stadium, he began to speak again, a slightly dreamy look on his thin face.

'When you're in the system, some of the people are nice to

you. They take you to see a film, they buy ice cream. But every time, they ask for a receipt, even for a fucking ice cream. I noticed the difference when we went to Llanerfyl Fair for the first time. Dad gave each of us a fiver, with no crap about receipts. I was part of the family.' Cai turned to stare out through the window as they approached the Plas Coch roundabout.

'If it's any comfort to you, Phil and Nans would love to see you.'

'Would they really?'

Daf couldn't tell if Cai was being ironic.

'They would. But you were in the middle of telling me what happened when you met Gruff and Felicity.'

'That's her name, is it, Gruff's girl? Felicity?'

'Not sure she's exactly his girl, it's more like "it's complicated", but never mind about that.'

'I tried to forget about it but he didn't even look at me, though we were like brothers, *were* brothers once. When they walked off towards the cinema, she slipped her hand into the arse pocket of his jeans.'

Cai turned to face Daf for a moment. 'I'm not gay but it's over three years since I went with someone who wasn't a man, and do you know why? Because women don't pick young men up off the street, fill them up with all kinds of shit then satisfy their lusts on them, not round here at any rate. I saw her, Felicity, and how easy things were for Gruff, and I started doing some remembering.'

'I'm sorry for you, *lanc*, I really am.'

'No, it did me good. I'd been too long looking for forgetfulness.'

His thin fingers were constantly moving, and Daf had no trouble working out why.

'Do you need a smoke?'

'In your car? Am I allowed?'

'Makes no odds to me.'

'There's a baby seat in the back.'

'But there isn't a baby in it, Cai, just don't worry about it.'

Cai sighed. 'You know what? Apart from the fucking predators, the worst thing about living on the streets is how many fuckers know exactly what you're doing wrong. One day, I'll give up the fags, eat five portions of fruit and vegetables, do an hour of exercise, the fucking lot. May even give safe sex a try, who knows? But I can't sort everything overnight, OK?'

'I understand that perfectly well, *lanc*. And you've got off the H, haven't you?'

'Yeah. But he said, that Father Doctor Parr, from the clinic did, that I needed to get the things in my head sorted, and he was right.'

'So, you decided to confront some things?'

Cai lit a thin roll-up.

'Yes, Mr Dafis, because of my Taid, Mum's dad. I gave him a promise, whatever shit happened, I'd get through it. And I am going to survive, one way or another.'

'Of course you will. I know it sounds simple to say it, but you've got a fair few people on your side, people who can help you find a life that's better than this.'

'I'll be going back to prison whatever happens.'

'Could be. But if you're prepared to tell me the truth, that'll be the best thing, the next stage in rebuilding your life.'

'The truth? That's a nice idea – what the fuck is truth?'

'Want anything from Starbucks, since we're passing?'

'Better not, I might spoil my dinner,' Cai replied scornfully.

Daf remembered the meal he had enjoyed the night before, and the atmosphere in the crowded house, which had been warm, if not exactly normal.

'You can have pizza, kebab, chips, whatever you fancy for your dinner.'

'Fair play to you, Mr Policeman, you're working hard to make a session of questioning at the police station sound attractive.'

'Back to your story. After you saw Gruff...'

'Like I said, I tried to forget but … Well, I was trying to sleep in a smokers' shelter, outside a country pub. I was offered a meal and a bed for the night by a man round about fifty. His house was full of pictures of his wife, who was off on a course, and his kids in college. Filthy bastard. When he was finally sleeping, I went to his son's lovely comfortable room and helped myself to a fair bit of stuff – jeans, hoodie, these trainers and, best of all, this.'

He pulled a T-shirt from his bag: he'd wrapped it carefully in thick plastic. As he was driving, Daf could only take a glance at it but it sent a shiver down his spine. The design on the front of the T-shirt wasn't a logo from Jack Wills or Urban Outfitters, but the cover of a famous Welsh 20th-century novel, depicting a large farmhouse with a sickle around it.

'Mrs Evans always said we should be careful with our Welsh because we were the inheritors of the tradition of that book, the tradition of Lleifior.'

'And you took the T-shirt from the house where…?' Daf was struggling to find the words.

'I'd love to be a fly on the wall when the respectable Dad explains to his son that his prized possessions have been stolen by a dirty little rent boy.'

There was no particular reason for the tide of sorrow which engulfed Daf, but he promised himself to do all he could for this damaged young man.

'Next morning, I thought I'd take my new trainers for a walk, down to Dolfadog. I wanted to ask them if they knew exactly what they'd done to me. Her, especially.'

'What time was it when you got to Welshpool?'

'I walked all the way. I don't have much luck with lifts because I look like what I am, a druggie who's been in and out of prison all his life. Nobody offers a lift to someone like me unless they're after something, usually a chance to make themselves feel good by hurting and degrading me. I arrived there on Monday, just after dinner time. I sat on the new roundabout for a while, watching the Landies come and go, recalling me and Dad going to market together. Then I looked for something to eat.'

'How much money did you have, *lanc*?'

'You just don't get it, do you? If you live like I live, every time you fall asleep, people just like yourself steal everything you own. There's no point doing odd jobs for twenty quid if it ends up in someone else's stash tin. On Monday, I didn't have a penny.'

'What about the food bank?'

'Only open on Tuesdays and Fridays. I sat outside the Town Hall and played my tin whistle. I've got Grade Four on the piano but you can't just pull a piano out of your pocket and entertain the public with a bit of Ravel. Mrs Evans always said I was the best at piano, even better than Nansi herself.'

Cai was rubbing the fabric of the T-shirt between his fingers as he spoke, then he stashed it away carefully in his bag.

'Got any brothers or sisters, Mr Dafis?'

'No. After my parents saw what kind of a creature they made first time, they went into early retirement, for fear of creating something even worse.'

Daf got the impression that Cai enjoyed a bit of banter, almost as if he was looking for a reason to laugh.

'Nor me, before getting to Dolfadog. Talk about a shock to the system. I remember going mental the first time I saw Gruff wearing my slippers but when I had a bit of bother in school, Jac stopped by and threatened to punch anyone who gave me hassle. After a bit, I got to like it. Dolfadog was a busy place, always a lot of coming and going, always someone to chat to, to just talk about nothing with, instead of those fucking deep bollocksy talks with the social workers. "How do you get on with your mum?" "I hate her." Talk about a fucking stupid question. "Why's that?" "Because she's a smackhead, that's why." At Dolfadog, there was a lot of small talk, a lot of, "How are you, *cog*?," and no one expecting more back than a "Grand, thanks," a word about the weather and a polite question about how their harvest was going. I liked that, big time. Just everyday rubbish.'

'I understand. But look where we are, Four Crosses already, let's get back to Monday, eh?'

'Welshpool people have got deep pockets and short arms, haven't they? I only got three pounds, the whole afternoon.'

'Did you see any police at all?' Daf asked, remembering that there was a multi-agency strategy which was supposed to engage with the homeless.

'No, not until the end of the day when the Jac Sais who runs the pub came out and told me to move on. I couldn't be arsed to start anything with a knob like him and I'd got enough to buy a few chips, so it was time for me to go.'

'Then?'

'I went into the library first because the chip shop would still be open when the library was closed. I was reading the *County Times* and I read that Mrs Breeze-Evans was standing in the Assembly Elections. There was a picture of her outside her office, receiving some petition with a right busy expression on her face. Fucking hell, Dad deserved better than that.'

Daf was glad to hear the way the young man's voice softened as he discussed Phil; it might pave the way for some sort of reconciliation. It also seemed symbolic that he called Phil 'Dad' whereas, like Gruff, he wasn't prepared to call Heulwen 'Mum'.

'Then I read the other papers till the library closed. I couldn't use the computers because I don't have a membership card. And I can't get a card without a permanent address and I can't look for help in finding a place to stay without using a computer. It's a vicious circle, Mr Dafis.'

'We can certainly do something about that. I'll speak to Joe, and to the County Council.'

'But, don't forget, I'm not the responsibility of Powys County Council – I'm not a local resident.'

'*Nefi blw!* You were raised in Dyffryn Banw, *lanc*. We can surely sort something.'

'That's not your responsibility. Your job is to arrest me, then I go to jail, then I come out and commit another offence and – '

'Come on, *cog*, we can do better than that. We will sort something.'

Cai turned to Daf, showing the cynical expression in his eyes.

'Whatever. After my chips, I was on my way over to Tesco's to buy a bit of chocolate and, before you start, I know I should have chosen fresh fruit instead but...'

'I've got no intention of preaching about your diet, lad. After what I've eaten in the last forty-eight hours, I'm in no position to give anyone any advice at all.'

'But on my way to Tesco's, I saw her again, the girl with the red hair, going for a meal with Gruff. Have you seen the two of them together?'

'No.'

'I watched them for a couple of minutes. It was right odd, as if they were trying to convince everyone, even themselves, that they were just friends but still, it was obvious that they were shagging.' Daf smiled at this sharp observation. 'And they drove me mad, Mr Dafis with ... well, with the future they've got for themselves. The wedding, the babies, the Section A for the little girl and every fucking thing. And Margaret would be ready to babysit for them to go to the Hunt Ball together and the Severn Valley Pony and Cob Society dinner, with Gruff in his fucking dickie bow and her in some fancy long dress, looking like a film star. Margaret offered to have me live at Tanyrallt but she was turned down for three reasons. She was single, so there wouldn't be a suitable male role model for me, Tanyrallt was too close to Nansi, and because she smoked. As if a bit of passive smoking would do me more harm than what happened to me at the hands of that piece of shit in the Home at Derwenlas.'

Daf didn't venture any comforting words, fearing his sympathy would sound shallow to the broken young man, but had to say something. 'By the way, do you prefer to be called Cai or Kyle?'

'Cai. That name's a comfort blanket to me, like the language is.'

'Even after what … what happened to you in the house where you got those trainers?'

'Yes. My Taid was a Welsh speaker, from Rhos. The best times in my life were with people about me who spoke Welsh, even if there are bastards that speak Welsh as well.'

'Back to that Monday night?'

'OK. After I saw them eating their nice tapas, all I wanted to do was forget. I can't always keep going over everything, time after time. There was a car in the car park with a sign, Vet on Call, in the window. It wasn't even locked and the bag was on the back. I wrapped up the bag in plastic because a homeless man with a smart leather case looks so fucking obvious. I went into the Castle Park to find a quiet place to open it. Then, bingo. Three bottles of ket.'

'You do know Felicity will be in serious trouble for leaving her car open with restricted drugs in it?'

'Felicity?'

'The girl with the red hair, Gruff's friend. She's a vet.'

'You said before but I forgot. That's handy, for a horse-mad man to be shagging a vet. If she's in trouble, I'm sure Gruff can think of some way of cheering her up.'

'What did you do with the ket?'

'I had a hell of a good idea. Go to see Mrs Breeze-Evans in her office and…'

'And what, Cai?'

'You said you hadn't taken acid, so I don't suppose you've ever been in the K-hole, have you?'

'No, but I've seen a couple of people who were.'

Cai paused as if he were considering his next step. 'Fuck it,

I might as well tell you. I'm in the shit anyway, and I'm not ashamed.'

'Ashamed of what?'

'When you're in the K-hole, you can sense everything going on around you but you can't move or speak. Did you know her?'

'Mrs Breeze-Evans? Only by sight.'

'She never listened to anyone. Anytime anyone tried to explain anything to her, she would just walk away. More important things to do. But if she was in the K-hole, she'd have to listen and for once, I could tell her my story. I know I sound like a total fucking nutjob.'

'I can follow your reasoning, even though it would be a crazy thing to do. Lots of us have mad ideas but we don't all put them into practice.'

'Do you know how many times people have put their fantasies into practice on me, Mr Dafis? Not sexy things, but their dreams about cruelty and pain? High time I did something to someone else for a change. So I went round to the office where some girl said Mrs Breeze-Evans was busy speaking to someone. I waited for a while and I heard the sound of a row from the back office. I'm pretty sure I heard a slap, then a woman marched out.'

'Did you see this woman?'

'Through the door of the waiting room, yes. Thirties, smart but not sexy smart.'

'Would you know her again?'

'Reckon so but it was only for a moment I saw her.'

'OK. Now then, Cai, I just need to tell you that this is just a chat, not a formal interview, yes? I get the feeling you could be about to tell me something that's bound up in a serious criminal offence but I'm not trying to set any kind of trap for you. If you want to wait until the tapes are on and you've got a lawyer, you just say.'

'Can't no one fuck with me, Mr Dafis, it's not my first day at the rodeo. I've been in and out of prison all my life.'

'But...'

'But every time I've been prosecuted, everything was done by the book and it did me no fucking good at all. So far, you've listened to me, fair play to you, and at least I'm warm here in your car.'

'Fine. As long as you understand that this is just an informal chat.'

'Right. Then the girl, secretary or whatever she was, went in and came back after a minute, saying Mrs Breeze-Evans was too busy to see anyone, but she changed her tune when I sent my name in. I got a nice invitation then, to come in for a cup of tea.'

'And how was she with you?'

'To start, very nice, like she could be, but she kept on saying, time after time, "There is no connection between you and my family." I had hoped she might have thought of "rescuing" me once again, to make a story about it like before, for the election this time. But she wasn't willing to listen to me. When she shifted about in her chair, like she was about to stand up, I leant over the desk and took her hand. I don't know what she thought I was doing but the last thing she expected was what happened. I turned her hand over and stuck the needle in, straight into one of her veins, just above her wrist.'

Cai blew out through his lips as people do when remembering a piece of excellent craftsmanship.

'She was a classic. Straight back in her chair, mouth open, eyes staring. So then, I had the fun of telling her everything: every fucking detail, especially what happened to me after she threw me back onto the scrapheap. After half an hour, my mouth was rather dry: it's a hell of a thing to talk that long without a drink. Of course, she couldn't show that she understood but I could see from the light in her eye, she understood every word. Graham Parr at the clinic was right. I felt some hell of a release, as if the words had killed some of the old pain. I went to get a drink from the front office and found that the girl there had gone but, looking through the bay window, I saw someone by the front door.'

'Did you see this person's face?'

'No, only the back of his head. He was a heck of a big man, tall and heavy.'

Daf tried to hide his interest.

'What did you do then, *lanc*?'

'One thing I have learnt over the years: always check you've got a way out. I'd noticed there was a back door so I slipped out right handy.'

Daf recalled how hard it had been to shift the bolt on the door in the wall between the back yard and the alley.

'Then out through the back door?'

'The bolt was too stiff so I climbed the wall, and off I went.'

'Did anyone see you?'

'Not as far as I know. I planned to go back to the Castle Park, find a place to sleep, so I went up through the car park and through the corner of the Oldford estate.'

'And did you see anyone?'

'There was some guy from the council at the top end of the lane behind the office, wearing a hi-vis jacket. No one else. I was getting cold and the buzz was starting to wear off, then I got an idea. I went back to the office and waited for a while outside the back door: it was dead quiet. There was a weird smoky smell, like someone had been trying to light a barbeque but there wasn't any flame and there certainly wasn't any heat. I went back in, no one there but her. I remembered her car keys were on her desk so I picked them up and waved them in front of her eyes and she couldn't do jack shit about it. I can't think now why I didn't pick up her bag, she usually kept a fair bit of cash in her purse but I didn't, so I've just got to shut up about it. I found her car easy enough; all I had to do was press the button and wait for the lights to flick on. The tank was three-quarters full so I went for a grand spin, up to Lake Vyrnwy, keeping off the main road because of the police. That big man, whoever he was, he would have been sure to call the ambulance and probably the police so they'd be looking for the car. And I haven't got a licence: Dad taught me to drive on the farm but they don't give driving lessons to scum like me. I drove back through Llanfyllin, over Pentrebeirdd and then for fuck knows what reason, I looped back. When I was going down Red Bank into Welshpool, I saw the smoke rising. I drove past Tesco and turned by the station but the road was closed. I had the window open and I heard the policeman tell the guy in the car ahead of me that an office was on fire on the other side of the canal, the Plaid Cymru office. I turned round sharpish. I knew I had to get rid of the car.'

'What about the ket bottles?'

'I'd left one in her office, on purpose. I wanted people to think she was a user. When I was up by the lake, I tipped the rest of the stuff into my stash bottle.'

The empty bottles Nev had found in the car, Daf thought, balancing his concentration on Cai's story with the need to pass a tractor ambling along the straight by the turning for Arddleen. By coincidence, they weren't far from where Heulwen's car had been found.

'And what happened to the liquid after that?'

'After I got shot of the car, I walked for a couple of miles and found a barn near Pool Quay where I could stop overnight. I needed a bit of something then.'

'What did you think when you heard Heulwen was dead?'

'I'm not very proud of myself, Mr Dafis. I don't live the kind of life a man can be proud of. But I know myself better than to pretend I could kill anyone. I'm too much of a yellow-belly.'

By now, they had reached the roundabout to the north of Welshpool.

'You've got to be right clear on this, Cai: you gave the ket to Heulwen to give her a high, not to kill her, yes?'

'I know where you're going on this one, Mr Dafis. *Actus reus non facit reum nisi mens sit rea.*'

'Spot on,' Daf answered, having understood the last few words of the Latin: *a crime is no crime without intention*. He remembered Nansi speaking of Cai's ambition to be a lawyer.

As they arrived at the police station, Daf noticed a physical change in Cai, as if he were tensing his muscles for the trouble ahead.

'Don't worry, *cog*. Whatever you think, this place is my little castle and nothing bad will happen to you here, right? Shall we order ourselves something to eat and carry on talking as we eat, eh?'

They were sitting quite still in the parked car, as if Cai had a say in what happened next.

'OK.' After a half minute silence, he asked, 'What's your angle, Mr Dafis? When people are nice to me, they always have an agenda, wanting to scratch some itch, like the man in the house where I got the trainers, or because, like Joe, they think that Baby Jesus cries a diamond tear any time a junkie jacks up. Professional people usually see me as a chance to help their stats in some way: if I confess to every fucking thing that's been done in their area since the war, their clear-up rate goes through the roof. But you, I don't get at all. What do you want, Mr Dafis?'

A hell of a question. Daf was quiet for a moment before framing his reply. 'Justice is my thing, I suppose. A bit of order and fair play for everyone.'

Cai didn't say a word as he got out of the car. Daf opened the door to the station and there, on the bench in the reception area, he saw the only man who had ever been a hero to him, and who had held that status since Daf was Rhodri's age. Gwynlyn Huws: poet, politician, actor, man of principle. A bit of everything, but one hell of a Welshman. By now, he was semi-retired but still achieving more in a week than most men could in a month. All his adult life, Daf had longed to meet him, to discuss the future of Wales and how to interest young people in their own culture instead of American rubbish. Huws was still a handsome man in his seventies, with a mane of thick white hair and the sort of profile usually seen on statues or ancient coins. By his side on the bench was a woman of his own age, but not his wife, who was a well-known children's author. Huws rose to his feet and extended his hand towards Daf.

'Inspector Dafis, we know how busy you are in the midst of all this trouble, but would it be possible to speak to you? This is Dr Elizabeth Wilkes, Janet Cilgwyn's mother.'

Daf was in a dilemma. Huws was an important, busy man, a man who deserved to be treated with utmost respect. Yet Cai had not finished telling his story, and Daf had promised to have lunch with him. He would have to be less than courteous to someone and he didn't want to lose the trust of the young man with the track marks on his arm. He sighed to himself as he announced his decision.

'It's a pleasure to meet you, sir,' he began, turning to English to add, 'and you too, Dr Wilkes.' He could feel Cai's eyes resting on him. 'But unfortunately, I'm not free just at the moment, shall we say an hour from now? Very sorry to be so discourteous but...'

'We're the discourteous ones,' replied Huws. 'Turning up here without notice. But we do need to speak to you, Inspector Dafis, so shall we get some lunch and come back to see you then?'

'Very grateful for your understanding, Mr Huws.'

As he closed the door behind the dignified old man, Daf felt compromised and frustrated, but he remembered a saying which had been a favourite of his grandmother, Nain Siop: 'If you can't help hurting someone, hurt the one who can bear it best.' He was certain the broad shoulders of Huws could bear the snub better than Cai.

'Come on, *cog*, what are we going to get for our dinners, eh? Just say the word, and I'll get one of my lads to fetch whatever you'd like. And a cup of tea in the meantime.'

Over his kebab, Cai finished his story. He had walked back to Welshpool and spent the day in the library. He read the weather forecast in the paper and decided to go and ask Joe for a bed for the night. He spent a comfortable night there but, having heard so much about the inquiry into Heulwen's death, he decided to leave in the morning. And he had several interesting observations to make on his fellow occupants of the presbytery.

'I had been worried about Joe, with so many of their priests being perverts, but I got the picture on Tuesday night. Joe is head over heels in love with her, the Polish woman, but she doesn't see him as a man at all, just a priest.'

'And she's taken, anyway, Cai. You may as well get used to the fact that she's in love with your dad, Phil Dolfadog.'

Cai whistled. 'Handy that Mrs Breeze-Evans is out of the picture, then, eh? Because if there had been a divorce, her money would have had to come out of the farm and I can't see Jac allowing that.'

A new angle on the situation. Whatever had happened to Cai's body over the last decade, his mind was still very sharp. He continued his account of his movements. He had left Joe then been seized with a desire to see Dolfadog, so he had walked from Welshpool to Llanfair Caereinion. After buying a sandwich with some of the ten-pound note Joe had given him, he walked in the direction of Dolfadog. He had no specific idea why he was going there but, judging from the smile on his face, it would be enough for Cai just to be there, Daf assumed.

'Jac's never done me any harm, except been a bit too much of a big brother at times. I went into the little wood, where me and Gruff and Nans built a den once. From there, you can see most of the farm, and Tanyrallt as well. It was good to sit there in the shade, watching the comings and goings. I heard Margaret far off, calling Gruff in for a cup of tea, then I heard Jac's hammer banging on the posts as he mended the fence between Dolfelyn and the Ffald. I sat there through the rest of the day, half thinking of sheltering the night in the den. I've slept in worse places many times.'

But in the twilight, his memories and anxieties were boiling in his brain and he wanted to forget. He thought there might be ket in Tanyrallt and waited until it was fully dark before walking up the familiar lane. The yard was quiet and the tack room door open.

'Wasn't there a padlock?'

'There was a padlock there but it hadn't been closed.'

Daf remembered the padlock with the neat cut through the closure; it seemed that Margaret and Gruff were pretending that their ket had been kept more securely than it was. Daf tended to believe Cai's version of the story.

Cai used the first bottle of ket on his way down the lane. It began to rain and he sought shelter in the open-fronted shed in the meadow, which was where he saw the Section As.

'I thought about Gruff and about the care those horses got. It wasn't fair. There was a head collar hanging on a nail in the shed: I caught them up easy enough, one by one, and I trimmed their hair with my little pocket knife.'

'Didn't they make a lot of noise?'

'No. I didn't hurt them and they're used to being caught up. It was a grand feeling, like pissing in Gruff's beer.'

'What about Margaret? They're her horses, her pride and joy that she's taken years to breed; she's never done you any harm.'

'Oh, I know that, but things aren't always that clear in my head, to tell the truth, Mr Dafis. The images, they run into each other and into nothing, like pavement drawings in the rain. I could see Gruff's hands, his long fingers, stroking that girl's hair, Felicity's hair, getting his pleasure from owning her. Then, the ponies' manes were that grand, one coppery just like her hair, and he owned them too. My aim was ... no, that's just shit. I didn't have any aim in mind, except hurting Gruff, because he was the one who told Mrs Breeze-Evans about ... about me and Nansi.'

Daf leant forward slightly as if his movement would narrow

the width of the desk, setting Cai at his ease. 'What was there to tell about you and Nansi, Cai?'

'We were playing. The three of us had been fast friends, then suddenly, Gruff was off, leaving us behind. Up till then, I'd shared a room with Gruff and we'd got along fine though I was fed up with the stories of all his success, especially with girls. He moved to sleep in a little attic in the old part of the house, near the back door so he could come and go without anyone knowing what he was up to. Nans and I talked about his stories, about how much was bullshit and how much was real and she was right jealous. We knew all about Dad and how he was always organising some sly little fuck for himself.'

'Did you love Nansi, Cai?'

'We were children, Mr Dafis. It was more like a game of Doctors and Nurses than Romeo and Juliet. I did love her, but like a sister, but a sister who wasn't really a sister either. We were close before the physical stuff began and closer still after but there wasn't any romance between us. We shared a bit of pleasure, not that different to if we'd decided to go to the gym together.'

'And who started the relationship?'

'She did. She was very keen on discussing what Gruff was up to and even a lad like me could see the subject really interested her. She wanted to show him that she wasn't an innocent little girl, even if he didn't have any idea what was going on. The secret itself gave her a buzz, I reckon.'

'And you, Cai?'

'There's got to be something special about your first time, hasn't there, Mr Dafis?'

Daf remembered a warm September night when he had been seventeen and Falmai had just come into the Sixth Form, when they had cuddled up together in her father's haybarn, with a blanket and a bottle of wine Daf had stolen from the shop. Despite their ignorance, lack of technique and the odd thistle in the hay, the two had shared an unforgettable experience, something more than just sexual activity. It had been love and it laid down the foundation for a marriage and a family. Thinking of the way in which Nansi had attacked her mother, Daf considered that something more than fun had taken place between Cai and his foster-sister.

'You had a hard time of it after leaving Dolfadog, I hear?'

'You don't have to ask about that. It's all on my file.'

'Did you tell Nansi what had gone on?'

'I only got a chance to speak to her twice. They were all calling me an abuser so I wasn't allowed to talk to her, but I did have to tell her what it felt like to really be the victim.'

'Did you know that Nansi attacked her mother after hearing what had happened to you? Tried to slit her throat.'

'Fair play to her.'

'That's not a very sensible thing to say, given that you have just admitted to delivering a dose of ket to Mrs Breeze-Evans.'

'I didn't kill her, but I'm fucking glad she's gone.'

Daf didn't see any untruth in Cai's eyes and he had, after all, readily admitted to a number of offences.

'What are we going to do with you?'

'One thing for certain, you can't bail me.'

'Why not?' Daf raised his eyebrows at Cai's certainty.

'No one's ever offered me bail before.'

'Where could you go, if you were bailed? You have to have a fixed address, you know that.'

'To Joe.'

'With other witnesses in the case under the same roof? That's not the smartest idea you've ever had.'

'Dolfadog. Or Tanyrallt. Give Margaret a ring.' There was a new look in his face, as if he could take action to determine his own future.

'What, after you just wrecked her chances in the Royal Welsh? Don't see that working. What about that place in Conwy? Hafod House?'

'It's OK there but who's going to pay for me?'

'Shall we have a word with Joe?'

Silence fell between them. Cai was obviously exhausted. He coughed again, trying to stop himself from spitting.

'You're not well, lad. You need somewhere to rest for a couple of weeks.'

'And what after?'

'Whatever happens after, you're not on your own any more. I heard your story yesterday from Phil and Nansi; they're so full of regret for what happened to you and they're eager to help. And Basia is as well. We can't forget about your offences but if we work everything through, we can start putting you on the path to a better life.'

'I can't get back what I've lost.'

'It won't help to think like that. You like Basia, right? Well, she's going to be your step-mother and you can rely on her. You should have heard Phil talking about you, about how much he enjoyed having you about the place, helping him about the farm.' Daf deliberately didn't mention Nansi.

Cai nodded his head several times then released a cry which seemed to come from the depths of him. He began to strike his forehead against the surface of the desktop, howling like a wolf.

'Don't Cai, please, you'll hurt yourself.'

Daf pulled off his jacket, folded it and laid it on the hard wood of the desk to protect the young man's head. Breaking every rule, he put his arm around his thin shoulders.

'All you've got to do is get well, Cai, then you can move forward. Go off to college. Get a job, a home, friends, a girl, children, just like everyone else. You don't need to be on the outside anymore. Joe believes in you, I'll do all I can, and your Dad, knowing full well how badly he's let you down, well, he's willing to do anything to help you, to make up for letting you down.'

Daf considered discussing just what charges Cai would face, but the young man was in no condition to face such a conversation. Of course, he would have to be punished but how strictly? If the object of any sentence was to reform him, then he should be punished with security and care, not prison. Daf rang Joe: no reply, so he left a message. He went to look for Nia but Cai became agitated at the thought of Daf leaving him: Daf reassured him that he was safe.

'Nia,' Daf began, in a low voice, 'look after him, can you? I know he's an offender but he's also a victim, right? He's heckish fragile.'

'I get it.'

'And while you're about it, can you show him a couple of pictures, see if he recognises Lisa Powell or Rhys Bowen?'

'No worries.'

'Is there any Glade in the cupboard behind the desk?'

'Should be.'

Daf sprayed a bit of lavender-ish scent around his office to get rid of the strong smell of kebab. Then he sat down to await the arrival of Gwynlyn Huws. That man's life was a series of successes, a list of good deeds done on behalf of his community, for Plaid Cymru, for the Welsh language. In his time in Parliament, he had won respect for his contributions, but had remained close to his roots, raising his family in a little stone cottage not far from Bala. He had led his Party for a decade, but like all leaders, there were those waiting for an opportunity to take his place. Their chance came when Huws was arrested in a protest against the closure of a small rural school. Speaking of his 'old-fashioned image' and the need to 'appeal to voters outside the Welsh heartland', his enemies succeeded in creating the impression that Huws was a stumbling block to progress for Plaid Cymru instead of being its foundation stone. He had to resign, which he did with good grace, choosing to concentrate on his writing, he said, and his role as a grandfather. Daf had to admit, as a long-term admirer of Gwynlyn Huws, that he felt nervous when he heard a knock on the door.

Like the gentleman he was, Huws opened the door for Dr

Wilkes and pulled out a chair to allow her to sit; Daf would not have expected less. Dr Wilkes looked very like her daughter but the passion and unhappiness Daf had seen in the eyes of Jan Cilgwyn weren't present in her mother's steady gaze.

'We are very grateful to you Inspector Dafis, for finding time for us. Dr Wilkes doesn't speak Welsh but she understands every word.'

'Fair play to her, indeed.'

'Not to waste your time with preambles, we're concerned about Jan. That girl came into Plaid under my wing, as you might say, and I've always kept an eye on her. We're worried about her relationship, and not because Lisa is a woman. You must understand that there is no element of homophobia in this, but genuine concern. Lisa tries to control Jan in all matters, and she can be violent at times.'

'An angel abroad, a devil at home,' Dr Wilkes explained, cautiously drawing on a Welsh proverb.

'I see,' replied Daf.

'We haven't come all the way to Welshpool for a chat about politics,' Huws continued. 'But by now, Jan's sexuality has become a part of how Plaid itself communicates with the world, a statement that they're no longer a fringe group from the Celtic twilight but a modern party. But, and this is the problem, if you incorporate your lifestyle into the message you give the world, it's very hard to admit when something is wrong. It becomes an issue of integrity.'

'Jan can't admit anything is wrong between herself and Lisa, because of her high profile,' Dr Wilkes added.

'Do you read *Golwg*, Inspector?' Huws asked.

'Not as often as I should, I must admit.'

'Two years ago, there was a feature article in it about Jan and Lisa, with pictures of their lovely home, describing them as some sort of 'golden couple' and saying how far Plaid Cymru had moved since the days of dinosaurs like me.'

'You're not a dinosaur, sir,' Daf felt compelled to say.

'If you say that, you must be one yourself, Inspector. Anyway, the image of Jan as a woman totally content with her life, a woman who has fulfilled herself, that image is very important to her. More important than her own safety, maybe. She doesn't want anyone to think of her as a victim.'

'I can appreciate that.'

'And it doesn't help that she has been so prominent in the campaigns to prevent domestic violence, talking about our duty to raise our sons to be caring, not cruel, never once talking about the violence women can inflict. Domestic violence is a hidden factor in the lives of too many in the LGBT community.'

'People are people, when it comes down to it. Some are more given to flaring up than others,' Daf opined, thinking of the Humphries family. Chrissie was prone to slapping Bryn hard enough to leave a mark, but he had never raised a finger against her, as she often acknowledged.

'Exactly, Mr Dafis.'

'She's painted herself into a corner,' Dr Wilkes said, using an image which seemed strange to Daf for a moment.

'And a dangerous corner at that,' Huws added. 'We had hoped that the new law on coercive control might be of help to her but she's wandering around as if she were blind, talking about hate crimes while ignoring the facts of her own life. Lisa is an obsessional woman with a history of violence, and she had every reason to hate Heulwen Breeze-Evans. And she had come up to mid Wales on the Monday, arriving in the afternoon.'

'We've done some amateur sleuthing,' Dr Wilkes explained.

'But Jan is the focus of our concern, Inspector Dafis. How can we keep her safe? In my opinion, Lisa Powell may well have killed once. What's to stop her from killing again?'

'We need your help, Inspector.'

'Is there any way to use the new Act, Mr Dafis? Coercive control?'

'If Ms Cilgwyn doesn't want to lodge a complaint, that puts

us in a very difficult situation. But whatever I can to do help, I promise you, I will do.'

Daf let out a deep breath as they left. He felt as if he had been running over soft sand. He needed quiet, half an hour of headspace, to attempt to process the new information; to make a judgement on how much truth lay behind Cai's words and to plan a response to the concerns of Gwynlyn Huws. The old man had come close to rebuilding Daf's respect for politicians, and it had been a pleasure to spend some time in the company of people who were both concerned and intelligent, especially after starting the day with a conversation with Mrs Rhys Bowen.

Daf nipped out to make a cup of tea for two reasons. He had asked a lot of his team over the last few days and it would do them good to see him making an effort in return. The second reason related to Nev's secret biscuits. Nev always denied that he had a hidden stash of private treats but the crumbs on his keyboard told a different story.

A man was standing rather uneasily in the reception area: Gruff. There was no one behind the desk to speak to him and, before Daf could call out to him, the toilet door opened and Cai emerged. Gruff turned his head slowly and stared at him. Daf stepped back for a moment, to observe how the drama would unfold.

'Cai,' Gruff exclaimed, in a small flat voice.

Cai stared back at him for a long interval. Like a ten-year-old boy, Gruff raised Cai's hand, closed the fingers into a fist and used that fist to punch his own jaw.

'Belt me one, Cai, you know I deserve it.'

Remembering the bitter words Gruff had used to describe Cai, Daf was startled. Perhaps Gruff had created a monster and given it Cai's name as a way of dealing with his own guilt but had then forgotten it all when he actually saw the condition of the man who had once been his brother. Cai managed to free his hand, then presented his own chin to Gruff.

'I deserve to be punched. It was me that spoilt Margaret's Section As.'

'They're only fuckin' ponies.' Gruff managed to speak between his trembling lips and he put his arm round Cai's shoulder. Cai responded with a friendly blow aimed at that arm. 'I acted right dull, fuck knows how dull I acted.'

'Wankstain. You behaved like a total wankstain.'

'I did, fair enough, but what about you, you loser?'

Cai gave a punch to Gruff's muscled belly and for a moment they stared at one another.

'Your monobrow's got worse,' Cai observed.

'You're not exactly a film star yourself.'

Daf had no further opportunity to study the interaction between the two young men, as the door opened. Joe entered, accompanied by a woman in her seventies in an expensive Loden coat and brogues. Daf recalled noticing her in the congregation at the strange service on Tuesday: she was the mother of the Tory MP, Mostyn Gwydyr-Gwynne. Her long white hair was wrapped around her head like a crown, making her look taller than her six foot, and her back was as straight as any girl in her teens.

'Cai,' Joe began, 'I'm not going to be able to take you over to Conwy tonight, but Lady Beatrice can take you. Daf, do you need anyone to put up bail?'

'Are you offering, Joe?' Daf asked, slightly surprised.

'The bishop's not mad keen, to tell the truth. And I don't exactly have many resources to offer, in terms of cash.'

'If bail is required,' said the old lady in a voice which reminded Daf of the irritating certainty of her son, 'I will provide it.'

'I'm not sure that will be necessary, Lady Beatrice,' Daf replied. 'If he settled in that place before, I'm sure he will be fine there.'

'Thank you, Daf.' Joe was clearly relieved. 'Graham Parr will keep an eye on him.'

'Hang on a minute,' growled Gruff, pulling his battered wallet out of the back pocket of his jeans. 'If anyone needs to pay his bail, it'll be me. Cai shouldn't be dependent on the charity of some old snob.'

'My Welsh is bad, young man, but not non-existent,' responded Lady Beatrice abruptly.

'I'm not asking anyone for money,' Daf explained. 'If Cai will undertake to stay at the centre until the investigation is completed, that's good enough for me.'

Cai nodded his head. Daf observed his response to Gruff's sour and ungracious offer; it was clear that the angry words had counted more than any flowery statements of affection.

'I'll give him a lift,' Gruff added, glancing sideways at Cai as if he could not bear to look at his frailty for more than a moment.

Things were developing rather too rapidly for Daf's liking. These weren't two loving brothers being reunited, but two unpredictable young men who had every reason to hate one another. A two-hour car journey together was not a good idea at this stage.

'Cai, how did you get to Hafod last time?'

'Lady Beatrice gave me a lift.'

Daf did not have enough officers to spare for taxi duties but neither was he comfortable about letting the old lady travel alone with an offender who had just admitted to attacking Heulwen Breeze-Evans, even if he hadn't killed her. Daf pulled the duty rota out from behind the desk: there were three CPSOs available.

'Lady Beatrice, Cai is currently involved in the investigation of a serious crime so I will have to send one of my community officers with you, if that's acceptable?'

She looked over at Joe for his response: he nodded.

'Certainly, Inspector.' She steered the conversation onto lighter matters in a manner characteristic of her age and class. 'I believe we are to see you at Plas Gwynne next month, Inspector, for my son's engagement party?'

'Looking forward to it, Lady Beatrice,' Daf replied, which was an utter lie. He really wanted to answer something more like 'I knew the bride when she used to rock and roll', but he knew it was useless.

Daf left Nia to sort out which CPSO could go with Cai whilst he led Gruff through into his office. Gruff collapsed onto one of the chairs, his long legs sticking out rather awkwardly in front of him.

'Now then, Gruff, what are you doing here?'

'Well, Mr Dafis. Cai...' he attempted, after a short silence. 'Nans has been talking to me. I never wanted ... all that shit to happen to him. I thought there was something wrong about what was going on with him and Nans. I tried to stop it myself and when they wouldn't listen to me, I thought the grown-ups would get it sorted. Because, never mind about blood, he lived with us like a brother and he should never have gone with Nans like that.'

'And Nans shouldn't've gone with him either.'

'Fair enough, Mr Dafis, but it's always the lad's fault, isn't it? Whatever, he deserved a bit of a lesson, a belting maybe, not all that crap. Is he ... is he going to die?'

'Not unless Lady Beatrice is a very bad driver.'

'Why are those people potshing about with Cai anyhow?'

'Don't get angry with them, Gruff. Joe Hogan has always been good to Cai and the old lady is just following his example.'

Daf's phone rang but he ignored it.

'I made a mistake yesterday, Mr Dafis,' Gruff began, displaying almost every one of the signs which indicate that a person is telling lies. 'There were three other bottles of ket in the tack room, a prescription I'd got from Felicity because...'

'Have you spoken to her since yesterday?'

'No. The charger for my phone wasn't working.'

And, Daf thought, Gruff wouldn't want to speak to Felicity when he was full of guilt about the fun he'd had with the photographer.

'Do you play poker, Gruff?'

'Have done once or twice but not often, no.'

'Well, don't take it up. You're a hopeless liar. I had a long talk to Felicity yesterday and she explained to me all about your little conspiracy.'

Gruff blushed like a schoolboy.

'I was ... well, the whole business was my fault. If I'd been a bit cooler with Clara, then Felicity wouldn't have been that keen to speak with me Monday night so she wouldn't have left her car open, I bet.'

'You told me that you weren't a couple.'

'We're not, yet. We will be, when the time comes.'

'But she's not too keen on you going with other girls, is she?'

'Depends on the girl. Felicity was worried about Clara, in case she becomes a nuisance. And it's not like Fliss can't have her own fun, of course. But never mind, it was all my fault, all this hassle. I'm going to say that I stole her bag because that way, she doesn't get into the shit for failing to lock her car. That's what happened, Mr Dafis. I went for a spin with Felicity, in her car, and when I left her, I nicked her bag because I knew there'd be some ket in it and I fancied selling it for a bit of pocket money.'

'Oh, shut your face can you, Gruff Evans? I haven't got the faintest interest in Felicity's sloppiness. I know she must be pretty half-soaked to be interested in a bonehead like you. You may be shit hot at the Chase Me Charlie, Gruff, but you are bloody rubbish at conspiracies. Get out of here before I charge you with wasting police time.'

'Is Felicity going to be OK, then?'

'God knows, given that she likes a *lembo* like you. But I don't intend to make a fuss about the order Cai got each bottle of ket. Listen to me: you stick to the truth in future, right?'

'OK, sir. Sorry, and thank you.'

'And remember this, *catffwl*: for God knows what reason, two top quality women, Margaret and Felicity, think the world of you. You need to think about what you do to deserve the faith they have in you.'

'I understand. I don't always think before I act, that's the trouble.'

'I don't believe you think at all, Gruff. Like cutting through the padlock, whose clever idea was that? Yours?'

He nodded his head.

'Conspiracy to pervert the course of justice, that's what that was. Just behave yourself, *lanc*, can you?'

Gruff paused for a moment, his hand on the door.

'Something odd happened Monday night, Mr Dafis. I was right late getting home, after eleven, and I saw lights in one of the fields by the brook at Dolfadog, the Ffald, we call it. There's a fair bit of stock been taken locally over the winter, as you know better than I do, and even if Jac is a bit of a knob, he's still my brother. So, I took one of the dogs, old Pero, and went over to check what was going on. But the odd thing was, it was Jac himself, unloading a trailerful of stores at that time of night. Right odd, because I know he'd bought them early in the afternoon.'

'Thanks for the information, *lanc*,' replied Daf, secretly considering that he would almost rather have to deal with Gruff the conspirator than helpful Gruff.

He looked at his phone after Gruff had left the room: it was the High School. Like all parents in such circumstances, he experienced a moment of panic. He rang Rhodri: no reply. He rang the school, his hand shaking as he heard the options on the system: 'If you want to inform us of your child's absences, press one; for the finance department, press two. If you want to speak to someone in reception, press three.'

'Daf Dafis speaking. You rang me about twenty minutes ago.'

'Oh yes, Mr Dafis, thank you for calling back. We're trying to arrange a meeting of the Exclusion and Disciplinary Committee next week. Are you available at all during the day on Tuesday?'

'I have no idea at present.'

'I'll send you the details in an email. The Head wants the issue dealt with as quickly as possible. It'll be a permanent exclusion, a boy in Year Ten, Robert Humphries.'

Daf experienced a suddenly torrent of emotional relief that Rhodri was not sick, injured or in trouble, mingling with annoyance that they should bother him during the working day when he was so busy. Whatever Rob might have done, Daf could not imagine that he deserved to be excluded. Chrissie had raised her children to be polite and hardworking, as Daf knew from experience. He recalled Chrissie's care for Gaenor and made a sudden decision.

'I will be available on Tuesday, just let me know the details.'

He put his phone down on the desk and tried to turn his mind back towards the investigation. Someone needed to speak to Bowen's young sidekick, Tory Boy. He would have to find out the truth from Lisa Powell and try to manage the threat to Jan Cilgwyn. A full timetable of the comings and goings at the office needed to be created; Anwen's testimony would be essential there. And Daf was now very curious to find out why Jac Dolfadog had been unloading store cattle quite so late at night.

Sheila opened the doorway but paused before entering the room when she saw the expression on Daf's face.

'I've seen you more cheerful, boss.'

'I'm trying to create a pattern, *lodes*. I always look pretty terrible when I'm thinking.'

'Good job it doesn't happen very often then,' responded Sheila, sharp as a tack and confident enough to venture a joke in her newly acquired Welsh.

'Anyway,' she added, 'Cai has confirmed that the woman who was arguing with Heulwen in the back office was Lisa Powell. He wasn't quite so sure about Bowen because he didn't see his face but he said he'd know the jacket again, rough brown tweed, like a shooting jacket.'

'Great, that's a big help.'

Sheila waited a moment before continuing. 'And I had a word with my friend, the one we saw in the pictures with Rhys Bowen. She was a bit shy to start with but I think I've got a good idea now of what was going on there.'

'Which was?'

'She talked about how she feels after a flat-out busy week, paperwork up to her ears, moaning clients, partners stalking about in the background. She's often too tired to put make-up on and go out but doesn't necessarily just fancy a night in by the telly with just the cat either. When she feels like that, she sends Rhys Bowen a text and if he's about, he nips over with three bottles of Prosecco, the best steak in the world and enough bacon to feed a regiment.'

Daf smiled. He had never before considered the erotic potential inherent in the life of a butcher.

'She says he's always in a good mood, never asks awkward questions and is a good listener. When he leaves, whether in the middle of the night or in the morning, she'll have a smile on her face for the rest of the weekend.'

'Fair enough. That seems to confirm what I've been thinking, that maybe Heulwen didn't succeed in her attempt at blackmail. To put pressure on someone, you've got to have a secret to hold over them and it looks as though, whatever else we can say about our Assembly Member, he wasn't deceiving anyone.'

'At least not in his personal life.'

'Good point, Sheila. We need to find out a bit more about his business affairs. Can you get on to Companies House and all that stuff? Ask Nev if you're stuck.'

'No worries, boss. Don't you stay too late tonight, will you?'

'Why do you say that?'

'Because you look shattered.'

'I'll just have a browse through the crime scene report then I'll go home. It's a real balls-ache about the warrant, I'm almost one hundred per cent sure that Bowen would have plenty of meths about somewhere.'

'Nothing we can do, though, is there? Can I ask a question, about that lad, Cai?'

'Of course.'

'Nia said Lady Beatrice offered to stand bail for him, but why? It's a very strange thing for a woman in her position to do, to get involved with a young fellow who's homeless and uses ket.'

'I think Joe Hogan reminds her very often how fortunate her life has been and she responds by sharing a little of her wealth with a view to seeing she will be alright on Judgement Day.'

'Judgement Day? Oh, I see.' There was a suppressed note of scorn in Shelia's voice. 'Good luck with the report.'

Daf spent a little over half an hour taking in the detail of the report, his respect for Belle and her dogs growing with every page. Just inside the front door, a smaller fire had broken out and on the paint inside the letterbox four small circles had been noted, traces of the matches someone had flicked through it in an attempt to ignite the meths. In the case of the main fire, several litres of inflammable liquid had been distributed fairly evenly throughout the office as if a methodical fire-starter had been given enough time to do a thorough job. Two-stroke and meths, two different catalysts: did that mean two different arsonists? Had two different people tried to kill Heulwen Breeze-Evans on the same night?

He had an email from Nev. Before joining the force full-time, Nev had been a CPSO whilst working at the bank, so whenever a case involved financial matters, Nev was always available, making sense of financial records in a fraction of the time it would have taken Daf to examine the same material. He was well organised, Nev, and he had set out the main points of his research in order:

- Nothing out of place in any of Heulwen's four bank accounts. No sign of blackmail money being paid or the costs of a private detective.
- After raising the laying unit, little spare cash left at Dolfadog. The fall in fat lamb prices was a serious blow to their turnover and apart from the hens, which Nev described as 'profitable but over-geared', the most profitable part of the business was the suckler herd. And to keep the suckler herd going, the farm needed the land they had taken on tack in Llangadfan.
- Heulwen had suggested dissolving the partnership, asking for her share of the assets of the farm. This wasn't an empty threat: she had employed a team of experts to advise her. Her valuers had suggested that negotiations should begin on the basis of a sum of £1.8 million.

Daf recalled Jac's description of his burden of debt. He was stubborn in his attitude towards the farm; even though his brother and sister had left, he was going to stay to fight for his inheritance. He reassessed the information he had received from Gruff; suddenly, it seemed significant. If Jac was unloading stock so late at night, where had he been until then? Another question: if Heulwen was not making money from the blackmail, what was her purpose? Perhaps Sheila had been right and the information she had collected was some form of insurance, just in case. But if that was the case, how had she obtained all this information? Daf sent a reply to Nev, thanking him for his sterling work and asking if there was any way he could trace the origins of the pictures of Rhys Bowen.

The next item on Daf's to-do list was a phone call to Jeff, Gaenor's brother. The whole family were great, Daf considered: hardworking, full of humour and totally without airs and graces, just like Gaenor herself. Jeff was a carpenter who had spent five years building his family a lovely home, but they had lived in a caravan in the meantime. His wife, Del, always said that she could face any challenge in the world after surviving life in the caravan with Jeff. In their spare time, Jeff and the children travelled the length and breadth of Wales racing quads, returning home covered in mud and full of stories.

'How are you, *cog*?' was Jeff's cheerful greeting. Daf hoped he read things right and Jeff genuinely did like him, as that was how it seemed.

'Alright, Jeff. A bit on the busy side.'

'Who did it, then?'

'If I knew that, I'd be at home by now with my feet up.'

'Gae said you wanted a bit of a chat about Rhys Weirglodd?'

'If you've got a minute.'

'No worries but I'm on the hands-free on the back road from Oswestry so sorry if I lose the signal.'

'How well do you know him?'

'We're still good friends, despite living pretty different lives.'

'And his wife?'

'That stuck-up bitch. He should never have taken her on, but I think he was dazzled a bit by how she looks and her fancy ways. He doesn't give a shit about her now, and she returns the compliment.'

'The girls Rhys sees, they're just something to pass the time, are they?'

'Just fun, yes. Del worries that he's a bad influence on me but there's no one else like him. You remember how they used to say on *Blue Peter*: "Don't try this at home"? That's what I think every time I hear the latest about Rhys Weirglodd.'

'He boasts a bit then, does he, about all these girls?'

'No way, Daf, he's not like that. I hear tales about him from other blokes, mostly jealous, but now and again, I hear he's got a soft spot for some girl in particular.'

'And is there a favourite at the moment?'

'*Duwcs*, yes. A cracker of a blondie from over Bettws way, Daisy Davies. We had a hell of a sesh with them in the Bull and Heifer about a month ago, Del and me.'

'Is Rhys a violent man?'

'Always been handy enough with his fists but it's usually self-defence. He's a bit of a target on a night out, being such a big lad. And it doesn't help that the women are all over him like chicken pox. We've had any number of fights in our day, I have to admit. Sorry about that, Policeman-in-Law.'

'Could he kill someone?'

'I wouldn't say so. He isn't a cruel man and that's what makes him so good at killing ... animals, I mean. He explained to me one time how important for the standard of the meat it is for everything to be quiet and calm around a bullock before they get stunned. To keep the level of some acid in the meat as low as possible. He still kills now, you know, even though he's got plenty of people to do the job for him, to keep the craft of it. He killed us a pig last year and made a grand job of it. But to kill a person? I'd say no.'

'Thanks, Jeff. I'm sorry to have to ask.'

'It's fine, you have to find whoever killed that woman, don't you? But you know what, Daf? Rhys is loving life, big time. I've had the chance to go to the rugby with him a couple of times and bloody hell, he's a genius at a spree. Great company, money in his pocket, smart little flat in the Bay, a job he likes and enough nice girls coming and going without bringing him any hassles; he's got too much to lose to do anything daft.'

'I really appreciate your help, Jeff.'

'Happy to help. Let us know when you can leave Miss *Fech* and have a night out, the food's grand at the Gwynne Arms just now.'

'I will.'

Daf had enough time to read the SOCOs report over again and he began to feel that he had a handle on the detail. He was about to get himself one last cup of tea before taking a few notes when there was a knock on his office door. It was John Neuadd, looking, as ever, slightly out of scale in normal-sized rooms; he belonged outdoors or in the echoing cavernous rooms of his home. At his tail was a thin man in a good suit. From his orange tie and aura of misery, Daf guessed that this might be the Lib Dem candidate.

'I know you're heckish busy, Dafydd,' John began, standing in front of Daf's desk like a giant version of a boy expecting a telling-off from the headteacher, 'but Crispin here needs to know what's happening about the future of the campaign. Tonight, for example, there were supposed to be hustings in the Town Hall but Crispin got a message from the Town Clerk saying they were cancelled.'

Daf sighed.

'I've already had this conversation. The police have no influence on the decisions of the Town Clerk.'

'But Crispin says that Brian UKIP said that he'd said to him that...'

'John, for Heaven's sake, don't start playing Chinese whispers with me. Hasn't Crispin got a tongue in his head?'

'Yes, but he only speaks the Thin Language and he doesn't want to appear stupid.'

'He looks totally stupid standing there opening and shutting his mouth like a goldfish.'

John nodded his head in the direction of the candidate to encourage him to speak. When he began in an accent totally devoid of character, Daf once again considered putting a cross in the box marked 'Bowen, Rhys'.

'Brian Clarke says you banned the hustings because you had public order concerns, with migration being such an issue locally and one of the candidates having been killed by a man from Eastern Europe.'

Daf jumped up to his feet and leant forward, pressing downwards on his desk.

'Total nonsense. If I were certain who had killed Heulwen Breeze-Evans, I would have made an arrest by now. Mr Clarke appears to have a vested interest in damaging community relations, but I will not tolerate any insinuations being made about this inquiry.'

The candidate began to tremble visibly and Daf felt some sympathy for him.

'Cool down, can't you, Dafydd?' John suggested. 'Crispin was only repeating what Brian Clarke said.'

'And what did the Town Clerk himself have to say?'

'Well, that Bowen was unwilling to take part in any election event which wasn't totally fair, and until Plaid had chosen a person to replace Heulwen, it couldn't possibly be fair.'

'There we are, then.'

'But, and that's the reason he's here tonight, it's really hard to plan a campaign when things are so uncertain. The Lib Dems want to know what's what, who's going to be arrested and when that is going to happen.'

Daf saw a flicker of uncertainty in John's eye and he had to explore this a little further.

'John, when talking about the Lib Dems, you don't seem to be saying "we" at all. Why is that, when the Joneses of Neuadd are one of the most famous Liberal families in the county?'

John bent over the desk and whispered in Daf's ear. 'I'm going to vote for Rhys Bowen but I don't want to upset them by saying it. Sion, too. Crispin here doesn't stand a canary's chance, to tell the truth.'

Daf glanced out of the window over John's broad shoulder and noticed that the sunshine was weakening into twilight. He recalled Sheila's suggestion about getting home early and he also recalled that he had more important things to do with his time than waste it in empty conversation with John Neuadd before he could return to Gaenor and his children.

'Gentlemen,' he began, in English for Liberal Crispin's benefit, 'you really must excuse me. I'm in the middle of a very complex inquiry at the moment and I'm not able to spare you any more time. Let me just assure you that the investigations are proceeding with all possible speed.'

He extended his hand to Crispin but immediately regretted it. The candidate's hand was cold and rather damp, like a piece of meat which has been sweating in its plastic on the seat of a car. The unfortunate Crispin went out first and John paused to speak to Daf in private.

'She came up to Neuadd, the girl with the dogs, on Wednesday morning, Dafydd.' He stumbled over his words, his usually deep pink face brick red. '*Duwcs*, she's a smart girl and right pleasant in her ways as well. You never said she was as smart as that, Dafydd.'

'I definitely remember saying...'

'He's very lucky, that lad of mine, and fair play to him for trying. What's her history, eh? What sort of family are they? Would you say she's ready to settle down?'

'I've only just met her, John, just like you. And Sion, for that matter.'

'You know what, Dafydd, Belle reminds me of someone. Just you guess who.'

'Oh Jesus, I've got no idea, John. Cameron Diaz? Little Mix? One of the girls who presents *Ffermio*?'

'Chrissie Berllan. Not because they look alike, but the way she moves and something about her attitude, somehow. And Chrissie is definitely coming to scan for us at Neuadd.'

'And what will the lady from the jewellery shop say about that, I wonder?' Daf asked, tormenting John.

If it was possible for John to go even redder, he did. 'That was a mistake. She came across as a nice woman but I saw the other side of her nature on the night of the fire. Talking about nothing but money when someone had been killed.'

Fal would be relieved to hear this news, Daf thought.

'Was it them who did it, Dafydd, those big Polish lads? Because they say that Phil Dolfadog is carrying on with...'

'John, I've got a hundred and fifty phone calls to make. When this business is over, let's have a talk over a quiet pint, shall we?'

Daf couldn't physically push John out but he managed to guide him through the door. When he saw the light flashing on the desk phone and the caller display indicating that Diane Rhydderch wanted to speak to him, Daf decided to escape. He collected the papers from his desk, stuffed them anyhow into his laptop bag and hastened through the door.

He didn't have any particular intention, but Daf drove over to Bowen's factory, deep in the industrial estate. He parked outside the site and looked at the high fence, the featureless building and the sign which read: '*Cig y Canolbarth* Mid Wales Meats'. The sense of frustration was boiling within Daf; he was desperate to get in there, to see what he could find. He heard a faint clinking sound from his jacket pocket and suddenly recalled the keys, Basia's keys which he had picked up in the flat. With everything else which had been going on, he had totally forgotten to give them back to her. He sent a text to Nev, who was on duty at the station:

'If the alarm goes at Mid Wales Meats, pay no attention.'

Nev replied with a winky face.

Daf saw the bulky padlock on the high gate and looked through the keys: a large, heavy key was made of similar metal. The lock opened easily. Following the signs directing visitors, Daf reached the reception area; the door was closed with a Yale lock. He blessed Basia for her organisation: there were tiny stickers fixed to each key and Daf easily found the correct one: 'MWM 1'. Another key had the label 'MWM 7568' so when Daf noticed the alarm box, he opened its plastic cover and keyed in the appropriate digits. The light on the alarm box changed from red to green. Relaxing a little, Daf looked around the reception area in the light of his torch. The area was dominated by a large bronze statue of a bull, and the walls, from floor to ceiling, were covered with framed certificates and awards: 'Best Faggot in Show', 'All-Wales Unusual Sausage Champion 2013', 'Steak and Kidney Pie Best in Show, Winter Fair 2012', 'Taste of Wales:

Rissole of the Year' and so on. Daf could scarcely believe so many prizes could be won for meat products. Behind the reception desk were a row of doors with names on them and the name 'Rhys Bowen' was on the door nearest to the factory's shop floor. 'MWM 2' opened that door. Using his handkerchief to avoid leaving fingerprints, Daf switched the lights on.

Rhys Bowen's office was a stylistic mash-up between *The Apprentice* and a traditional country house. There was a vast desk made of shiny steel and some black wood, modern light fittings and a huge Apple computer but, in contrast, there was a stag's head hanging in the corner and a wide leather Chesterfield filled the room opposite the desk. A coffee table stood by the Chesterfield and on it was a framed photograph, clearly highly prized. The photo showed Rhys Bowen in a white stock coat standing beneath a banner proclaiming: 'All-Wales Unusual Sausage Champion'. He was offering his unusual sausage to a woman in a very well-cut coat who was weeping with laughter: it was Camilla, Duchess of Cornwall. Daf had to admire Bowen's nerve; he had clearly been flirting with the wife of the Prince of Wales exactly as he had flirted with Gaenor.

One wall of the office was covered by curtains. It was hard to be certain in the darkness, but Daf thought it likely that this window afforded Bowen a view of his shop floor so that he could keep an eagle eye on his workers. Opposite the main door was a smaller door and set on the wall beside it was a great glass-fronted case displaying butcher tools, knives of all sorts, hooks and several different sizes of hatchet. This gave visitors a clear message, Daf thought: Bowen was a butcher who happened to be a businessman rather than a businessman who had invested in the meat trade.

Every one of the four filing cabinets was locked but the desk drawers were open. In the top drawer, Daf found several biros and a diary which revealed nothing more personal than the dates of sales in the Smithfield and the timetable for meat deliveries. The next drawer felt more representative of the man Daf had come to know: a recently-filled hip flask of brandy, two packets of Custard Creams and a small leather pouch containing various different types of condom. The bottom drawer, which was considerably deeper, contained a muddle of rosettes, shields and cups, all heaped in *sang-di-fang* as if Bowen had won too many prizes to care very much about them. Underneath this triumphant jumble was a manila folder. Given that this had clearly been hidden, its contents were a considerable disappointment to Daf: nothing but a pile of delivery notes and invoices from meat companies throughout Britain. Daf's eye rested on the name of one company: 'Fazakerley's Premier Meats, the North-West's largest supplier of Premium South American Beef'.

Still taking care not to leave fingerprints and wishing he had thought things through, given that there were plenty of rubber gloves at the station, Daf opened the smaller door. He saw a cell-like room without a window. Above his head ran two rails, both with a number of hooks hanging from them. The walls and floor were made of concrete but there were little patches of gleaming surface here and there, as if years of fat had created a sheen impervious to the most assiduous use of a pressure washer. A solid wooden table stood opposite the door, its thick surface worn into a concave shape by years of cutting, and there was an external door, like a smaller version of the doors seen on a shed, to allow animals to enter from outside. The tang of blood hung in the air. A tall metal cupboard stood in one corner and in the other corner, the floor sloped slightly towards a grating which was fed from an open gutter designed to dispose of blood and water. It was Rhys Bowen's killing room.

In the locker, several long aprons were hanging. Protective gloves of varying thicknesses were piled neatly on a shelf and, in a case similar to a briefcase, rows of gleaming knives. Beside the case of knives were three well-washed empty Fray

Bentos tins and a large bottle of purple liquid: methylated spirits.

Daf felt a spike of adrenaline: he had ventured into the factory on the off-chance and had found exactly what he needed to find. He took a picture of the contents of the cupboard on his phone, his back to the door. Suddenly Daf became aware that someone else was nearby, not from any sound but the movement of air. Heart pounding, he turned around. Instinct alone made him duck, as a hatchet flew through the air over his head, hitting the opposite wall and falling to the floor with a loud clattering sound. Daf rose to his feet and stepped back into Bowen's office. The case on the wall was open and one of the hatchets had been removed but no one was there. He ran into the reception area: it was also empty but the door into the main factory space was ajar. Cautiously, Daf stepped into the great echoing space, searching for the light switch. He found a panel to the left of the door and pressed every single switch. Powerful white light flooded down, showing row upon row of stainless steel benches. No one was there. He heard the sound of a car engine firing and ran out through the main entrance: still no one to be seen but the fading scent of diesel reached him from the road. In the distance, he heard an engine sound retreating into silence.

His skin crawling with cold sweat, Daf stood outside in the soft air. Now the threat to his life was receding, he had to consider another threat, the threat to his career. At least one other person now knew that he had been trespassing in the factory without a warrant and that person, as Daf had just discovered, was a very dangerous person indeed. Walking on the balls of his feet, Daf returned to the killing room. He carefully picked up the hatchet and replaced it in the display case; the quiet click of the door of the case closing was like a gunshot in the deep silence. As he was re-setting the alarm, he noticed damp footprints on the floor which he had not seen before. He took a picture of them on his phone and as he did so, realised that his hand was shaking. He locked the door behind him, then the big padlock on the gate, jumped into his car and drove away.

Daf was used to violence. No policeman, even in the gentle loveliness of the Montgomeryshire countryside, could avoid it. He had spent two periods in hospital after being attacked: once, an unlucky punch had dislocated his jaw and led to surgery on his cheekbone and on another occasion, he had been stabbed in the stomach by a lad who was full of cocaine. He had never before been attacked out of nowhere. He stopped the car in the Sylfaen lay-by for a breath of fresh air. As soon as he was standing upright, he was seized by a bout of retching and vomited his guts up into the long grass.

He leant on the car to get himself together. Bowen. Who else could have opened the place up? Then he recalled that he had not locked himself in, and therefore anyone could have followed him into the factory. But who else would do such a thing? Who would benefit from killing him? As his stomach began to settle, Daf remembered how long ago it was that he had shared the kebab with Cai and that he had failed to find Nev's secret biscuit stash. High time that he went home for a meal and a cuddle with Mali.


No home could have been more homely. The smell of bolognese, the telly turned down low and faces full of love. He lifted Mali from her mother's arms and hugged her tight, thinking of what might have happened if he had not avoided the blade of the hatchet. He smelt something unusual in the room: aftershave.

'*Nefi blw!* It's good to be home. Today's been a hell of a day. Have we had visitors?'

'Sion's just left, he had his supper with Rhods.'

If Sion had started to smell of expensive aftershave instead of his usual mixture of silage and strong soap, Belle's influence was being felt already.

'Listen, Daf,' Gaenor began, getting to her feet to embrace him, 'Rhodri's in a peculiar mood. Can you pop up to see him while the pasta's boiling?'

'Sure.'

Daf wasn't sure he was in the best frame of mind to deal with his son's adolescent troubles after his terrifying experience, but he tried to psyche himself up to listen.

'How's it going, *cog*?'

Rhodri was on his phone, on his iPad and playing 'Call of Duty' on his laptop all at the same time.

'Hi, Dad. How's the investigation?'

'Like a bowl of lobscouse, full of lots of bits of different things. Got time for a chat?'

He put the game controller down but kept hold of his phone.

'You've got to help Rob, Dad. He's in the shit at school and it is totally not his fault, not at all.'

Daf knew that as a member of the Exclusions Committee, he should have silenced Rhodri at once, but he didn't.

'What's going on?'

Rhodri couldn't meet his father's eyes, and for the first time ever, Daf felt uneasy about him.

'They want to get rid of Rob because of his impact on the attendance figures. They're looking for a reason to get him out.'

'I'm sure that isn't the case at all. But what's he done?'

'He had a picture of a girl on his phone.'

'Ah.'

'She took it and sent it to him.'

'But did he keep it?'

'He did, but for a good reason. Do you know Ben Jones, in the year above us?'

'I know who you mean, I think. Tall lad, plays a lot of football?'

'That's him. Well, Ben's got a girlfriend and, Dad, I'm not being sexist when I say this, but she is a real floozy. She's after the lads something serious, especially Rob. But Ben thinks the world of her and he's a right good friend of Rob's so the whole thing is dead awkward.'

'I get it.'

'Rob knows the score, he's way more mature than the rest of us. This Lwsi's been contacting 'Brillwen, telling her that Rob's shagged her and all kinds of stuff. It's a good job 'Brillwen has got her head screwed on.'

Ebrillwen Pennant, Rob's girlfriend, lived somewhere the other side of Aberystwyth but they had been together since the previous summer when the National Eisteddfod had been in Meifod. Their relationship did not meet with the approval of Ebrillwen's father but, despite his best efforts, the young couple were still together.

'It was a picture of Ebrillwen, was it?'

'No, no, Dad; it was a picture of Lwsi Lewis. She took it and sent it to Rob. Rob's been worried about Ben because he's not the sharpest knife in the drawer and he never believes anything bad about her. And fair play, she is good-looking, especially her figure, but he deserves better than to be mucked about. So, Rob decided to show Ben the image, to convince him what sort of girl Lwsi is.'

'But?'

'But Lwsi told her dad, who's on the staff. I haven't seen it but apparently, it's a heckish dirty picture. Rob said she was ... no, I can't say it. But what I'm trying to say is that it wasn't just her naked skin, if you get what I mean.'

'I can imagine.'

'She's the same age as us, is Lwsi, fifteen. So now she's saying that Rob's a paedo, collecting filthy pictures of children.'

'That's ridiculous!'

'But they believe her! She says Rob badgered her into taking the picture. They are definitely going to exclude him.'

'What rubbish!'

'The truth is, Dad, Lwsi's angry with Rob because he doesn't fancy her. You're on the panel, aren't you?'

'Supposed to be, Rhod, but thinking about how close our two families are, I had better stand down from the panel and represent Rob instead, to ensure it's fair all round.'

'Can you tell him that? He's that worried about it, especially because he doesn't want to worry his mum.'

'Of course.'

Gaenor called up the stairs to announce that the spaghetti was ready. Daf explained the situation to her over the meal and they had almost finished when Rhodri came into the kitchen, phone in hand.

'Rob rung. He wants a word, Dad.'

Rob's voice, which was normally low for a lad of his age, was higher than usual.

'Mr Dafis, I'm that sorry to be a pain to you, really I am, true to God.'

'Rubbish, *lanc*, your mum's been a great help to us this week so I'm more than happy to do anything I can to help.'

'I don't like the girl at all, Mr Dafis. I've got no interest at all in seeing her lady garden.'

'I believe you.'

'You know better than anyone, Mr Dafis, I'm a steady one, me. 'Brillwen suits me champion.'

'Why didn't you get rid of the picture?'

'I wanted to show it to Ben. He's a grand lad, Ben, but his mum comes from over Llanidloes way and you know what people say about them: "Llani born and Llani bred, strong in the arm, weak in the head." That Miss Lwsi Lewis treats him like shit. Sorry for the language, Mr Dafis but I can't think of another way to say it.'

'This is important: apart from Ben, did you show or send the picture to anyone else?'

'No way. I described it to Dad Bryn.'

Daf always liked the way Chrissie's children referred to their uncle who was now their mother's husband. Bryn had always been a presence in their lives and when his brother was alive, he too had been described using his first name, as 'Dad Glyn'.

'What did Bryn say?'

'He said to delete it straightaway.'

'It's a shame you didn't.'

'I know, but Ben's such a *twmffat*, I have to take care of him. I really want to stay on in school for my exams, Mr Dafis.'

'Of course you do.'

'I've got plans: I've sorted an apprenticeship with Fowlers, down Chirbury way.'

'I shouldn't think there's anyone in Fowlers knows more about tractors than your mum.'

'Right enough there, Mr Dafis, but she's got a bit of a thing for them old Masseys. Claas and John Deere, they've got down Fowlers and a fair bit more work with the arable kit into the bargain. So, I go to Fowlers, stay on with them for two years after I'm qualified, work for Mum for five years then set up in business on my own account, sales and repairs. I'll be building my own house when I'm twenty and then, that's me sorted. But I need my exams to get my apprenticeship, so I've got to stay on at school.'

'I'll do my best for you, *lanc*.'

Somehow or other, Daf didn't find the right moment to tell Gaenor about what had happened in the factory. In the middle of the night, he woke from a nightmare, relieved to see her sleeping soundly by his side, making that toffee-chewing noise of hers. In Daf's bad dream, Gaenor had been hanging, a sharp hook through her throat, from the rail in Rhys Bowen's killing room.

# Chapter 12

## *Saturday morning, April 16, 2016*

Daf was surprised by how quiet the house was when he woke up, before recalling that it was Saturday. He felt like a burglar, or some illicit lover, slipping out of the house without having spoken to anyone or even making himself a cup of tea, but time was short. He had a list of things he had to get done, at the top of which was going after Bowen, restarting the warrant application process if necessary. On the one hand, it seemed to Daf that Bowen could only be part of the explanation because of the second fire, but it would have been possible for him, having failed in his attempt with the meths, to have tried again with another catalyst. Two fires but only one fire-starter, perhaps?

Before turning Heniarth corner, less than three miles from Llanfair, he heard the sound of a text arriving. He turned into the gateway at Tŷ Brith to read it: it was from Nia.

'Sorry to be a nuisance, boss but could you go and see Jac this morning first thing? He's behaving oddly and Low is worried.'

Daf replied: 'What's Lowri's number?'

He sent a text to Lowri and she messaged straight back:

'If you could come early, that would be great.'

Daf turned the car around and reached Dolfadog in ten minutes. The dew was still on the pastures and the spiders' webs on every hedge were heavy with tiny pearls shining in the morning sun. Daf noticed for the first time the little piece of woodland where Cai used to play with Nansi and Gruff, and he could not keep himself from wondering what kind of future there might be for the family and whether relationships worth treasuring might be rebuilt.

When Daf arrived at the door of the cosy little house which

had been created from the farm buildings in the rickyard at Dolfadog, he was warmly greeted by Lowri. She showed him into the kitchen where every beam gleamed with preservative oil and, in total contrast to the farmhouse itself, everything was in its rightful place. The house was filled with a delicious smell: Jac was struggling to free a loaf of freshly baked bread from the bread-making machine.

'Dough was a bit on the wet side, I reckon,' Jac observed.

'Fingers a bit on the clumsy side, I reckon,' retorted Lowri, taking it from him and releasing the golden loaf without difficulty.

Jac sat in the chair at the head of the table. All his movements were indeed clumsy, as if he had drunk several pints of beer, and there were shadows under his eyes. He raised the bread knife to cut the loaf, but the blade slipped from his hand and clattered to the tiled floor.

'What's the matter with the fucking thing?' he thundered.

'No, Jac,' Lowri said, in a low voice as she picked up and washed the knife before tucking the warm loaf under her arm in the old-fashioned manner, 'what's the matter with you, is the question. Mr Dafis has come up here to speak to you. I'm going upstairs to change the bedlinen. Can you please tell him what's chewing you? And don't pretend it's this business with Cai, because you know that isn't it.'

She arranged four large slices of bread on a plate for them before leaving the room.

'Will you have a cup of coffee, Mr Dafis?' Jac's voice had diminished to a civil tone.

It was good coffee, too, from a cafetière.

'By heck, you live pretty nice here, Jac! Fresh bread, snug little house, grand wife and the best coffee in the county.'

The young man lowered his eyes.

'And what have I done, Mr Dafis? Put the whole lot under threat.'

'How's that, then?'

'I haven't eaten or slept properly since Monday night. I can't carry on like this. I've even been ... letting Lowri down, which I've never done before.' Daf took this unclear expression to mean that Jac had lost his sexual appetite too and he rather liked the young man for expressing this in such delicate terms, focusing on his duty to his wife. 'Can I ask, Mr Dafis, when a man goes to prison, do they take away all his belongings: his ground, his stock, his whole business?'

'Not necessarily,' said Daf. 'If a person had profited from crime, they would confiscate the proceeds.'

'Oh.' A look of hope came over Jac's face. 'So, the money you've got through hard work, they wouldn't necessarily take all of that?'

'Every case is different but usually not.'

There was a moment of quiet whilst Jac refilled the cafetière.

'I did something mad on Monday night, more than one thing, actually, and in my head, I can't get round these things. Am I having a nervous breakdown?'

'Sounds more like the normal action of conscience to me, *lanc,* and the best way to deal with that is to tell the truth. On you go.'

It was a simple enough story to begin with. In order to try to persuade his mother to sign the lease, Jac had called to see her late in the afternoon. She had refused.

'She was that full of spite, talking about getting her share out of the farm, time and again, like a stuck record. She had that false smile of hers on her face as she kept on saying: "Here are my terms: give me my inheritance from Dolfadog and I'll sign any document under the sun." I wasted half an hour trying to change her mind, saying her best chance of getting something out of the farm was to help it prosper but she wouldn't budge. Then ... then I decided to do something stupid, bad and stupid. I thought that if I waited till that girl left the building, I could go back and force her to sign the lease.'

'How?'

Jac coloured and could not meet Daf's eye. 'It's a terrible thing to say about your mother, but I thought about breaking her fingers, one by one. She'd never call the police, because of the disgrace, and I'd seen, after Nans went for her that time, that she treated her with a lot more respect afterwards.'

'You're right, it is a terrible thing to consider doing. But you didn't put that God-awful idea into practice, did you?'

'How do you know that?'

'By now, I've collected a fair bit of detailed information about what went on in that back room. And her body would show the evidence of that. Anyway, on with the story: how did you know when Anwen had left the building?'

'I parked the Landy just outside Gwilym Bebb's office. There was a reason for me to be there, of course, because of the lease. I got myself a bag of chips to fill a hole and I waited.'

Daf could barely believe his luck: talk about a good witness! 'How long were you there for, Jac?'

'Three hours. Didn't move except when I realised I was blocking the lane, you know, the lane which runs up behind the houses. There was a car, well, a pick-up, wanting to go up so I moved.'

'What kind of pick-up?'

'Carwyn Watkin's pick-up, it was. Brynybiswal. He does odd jobs; did odd jobs for her, and for a few other people. He was on his odd jobs on Monday, I suppose, because he had a lawnmower on the back.'

This was interesting, and new but Daf wanted to move the conversation on quickly. Jac was in a strange state and might clam up at any moment. 'So Jac, and this is important, who came in and out of the office in that time?'

'I'm trying to recall.'

'It is important, for you as well as for me, Jac. I'm going to ask you, straight out: did you kill your mother?'

'No, Mr Dafis, but I didn't rescue her either.'

'OK. So, who did you see?'

From the kitchen drawer, Jac took a little stub of pencil and a neatly cut piece of a cereal packet, designed to be used as scrap paper. For rich farmers, they were careful with their pennies, Daf observed. Jac created a tally.

'To start, there were three people went in, a man and two women. I knew him, he's from just by Mach somewhere. He was in Young Farmers same time as me, one of the Bro Dyfi lot, and now he teaches in the school there.'

The only meeting in Heulwen's diary: the Welsh Teachers' Union.

'Then, maybe an hour after they left, Rhys Bowen came to the office, he didn't stop for long. Then Carwyn Watkin, then a businesswoman in high heels, right smart but not sexy.'

Carwyn Watkin again, Daf thought to himself, nodding his head to encourage Jac to resume the narrative.

'Before the posh woman came out, a rough-looking young man went in. Thin he was, with a straggly beard. I didn't know who he was but there was something familiar about him, somehow.'

'It was Cai.'

'Shit, no! There never was much meat on him but...'

'We can talk about Cai later. When did you see him leave?'

'I didn't. That Anwen left not long after the posh woman. Something weird happened then. It was almost dark by then but the young man, Cai, didn't come out through the front door at all. He came into sight from down the back lane and at the same time, Bowen came back to the front door. He stood on the doorstep in front of the door, and this is going to sound right mad, I know but...'

Jac mumbled the rest of the sentence so Daf could not make out the words.

'What did you see Bowen doing?'

'Well, the way he was standing and that, I thought he was pissing through the letterbox.'

Bingo, Daf thought.

'What next?'

'The rough chap, Cai, came back, going up the lane again, then came back down again, as if he'd just nipped back to get something. I waited for maybe ten more minutes, until the place was quiet then I went in through the front door. There was a strange smell and a pool of liquid on the floor but it wasn't the smell of piss, more like that old spirit stuff Nain Maesgwastad used when she was cleaning. Not that I took much notice, because I went straight in to speak to *her*.'

He hid his face in his broad left hand.

'When you saw your mother, was she still alive?'

'Yes, I think so.'

'Only think so?'

'Her heart was beating and her eyes were ... well, there was something there, in her eyes but she didn't move or speak a word.'

'That was the effect of the ketamine.'

Jac showed little reaction as Daf named the drug, as if he had gone beyond surprise. 'Whatever the reason, I couldn't get her signature so I copied her name from a letter which was on her desk. She could see what I was doing but she couldn't do fuck all about it. And I have to say, I got a bit of a buzz to see her like that. After I'd sorted the lease document, I had a stupid idea: I picked up her hand and put it on the contract to make sure there were enough of her finger prints on it if there was ever any questions asked.'

'And then you left her?'

'Yes. In the chair, unable to move or speak, unable to help herself. I'm not at all proud of what I did, Mr Dafis, not a bit proud.'

'And you went out through the front door?'

'Yes. I was halfway home when I recalled I'd still got the lease in my jacket pocket. So I went back to Welshpool and just before the Raven, Carwyn Watkin came up in my direction, driving flat out. I had a chance to put the lease through the door of Gwilym Bebb's office but when I drove past the Plaid office, the window looked odd. There was light inside but not like electric light, it was too orange. The place was on fire. I had to call the fire people but I couldn't use my own phone in case the call was traced. I used the kiosk outside the Pinewood. Fair play to them, it was only ten minutes before I heard the siren going.'

Once again, Belle had been right: she had said the fire had been extinguished quickly. Jac seemed to be struggling to finish his account of the events of Monday night.

'I saw the Llanfair tender go past as well and ... They, my neighbours and friends, were going to risk their lives to save *her* when I couldn't be arsed to even call for help until the whole place was ablaze.'

'No one could have known the place would go on fire, Jac.'

'But I could have known something bad would happen to a woman hanging like that between life and death. I was dying for a pint after so I took the back road home and stopped at the Beehive in Castle. Home then and Low was fretting something serious. Looks like she was right to worry, eh?'

'Jac, if we decided to forget for a moment the business of forging your mother's signature, what exactly do you think you've done?'

'Well, I left her.'

'I'm not saying it's the nicest thing I've ever heard anyone doing but that doesn't make it a crime. In France, everyone is under a legal obligation to help one another but not here in Britain.'

Jac rose to his feet and walked over to the window. He changed the subject, his voice lighter.

'We haven't shown you Mum's study, have we, Mr Dafis? Over in the house. Not the big room but her little private study. Do you want to go have a look?'

'Please.'

Jac's body language had eased, his stride lengthened as they crossed the yard to the farmhouse, his shoulders had come down from their clenched state. He might not be the arrogant young master of Dolfadog but neither was he the haunted criminal Daf had met earlier that morning. And he had added considerably to Daf's understanding of exactly what had gone on in the Plaid Cymru office on Monday night.

Nansi and her family were the only people staying at Dolfadog. Jac opened the back door without knocking, as Seth was saying grace before they began their breakfast. Jac rolled his eyes scornfully but what Daf saw was a united and loving family, even if they were a little old-fashioned in their ways.

'I'm taking Mr Dafis to see Mum's things,' Jac explained.

Nansi nodded but continued to focus her attention on cutting slices of toast into strips thin enough to dip into soft-boiled eggs.

'Where's your dad, Jac?' Daf asked as they followed the corridor through the labyrinth of the old house.

'Fixed himself up with a love nest in Welshpool, so it seems, handy for that piece of his. Apparently, she wants to keep on working until they marry but the old bugger will have to carry on doing his share here, wherever he's living.'

'Fair enough.'

Jac opened the door of a small room, scarcely more than a large cupboard: it contained a desk and chair, a printer and, very interesting to Daf, a laptop.

'Have you got a bin bag I could wrap this in, Jac?'

'Yes, sure.'

With the laptop under his arm, wrapped in one of the purple bags provided by the council for unrecyclable rubbish, Daf returned to the kitchen where Nansi was carefully crushing the empty shells of the boiled eggs. Daf's Nain Siop had always done the same, in case witches might take your eggshell to use as a boat.

'I've got work to do, if that's OK with you, Mr Dafis?' Jac asked in a milder tone than he had used before.

'No problems, *lanc*. And thanks for the chat before, very helpful.'

Daf stood in the kitchen waiting for an offer of some kind which eventually came from Seth.

'Nancy, I think Mr Davies would like a cup of tea.'

'Of course.' She changed to Welsh to make the offer. 'You'll have a cup with us, Mr Dafis?'

'Thanks very much.'

As his wife filled the kettle, Daf noticed that Seth was avoiding catching his eye. When the children had finished their breakfasts, he ordered: 'Now, children, you go quietly to the parlour to play. I will be with you in a few minutes.'

The atmosphere in the room changed after they left. Nansi's face seemed to close in, as if she were preparing herself for whatever was to come.

'Mr Davies,' Seth began, rising to his feet as if he were preparing to preach, 'I do not know if you are a man of faith but you probably know that for us, the service of the Lord is at the heart of our lives. We strive to avoid sin though we do care for sinners. But those who find themselves deep in sin in this modern world often choose to describe their actions as choices which they have a right to make. Those people are dangerous because they infect others with their wrongdoing and that, Mr Davies, is the difference between Nancy's parents.'

Nansi's cheeks were flaming with embarrassment. She set his tea in front of Daf: a cup and saucer, not a mug. It was obvious that Seth had not finished making his statement.

'Nancy's father is a fornicator but, to give him his due, he did not want the God-gifted institution of marriage destroyed. Last year, when she was a guest in our home, Nancy's mother chose to ... indulge her unnatural desires in our spare bedroom. When I confronted her and the degraded woman she described as her "partner", she started to recite a confection of dangerous nonsense, describing the unnatural lust they shared as "love".

345

I was obliged to expel her from my house, and from that time, my family have had no contact with her. It is not easy to say this about the mother of my beloved wife, but she was a corruption, an evil influence who was not to be permitted to imperil my family.'

With this judgement, the Reverend turned slowly and walked out of the room at a dignified pace. A silence fell, deep and full of embarrassment.

'He's a good man,' Nansi ventured after a while. 'It's a different tradition, you understand, Mr Dafis. In the Gambia, where Seth is from, it's still against the law to...'

'I get that, but Nansi, if someone speaks as Seth has just done about someone who has been killed, it raises questions.'

'When he opened the bedroom door, he had a serious shock.' She smiled and Daf had a glimpse of the lively young girl Nansi must have been before the shadows closed in upon her. 'And I know many men have a fantasy about seeing a couple of girls in bed together, but not my mum and Jan Cilgwyn.'

Daf had to laugh but Seth's words were still ringing in his head. He had been speaking of his mother-in-law as if she were a bacterium instead of a woman with a soul, with choices, with rights.

'Nansi, where was Seth on Monday night?'

'On his way back from a meeting.'

'And where was the meeting?'

She lowered her eyes before replying. 'A place up above Newtown. Dolfor.' There was a low sigh in her voice, as if she foresaw further troubles.

'What sort of meeting was it?'

'There's a strong community in Newtown, looking for a pastor. The salary is a fair bit more than we have at present, including a job for me as Family and Youth Leader, and there's a fair-sized house into the bargain.'

'But?'

'But no man can lead a flock in good conscience if his mother-in-law doesn't conduct herself properly. We had a long talk about it on the Sunday, before he went up to Dolfor; Seth would have to turn down the offer because of my mother's scandalous conduct.'

'And what was his response to that?'

'Of course, he was angry. It would have been a great opportunity for us as a family, and I would far rather raise my children in Montgomeryshire than in Cardiff, if I had the choice.'

'What time was it when Seth arrived home?'

'Just before seven. He always makes an effort to get home in time to read the children a story, even if he has to go out again afterwards.'

'And did he go out again on Monday night?'

'Only to the hall, which is just next door to the house. Finance committee.'

'So Seth wasn't in Montgomeryshire at say, nine o'clock...?'

Nansi jumped out of her chair, cheeks blazing, eyes grown huge with emotion. 'I get what you mean, Mr Dafis, and you're totally wrong. Seth is a kind and gentle man. I'm surprised at you. Seth may not have condoned Mum's behaviour but that is a very long way from killing her.'

'I never said any such thing.'

'But I could see the suggestion in your eyes, Mr Dafis. I know these days that young people are encouraged to break all the rules, to do what they like and to hell with the consequences but, from my own experience, sex isn't a thing to take lightly, like choosing to go for a country walk. It was my lust which destroyed Cai, and it was my parents' sexual unhappiness which wrecked our chances of a comfortable, safe life. They couldn't put us before the itches they wanted to scratch, though we were their own children. Sex is like a fire; you can get warm, of course, but you have to take great care or people will get injured and that leaves scars on everyone, scars that will never heal.'

'I've seen that myself many times, *lodes*.'

'Don't judge Seth for speaking the truth. My mother's lifestyle was pure selfishness and I am glad she's gone.'

Nansi ran out of the kitchen like a ten-year-old girl who couldn't win an argument. Daf picked up the laptop and paused for a moment on the threshold, considering the difference between the welcoming little kitchen the other side of the yard and the emptiness of the farmhouse. He hoped, as he closed the door, that Low's influence could make a home of the echoing cold house.

His mobile rang again opposite Tŷ Brith: Dilwyn Puw the Deputy Chief Constable, on a Saturday?

'Seen the papers, Dafydd?' he asked.

'I've been at Dolfadog with Heulwen Breeze-Evans's family till now, boss.'

'You'd better look at them. There are a couple of articles which deserve a bit of attention, in my opinion.'

'Why's that, sir?'

'In the *Express*, the headline runs: "Fear of unrest prevents arrest in Welsh killing". They've got a long piece from some chap called Brian Clarke, who describes himself as a "champion of the local community". God knows what that means.'

'He's the UKIP candidate in the election, sir, and he's trying to stir things up.'

'I take it there is no truth in his suggestions, Dafydd?'

'Not a *smic*. We have been talking to two men from Poland, one of whom has a violent record, but neither of them has a motive to kill the victim and they have an alibi: they were in a crowded pub when the killing took place. There was a sort of storeroom in the top flat above the office, cigarettes, vodka and so on. I can't see them setting a fire without moving their stuff first.'

'Smuggling?'

'Could be. But whether or not they'd paid their excise duties, they certainly valued what they had stashed away.'

'Fair point. I think you should speak to Diane Rhydderch as soon as you can, anyway.'

'Is that all, sir?'

'Unfortunately not, Dafydd. There's more to worry us in the *Guardian*. "Rural forces fail on hate crime, says victim's lover." Then there follows a description of you which is far from fair but could cause us a lot of bother if this is the line the press are going to take. They call you old-fashioned, the sort of policeman who would help the Famous Five capture some smugglers, suggesting that your lack of experience prevents you from leading an effective investigation. At least they didn't actually call you a homophobe.'

'Absolute rubbish. I'm not stupid, nor am I prejudiced. If you aren't sure where I stand, sir, ask Mei Martin from North Wales Police.'

'I've already spoken to Inspector Martin this morning.'

There was a short silence whilst Daf processed the idea of the Deputy Chief Constable ringing Mei on a Saturday morning. Mei moved heaven and earth to avoid working on Saturday mornings if he could, in order to be able to spend the whole day with his partner, Graham, and their large untidy dog, Faggot, who was constantly coming close to structural damage with the chaos he wrought in their home. Daf hated the idea of his friend's free time being disturbed without reason but he was certain Mei's response to the call would have calmed Puw's anxieties considerably.

'What exactly do you suggest I should do, sir?' Daf asked, managing not to be too abrupt.

'Tread carefully, that's all. And Dafydd, please do use the skills Diane Rhydderch has, she's there to help you.'

'OK, sir.'

'Could Diane draft a statement of some kind in time for the Sunday papers?'

'That's possible, sir.'

'Divert their attention, that's the idea. By the way, Dafydd, did you get on OK without the warrant?'

'Yes, sir,' Daf replied, the web of lies extending.

Puw changed his tone of voice as if he were speaking to a friend rather than a subordinate.

'Get in touch if you need to, Dafydd. Over the weekend, if need be, just pick up the phone.'

'Thank you, sir. It is a complex business.'

'I'm sure it is. Bye for now.'

Daf was by nature an anarchist, unwilling to accept any form of authority, therefore it was a peculiar experience for him to receive support from a man like Puw; as they said in Carys's favourite film *Notting Hill*, "surreal but nice". Driving past the lay-by where he had vomited the night before, he was full of energy, ready for any challenge. Even before he'd greeted his team, he presented the laptop to Nev.

'Bit more work for you, *cog*,' he said. 'And the moment you've worked out where those pictures of Rhys Bowen came from, bring me the info, together with two Garibaldis. Don't deny you've got a secret stash of biscuits, I'm not daft, you know.'

'No idea what you're talking about, boss, but thanks for the laptop. The Plaid girl is here, and that Tory lad and I believe Bowen himself is on his way over.'

'Fine. I also need a word with Carwyn Watkin Brynybiswal. See if you can get in touch and arrange for him to come in to see me, please. Where's Steve?'

'Gone to play football. Away, in Flint.'

'Part-timer.'

'It is a relegation decider, boss.'

Anxious to avoid a discussion of minor league football traumas, Daf went to find the young politicos. They were sitting side by side on the bench in reception, discussing Einion's book *Sex, Lies and the Ballot Box* and, despite their different perspectives, were clearly getting along famously.

'But according to Piketty...' Anwen was protesting.

'Stuff Piketty,' answered Einion abruptly. 'His sums don't add up, I'll send you a link. Anyway, he's a Frenchman. How many top-flight French economists can you name? Go on, just name three...'

Daf had seen something like this before and knew that Carys had a name for it: 'geek love'. Talking about this abstract subject, their eyes were wide, their hearts thumping like steam hammers. Before long, discussing some other dry topic, such as the sustainable development of rural Wales, they would suddenly find that they were ripping each other's clothes off.

Their debate was interrupted by Anwen's phone ringing. She opened the text message and all trace of colour vanished from her round cheeks.

'*OMB*,' she gasped,

'Are you OK, Anwen?' asked Tory Boy courteously.

'They've chosen a new candidate for this seat.'

'Who?'

'Me, if I accept.'

Without thinking, Einion wrapped his arms around her and squeezed her tight.

'That's awesome, Anwen!'

Bowen walked in through the door before Einion had let Anwen go.

'Well, I can't say that I'm surprised,' Bowen observed, throwing Daf a suggestive glance. 'I've been expecting something of this sort for a good old while, to tell the truth. *Plantos*, we have got to create a coalition against Labour and I'm delighted to see you are getting your own coalition process underway.'

Daf looked at Bowen with his wide smile and eyes full of affectionate humour. It was difficult to believe that the man in front of him was the person who had tried to kill him the night before. He recalled Jeff's observation about Bowen: his singular talent was to relax the animal he was intending to kill.

'Anwen, Einion, I'd like to speak to Mr Bowen first, if you wouldn't mind waiting here for a little longer?'

'It's no problem for me,' answered Einion, and Anwen nodded her head. The offer she had just received had obviously given her a considerable shock.

'Hey, Einion,' Bowen suggested, looking over at the young people with a paternal air of indulgence. 'Why don't you take Anwen up to the office and print out a set of our canvass returns for her? On the same lines as showing a girl your "etchings" as they used to do.'

'We lost our database in the fire,' Anwen said, her eyes filled with longing. 'It took me months to build it up. I should have loaded it onto the Cloud, I know.'

'I'm not joking, *lodes*,' Bowen added and Daf could not help noticing that the generous-spirited offer was being made at the same time as the Assembly Member was admiring Anwen's large, firm breasts. 'You're starting late and in very tricky circumstances. It wouldn't bother me if you had a look at our returns, you've got no time to waste. For example, you've got a good lot of firm support promised in Mach and you probably know exactly where they are, but what about those who are on the ding-dong, not decided yet? We've had people over the town like ants. Nip up to the office with Einion, see what we've found out. And Einion, if any of the old ladies kick up about Anwen here, you refer them to me, eh? I'm going to win this election, but I don't want anyone saying I didn't win in a fair fight.'

'That's so kind of you, Mr Bowen.' She smiled broadly.

Daf opened the door to his office and Bowen strolled in behind him, whistling. Daf struggled to remember the hatchet and, in his haste to find out the truth, dropped all formality.

'You're in a good mood, Rhys.'

'The sun's shining, I had a cracking breakfast, the local polling shows I've got a ten-point lead and I spent a very worthwhile night last night.'

'Worthwhile in what way?'

'Filled in some right promising Voter Intention Sheets in the Bull and Heifer then got busy on some different sheets after.'

'Daisy Davies?'

'You're a right nosey bugger, aren't you, Daf Dafis?'

'I'm a policeman. So, it was Ms Davies's turn for the steak, bacon and Prosecco treatment last night, was it?'

'The Bull and Heifer just bought a Welsh Black bullock off me, I needed to make sure it was being cooked right.'

'And how was it?'

'Grand.'

'Can I ask what time your date was?'

'Eight.'

'And before that, where were you?'

'I can't say.'

'Why not?'

'Because I stopped by to visit a girl and I can't give her name to anyone unless she says that's fine by her.'

Chivalry from such a shagger began to thoroughly irritate Daf.

'OK. Perhaps this will help you be a bit clearer. I have reason to believe that last night, at around quarter to eight, you tried to kill someone.'

'Fuck's sake, Daf Dafis, what is the matter with you?'

'What's the matter with *you* is more the question. I've been pretty patient in dealing with you but now it's time for a bit of plain speaking. I know you went to see Heulwen on Monday. Why?'

'She asked me to come down and visit her.'

'And what were you discussing, the two of you? Education policy?'

'No.'

'What then? How will your local polling look if you get arrested for wasting police time?'

353

'Listen, the old bitch is dead now. What difference does it make what poison she was trying to spread around?'

Daf pushed the envelope of pictures across the desk.

'It was very important for Heulwen to beat you, Rhys. Her aim was to start a new life with her partner down in Cardiff and you were the only thing which was standing in her way.'

Bowen was browsing through the photographs with a connoisseur's eye, remarking from time to time on what he saw.

'Real identical twins they were, and double-jointed too: hell of a good night and worth every penny ... Here's a lovely girl and a half: hardworking, honest, cracking tits on her. What is the matter with these single fellows, eh? I picked this one up in the Eli Jenkins when her date stood her up, poor girl, but she wasn't disappointed in the end...'

Daf snatched the photos away from him, annoyed.

'Do shut up, Rhys. We got these from Heulwen's safe: was she trying to blackmail you?'

'Yes, yes, she's always been Mrs Background Knowledge, which is how she's kept that wimp Car Wat on a piece of cord since forever.'

'Did she succeed in blackmailing you?'

'What was it the Duke of Wellington said that time? "Publish and be damned", wasn't it? That's what I said, and I asked her to get out of that office because I wasn't prepared to rent any property of mine to someone who behaved like that. She told me the lease ran till June and she'd see me in court if I tried to get her out. I was seriously fucked off with her.'

'What did you do after?'

'I think I know what you think about me, Daf Dafis, and you're probably right; I'm a lad who's never really grown up. I was feeling that tied down and frustrated, and what's the best cure for that?'

'I can imagine.'

Bowen put his large hands flat on the surface of the desk and looked at their hairy backs as if he'd never seen them before.

'You know how I live, how I've lived for a fair bit now. Coldness at home and fun round and about. I had one hell of a telling-off yesterday from an old friend, someone I'd known since way back. And you know what? She was spot on. I am right lonely. But I've learnt what it is I want: friendship, a bit of company in the evening, maybe even children. Monday night, for example, I wanted to see someone in particular, not just any girl I could fuck, but she had a parents' evening till later. I've thought since that if I'd been able to go straight over to see her, perhaps I wouldn't have...'

'It's not the girl's fault if you did something stupid.'

'I've got a little room at the factory,' Bowen began to explain. 'Where I kill. I still kill right often. People are always asking, especially if it's a beast they've reared special. And some old friends, people like Jeff Morris, they ask me for help, with their fowls at Christmas, say, and that nice porker Del raised in the back end. It's cold in there so I've always got a couple of bottles of Prosecco there; the ladies love the stuff though I prefer a nice South American red myself...'

Lonely was the right word, Daf observed. Bowen reminded him of the old farmers who would come into the shop when he was young, the ones who would take the best part of an hour to buy a packet of tea, taking every chance to speak.

'Whatever, I went to get her Prosecco and that's when I saw the meths. I still use it now and again, to get rid of the down on ducks, and some types of chicken.'

'What were you thinking of doing?'

'I thought I could create a bit of hassle for Heulwen, that's all. I thought, if I did something a bit like what the lads from Meibion Glyndŵr used to do...'

'Why would Meibion Glyndŵr, even if they still existed, which they haven't for at least twenty years, target a Plaid Cymru office?'

'I don't know. I wasn't thinking that straight or I wouldn't have considered such a fucking daft thing. A bit of smoke, I thought, and she'd have to run out, her secret file tucked under her arm...'

'And what about the Bartoshyn family? How would that kind of stunt affect them, eh?'

Daf felt as if he were talking to a lad of eighteen, not a citizen of substance who was fulfilling an important role as a lawmaker.

'I only intended to make a bit of smoke. Anyway, I've got a tidy house available up Bryn Siriol which would suit them better than the flat. Basia keeps things real nice, she deserves a better home.'

'So what you decided to do was make a firebomb to set fire to your own property?'

'It wasn't a bomb, only a rubber full of meths. I didn't light it, anyway.'

'I know that. Five matches, was it, or six?'

Bowen was startled. 'How the heck do you know that?'

'That's my job. I must say, the idea of a man like you standing by the front door of a building in Canal Street, flicking matches through the letterbox is almost unbelievable, but as Sherlock Holmes always says...'

'Oh, please don't moither me with Sherlock fucking Holmes. Are you going to arrest me?'

'Possibly, but just at the moment, I've got an important question to settle. If you didn't manage to light your fire, who was responsible for the other fire which killed Heulwen Breeze-Evans?'

'No idea.'

'OK, let's get back to Monday night then. You tried your nonsense with the matches, then what?'

'I went to the Oak for a coffee.'

'A coffee?'

'I've said to you before, Daf, I'm not stupid enough to put my whole campaign in danger over a glass of wine. I'd get a nice drink later anyway, over Bettws.'

'And how did you feel, sitting in the Oak, sipping your coffee?'

'Like a fucking fool. It had scared me, to tell the truth. Not the business with the ladies because everyone knows what sort of chap I am, but nobody likes the thought that someone's creeping about, trying to discover all their secrets.'

'What secrets would those be?'

'I'm in business. No one ever made a fortune by following every little rule.'

Time for a bit of fishing, Daf thought.

'Such as, for example, selling top quality Welsh produce whilst at the same time importing a fair bit of meat from Argentina through Mr Fazakerley?'

'Ooh, you are a sharp old beggar, Daf! This is how it is. Take a meat pie, now. Some are prepared to pay four pound for a top-notch pie, high quality ingredients, everything tip-top. Others are looking to be able to feed their kids on cheap rubbish and they aren't going to pay over a pound. Keeping the customer satisfied, that's my game, but I've also got a good name to keep up. A reputation's hard to get and easy to lose.'

Daf had to ask, purely out of interest, a question which was unconnected to the investigation.

'What about horsemeat? Have you put a bit of minced Shirgar in your rissoles, Rhys?'

'No way. I've got a simple rule: I'm not prepared to process anything I can't understand. I've never killed a horse, got no idea how to butcher one, which means if I was in the market for horsemeat, I wouldn't be able to judge the standard of what I was buying.'

'Right. What happened after you had your coffee on Monday night?'

'I nipped into the office to check my emails, nothing important, then over Bettws, to see my friend.'

'Daisy Davies?'

'Daisy Davies.'

When he said her name, a romantic expression came over Bowen's broad face.

'Stay the night?'

'I went home in the morning to change my shirt.' He paused for a moment. 'You know what? When this business is all over, the investigation and the election, I'm going to sort things out a bit. Settle down, maybe.'

'With the greatest respect, Rhys, I don't have enough time to discuss your plans at the moment, I just need facts. So it went like this: fire bomb, coffee, office, Bettws, right?'

'Yes. I did pop into the shop in Berriew, for a bunch of flowers on my way over to Bettws.'

'Fine. What about yesterday afternoon?'

'Canvassing in Newtown until four, then Einion went with the rest of the team back to the party office. I had to go to the works: HR problem.'

'HR problem?'

'You know what was at the root of the HR problem? Same as always, the bother comes when I employ English people. Always complaining, bleating on about their rights, never roll their sleeves up for a bit of hard work. Welsh and Poles I can manage but the bloody Saxons...'

'There is such a thing as the Racial Discrimination Act, you know.'

'They deserve being discriminated against, the lazy bastards.'

'What time did you leave the factory?'

'We don't have a late shift on Friday. It's hard to fill the line and there are always no end of problems. The type of people that work for me, they like a bit of a spree on a Friday night but they're fine for doing a Sunday instead. So the place shuts down right early on a Friday, office hours. I left a bit before six.'

'Left to go where?'

'I can't say.'

'So you can't tell me what your movements were between leaving the factory and arriving at the Bull and Heifer?'

'Sorry, no.'

'Why are you so stubborn? You do realise that I have the right to arrest you now?'

'*Twt lol.* Won't make a difference to anything, I've got no right to say.'

'Why not?'

'Because it's a private matter.'

'We could use your phone data to find out where you were, you do know that?'

'Knock yourself out.'

'I'm almost certain you're not being silent to conceal a crime so why won't you make matters that much simpler for yourself by saying?'

'What if I have a word with my friend and if she's fine with it, then I'll say, OK?'

'Fine. Time for a cup of tea, my mouth's as dry as a cat's nest.'

By this time, Anwen and Einion had returned and were absorbed in the contents of a brown folder, their heads close enough to be touching. The station was quiet. Nev was no doubt working steadily on Heulwen's laptop and there was a CPSO on the desk. Daf made tea and had a flash of inspiration. In the filing cabinet, the file marked G was hanging askew. In the bottom of the file was a lump, a packet of Garibaldi biscuits. Nev was a tidy-minded young man, hiding his biscuits in alphabetical order. Daf's phone rang, Gaenor.

'Morning, *cariad.*'

'Good morning, Daf. I know how busy you are, so I won't waste your time. Don't make a big thing out of this but Rhys called by yesterday for a cup of coffee and a chat. Rhys Bowen.'

Daf felt the muscles of his stomach tightening as if he had received a physical blow.

'What?'

'You were asking where Rhys was yesterday evening, before going over to Bettws. Well, he was sitting on our sofa, drinking coffee and admiring Mali.'

Rage and jealousy rose in Daf's throat like vomit.

'What the hell did you invite Bowen to our house for? A bit late in the day for him to call by to see you, wasn't it? If he'd come earlier, Rhodri wouldn't have been about to see whatever you were getting up to.'

There was silence at the other end of the phone for some moments.

'Daf, I didn't invite anyone,' Gaenor replied at length, in a sad, low voice. 'He was on his way to visit some lady friend; he wanted a chat. But it's very clear that you don't trust me, so we'll have to have a proper talk later on. I really don't deserve this from you, Daf.'

She ended the call. Daf buried his head in his hands for a moment and forced himself to return to his office. The Horlicks clock seemed to be judging him, reminding him of his parents who had succeeded in creating a relationship which had survived for almost fifty years. He almost threw the mug of tea on the desk in front of that snake Bowen, as Jan Cilgwyn had described him.

'Gae gave me a hell of a bollocking,' Bowen explained. 'I was worried, when you kept on asking, that she hadn't told you I called by to see her. *Duwcs*, that's a lovely baby you've got.'

'Please don't discuss my family.'

'OK, but she's a real looker, just like her Mum.'

Daf smashed his fist down on his desk.

'How do you have the right to discuss every woman as if she was a piece of meat? Gaenor Morris and I love one another, love which is something very different from the way you treat women. The fact that you knew Gaenor as a young girl does not allow you to have any contact with her now. You are under suspicion in a case I am investigating, you are not a friend, right?'

Daf had never raised his voice like that before in the police station. He fell back into his chair, his hand hurting. Nev popped his head round the door.

'All good in here, boss?'

'No problems,' answered Daf untruthfully, shaking from his head to his feet.

After Nev had closed the door behind him, Bowen extended his great paw to touch the back of Daf's hand.

'I know you and Gaenor are in love. She was telling me how good her life is now, sharing her days with someone who's not only the best lover in the world but also her best friend. She was saying how empty and dull her life was at Neuadd, before she loved you and she said, no, more than that, she ordered me to go out and see if I could find a better life for myself, like you two have. "An unhappy marriage isn't a life sentence" she said to me, so I went over Bettws and when we were having our pudding, I asked Daisy if she'd be willing to give it a bit more of a go between us, get something permanent together. She did agree, after a fair bit of persuasion. So, when you see Gaenor, can you tell her I've been a good boy and followed her orders?'

Daf was determined that the tears he could feel pressing on the insides of his eyelids would not escape. He rose slowly.

'Sorry. I'm real sorry for flying off like that.' He suddenly decided to trust the big man, without knowing why. 'I went into your factory last night, to have a bit of a sprot about.'

'Without a warrant?'

'Without a warrant. And when I was in there, someone picked up a hatchet from the display case in your office and tried to kill me.'

'What?'

'Have you got any idea who might do a thing like that?'

'No, not at all. How did you get in?'

'Basia's keys, without her knowing. She didn't give them to me, I picked them up when I was searching their flat.'

An explosion of laughter rocked Bowen.

'Me with my fire bomb and you with your breaking and entering, talk about a couple of scoundrels! I'm not surprised you're feeling right angry today.'

'So no one has a reason to be wandering around your factory at night?'

'No. There's a security system on the estate, with one fellow watching the feed from all our cameras. But you know what? I've had a strange feeling for a while now, like I was being followed.'

'Use your brain, Rhys Bowen, think of those photos in the envelope. They couldn't have been taken without someone watching you.'

'Perhaps it was the same person!'

'Taking a few dirty pictures with a long lens and trying to kill someone with a hatchet are two pretty different things.'

'Which hatchet was it, as a matter of interest?'

'I've got no idea. They all look the same to me.'

'Doesn't matter. Can I go now? We're doing Carno, Clatter and Caersws today and I always get a bit of a rough old ride in Carno, because they love their fucking windmills there.'

'Sure. And sorry again for flipping like that.'

'Don't think twice about it. You've got yourself a woman well worth keeping. You wouldn't want to lose her.'

Nev was not best pleased to be given the task of interviewing Einion and Anwen, but he knew, the moment he saw Daf's face, that something wasn't quite right, so he didn't make an issue of it. Daf drove home, trying to think of absolutely nothing, since all his thoughts turned back to Gaenor. When he opened the front door, he saw Mali in her buggy, ready to go out.

'Rhods!' he called. 'Would you be able to take Mals out for a breath of air?'

'No worries.'

After the children had gone, Gaenor ventured a small joke. 'He's sharp enough to realise how much a lovely little baby turns him into a babe magnet.'

Daf took her hands because he felt he didn't have the right to take her in his arms.

'I've come back to apologise for being such a ... such a ... well, there aren't words in any language to describe what an idiot I've been.'

'I was sympathising with Rhys, comparing the emptiness of his life with everything we've got together.'

'I know, I know. I don't know what's the matter with me.'

'I know exactly what the problem is because I'm suffering from the same thing. You don't have to go straight back to work, do you?'

'Well, I suppose I've got ten minutes or so.'

'Pace yourself, *lanc*, I'm feeling ready for something that's going to take us more than ten minutes.'

Gaenor led him up the stairs.

# Chapter 13

## *Saturday, April 16, 2016 – later*

Daf, holding her gently in his arms, was about to remark on the power she had over him, changing his mood completely, but Gaenor interrupted his thoughts, admitting that she had received some confirmatory advice about him from Chrissie.

'We were talking about the business of giving birth,' Gae explained. 'She was saying that twins are comparatively easy in one way because each one tends to be smaller than a single baby but of course, she was anxious, because they'd lost Rob's twin.'

'So many crap things have happened to Chrissie over the years, but she always manages to push through somehow.'

'She's a big fan of yours, as you know, and she knows you better than you think. I was telling her about the stitches and she said, "So that's why Mr Dafis looks like Krakatoa, is it? I reckoned you two hadn't got back to the loving yet." Sharp as anything, isn't she?'

'Krakatoa?'

'Volcano. It was an old film, *Krakatoa: East of Java*. Well, you've been Krakatoa, West of Welshpool. And that was a very nice eruption indeed.'

They were right, these wise women, though it was rather odd to think that they had been discussing his level of sexual frustration. It had made quite a difference, though. As he lay contentedly on his back, gazing at the ceiling, Daf felt as though he had found another gear, a higher gear and that he was ready to concentrate on the case. He heard the sound of the front door opening without worrying, as Rhodri was a sensible lad and not given to interfering. But Rhodri's voice came clearly up the stairs.

'I'll get him for you now, Mrs Humphries! Would you like a cup of tea?'

'I'm grand, thanks, *lanc*; I only nipped into Wynnstay for a bag of Ovilac.'

Daf hurried to pull his trousers on but found himself unable to leave Gaenor without giving her another long kiss, so he was still fastening the bottom button of his shirt when he came down the stairs which led directly into the sitting room. Chrissie noticed at once.

'Mid-morning nap, Mr Dafis?' she asked, with a wink.

'Something like. How's things, Chrissie?'

'What's the best thing to do about this exclusion business, Mr Dafis? He's a right tidy lad, is Rob.'

After releasing Mali from her pushchair, Rhodri handed her to Chrissie before tactfully disappearing into his room.

'I know exactly what sort of lad he is, Chrissie, and you should be proud of him, but it doesn't make matters easier that he's missed so much school lately.'

'What could we do? Bryn was booked out on any number of contracts before we knew I was carrying.'

'But education is important, isn't it?'

Chrissie licked her lips. 'Oh, Mr Dafis, I feel like a naughty little girl who's getting a good telling-off from her favourite teacher. So sorry for being such a bad girl, Mr Dafis.'

'You're not allowed to change the subject that way, miss, you've got to try to improve his attendance.'

'I promise, Mr Dafis. It was a one-off. Usually, I go straight from the labour ward into the shed, but everything takes that bit longer with the two.'

'Of course it does,' Daf agreed, noticing the cloud in her usually bright eyes. She had given birth to twins before but not had the chance to raise them both. 'Anyway, that shouldn't be relevant to the business of the picture. You are sure Rob didn't ask the girl for the picture?'

'I don't know where you stand on this business of porn, Mr Dafis. I'm not a shy girl and I take a good interest in sexy things but films and pictures don't do anything for me. Bodies together, that's the magic, not some stuff on a screen. This nasty porn stops the lads from understanding that us girls are people, people with tits, of course, but people just as much as they are.'

'Totally agree.'

'I don't want my lads growing up with the idea that there's thousands of girls to be had just by swiping on a screen. To catch a girl, they need to be acting nice, especially when you think of how scarce girls are in this square mile. They shouldn't be thinking about girls as toys.'

'Wow, Chrissie, you should be giving lectures to the kids in the High School.'

'Don't be daft, Mr Dafis. But Rob knows well enough not to go down that line. Bryn's taught him right, anyway.'

'Taught him?' Daf asked, with more interest than he could justify.

'Just the basics, Mr Dafis, half a dozen simple tricks. He'll need to develop his own style in time.'

The family at Berllan, it would appear, discussed sex like other families discussed cookery, handing down sex tips to the next generation like recipes.

'So Rob wouldn't send a picture, or ask for one?'

'Hand on my heart,' Chrissie said, placing her small hand on her breast in a gesture she knew perfectly well would prickle up desire in him. Daf smiled, looking forward to discussing this with Gaenor later on.

'Leave it with me, Chrissie. I'll sort it.'

By now, Mali had turned her face to Chrissie's breast, nuzzling in to look for milk.

'You'd better go to your dear mum, *cariad bach*,' Chrissie said as she put Mali into Daf's arms. 'Thanks so much, Mr Dafis. I'm not good in situations like this, because I just want to give the girl a right good slap.'

'Her mum left home a couple of years back. It's not easy for a single man to raise a teenage girl.'

'Well, he's raised a real piece of work there. I saw her at

the Winter Fair last year, making poor Rob that embarrassed.'

'Don't worry.'

Gaenor came down stairs just in time to see Chrissie, by the door, go up onto her tiptoes to give Daf a kiss on his cheek.

'Thanks again, Mr Dafis.'

Daf shut the door and turned to Gaenor, who was laughing aloud.

'You two are so hilarious, you really are. Chrissie is flirting flat out and you're pretending to ignore her whilst sticking your chest out like a turkey or something.'

'I don't deserve you, Gaenor.'

'I know that perfectly well. We're out of broccoli so if you get a chance between solving every case and flirting with every woman, can you pop into Tesco's?'

'OK, boss.'

Daf was in Tesco's, buying not just the broccoli but the biggest bunch of flowers they had, a box of seashell chocolates and two packets of Garibaldi biscuits, when he received a text from Nev.

'Photo problem solved.'

Daf picked up another packet of Garibaldis to thank him.

'It was simple enough in the end,' Nev explained, all smiles, when Daf presented him with the biscuits. 'Whoever took those photos needed to send them to Heulwen. They weren't stupid enough to send them through an open email server but not experienced enough to venture out onto the dark net either, so the logical thing was to use PGP.'

'PGP?'

'Pretty Good Privacy. The messages are encrypted but it's easy enough for anyone in the same web of trust to read it. Then they can send anything by Hotmail or whatever and that's just what they did. I've found the IP address and got in touch with the service provider, which in this case is Microsoft. They've promised me a response within an hour.'

'Well done you, Nev, I couldn't have got that far in months. And I couldn't have sent it down to Carmarthen for the geeks to look at because I just would not have known what question to ask.'

'I had enough time left to make a bit of a timeline from the evidence those young people gave, one document showing the movements of Bowen and the other showing who came and went from the crime scene.'

'I may have a bit to add to that. Turns out Jac Dolfadog was sitting outside the office for hours, looking for a chance for a quiet word with his mother.'

'In Bowen's case, there's only one gap in the information, which is yesterday, between finishing canvassing and going for a date with someone called...'

'Daisy Davies.'

'Do you know her, boss?'

'No. Bowen's an old friend of Gae's,' Daf clarified, amazed how easy it suddenly was to say that sentence. 'In the gap, Bowen had an HR meeting at the factory then popped in to see the baby, Mali, on his way over to Bettws.'

'Right.'

'Do we happen to know where that Lisa Powell might be, Nev? Is she still stopping at the Oak?'

'No, boss. Apparently, she made some enquiries about renting a cottage. The girl on reception had suggested Nantbriallu but didn't know if she'd had any luck.'

'I know Derek Nantbriallu. I'll ask him.'

Daf felt a fair bit of sympathy for poor old Derek, who he'd known since school. A year younger than Daf, Derek had married a girl from over the border who was some serious snob and there had had to be major diversification to keep her in the style she wanted, to pay for the extension to the house and holidays in villas in Portugal. They had two children in a place Derek described as pre-prep, whatever that might be, and the row of stone outbuildings on the far side of the yard had been transformed into four holiday lets. Daf rang Derek to enquire but there was no answer.

Nantbriallu stood at the bottom of a cup in the hills between Guilsfield and Llanfair, amidst a maze of narrow lanes. In a stand of fine woodland on the edge of the farm, the oaks, beeches and chestnut trees were displaying their new leaves in a tapestry of verdant freshness. Daf wondered exactly where the edge of Derek's ground lay; he couldn't imagine Mrs Nantbriallu allowing so much valuable standing timber to remain unscathed when it could have been chopped down and turned into school fees and Audi 4x4s. Daf paused for a while at the top of the lane by the sign which read 'Primrose Brook Holiday Homes'. Primrose bloody Brook! Daf startled himself by his reaction to this plonking translation of a lovely traditional name, making a snorting noise like some disgruntled elderly colonel.

The yard was as neat as a pin but Daf could not be certain whether that was because of effective farming practices or, as he rather suspected, that very little proper work was ever done there. He parked in front of the farmhouse and knocked on the door: no reply. There was little sign of activity. The only car visible was parked outside the third of the holiday lets. Daf also noticed that the window was open and, as he walked over the yard, he heard the sound of quiet sobbing.

Over the years, Daf had become accustomed to every emotion under the sun: fear, rage, guilt and more than anything, mourning after bad news. The moment he heard the weak, muffled sound coming from the cottage he knew that someone was trying to quieten themselves to avoid the anger of another. The pattern was pretty familiar: he was expecting a scene of domestic violence. He stood for a moment by the window, out of view.

'I've heard enough of that noise, my girl.'

'Sorry, Lisa, I'm so sorry.'

'Well, I'm glad to hear that you're sorry after all the trouble you've caused with all your nonsense. Blow your nose, can you? You're plain enough as it is.' Then she changed the tone of her voice and to Daf's experienced ears, her patronising words were far more frightening than temper. 'You come here, you dirty girl, so I can sort you out.'

Through the window, Daf saw Lisa take hold of Jan's head, turning her face up with such force it must have been painful. She was drying her partner's tears with one hand whilst the other gripped her hair in a savage hold. The grief in Jan's eyes was pushed out by fear. Walking quietly, Daf reached the door and opened it without knocking.

'Ms Powell,' he declared, in a clear, strong voice, 'that's enough.'

'What are you doing here?' she replied abruptly. Jan didn't say a word but raised her hand to rub the back of her head.

'First of all, one of you is going to leave this house.'

'But we've booked...' Lisa protested.

'I'm not going to permit behaviour of this kind.'

'Behaviour of what kind? Jan and I love each other very much.'

'I saw you hurting her.'

'Jan has no reason to complain. She's very glad that I love her, that I take care of her. There's nothing amiss in our relationship, thank you very much, and perhaps all we're seeing here is another example of your homophobia.'

'I saw through the window the kind of care you provide, Ms Powell. Do you need a doctor, Ms Cilgwyn?'

Jan shook her head and Daf noticed that she couldn't move freely: there was a substantial, fairly fresh bruise on her neck. Looking straight into Lisa's eyes, Daf pulled his phone out of his pocket.

'Huw, can you come over to Nantbriallu? Couple staying in the cottages there. OK, thanks.'

'I'm fine, truly I am. Lisa will look after me,' Jan stated in a soulless little voice.

'The situation is out of your hands now, Ms Cilgwyn.'

'But I don't want...'

'It isn't your decision.'

Daf decided to ring Sheila as well because she was always ready to help in these situations, even when she wasn't on duty. The third phone call was rather difficult for Daf but what was the risk of causing embarrassment in comparison with the importance of keeping a vulnerable woman safe? The call went straight through to her answer machine.

'Hiya, Haf, Daf here. I've got a DV who could do with a bit of legal advice from you. Nantbriallu, between Llanfair and Guilsfield, turn up by Shinglers. As soon as possible, if you can. Oh, and thanks for the invititation, Gaenor and I would love to come to your engagement party.'

Daf sat down at the head of the table and ordered Lisa and Jan to join him, one on each side.

'Right, ladies, we need to face this situation head on. Lisa, I don't doubt for a minute that you love Jan very much indeed but you're also hurting her and that isn't acceptable. This situation can't go on. In Powys, we've got a scheme to help people with violent tendencies, women as much as men.'

'I'm not violent.'

'Lisa, I saw you with my own eyes, pulling Jan's hair in a way which must have really hurt her.'

'I was hugging her, a gesture of love, that's what you saw. We're fine, aren't we, Janni *fach*?' Jan didn't say a word. She was staring at her hands, scratching at the edge of her thumbnail. Lisa pressed on, trying to justify herself. 'He's the bully, this macho man, bursting in here and...'

'Listen, things can get better, if you two are prepared to admit that you've got a problem. And whatever else happens, it's not safe for Jan to stay with you at the moment, Lisa. Why don't you give your mum a ring, Jan? She came up to see me because she was worrying about you, and Gwynlyn Huws came with her.'

Lisa gave a spiteful laugh. 'That's an old, old story by now, isn't it, Jan? Jan introduced him to her family and before long, the old bastard was shagging her mother.'

Jan jumped to her feet, her eyes blazing. 'It's not true! It's another of your sour stories, Lisa. I'm going to phone my mother now.'

'I understand how badly you feel about it, *cariad*. You destroyed your parents' marriage by pulling Huws into their orbit and that's hard to accept. You made so many mistakes and you keep on making them and I am the only person willing to forgive you, because I love you so much.'

Lisa stretched her hand across the table to stroke Jan's hand. Jan sank back into her chair like a punctured balloon.

'Don't trouble your mother. She has enough on her plate, dealing with all the troubles you've caused her. You're a silly girl, Jan, and you know that as well as I do.'

Daf had heard this many times before, the gentle words which undermined a person, which ran like poison in their blood. After years of this, escape became very difficult.

'And think of the harm you've done Heulwen as well. You dragged her into your problems, tried to lean on her like you lean on me and her family decided to kill her, to avoid scandal. It's your fault again, Little Miss Raincloud. Every time you behave in a silly way, someone else gets hurt.'

'That's enough,' Daf commanded, in a voice full of quiet authority. 'No one's been charged with the killing of Heulwen Breeze-Evans, so stop talking nonsense. Jan, I'll ring your mother if you don't.'

Jan nodded. 'Can I go to rest for a little while, please, Mr Dafis?' she asked like a little girl rather than an Assembly Member.

'I'm afraid you can't yet, Jan, you need to see the doctor and a lawyer. A member of my team will be here in a minute and she'll look after you.'

'I look after you, Jan, you know that. You won't be able to cope for a moment without your darling Lisa.'

Daf picked up his phone again, silently grateful for the fact that there was a decent signal, a rare phenomenon in that area.

'Nev? Can you look through yesterday's log: I spoke to a woman called Dr Wilkes, early afternoon. Ring her and tell her she needs to come and pick up her daughter, and give her the postcode for Nantbriallu to put in the sat nav.'

Lisa struck the table with the palm of her hand. 'You can't do this. I know how much of a homophobe you are and I will destroy your career. Your reputation will be ruined.'

'As the young people say, Ms Powell, bring it on. Jan deserves a better life than this, a life without fear.'

'But I'm so tired...' whispered Jan.

Once again, Daf's experience was essential to him. Twice, in similar situations, he had seen the victim react to the opening up of the misery of her marriage by attempting suicide. One of the women succeeded, leaving behind three children.

'Just stay where you are for a few minutes more, please, Jan. Sheila will be here any time now.'

'See what a bully he is, Jan,' Lisa urged.

They were still sitting around the table, Daf in control but Lisa endlessly sniping, Jan collapsed into herself, when Haf Wynne and Hugh Mansell arrived at the same time, with Sheila a few minutes later. Daf noticed the Victorian ring on Haf's left hand and had to admit that it was tasteful and suited her well: a family heirloom, he supposed. And she'd cut her hair to get rid of the last trace of hippydom; Daf felt a twinge of regret that the slightly untidy mane of golden hair was now a sleek bob.

'Jan, you go to your room with Dr Mansell, please, so you can have a quick check-up and when you've done that, Ms Wynne is here to speak to you, to help you decide what to do for the best. In the meantime, Ms Powell, I need to speak to you, right? Are you happy to talk here or would you rather go down to the station? Sheila, if you could stick close to Ms Cilgwyn, that would be helpful.'

'I refuse to leave this house whilst Jan is still here,' was Lisa's retort. 'I have no idea what you might do to her.'

'We'll talk here then. Haf, are you willing to wait in the

sitting room till Dr Mansell has finished checking Ms Cilgwyn over?'

'Always willing to obey your orders like a faithful little pup,' Haf answered with a cheerful smile. Daf had to admit, reluctantly, that she did smile more frequently since starting her relationship with that Tory.

When they were alone, Lisa hissed at Daf, 'If you think that you can just call up your gang of hambones and split up Jan and me, you're wrong.'

'Ms Powell, I can arrest you for what I saw through the window. Perhaps a night in the cells would help you think more clearly. But for now, let's concentrate on Monday night, and I am expecting to hear the truth.'

'Monday night? I went to my yoga class after work, then...'

'You weren't in work on Monday. And I know you were staying in the Oak using a false name, Mrs Wilkes, as if you were Jan's wife.'

'We're getting married next year; what difference does it make?'

'Never mind that now. Why did you come all the way up to Welshpool?'

Lisa looked at her hands.

'Can I jog your memory? You'd arranged a meeting with Rhys Bowen, of all people. Why, Ms Powell? Jan's a vegetarian so it can't have been rissoles you were after.'

'I was ... Well, he deserved a few remarks about his bullying behaviour towards Jan in the Senedd.'

'That's been a problem for the last five years, so Jan says, and you haven't intervened before now. No, you wanted to talk to him about the campaign in Montgomeryshire.'

'How do you know that?'

'Because Bowen, who may be many things but is not a fool, arranged to meet you in his office, with his assistant next door recording all that was said, on tape and in shorthand. He didn't trust you at all, Ms Powell, so when you suggested meeting alone, just the two of you, he was naturally suspicious.'

'You have to have a person's permission to record them, it's an offence to record them secretly.'

'And blackmail is a much more serious offence, Ms Powell.'

'What are you talking about?'

'You provided Bowen with information about the relationship between Jan and Heulwen.'

'It wasn't blackmail. I never asked him for a penny.'

'The crime isn't confined to asking for money. You were trying to damage Heulwen's chances in the election and that is plenty enough to meet the requirements of the 1968 Theft Act. But Bowen didn't fancy publishing the information: instead, he marched down to see her as if he had just got hold of a nuclear missile. But unfortunately for you, Heulwen herself had a package of interesting information to use against Bowen. What they used to call Mutual Assured Destruction usually leads to a stand-off. Nothing happened.'

Lisa frowned. It seemed to Daf that she had trouble coping with any type of authority.

'What did you talk to Heulwen about on Monday evening?'

'I didn't see Heulwen.'

'We're wasting time, Ms Powell. I have at least three witnesses who saw you there, including Heulwen's assistant who spoke to you.'

'OK, I did go and see her.'

'And you gave her a bit of a slap?'

'You have no evidence of that whatsoever.'

'Oh, but I do. Two witnesses who were on the other side of the door and confirmation from the forensic report.'

Lisa lowered her head. 'She said, she said something disgusting.'

'What?'

'She said I had never been able to satisfy Jan, in bed.'

'That's a cruel thing to hear. So, you came back later and burnt the place?'

'How could I burn the place? What with? And all the time I was setting this big fire just outside her office door, what would Heulwen have been doing? Knitting?'

'How do you know the fire was started by the door?'

'I don't know. It was a guess. If I had started the fire, which I didn't, I would have chosen the end of the corridor, just outside the door.'

'Outside the door? Not inside?'

'But, Mr Dafis, Heulwen wouldn't just sit still in her chair as someone was burning the place down! What a stupid suggestion!'

And so Daf was convinced that, whatever other cruel things Lisa Powell might have done, she was not guilty of the murder of Heulwen Breeze-Evans; she had no idea that the victim was unconscious before the fire.

Daf took Lisa Powell down the station to charge her with actual bodily harm, assault and blackmail. He was willing to bail her on the condition that she kept well away from Jan and from Jan's parents' home, then he gave the heads up to South Wales Police to keep an eye on the address. The duty solicitor came in and there was some discussion of these terms but Daf was sure of his ground. The magistrates would not be willing to alter any terms which had been put in place to protect a vulnerable person who was under continuing threat. And in this particular case, it didn't harm Daf's confidence that the Chair of the Bench was well known for her firm line on domestic violence cases, and that she happened to be Lady Beatrice Gwydyr-Gwynne.

By this time, Daf was tired and seriously hungry, and starting to consider how tasty raw broccoli might be if it had spent half a day in the boot of his car. But the piece of paper on his desk contained a name which woke him up like a bucket of cold water. He called out, 'What does this mean, Nev?'

Nev was clearly having a good day at the office, Daf had never seen him with such a spring in his step.

'Those photos, the ones Heulwen Evans had in her blackmail file, they came from the computer of County Councillor Carwyn Watkin, Brynybiswal, Bettws Cedewain.'

'Ring him, Nev, and get him to come in and talk to me at ten o'clock tomorrow morning and don't take any shit from him about missing chapel. Then get hold of his bank accounts and see if you can find any evidence of blackmail-related payments going through, or any financial connection with Mrs Breeze-Evans; they could have used his accounts to keep a bit of a distance.'

'OK, boss. And while you were out, another little job has come up. West Mercia Police have been in touch, they need someone to arrest Gwilym Bebb.'

'What, Gwilym Bebb? Another county councillor? There'll be no one left in County Hall soon.'

'Not sure how much we'd miss them, sir. Anyway, as you know, we inputted the contents of Mrs Breeze-Evans's safe into the national database and West Mercia have slotted Gwilym Bebb into a widespread pattern of deception they were investigating, and the info we provided means they're ready to act. I'm not sure of all the details but it seems that some of the people involved are likely to try to dash off abroad somewhere if they have any idea the game is up. So every one of them must be arrested by eight o'clock tonight.'

'I've got too much on my plate to deal with this.'

'But he lives just outside Llanfair, boss, you could just drop by.'

Daf sighed and picked up the phone. He called Banwy Hall, Gwilym Bebb's home. His wife, whom Daf considered a heartless, sour creature, answered.

'Oh. Deifi Siop. I'm almost certain that Councillor Gwilym Bebb is too busy to speak to you.'

'I am sorry to trouble you, Mrs Bebb, but it is an important matter.'

'Important indeed! Important to you, Deifi Siop.'

Daf was kept waiting for several minutes whilst Mrs Bebb looked for her husband.

'I was right, Councillor Bebb is not available.'

Diane Rhydderch appeared in the open door of Daf's office just as he was putting the phone down.

'Miss Rhydderch! Working on the weekend?' Daf attempted to greet her courteously.

'I always put one hundred per cent into a case like this. We had a lot of rather unfortunate press this morning, we need to give the sharks something else to feed on, agreed?'

'Agreed. I just arrested a woman.'

'For the murder?'

'No, unfortunately, though she is a witness in the case. Blackmail and assault on her partner.'

Ms Rhydderch shook her head a little.

'Not Jan Cilgwyn's partner, surely?'

'Yes. Jan Cilgwyn has been the victim of domestic violence over a considerable period of time and...'

'Oh, Inspector Dafis, you've arrested the second lesbian you've ever met in your life! This is not going to look good, not at all.'

'She's a dangerous woman, controlling her partner through fear,' Daf protested.

'I don't doubt that for a moment, but what we need is a totally fresh angle on this investigation, to make people totally forget issues of sexuality.'

'Well, we have got evidence which has come to light as part of the investigation which is proving vital for the exposing of a number of serious frauds and conspiracies in Wales and beyond, and there are some well-known names amongst those who are going to be arrested.'

'Now that's very promising. It may not be as attractive to the press as historic child abuse but perhaps there's enough there to tempt them to follow a new line.' She touched Daf's arm in a patronising gesture. 'Change the narrative, that's the trick. By tomorrow morning, you won't be an old-fashioned homophobe but a sharp and effective policeman who has unmasked a powerful criminal conspiracy.'

'I'm not a homophobe.'

'Not everyone has had the privilege of getting to know you, Inspector Dafis,' she said, in a voice pitched a little higher than usual. Daf struggled to suppress a shudder down his spine and he considered for a moment asking Rhys Bowen for help: if Ms Rhydderch was given a bit of attention by the ever-ready AM, she might not be so likely to flirt with Daf.

'Anyway,' Daf began, rising to his feet, 'you can get all the details from DC Francis, and more information will be released at eight o'clock tonight.'

'Exciting! The media always thinks things are way more important if they're under an embargo. If I put my shopping list under an embargo, they'd all be desperate to take a look.'

'Thank you for your help, Ms Rhydderch. I really appreciate your contribution.'

'Are you expecting any further major developments over the weekend, Inspector Dafis? I was thinking of going home until Monday, another boring evening in the Oak would be too much for me.'

'That's fine by me,' replied Daf, still very uncertain as to her attitude towards him. 'But Saturday nights in Welshpool can often be pretty lively.'

'Lively isn't much fun unless you've got company. I'm off home then.'

Daf started his journey with a sense of release, despite the Gwilym Bebb business. He tried to think of the pleasant company of his family and the prospect of a tasty supper as he drove to Banwy Hall. There was no car visible on the gravel outside the elegant Queen Anne house and when he knocked on the green-painted door, there was no reply.

He decided to stop at the Spar for a bottle of Shiraz and, from the look of things, Margaret Tanyrallt had had the same idea. Unlike many local women who tended to hide their bottle of rosé deep in their capacious bags, the top of a litre bottle of Bells was visible in the outer pocket of her oilskin.

'Well, *cog y siop*, it seems that Gruff has made quite a fool of himself.'

'He's young and he was trying to defend Felicity.'

'Hmm. She's a steady sort of a girl, that one.'

'And she thinks the world of Gruff as well.'

'Hmm. I'm a bit old to start out life in a caravan, you know.'

'You wouldn't need to. They could build a house; vets are on a decent wage.'

'Or, I could rent Jac's place, in the *helm* at Dolfadog. Whatever, thank you for being kind to that pair of young fools.'

'I was just doing my duty, finding out who killed Heulwen is the priority.'

'So why haven't you asked where I was on Monday night?' Margaret's eyes twinkled as if she were relishing being under suspicion. 'To save your trouble, I was in a WPCS meeting on the other side of Tregaron and I didn't get back to Tanyrallt till half past ten.'

'I didn't ask because there was no evidence linking you to the scene of the crime.'

'I'm very glad she's gone. If I'd known all that had happened to poor little Cai, I would have killed her myself, the old bitch.'

She lit a cigarette.

'And is it true that she went with women?'

'She did have a relationship with a woman, yes.'

Margaret looked into Daf's eyes.

'Usually, Daf Dafis, you men think you're the passionate ones but that's not true. You, for example, could not have persuaded your lady to leave Neuadd for that hen coop opposite the Goat unless there was a fair old bit of lust involved. Phil's got a good name for being able to please the ladies and yet Heuls never spent a single happy hour as his wife. I used to think it was the shadow of How's death lying over their relationship which was responsible, but perhaps it was something else, deep in her nature.'

'Very likely.'

'And how did the Reverend take the fact that his mother-in-law was gay?'

'That's not a police matter.'

'Gruff said that the Reverend had walked in on Heuls, on the job with some girl. Is that true?'

'No comment.'

Margaret laughed. 'Which means it is true! Priceless.'

'I've got to go, anyway.'

'Call by some time, when you're free. We'd better start thinking about a Section A foal for that little girl of yours, so they can grow up together.'

As he turned to leave, Daf noticed a poster in the window of the butcher's shop: 'Fundraising Concert for the Urdd, Saturday Night, The Institute. A Feast of Local Talent including National Under 21 Solo Winner Carys Dafis, Parti Cut Lloi, Pontygaseg Trio and many more. Accompanists Mary Morgan and Sion Jones. Compère, Councillor Gwilym Bebb.'

He pulled out his phone as he stood on the step of the shop and sent a message to Steve. Almost immediately, he received a text from Nev: 'West Mercia getting a bit jumpy. Seems one of the gang went into Birmingham today and changed a fair bit of cash into Brazilian reals.'

Daf replied: 'Come up to Llanfair and bring Steve with you. The man himself is compèring a concert tonight.'

'Sweet, boss, sweet.'

Daf didn't find the situation sweet in the least. As the worst father in Wales, he had forgotten that Carys was taking part in the concert, and since leaving Falmai, he had very little connection with the Urdd. He climbed the wide stairs of the Institute to speak to Mrs Howells who was on the door.

'May I have a word with Mr Bebb, please?'

'Shame on you, Deifi Dafis, the tickets are eight pounds.'

'But I haven't come to listen to the concert, I have to speak to Mr Bebb.'

'You haven't come to listen to your daughter's beautiful voice? Or support the movement which has given her such a platform over the years?'

'Alright, alright, give me a ticket.'

He pulled a ten-pound note out of his pocket very reluctantly.

'And you'll take two strips of raffles with the change, I'm sure?'

It wasn't a question. Daf stepped into the hall and was surprised to see how many people who were involved with the investigation had ventured out. In the front row, his long legs creating a significant obstacle, was Rhys Bowen. Daf noted no fewer than five of the women he had seen with Bowen in the blackmail pictures, all looking perfectly respectable in their asymmetrical cardigans and chunky jewellery. Daf couldn't name them and tried without success to work out which one might be Daisy Davies. Unexpectedly, Nansi and Seth were there, accompanied by their smartly dressed children. The poster had warned Daf to expect Carys and Sion, and Falmai was there, of course, smart without being attractive somehow. Since Daf left, she had lost a stone and a half and coloured her hair, enough to attract Jonas Bitfel but not enough to persuade him to attend a concert with her. It was obvious that Ivy of Hair by Ivy had had her way with Falmai, highlights, lowlights and every other colour that chemistry could provide. At Falmai's side was her brother, as was to be expected, but on the other side of John, Daf was surprised to see Belle. Given that her sister was an Urdd organiser, there could be no excuse for such a tight, short leather skirt, and when she bent over to put her bag on the floor under her seat, John went as red as a beetroot.

On the other side of the hall, chatting over the price of hay, was Carwyn Brynybiswal. He didn't look like the sort of man to be involved in any form of conspiracy, with his open face and innocent eyes. Daf watched him for a moment: when one of the girls from the blackmail pictures walked past him, her lambswool sweater tight over her breasts, Carwyn grew red and dropped his eyes. Daf decided he would have a quick word.

'Sorry to pull you in tomorrow, Carwyn,' he began, in a leisurely tone. 'Nothing serious.'

'No problem, Dafydd. I can't get over this business.'

'Yet life goes on ... enough people have come here tonight, for example.'

'Good turnout.'

'You know what, Car, there's that much coming and going in this area, by now, I don't know half these people. Who's the fair girl in the blue jumper?'

'A neighbour of mine,' mumbled Carwyn. 'Teacher. I do a bit for her, in the garden and that.' Daf thought of the usual local meaning of the expression 'he does a bit for her', but doubted that Carwyn did anything more than garden. 'Who's that sitting by John Neuadd?'

'Sion's new girlfriend, from the north.'

'Www, she's a smart piece, isn't she?'

'Well, old friend, we've got to the age when all the girls look smart to us.'

Carys stepped out of the door by the stage in her long black gown, her favourite singing dress. Every time Daf saw his daughter, he felt so proud of her, and not just because of her talent. She was a girl of great qualities, kindness, generosity, intelligence and determination, to say nothing of her ability to perform. Carys went over to Mair, her best friend who was in the audience with her boyfriend, who happened to be Gwilym Bebb's grandson. Daf went after her.

'Dadi!' Carys exclaimed. 'I wasn't expecting you here tonight. How goes the great investigation?'

'I'm still working. I've got to have a word with your grandfather, Arwel.'

'Please don't tell me that Taid killed Heulwen?' asked Arwel with mock seriousness.

'No, no, but I need to speak to him at once.'

'I'll go and get him now,' Carys offered. 'He's at the side of the stage.'

Daf glanced back at the clock which was above the double doors. Before eight, West Mercia had said. It was half past seven already and the hall was full.

Daf chatted with Mair and Arwel about their college courses whilst he waited for Carys to return, keeping an eye on the comings and goings. After some minutes, Carys returned from the stage area with a puzzled expression.

'He's not willing to come to speak to you, Dadi. He says whatever it is will wait until the interval.'

Daf pulled at the corner of the curtain and shouted into the darkness. 'Mr Bebb? Mr Bebb, I must have a word with you right away.'

From the darkness came a loud, melodious voice. 'I have no time for your nonsense now, Deifi Siop.'

Falmai was pulling at his sleeve. 'Do you have to make Carys embarrassed? As far as I am concerned, it would make no difference to me if you walked in stark naked because you've already humiliated me as much as it is possible for one human being to humiliate another, but you are still her father.'

'I know that very well but I'm here on duty. I have to speak to Mr Bebb before eight o'clock tonight.'

'Oh, I can see you haven't lost your taste for drama, Daf. Bit quiet for you with the tart and the by-blow in that chicken-coop, is it?'

'I'm serious, Falmai. And I'm not sure there's anything to be gained by talking about Gae and Mali like that.'

The curtains opened and Gwilym Bebb stepped onto the stage to open the concert. Falmai slipped back quickly to her seat beside John.

'Is it important, Dad?' Carys whispered. 'I could refuse to

perform until he's spoken to you but I'm not supposed to be going on until the end of the second half.'

'Thanks for the offer. During the next item, tell him that it is a serious matter.'

Under the clock, which showed that it was now quarter to eight, he saw Steve and Nev. Frustrated, Daf turned his attention to the two-voice party from the high school, and during their performance, Daf recognised the bottom of the conductor, which was moving to the rhythm of the song: another of Bowen's lady friends.

The next item was a comic song by two members of the Young Farmers' Club, Ed Mills and Tom Topbanc, who were dressed up as old ladies. They received a very warm reception despite their poor singing. As they were singing their final chorus, Carys returned, shaking her head. Daf turned to see Steve at the back of the hall raise his arm and point to his wrist to remind Daf of the time. Daf took the brown envelope from his jacket pocket and looked at the Post-it note which had been stuck on the corner of the official document:

'*To be served by 8pm 16th April 2016.*' Daf pulled the Post-it note off and stepped up to the side stage area. Bebb had moved to the centre of the stage.

'Mr Bebb, Mr Bebb, I must speak to you at once.'

The old solicitor raised his hand as if he were swatting away an insect.

'Mr Bebb, I am serious.'

'And the next item is *cerdd dant* so please give a warm welcome to our harpist for tonight, Sion Jones, Neuadd.'

Sion began to push his Salvi into place on its little trolley but he lost all interest in the harp when he saw Daf walk across the stage, saying, 'Gwilym David Bebb, I have a warrant to arrest you, on behalf of West Mercia Police. You have the right to remain silent but...'

The next few moments remained in Daf's memory like a film: Bebb's mouth open, the sound of the Salvi falling to the ground, Falmai's voice screeching, Arwel's hand reaching up above the heads of the audience to film the event on his phone.

'You little bastard, Deifi Siop,' hissed Bebb, turning on his heel. One from each side, Nev and Steve reached the stage. Standing close to Bebb without touching him, they managed to escort him down the steps.

'Pull the curtains, Carys,' Daf shouted to his daughter.

In the darkness, he heard Sion's heavy tread approaching.

'You are a total legend, Uncle Daf.'

'Look after the bloody Salvi, or your mother will kill me.'

Daf stumbled down the steps into a tornado of sound. Falmai had decided to pretend to faint, an old trick of hers when she couldn't cope with any situation. Steve was standing by the rear door, Bebb by his side.

'Boss,' Nev observed, 'you're looking shattered. Can we deal with him?'

'Yes, thanks. Don't keep him at our end: I hate the idea of the old bastard hanging around my station, and Nev, make sure you're noting down all the extra hours you're doing, won't you? And take Bebb's phone off him.'

'I will. Seven minutes to eight: you like cutting it a bit fine, don't you, boss?'

As soon as Bebb was gone, the real chaos started. The crowd were discussing, in shocked voices, the best drama they had ever seen on the stage of Llanfair Caereinion Institute. Ed Mills and Tom Topbanc emerged from the changing rooms, their hair still full of flour, very disappointed to have missed all the excitement.

The chair of the county Urdd committee collapsed in sobs. Even though he had caused all the fuss, Daf felt under no obligation whatsoever to calm them down; leadership would have to come from a different direction. He walked down the hall between the seats and the wall, paying no attention to anyone.

'My friends,' thundered a voice from the front: Bowen had

risen to his feet. 'Looks like we've lost our compère for tonight but are you all keen to continue with the concert? The performers are here, all ready to entertain us, and if you're prepared to put up with me, I can do the introductions and what have you. What do you say?'

He was answered with a burst of applause and Daf headed out into the night, longing for Gaenor, his family and a glass of Shiraz.

'What about your raffle tickets?' yelled Mrs Howell after him.

'Stuff the raffle,' answered Daf, a sentence of pure heresy in Montgomeryshire.

# Chapter 14

## *Sunday, April 17, 2016*

At quarter past four in the morning, with his arm around Gaenor's shoulders as she was feeding Mali, Daf shared with her the story of his adventure in the Mid Wales Meat Factory.

'Who was it, Daf?' she asked, in a low voice, heavy with concern.

'Not that old fancy of yours, anyway, because while my life was on the line, he was sitting on the sofa downstairs eating my Hobnobs.'

'What about that young lad, Cai? If he had taken more of that stuff...?'

'No, he was halfway to Conwy by then, with two pretty good witnesses: Lady Beatrice and one of our PCSOs.'

'One of the Dolfadog lot?'

'Possibly. I'll have to check everyone but I do need to be a bit careful, given that I shouldn't have been there myself in the first case.'

'But if you've told Rhys about it, no one else needs to know that you were there without permission.'

'Good point.'

'Please, please be careful, Daf. I don't want to make a fuss but you are the centre of our lives. I don't know how Mals and I would last a day without you. And I don't want to think about it.'

'*Twt lol*. My side of the bed wouldn't be cold before you'd blown your nose and marched over to Bowen Towers, to raise Little Miss as a sausage heiress,' was Daf's cynical response.

'Or I might fancy popping over to Berllan, to see if Bryn had any needs I might attend to...'

By half past five, the grey pre-dawn light was visible behind the curtains, and Gaenor could not keep her eyes open a moment longer. Daf lifted Mali from her lap and set her down gently in her Moses basket but less than a minute later, the tiny creature had managed to generate a sound loud enough to raise the dead. Daf could hear movement from Rhodri's room. It would be totally unfair to the lad to expect him to put up with his little sister crying herself to sleep, so he dressed her, finishing with a quilted suit so they could go for an early morning walk.

Dawn was breaking in multi-coloured ribbons above Montgomeryshire, gradually filling the little dip in the hills with tender light.

'How about this for a grand morning, *cariad bach*?' he remarked to Mali, who was held firmly against her father's breast by the sling. 'Why don't we make a fair old walk of it, let your Mum get a decent rest?'

The ability to walk easily when little legs hang halfway down your thighs was something Daf had mastered when his older children were small. He turned up by the old Wynnstay pub, now divided into flats, past the old market site which was now a cul-de-sac of modern houses and up onto Gibbet Hill. The steep slope proved a bit of a challenge for Daf, especially as he was talking to Mali the whole time, explaining his progress in the investigation to his little daughter.

'It's easy enough to rule out Rhys Bowen, Cai Evans or Lisa Powell, Miss Mali, but where does that leave us? Can you help your daft old dad sort out this puzzle? Perhaps it's someone else, someone involved in the blackmail. It's going to be heckish interesting to see what Carwyn Brynybiswal has to say on the subject. If Gwilym Bebb was as deep in things as our friends from West Mercia tell us, who knows what other treasures there are in Mrs Breeze-Evans's files?'

By this time, they were standing on the crossroads by Penarth, the view before them extending to the blue mountains in the distance, the familiar shoulders of Cader and the Berwyn.

'Well, Mals, those old Romans knew their stuff when they built their fort up here. Look, you could see an enemy approaching from any direction. Your dadi's not always that lucky.' With his daughter's breath warming him through his jumper, he decided to do a circuit of the tops and come down Mount Road, past the football ground.

Daf didn't see anyone else until it was almost seven. Halfway between Rhosfawr and Mount Farm, a runner came into sight, puffing up the slope. His face was all white, not just pale but dead white, as if he was wearing a mask. As he came closer, Daf realised that it was some thick cream or ointment, the sort of stuff Carys used to put on her face when she was in Year Eight. It took a while for Daf to recognise him but just before he passed them, Daf realised that the runner was Lembo Lewis, father of the now notorious Floozy Lewis.

'Morning, Mr Lewis, you're up early.'

'And you, Mr Dafis, though I can see the reason you're not still asleep.'

'Right enough, but I'd still rather have half a dozen this age than a teenager.'

Because of the stuff on his face, Daf couldn't tell if Lewis had coloured with embarrassment at the reference.

'It's an ugly old business, this thing with the phones,' said Daf. 'We shouldn't discuss it.'

'I'm going to have to step back from the Exclusion Committee this time: there's a fair bit of coming and going between us and the Berllan family. My partner's friendly with Rob's mother and...'

'And you're pretty friendly with her yourself, I hear,' was Lewis's spiteful response.

'You shouldn't believe everything you hear in a little town like Llanfair, Mr Lewis. But I will be at the exclusion meeting representing Rob, and I can tell you with some certainty, he is not going to be made to leave the school. In the process, your girl is going to get herself a bit of a reputation, for telling lies and for taking the picture in the first case.'

'My daughter doesn't tell lies.'

'None of them are saints. She's gone too far, painted herself into a corner. Perhaps she thought she could play games with Rob because he comes from a family without much education but if so, she's made a big misjudgement.'

In the silence which followed, Daf could hear the laboured sound of Lewis trying to regain his breath.

'It's tough for a man to try to raise a girl,' he started. 'There are subjects I wouldn't dream of discussing with her and I still need to protect her, like all parents do.'

'Of course you do, but are you going the right way about it? If, and I've told you it's a very small chance in my opinion, Rob is excluded, he'll appeal, and his family have got enough money to take the matter to court if it comes to that, and how will that help Lwsi? If you really understand what a paedophile is, Mr Lewis, then you will appreciate that Rob does not deserve that description at all. I hope you've never had to look at the sort of images we come across, pictures so disgusting that a normal person has to throw up after seeing them. I do have to look at those type of pictures so I know what I'm talking about. This is far too serious a subject for anyone to play games with like this. If Miss Lwsi Lewis is uncertain what child abuse means, my colleagues in CEOP have got age-appropriate training she can attend.'

Daf knew he was preaching, not his normal style of communication at all. It was difficult to hold a serious discussion with a man with white paste cracking in fine lines over his whole face but that was no excuse. The reality was that Lewis represented to Daf all the middle-class parents who had driven him mad over the years by their refusal to think that their little darlings might have any responsibility for any transgressions, no matter how clear the evidence.

Though Daf felt uncomfortable about his didactic tone, it certainly had an impact on Lewis. He moved his mouth about in discomfort, cracking the surface of the mask around his lips and up to his cheeks.

'But Mr Dafis, how could anyone persuade her to step back before she does herself some real harm?'

'Does she have any close friends?'

'No sensible ones.'

Daf was tactful enough not to mention Lewis's wife who was rumoured to be living in Wiltshire with a soldier she met online.

'What does Lwsi think of my Carys?'

'She's always been a big fan, describes her as the girl who has it all going for her.'

'What if Carys called by this morning for a chat?'

'Well, Lwsi is a very stubborn girl but she'll give Carys a hearing, I'm sure.'

'Worth a try, then?'

'Yes. Thank you, Mr Dafis.'

As he strolled down the hill, Daf was feeling no small measure of sympathy for Lembo who clearly had no effective way of communicating with his daughter. At least he was taking some steps to try to do something about the yellow-topped pimples which disfigured his face and had been the subject of so many cruel remarks by the children he taught. But whatever the difficulties Lewis was encountering, nothing gave his daughter the right to play with others' lives.

Carys returned from Mair's house at eight, in time for the best breakfast possible. They needed to eat their way through all the bacon Chrissie had bought, and last night's leftover mash made hash browns to go with eggs, fried bread and sausages.

'Rob starts every day with a feed like this,' Rhodri remarked wistfully.

'No, he doesn't, he starts with two hours of hard work to justify his fry-up,' Daf corrected.

'You know Sion and Belle are coming to tea?' Carys asked. 'Would it be OK if Garmon called by?'

'Keen to meet Belle, is he?' Gaenor asked.

Carys went red. 'Not quite, it's Mali he's keen to see. It's been ten days since he saw her last.'

'Oooh, broody, is he?' Gaenor continued, teasing.

'Don't know, but he's certainly acting odd. Every time we go near any shops, he's looking for a place to buy her a new outfit, or a toy or a book.'

'Right,' Daf put in, not entirely happy with the direction of this conversation, given that as a new father, he did not relish the prospect of becoming a grandfather, 'time I was going. Carys, can I have a word?'

Carys quickly agreed to speak to Lwsi but Daf was rather troubled by what she said afterwards: 'The fact is, we've all got to get used to the fact we want to have sex with one of the Berllan family and can't; Lwsi's no different to me, or Gaenor, or Uncle John, or you yourself, Dadi. Or Mum, come to that, if she was honest enough to admit it. It's a waste of the world's resources for one family to be so damn sexy but there we are. There's nothing we can do about it.'

'Come on, Carys, Garmon's a heck of a good-looking chap.'

'Of course, but he's no Bryn Berllan.'

'Thanks for trying with Lwsi, anyway.'

Considering that it was Sunday morning, there was a lot going on at the station.

'Well, boss,' Shelia began, beaming at him, 'Tom's mother came home from the concert last night with the best story ever.'

'I wasn't trying to make any kind of story. The stubborn old mule wasn't prepared to listen and time was running short.'

'West Mercia are dead chuffed,' Nev put in. 'They've taken in half a dozen lawyers who were playing ducks and drakes with their clients' money, and a couple of dodgy financial consultants as well. And in the nick of time: one of them had booked a flight to Brazil, one way.'

'If I live to be a hundred and fifty and have the most successful career ever, they'll still be talking about the arrest of Gwilym Bebb at my funeral,' Daf concluded.

'Absolute classic, boss,' was Steve's contribution. 'And speaking of absolute classics, Ms Wynne is waiting to see you.'

Five minutes later, Daf was sharing a cup of tea with Haf, discussing Jan Cilgwyn's case.

'Dr Huw noted a number of bruises and an unhealed burn mark on her leg,' Haf began. 'From experience, I should say she's been suffering abuse for a considerable time.'

'But she was strong enough to have an affair,' Daf observed.

'Who was the strong one, her or Heulwen? I'm pretty certain Jan saw her relationship with Heulwen as a door.'

'What do you mean?'

'It happens very frequently. Someone feeling trapped, who can't see any way forward, may seek someone to help them escape.'

The sunshine streaming in through the window glinted on the diamond on her finger and Daf had to say something. 'Like you, I suppose, opening the door to Plas Gwynne?'

Haf set her mug down and sighed. 'I was so pleased when Mostyn said you had accepted the invitation. I'd be delighted to see you both at the party.'

'And we're looking forward to it as well, but just tell me, Haf, why on earth are you marrying him?'

'I don't recall asking any such question when you threw your whole family into chaos by running off with your sister-in-law.'

'I love Gaenor.'

'And I don't love Mostyn? Thank you so much for keeping me fully informed of my own emotional condition.'

'But he's so different from you. You're a leftie, he's a Tory. You work to help the disadvantaged, he follows the hounds. You love books and he ... well, I haven't really got much idea what he does, but he certainly doesn't read *The Guardian*.'

'You'd be surprised, Daf, you really would. We go to the theatre all the time, locally and in London. I love books, as you say, and there's a library at the Plas. You know I was very keen on my ponies when I was a girl, Mostyn's found me a beautiful hunter, though I'm not sure I will hunt. And you talk about helping people: who paid to get Cai Evans clear of heroin? Not the local Labour Party, nor *Guardian* readers, but Mostyn and his mother.'

'People like Cai need justice, not charity.'

'Good luck with the vision, Daf, but in the meantime, Cai's off the H, thanks to the good folk of Plas Gwynne.'

There was a long silence before Haf picked up the conversation again. 'You've forgotten one thing, Daf, in your socio-political analysis. I'm a lonely woman in my thirties and Mostyn is a lonely man in his forties. He's a good man, kindly and loyal, if a bit stiff and old-fashioned. I'll have a lovely life as his wife and I hope I'll raise the little Gwydyr-Gwynnes whilst I carry on working just as I am now. I'll have to go now, Daf, their church service will be over by ten.'

'You don't go with them?'

'I see plenty of your friend Joe Hogan in the bloody lessons.'

'Lessons? Do you mean the Pre-Cana?'

'Yes. Six weeks to teach an utter pagan like me to join a tradition going back to the Middle Ages. I'll have a lot of homework to do before this June wedding.'

'Lovely job.'

Haf laughed aloud. 'I just love it when you're sarcastic, Daf,' she said as she left.

The phone rang: Nev. 'Carwyn Watkin just rang. He's got a flat tyre and he's asking if it's OK if he comes in a bit later?'

'Fine by me. I could do with some time to look through the contents of Heulwen's safe.'

'I'll bring it all over to you now, boss. Have you seen the papers this morning?'

'No.'

'Full of praise for the investigation. Press very excited by all the arrests yesterday.'

Diane Rhydderch had been right, it seemed, which meant fractionally less hassle for Daf, but his heart sank a little to think that this might mean that he would have to pay greater attention to her pronouncements in future.

Daf spread the envelopes from Heulwen's safe across his desk and stuck the notes he had made onto each one. The set wasn't complete and he needed to know why, but before he could ask, the phone rang: Joe.

'Daf, you don't happen to know where Phil Evans is living now, do you?'

'Not sure, no.'

'I've got an address; 67, Bronwylfa. Can you get there at once? Preferably before Milek does.'

It took five minutes for Daf to reach the seventies house with its wonderful views over the Severn Valley.

Like many men, Phil was spending his Sunday morning tidying the garden, which wasn't quite a wilderness but was in need of a bit of attention. He was on a little ladder unhooking the withered hanging baskets by the front door as Milek pounded up the slope, yelling one word, time after time: 'Bastard!'

Milek ran right into the ladder and Phil fell to the ground before Daf was out of his car. Milek was thumping Phil, blow after heavy blow striking that handsome face, drawing forth spit, blood and tears. Daf leapt on Milek's back and pulled him off, knowing how to avoid the flailing fists. Phil rose to his feet, shaking, and stepped over to help Daf hold Milek, and between the two of them they had managed to put the big man on his back by the time Joe arrived. Basia got out of Joe's car, wearing a charming yellow dress highly suitable for a church service in spring. She ran across the lawn to embrace Phil and, after a couple of moments, the lovely dress was covered in blood, reminding Daf of Jackie Kennedy at Dallas. Milek sat up and remained on the ground as he received reprimands, first from Joe, then Basia.

'Right,' Daf said to him, 'on your feet. You're coming to the station with me.'

'I don't want it to go any further,' muttered Phil through his swollen lips. 'It's family business.'

'He near as damn it broke your nose.'

'I don't give a stuff.'

Basia went into the house and returned with a bowl of warm water to clean Phil's face. There were tears on her cheeks as she took care of her lover, reminding Daf of Pre-Raphaelite paintings. When she'd finished, she passed the bloody cloth and bowl of dirty water to her brother.

'What's it all about?' Daf asked Joe.

'Basia didn't come home last night. Milek was on tenterhooks, and when Basia refused communion, his fears were confirmed. We don't take communion unless we are in a state of grace, with no sins unshriven.'

'Pity Milek didn't have a bigger breakfast than a little wafer, might have steadied him a bit.'

'We're not allowed breakfast until we have received Our Lord in the Blessed Sacrament.'

'You know what, Joe? Old Karl Marx was right: religion is the opium of the people and you lot are all off your faces on it. I've got to go but I need you to keep an eye on the Polish Tyson Fury there.'

Carwyn Watkin was waiting for Daf, full of apologies.

'I must have picked a nail up somewhere,' he explained.

'Easily done,' Daf agreed, remembering, without knowing why, the pile of old pallets on the pavement opposite Bowen's factory. 'I got called out anyway.'

'*Duwcs*, you're always busy, Dafydd. I'm surprised your head doesn't get scrambled with all this coming and going.'

'I'm used to it, Car.'

A small sound from his pocket was a message from Gaenor to remind him that Belle and Sion were expected at three. Daf put his phone down on the desk and looked at the man sitting opposite him. He wasn't a tall man but, like many farmers, his body was solid and his hands strong. The only change in his clothes over twenty years was the addition of a Dectomax fleece, and Carys often said there was no excuse for wearing garments advertising treatments for parasitic worms. Daf raked through his cheerful memories of times at Brynybiswal but could not recall much about Carwyn in particular. Mr Watkin often teased his wife about spoiling their son but Daf had never seen any evidence of that. He recalled a quiet young man, rather in the shadow of his more gregarious parents. What did Carwyn like? Had he ever travelled? Daf had no idea of the answers. He observed Carwyn looking at the notes stuck to the evidence envelopes: he gathered them back into their file and closed it.

'Right, Carwyn, you know very well what I have here. I want the background and to hear about how you and Heulwen got along.'

'She was an able woman, Daf, always picked up on everything. We went down to Llandrindod together, to the County Council.'

'Before we go any further, Carwyn, why did you decide to stand in the first place?'

'I wanted to do something worthwhile, make Mum proud. I didn't know then how much paperwork there was in the job. To tell the truth, you need to be a bit of a brainbox to do the job well these days, not a pick and shovel lad like me.'

'And Heulwen joined at the same time, you said?'

'Yes, and she was a great help to me from Day One, explaining things, stopping me from making a fool of myself, helping me. And she was good company, the two of us travelled down in her car right often. Good chance to chat.'

'Man and woman, spending so much time together ... did you get to love her, Carwyn?'

It looked as if the very idea terrified Carwyn.

'No way, Dafydd. She was another man's wife and anyway, she's not my type.'

'Who is, then?' Daf asked.

'Well, I like 'em a lot younger than Heulwen, for a start. A lively girl, with a bit of twinkle in her eyes and enough meat on her bones, that's my type.'

Similar taste to Bowen, Daf thought, unwilling to consider that Gaenor also fitted the description.

'OK, but you and Heulwen were pretty close.'

'We were.'

'Someone said to me that you always obeyed her orders. Was that true?'

'That's not how things were, Dafydd. She always knew the right thing to do, so it was only plain common sense to listen to her.'

'But she did ask you to do things?'

'Indeed.'

'Fine. Now then, Carwyn, where did these pictures come from?'

Daf picked up the envelope containing the photos of Bowen and pulled one out at random to show Carwyn, who reddened.

'That's not the kind of thing I like to do but he had to be stopped.'

'Who? Rhys Bowen?'

'Yes, that bugger needs stopping. He gets away with anything.'

'You still haven't answered my question, Carwyn: where did the pictures come from?'

'I'm a bit of a photographer, Dafydd. There was a course in the village hall, some twenty years back. I went, just because you should support a local thing but *duwcs*, it was interesting. Mum got me a camera after.'

'You took these pictures?'

'I've got several different lenses and sometimes, I used a little hidden camera, like the ones you can get for going in nest boxes to film the little birds.'

'With the greatest respect, Carwyn, there is a hell of a difference between wildlife photography and pictures like this.'

'Some came from a detective in Cardiff.' He wasn't displaying the slightest sign of regret or shame.

'Not a great thing to do, was it? Taking pictures of people's private lives?'

'He was the one behaving badly, Daf. I pity all those poor girls.'

'What if I told you we've already spoken to one of these girls and she was perfectly happy with everything that went on?'

'He could persuade them to do all kinds of things.'

Carwyn took the envelope and browsed through the contents. He selected a picture and passed it to Daf. It certainly wasn't a particularly romantic image, Bowen sprawled on a sofa, legs splayed and his flies open, a naked girl kneeling in front of him, but Daf couldn't help noticing the two bottles of Prosecco and, just by Bowen's hip, the largest possible box of chocolates.

'Is that legal, Dafydd? It shouldn't be. Pity the poor girl.'

'Listen, Carwyn, I haven't got the least interest in what Bowen does with consenting women. No one here is under age, under the influence or being threatened in any way. It may not be particularly praiseworthy behaviour, but it is a completely private matter.'

'What about his status, representing us in the Assembly?'

'I don't think Bowen has ever spoken about his morals. He's a shagger, always has been, but that's not a crime. Blackmail, on the other hand, is a serious offence.'

'But...' Carwyn's voice dwindled away, as Daf had foreseen.

'Would you like a cup of tea, Carwyn?'

'Thank you. All this talking makes you dry.'

Taking the rest of the evidence file with him, Daf popped out to get the tea and to check up on the mountain of paperwork needing to be done, hoping to give Carwyn an opportunity to put his thoughts in order.

'The CPS are mad at you, boss,' Sheila said. 'They've put out an "all leave cancelled" statement.'

'Ha ha.'

'Not joking. Just count up how many cases we've got going on at the moment, to say nothing of Gwilym Bebb, because he's a headache for West Mercia, not us. Lisa Powell's not straightforward, and there's Cai Evans and his ket and the blackmail. We've got no time at all to deal with the assault which took place somewhere up on Gungrog Hill this morning, and then God knows how many other cases there are in that file under your arm.'

'I witnessed the assault. The victim, who happens to be Phil Dolfadog, doesn't want to prosecute, because it's a family matter, so you can at least tick one off your list.'

'This case seems to be spiralling off in all directions,' Nev observed. 'It's the gift that keeps on giving.'

'You're not wrong, Nev. Put the kettle on, would you, *lanc*?'

Carwyn did look better when Daf returned, he was sitting in a more natural way and breathing more steadily.

'Tea on its way,' Daf began, noting that his phone was not where he had left it. Carwyn followed his eyes.

'Sorry, your phone was ringing, and I tried to switch it off.'

'No worries. Back to business. Carwyn, I have known you all my life. You're not the kind of man to go about sticking long lenses through people's windows, I'd bet my life on that.'

'But someone has to do something to pull him down, that bastard Bowen.'

Daf couldn't remember hearing Carwyn swear before.

'Were you aware that Heulwen was keeping a little file on you as well?'

'Nothing but a misunderstanding, a couple of mistakes I've made,' he muttered, red to his ears.

'But they look bad, don't they?'

'Well, maybe.'

'Carwyn, I don't think you get what I'm trying to do here. If you have committed a crime, and we are looking at blackmail, conspiracy and God knows what else besides, you are going to be punished and I reckon you'll go inside: prison. But if you were forced to do these things because of the hold Heulwen had over you, then that's a totally different matter altogether. You had no choice. That's how it was, wasn't it?'

Sheila opened the door.

'Nev's getting worse with the tray, slops half of the tea about the place,' she began, looking for a place to set the tray down. Daf moved the photos. Carwyn grew even redder.

'Oh, hello there, Mrs Francis,' he muttered.

'Good morning, Mr Watkin. Do enjoy your tea.'

The presence of the wife of a well-known farmer in the same room as the pictures he had taken clearly embarrassed Carwyn. He glanced at the door to check Sheila was gone.

'Time for some straight talking, Carwyn. You had no choice in what was done; you were just doing what you had to do, obeying Heulwen to save your skin.'

'Well,' Carwyn began, sipping at his tea. 'It wasn't easy to say "no" to her, but we mustn't speak ill of the dead, must we?'

'We've heard plenty about Heulwen over the last few days.'

'Very likely.' Carwyn set his mug down with surprising delicacy, given his thick fingers.

'What did you do on Monday, Carwyn?'

'Nipped down to the Smithfield.'

'Buying or selling?'

'Neither, just checking prices and ... well, seeing people. I had my dinner in that little café they've got there.'

'Who with?'

'Well, Jac was there, Heulwen's son, but there's never much chat to be got out of him. Who else was there? Glyn y Rhos, Edgar Topbanc and Gethin Glanhafren. No one else.'

'Then what?'

'Did a bit of shopping, then I went to the Planning Office

to look over a couple of applications in my patch. I had a phone call from Heulwen reminding me that I'd promised to cut the grass for Mrs Richards, the old lady who lives behind the wool shop.'

'Next door to the Plaid office, you mean?'

'Yes, not right next door but close enough.'

'And that wasn't a problem for you, just obeying Heulwen like that?'

'No, it wasn't, Dafydd. She's a nice old lady, is Mrs Richards. Used to teach at the Grammar School and that goes back a bit.'

'I know fine well who Mrs Richards is.'

'So, I popped back home for the mower and strimmer, got myself a bag of chips and went to cut her grass for her.'

'And what time was that?'

'I can't rightly say. I had to do a couple of little jobs at home before going back to Welshpool, feed the dogs, check my messages...'

'Were there any messages?'

'Only Heulwen, reminding me about Mrs Richards.'

Daf realised that Carwyn's life was so empty that he actually relished obeying Heulwen's orders.

'But before cutting the grass, you went in to see Heulwen, didn't you?'

'Only for a minute.'

'What did you discuss?'

'Nothing important.'

'Carwyn, I am trying to do my very best here, but you are going to have to be honest with me. If you had nothing important to discuss, why were you wasting the time of a busy woman?'

'It was the business with Bowen. We needed to make a decision about publication but Heulwen was worried about the timing. If people had enough time to think about it, they could forget and vote for him anyway.'

Carwyn Brynybiswal was discussing his criminal conspiracy as if he were arranging a community project for the benefit of all, like painting the village hall or planning the Sunday School trip.

'And what did you decide?'

A sulky look came over Carwyn's face and Daf remembered old Mr Watkin's description of his son as spoilt.

'She'd changed her mind. She wasn't willing to do anything at all about it, after all that I'd done.' Tears of frustration shone in his eyes as if he were a boy of three in the throes of a temper tantrum. 'She said a right nasty thing when I spoke up against what she'd said. She said she was sure that I'd enjoyed watching … what I took pictures of … but she was wrong, it wasn't like that at all. They show plenty of spicy stuff on telly these days, man and girl in bed together. I love my history and, by gosh, there was a fair bit of sex in that series *The Tudors*. I really liked that Anne Boleyn, even though she was a bit on the slim side. Things like that I enjoy, not the business with Bowen. Sometimes, the girls got undressed real slow, to please him, I suppose, and that was nice to watch but I never enjoyed it. As if I could enjoy watching dear little Daisy bent over like an animal…'

'So, you were angry with Heulwen?'

'But Dafydd, what was the point? Over the last fifteen years, time and again she's done things I don't understand but she's always been proven right in the end. But I still want to do something about Bowen, spread some of his muck about.'

'Did you see anyone else in the Plaid office?'

'I was too angry to notice. But after I left the office, I had to ask Jac, Heulwen's son, to move his pick-up: he was parked outside Gwilym Bebb's office, with a trailer. He was blocking the narrow lane behind the big buildings; that's where Mrs Richards lives.'

'Did you speak to Mrs Richards at all?'

'I knocked on the door but I could see her sleeping in the chair by the stove. She's in her nineties, you know.'

'What then?'

'I cut her postage stamp of a lawn and left. I didn't see

anyone or notice anything. I went home and went straight to bed.'

'Early night?'

'I've got no reason to stay up, if there's nothing good on telly. I like drama or nature programmes, Attenborough and our Iolo Williams. Or history, like I said. Can't stand sport, can't stand all those game shows.'

There was no reason for him to be flexible, of course, since he lived alone, but Daf was aware that Carwyn was a man well used to getting his own way.

'OK, Carwyn, that'll do for now. We are going to need to talk again and, in the meantime, I want to see your computer and all of your cameras.'

'Will tomorrow morning be soon enough?'

'As soon as possible, please. If it isn't convenient, I can send an officer up to get what is needed.'

'I'll come back after I've had my dinner.'

'Champion.'


There were visitors waiting for Daf by the front desk: Basia and Phil. His face was far from attractive but she had certainly done her best to patch him up. She held a plate in her hand with a cake on it, and from the delicious smell, Daf knew it was freshly baked. Something else which was delicious was the look on Basia's face. Daf suspected that Milek was right about the previous night but it appeared to have been highly satisfactory as far as she was concerned.

'Sorry for all the trouble,' she began, handing Daf the cake. 'Milek acts like a fool sometimes.'

'Phil, you should get yourself to a doctor. You need a stitch just by your ear.'

'I'll be grand, Daf.'

'There'll be a scar if you don't get a stitch.'

'I couldn't care less if I'm scars all over,' Phil replied cheerfully.

'Are you sure you don't want me to give Milek a bit of a lesson? Bring him in overnight, maybe?'

Basia shook her head. 'Milek knows just what the inside of a cell looks like. He was trying to defend me, and he doesn't need to do that anymore.'

Defend Basia or her virginity, Daf speculated, trying desperately not to imagine what kind of night it had been.

'We'd better be off,' said Phil, slipping his arm around Basia's waist. 'We've got to get these bedding plants sorted.'

Daf shared the cake with the team, of course, after they had demolished a mountain of chips. Daf was on his third slice when Nev decided to remind them all of the policy on gifts from witnesses.

'Try not to be a lamb's cock, Nev,' was Sheila's robust reply.

'Excellent use of idiom,' Daf remarked. 'Nev, you need a bit of fresh air. Get up to Brynybiswal and check out what kind of lawnmower Carwyn has, electric or one that runs on...'

'Two-stroke!' they all yelled in unison.

'Not too late to get up a recitation party for the Powys Eisteddfod, friends.'

'Surely you don't think it's Carwyn who killed her, boss?' Sheila was full of concern. 'I was thinking of setting him up on a double date with a friend of mine...'

'Not the accountant, he's seen plenty of her already. And don't forget, even if the two-stroke came from Carwyn's pick-up, that doesn't necessarily mean he killed Heulwen, but there is no doubt that when we know the history of the accelerant, we'll be a lot closer to the answer.'

'OK. And, boss,' Sheila added as an afterthought, 'I did check up on Bowen's financial position: he's rolling in money.'

'We usually say "he's a rock of money" in Welsh, Sheila.'

'Well, it's a rock and a half then. As well as the Mid Wales Meats factory, he's got two abattoirs, one outside Oswestry and the other up near Liverpool. He owns that swanky house in the

Meifod Valley outright and his bachelor pad down in Cardiff Bay. And over the years, he's bought up houses to rent, over forty by now. And he's also got a cast iron pre-nup: if he and the wife split, she gets a million in cash and nothing more. Something to do with his late father-in-law's business, I'm told.'

Fair chance for Daisy Davies, if she fancied it, Daf thought to himself as he heard his phone bleep. He supposed it would be Gaenor, needing an extra pot of jam or something for the 'first impressions' tea party. Before checking his phone, he made a statement to the team.

'I'm going home this afternoon for a couple of hours, but I'll be back by six. Thinking it over, Steve had better be the one going up to Brynybiswal for a sprot at Carwyn as he's promised to drop his laptop off here and I want you to start work on it as soon as you can, Nev.'

'You do remember I'm not an expert, boss?' Nev protested. 'I can only do the most basic searches.'

'Still way better than me, *lanc*. And we're not battling "Anonymous" or China's cyber attack troops, just Heulwen Dolfadog and Carwyn Brynybiswal.'

Daf was glad to have a reason to escape the maze of paperwork, given that it was all in safe hands. Nia was a form-filling ninja; he could leave her to it. Sheila had mentioned something about leaving the station for a while and suddenly Daf remembered where she and Tom were heading on their Sunday jaunt. They'd been invited before Belle was a factor and Daf was not about to put them off. The little house would be crammed full but that made things easier.

Daf would have enough time to pop round to see Mrs Richards, to confirm Carwyn's story. He went via Tesco's and, in the car park, checked what he thought was a text from Gaenor. Instead, it came from an unfamiliar number:

'Important evidence about Monday night has come to light. Come to the factory to discuss it 3pm, RB'

Interesting. Only ten minutes until he was due at the factory, and he could go from there straight home. But first, Mrs Richards.

Every bit as much as Powis Castle or the Cockpit, Mrs Richards was part of the history of Welshpool. A former teacher and widow of the ironmonger, she was widely described as an 'institution' but to Daf, she was a nightmare. At one point, she was wildly anti-dog, taking pictures of canine crimes on her Instamatic and marching to the police station, demanding justice both swift and terrible. The next threat to the town she perceived was flooding, and her vendetta against crazy paving lasted years, though Daf eventually persuaded her that it wasn't his department. It seemed to him that every promotion he gained brought him more of her nonsense. She didn't venture out much anymore, which was a relief, but Daf still dreaded knocking on her door. Through the net curtains, he saw an ancient eye, like a dragon's.

'Mrs Richards? It's Daf Dafis, from the police.'

He heard her moving slowly and the sound of a little chain tinkling. When she opened the door, the heat and smell which flooded out were lethal.

'What do you want, Dafis?'

'Just the answer to a simple question: was Carwyn Watkin here on Monday evening?'

'He was.'

'You're quite sure? Because he said you were sleeping when he called.'

'I was pretending to sleep to avoid having to speak to him. He's an utter fool. And the cheek of him. Take a look at my gate.'

Daf followed her pointing finger towards a door in the wall, very similar to the one behind Heulwen's office.

'If I put the bolt over that gate, it means I don't want to be disturbed but what did he do? He fettled himself a little gadget so he can open the gate from the other side, the cheeky little maigrim.'

Maigrim. A word so ancient and local that no one knew if it was Welsh or English but it was certainly the word used to describe someone whose behaviour was highly unacceptable. As he was thanking her, Daf wondered if she would use the word to describe him to any later caller. He walked slowly over to the rear of the crime scene. If everyone who came in through the front door was ruled out, the killer must have come in through the back gate. Carwyn had been cutting the grass but had seen nothing. Plenty of two-stroke available and a gadget for opening bolts from the other side. And an almighty row with Heulwen about the pictures of Rhys Bowen. Daf decided he needed to check in with the team before going to meet Bowen.

'Nev? Has Carwyn Watkin dropped off his computer yet?'

'Not yet, no.'

'If he comes in, keep hold of him, *lanc*. Charge him if you have to.'

'What with?'

'Conspiracy, blackmail, wasting police time, whatever. Just keep hold of him. And tell Nia to take one of the CPSOs over to Bettws Cedewain, to find a Daisy Davies – teacher, fair hair – and check she's safe until further notice. I'm starting to feel very suspicious about our friend Carwyn. At the very least, he's got a lot more questions to answer.'

# Chapter 15

## *Sunday afternoon, April 17, 2016*

Daf expected the factory to be busy but, although the gate was open, all was quiet. He walked over to the door to the reception area, which was also open. In the reception area, there was a list of shifts on the wall which confirmed that the first shift on Sunday began at six pm. Like an invitation, Bowen's office door was wide open and Daf was surprised by the quietness of the place. Until now, every moment Daf had spent in Bowen's company had been accompanied by some kind of sound from the butcher: laughter, speech or whistling. Perhaps he was more restrained in his workplace, Daf speculated as he entered the office: the room was empty. He hoped Bowen had come across some information to reveal who it was who threw the hatchet; the weapon itself was in place in the case, but several other knives were missing. Daf recalled what Jeff had said about Bowen still killing on request: perhaps the blades were missing because he had promised friends he would butcher a pig for them. The full daylight flooded in through the window but there were pools of deep shadow. On the wide desk was a note on a piece of A4 paper, written in large, old-fashioned script:

'Second drawer, at the back.'

A note like this didn't somehow seem to fit with what Daf had seen of Bowen's nature thus far. He had come to the factory expecting raised voices and accusations flung about, not a neat little note. And where was the man himself? In the toilet? In the killing room? Daf shut the office door before sitting down in the leather chair in order to be able to reach into the drawer. He didn't hear or sense any movement.

Suddenly, Daf felt the pressure of the edge of a sharp blade at the side of his neck, under his ear. He hadn't heard anything.

Someone had been hiding in the shadow thrown by the tall filing cabinet beside the desk.

'That's your carotid artery, Dafydd,' began Carwyn Watkin, in a voice which was terrifyingly conversational. 'If I were to cut her, you'd be dead in less than two minutes. You wouldn't suffer much at all. Not like a little axe in your back. Sorry about that. On-the-spot decision. Sorry again.'

'What are you doing, Carwyn?' Daf managed to keep his voice firm and natural in tone, whatever thoughts were racing through his mind.

'It's been a right tough week for me, you know, Dafydd. I'd come to rely on Heulwen and she let me down serious. Looking out for herself, she was, not wanting Bowen to tell the world whatever her little secrets were.'

'What secrets?'

'You don't get to ask any more questions.' Carwyn's voice went up half an octave. 'I didn't like sitting at your desk like a naughty lad in front of the head teacher. You're not the head teacher, you're Deifi Siop, a lad who'd come up to us to play whist because he hadn't got any friends of his own.'

He pressed on the blade a little. Daf felt the warmth of liquid running across his skin but no pain. He stayed perfectly still, as he had done in similar situations in the past.

'You're not trembling, Dafydd? Why's that? I've got one heck of a big knife. Look over there in the big case, on the third row, that's where she belongs. I did take a few others, and the saw, because I did consider having to cut you up into pieces to get rid of your body. Starting another fire wouldn't be wise, I don't reckon. Then I thought, what about trying to kill two birds with one stone? And now here we are. You've come here to meet Rhys Bowen, and the message on your phone confirms that. When they find your body in his office, killed by his knife which has his fingerprints all over it, I will be rid of the two of you at once. I'm right proud of the plan.' Daf could actually hear the smug smile in Carwyn's voice. 'I should have thought more

411

like this before, more strategic, like, Dafydd. I didn't really need Heulwen and I'd gone right lazy, expecting her to organise every little thing.'

The little flow of blood had reached Daf's collar and the fabric sucked up all the liquid. Daf remembered the moss on his trousers from the bench at Dolfadog: he'd need the Vanish again for his shirt. He wasn't sure if it was Carwyn's adrenalin he could smell, or his own.

'Everyone says you're some bit of a clever fellow,' Carwyn was saying now. 'A bit of a scholar, but you weren't nearly clever enough to solve this little puzzle, were you?'

'Well, the two-stroke was a big clue.' Daf focused on keeping his voice level. 'Who else, of all the people who were around at the time, would have access to that quantity of two-stroke? And my opinion of you turned upside down when I learnt that it was you who took those pictures.'

'You're different from what I thought of you, too, Dafydd. I thought you were a steady sort of chap but after being on the news all the time, with the Plas Mawr business and the trouble at the Eisteddfod, your head's been turned for sure. You had a nice wife and lucky to have her, boy from the shop marrying into Neuadd, but all of a sudden, that wasn't good enough for you. You had to go chasing after that slut Chrissie Berllan, then, worst of all, you stole your brother-in-law's wife. Think you're a bit of a stallion, do you, Deifi Siop? Bit better than respectable men like me?'

'I don't think I'm better than anyone at all, Carwyn. And my family's right close to the Berllan family, that's all.'

'You think you're God's gift to women, men like you and Rhys Bowen.'

'With the greatest respect, Carwyn, I don't behave like Bowen in the slightest.'

'How many women do you want?'

'One's enough for me.'

'But she belongs to another man?'

'People don't own one another, Carwyn.'

In the half minute of silence which followed, Daf tried to see the world through Carwyn's eyes and suddenly understood the root of the problem. Whereas Basia, for example, had decided, battled even, to keep her virginity, Carwyn had never had another option. The sourness in his voice as he discussed Daf's life was proof of years of frustration and loneliness; you didn't need to be a psychiatrist to appreciate how pressures like that can twist a man's nature. Daf, his collar now sticky with blood, decided to try another tack.

'Nasty business taking those pictures, eh?'

'To be fair, Dafydd, I didn't think I could do such a thing until Heulwen asked me to. That was her mistake, forcing me to watch him, time after time. And they were all nice girls too, apart from the tarts he picked up in Cardiff. It was like he'd cast a spell on them somehow, to make them do all them dirty things.'

'Like I said to you before, they were all quite willing. You, more than anyone, should understand that: they'd ask him to come back to them, time and time again. Just lonely girls looking for a handy little spree, that's all.'

'Spree?' The blade suddenly pressed harder on Daf's neck. 'What nonsense! And they aren't lonely girls either: the one who lives in Bettws, she's got any number of friends. She had a party the one time and the house was packed. Any number of friends.'

'Daisy Davies? Do you know her, then?'

'More than that, Dafydd, she's going to be my wife.'

Daf knew from the tone of his voice that Carwyn was suffering from a pretty serious form of mental illness, and if he wasn't thinking clearly, he was definitely not a safe pair of hands for that knife.

'Congratulations. Have you named a day?'

'Not yet. She doesn't know yet but I reckon autumn half-term next year. Quiet time on the farm, especially if the cattle aren't in yet.'

'I didn't realise you were courting.'

'We do any amount together, Daisy and me. I cut all her firewood and her grass, of course.'

'Kissed her?'

'She kissed me New Year's Eve, under the mistletoe at the Bull and Heifer. She's got such nice ways about her, she's almost dainty, like the little Jersey heifer Mum had when I was a lad, something right special.'

'At the concert last night, was she the girl in the blue jumper?'

'Aye.'

'Cracking-looking girl.'

'More than that, Dafydd. Her nature, her ways, her voice, all real special.'

Daf ran through a number of scenes in his head, ideas of how he could escape from the situation without moving an inch. In the distance, the Town Hall clock struck the half hour. Half past three. No one was likely to turn up to prepare for the shift for at least an hour. Daf wondered how Carwyn had got into the factory but recalled Mrs Richards' complaint about the device for opening her gate; Carwyn was almost certainly far more resourceful than Daf had given him credit for. Daf tried to assess the situation logically. Though Carwyn had the knife, he didn't have experience of similar situations. Physically, Daf was the taller man, Carwyn more strongly built, so there was little difference. In the end, it would come down to a competition of nerves and reflexes, and of bladder capacity.

When Daf was a young policeman, an experienced officer had told him, 'Strange but true, but people who would cut your throat like they were cutting a jam sandwich aren't willing to piss themselves. Wait until they start to feel a bit uncomfortable, that'll be your chance.'

Daf needed to keep quiet, keep observant, keep his patience: play the long game. He managed not to think about the tea party, about Belle meeting Garmon, Sheila and Tom exchanging glances as they praised the baby, Gaenor giving everyone not just tasty snacks but her lovely smile. He wanted to be there so much that it was like a physical pain which hurt far more than the knife in his neck, but if he did not play this situation right, he would lose it all, forever.

'Does she teach at Davies Sisters' School, then?' Daf asked, accidentally pushing back very slightly towards the blade as he pronounced the name of the school.

'She does, and she's a brilliant teacher. I'm on the governors and even Estyn praise her standards. Nursery Reception.'

That's the reason he's so lonely, Daf thought. He's as boring as a gatepost.

'That's why it got so hard, to see her lowering herself with Bowen. They just weren't normal, the things he did to her. And it was Heulwen's fault I had to see that. It's one thing to know Daisy *fech* went with Bowen, but another thing altogether to see them doing it. He's a big man, you know, and heavy. Poor Daisy *fech*.'

His voice started to break, and Daf's hopes rose. It would be easy enough to escape from a man who was weeping like a flowing river. But Carwyn grew quieter, and when he resumed his story, there was a perilous note in his voice.

'I don't think she'd ever loved anyone, Heulwen. Not Phil, not even the children. I heard the story of that lad they adopted and what happened to him in the long run. I called her my friend, but she wasn't a friend to me. I was a weapon, something she could use against other people just as she liked. I asked her on Monday night, time after time, what was the point of taking them horrible pictures if she wasn't willing to use them against the bastard? And all she did was smile and remind me I had to cut the grass for that old witch up the lane.'

'Mrs Richards?'

'Mrs Richards. That old bitch wasn't even polite enough to offer me a cup of tea. She was pretending to sleep, I know that fine well. I started to think, what kind of a man am I, running about after all these old ladies but never getting to spend any time with any nice girl? I've been kept on a leash by them, Dafydd, by the fucking witches, and where's my life gone? While men like you get to keep company with lovely girls, get to raise a family, I was washing the support stockings and waiting for the fucking carer, who was always late. That's how it was, nursing the boss first, then Mum, as I watched people like Bowen feasting on a world of pleasure, with me never leaving the fucking yard. I went back in to see Heulwen, to tell her I was going to send them pictures to the *County Times*, whatever she said, but she was sitting in a chair, looking into the distance, with a false half smile on her face.'

'What did you think had happened to her?'

'Stroke. The boss was like that one time. And suddenly I thought, she can't turn me this time with her clever words. Then I had another thought: if I made sure she was dead, no one would have to nurse her, like I nursed Mum and the boss. Jac didn't deserve that responsibility and Phil would never give no help. She was in the road, she was, that woman made me do that many ugly things.'

There was pride in his voice as if he was expecting praise.

'And Bowen owned the building and all. A fire in the place would bring a fair bit of trouble for him. He'd have his insurance but it would still be a hassle and people would start to ask questions, blame him, maybe.'

'What about the people in the flat upstairs?'

'Two foreign thugs and a whore? What about them?'

'What if they'd been killed in the fire?'

'They're never in the flat in the evening. The men go out on the piss and she's busy chasing after Phil Dolfadog like a bitch on heat.'

Daf had never heard a less apt description but decided not to raise the point, given the position of the knife.

'So, you decided to set a fire?'

'Aye. It was easy enough, with enough of the two-stroke

from the can I'd got in the back of the pick-up. I've never smoked but I carry a lighter in my pocket in case. Things to burn on the farm, in the garden and what have you. It was a grand thing to see her face through the smoke. She couldn't say a word but *duwcs*, the fear was clear enough in her eyes. They went red, her eyes, from the smoke, and tears with no meaning behind them ran down her cheeks. It wasn't real weeping but at least there were tears in her eyes at last. Tears at last.'

This expression clearly pleased Carwyn; he turned it over and over in his mouth like a man savouring a good wine. His lack of any empathy for Heulwen made Daf afraid: he knew it as a sign of a psychopathic nature. Yet Carwyn seemed to want to make sure Jac did not suffer from the same issues which had soured his younger life. Was that real empathy, Daf wondered, or had Carwyn just decided to use Jac as a character in the drama of his self-pity? Daf recalled the old age of his own parents, and his Uncle Mal's illness, times of strain and anxiety caused by their illness and by the terrifying fees he had to meet for their care. But even in those tricky times, life had moved on; his children had grown up, his career had prospered, and they'd even managed the odd foreign holiday. Carwyn had been stuck at Brynybiswal, as if time had frozen.

A flood of memories of his family surged through Daf, and he tried his best to turn the conversation, lest he should display his weakness. Despite having a psychopath with a knife just behind him, Daf had to keep control of himself, and he needed to steer the conversation away from Heulwen, violence and the fire.

'I'd forgotten you were a governor, Carwyn; I'm on the board up at the High School. We've been working hard on the transition arrangements between the High School and primary. How's it going for you in Davies Sisters' School, may I ask?'

'Right well, thanks.' Carwyn's tone was conversational again. It sent a shiver down Daf's spine. 'We know full well how busy you are in the High School but I think we'd like to see the staff calling by a bit earlier in Year Six, if that could be arranged.'

Carwyn had heard someone else say this, Daf observed. And now here he was, parroting without understanding.

'Definitely worth discussing.' Daf tried to match Carwyn's conversational tone. 'Where does she come from, your friend Daisy Davies? Not a local girl, is she?'

'No indeed. From Llanfihangel y Creuddyn in Ceredigion, originally. I've not been there, not yet, but it's a remarkable village, seemingly.'

Daf began to wonder which would be worse, being stabbed or having to hear much more of Carwyn's crushingly boring conversation?

'One of the Grateful Villages, it is, one of the villages who lost no one in the world wars, no one at all. Which makes it a Doubly Grateful Village, as I understand it...'

'I think I saw something about it on telly last year.'

There was a silence. Daf had to make an effort to resurrect the conversation.

'How many places like that are there, who didn't lose anyone at all, I wonder?'

'Fourteen, throughout England and Wales.' He was like a page from an exceptionally dull textbook.

'It would make an interesting tour, to go round them all, I reckon.'

Then, without warning, Carwyn dragged the point of the blade over Daf's skin, leaving a shallow, long wound.

'Do you reckon you can play with me, Dafydd? Reckon you're a clever man and I'm some dull old fool? You're a fair way off there, a fair way. High time you did your homework. There's a biro there. Pick it up and write, on the back of that paper there.'

There was only one piece of paper on the table, the note Daf had assumed was from Bowen.

'Is it going to be a good idea for me to write on a piece of paper with your handwriting on the back, Carwyn?' Daf asked, playing for every second.

'You're right.'

'There's probably a bit of paper in the drawer here.'

'Open it, then.'

Daf knew from his unauthorised visit on Friday what he was likely to find in Bowen's desk. There had been some paper amongst the pens and other odds and ends in the top drawer, he was sure. He tried to remember, as his fingers reached into the corners, if there was anything which could be used as a weapon. As he bent his head forward, drop after drop of bright blood fell onto Bowen's stationery, onto the Post-it notes, the gel pens, the brown and white envelopes. He pulled a half-used pad of A4 paper from the drawer with his left hand and closed the fingers of his right hand around a small but heavy brass paperweight. With his little weapon safe in his right hand, he was obliged to write with his left.

'What do you want me to write?'

'Your name to start. *Duwcs*, Dafydd, for a scholar, your handwriting's terrible.'

'I had an accident when I was at college, some nonsense on a night out. Injured the nerves in my fingers and I've written like this ever since. Thank heaven for computers.'

Daf had no idea if Carwyn swallowed the story or not.

'Then, you write that Bowen had fixed to meet you here but now you know he's going to kill you.'

'Why's he going to do that, then?'

'Because you had found out that he'd nicked a whole can of two-stroke off me. And, you can write as well that you know Bowen was looking to shag what's-her-name, John Neuadd's wife.'

'OK, OK, I'll do it now.'

As he was struggling to write, Daf heard the sound of dogs barking outside, exactly as Belle's dogs had barked when they arrived at the crime scene on Tuesday afternoon, which now seemed like a very long time ago.

'Then you can write than Bowen had turned his back for a moment and you'd taken your chance to tell the truth. You need to say that Heulwen was just about to tell the world about all that Bowen had been doing, all the filthy things, and that's why he had decided to kill her.'

'..."All the filthy things"...' Daf repeated. 'Do you want anything more specific put in there, Carwyn?'

'No, I don't think so. Then, if you've got any messages for the children, you put them down, farewell and that. This game is coming to a stop now.'

As Daf finished writing, Carwyn tightened his grip on his shoulder, ready for the blow. At that moment, there was a strong knock at the window and Daf saw a face, a face which was very familiar but totally unexpected in this context: Sion.

'Hello there, Mr Watkin,' Sion called loudly and for half a moment, Carwyn seemed totally perplexed. Daf raised his right hand and struck where he thought Carwyn's wrist would be, hoping to find a weak spot. Carwyn yelped like a puppy but kept a tight grip on the knife. Daf kicked back suddenly but missed and he felt the pressure of the blade heavy on his skin, cutting his flesh. The door was opened with a loud click. In the next instant, the knife was on the floor and Carwyn was doubled up in pain, howling like a wolf. Belle spun around again, landing the side of her foot into him a second time, a powerful kick into his other wrist. Carwyn cried out like some fiend from hell. Belle looked down at him.

'One broken wrist hurts like hell, you fucker,' she said, in a low, threatening voice. 'But two are more than twice as painful, wanker.'

She aimed another kick at him, straight into his balls.

'Thanks, Belle,' Daf exclaimed, getting his breath back. Sion was standing in the doorway, his eyes shining like a child who has succeeded in watching a horror film without his mother's permission.

'Everything worked out just fine in the end, didn't it?' Belle